MEET ME ON LOVE STREET

Also by Farah Heron

Tahira in Bloom

How to Win a Breakup

Remember Me Tomorrow

MEET ME ON LOVE STREET

Farah Heron

NEW YORK   LONDON   AMSTERDAM/ANTWERP
TORONTO   SYDNEY/MELBOURNE   NEW DELHI

SIMON & SCHUSTER BFYR

An imprint of Simon & Schuster Children's Publishing Division
1230 Avenue of the Americas, New York, New York 10020
For more than 100 years, Simon & Schuster has championed authors and the stories they create. By respecting the copyright of an author's intellectual property, you enable Simon & Schuster and the author to continue publishing exceptional books for years to come. We thank you for supporting the author's copyright by purchasing an authorized edition of this book.
No amount of this book may be reproduced or stored in any format, nor may it be uploaded to any website, database, language-learning model, or other repository, retrieval, or artificial intelligence system without express permission. All rights reserved. Inquiries may be directed to Simon & Schuster, 1230 Avenue of the Americas, New York, NY 10020
or permissions@simonandschuster.com.
This book is a work of fiction. Any references to historical events, real people, or real places are used fictitiously. Other names, characters, places, and events are products of the author's imagination, and any resemblance to actual events or places or persons, living or dead, is entirely coincidental.
Text © 2025 by Farah Heron
Jacket illustration © 2025 by Maggie Roman
Jacket design by Krista Vossen
All rights reserved, including the right of reproduction in whole or in part in any form.
SIMON & SCHUSTER BOOKS FOR YOUNG READERS
and related marks are trademarks of Simon & Schuster, LLC.
For information about special discounts for bulk purchases, please contact
Simon & Schuster Special Sales at 1-866-506-1949 or business@simonandschuster.com.
Simon & Schuster strongly believes in freedom of expression and stands against censorship in all its forms. For more information, visit BooksBelong.com.
The Simon & Schuster Speakers Bureau can bring authors to your live event.
For more information or to book an event, contact the Simon & Schuster Speakers Bureau at
1-866-248-3049 or visit our website at www.simonspeakers.com.
Interior design by Hilary Zarycky
The text for this book was set in Calisto MT Pro.
Manufactured in the United States of America
First Edition
2 4 6 8 10 9 7 5 3 1
Library of Congress Cataloging-in-Publication Data
Names: Heron, Farah, author, illustrator/
Title: Meet me on Love Street / Farah Heron.
Description: First edition. | New York : Simon & Schuster Books for Young Readers, 2025. |
Audience term: Teenagers | Audience: Ages 14 up. | Audience: Grades 7–9. |
Summary: Seventeen-year-old Sana, a hopeless romantic, teams up with the cynical Miles to plan a festival to save her gentrifying neighborhood on Love Street, all while trying to prove that love can conquer even the toughest of hearts.
Identifiers: LCCN 2024052737 (print) | LCCN 2024052738 (ebook) |
ISBN 9781665957571 (hardcover) | ISBN 9781665957595 (ebook)
Subjects: CYAC: Festivals—Fiction. | Canada—Indians—Fiction. | Gentrification—Fiction. | Love stories. | LCGFT: Romance fiction. | Novels.
Classification: LCC PZ7.1.H49462 Me 2025 (print) | LCC PZ7.1.H49462 (ebook) |
DDC [Fic]—dc23
LC record available at https://lccn.loc.gov/2024052737
LC ebook record available at https://lccn.loc.gov/2024052738

For Khalil, whose lifelong obsession with making places livable and fair for all the people who want to live in them inspired this book.

CHAPTER ONE

THE VELVET FORTUNE COOKIE

My name is Sana Merali, and I am a self-identifying, card-carrying, cheese-loving, *hopeless* romantic.

I'm actually quite *hopelessly* hopeless. There's nothing in the world I love more than love. Reading about love. Talking about love. Seeing people in love. I even love helping people *fall* in love. I'm a total romance girlie, and I'm not ashamed to admit it.

It's inevitable that I would turn out this way because I *literally* live on Love Street, a quiet side street in east Toronto. I technically didn't grow up here—Mom bought Morgan Ashton Flowers and the apartment over it after my parents divorced when I was nine—but I spent my formative years on Love Street.

And I've been a superfan of everything love and romance since I first set up my bedroom. I painted the walls pink and covered them with hand-painted hearts and rainbows. I threw out my chapter books and switched to YA romance. I plastered my walls with pictures of couples from my favorite movies and TV shows. To this day I have a two-book-a-week romance novel habit, and I watch holiday rom-coms year-round. *Seriously*. I freaking *adore* love.

And that's why I was happier than a raccoon on trash

day when Priya, my ex-girlfriend, told me today that she couldn't go to prom with me anymore because she'd fallen in love.

"She's so smitten!" I tell my friend Cara. We're at Cosmic Vintage, the store where Cara and I work part-time. This job is perfect for me because not only do I almost exclusively wear vintage, but it's also on Love Street, right across from Mom's flower shop. "I don't know why I didn't see it before, but Priya and Amber are *made* for each other. Somehow they hadn't even met until I introduced them last week!"

"You introduced them?" Cara asked. "That's odd. She's literally your ex. Now you don't have a prom date."

Cara is standing behind the counter with me, helping me sort through donations for Cosmic Vintage's annual prom drive. The store partners with a local youth drop-in center to donate prom clothes to kids who need them. It's my favorite thing to do at the store because going through other people's prom memories feels like getting a peek into their happiness. Cara pulls a pale blue off-the-shoulder tulle gown out of a garment bag. It looks a lot like my prom dress, except mine is dusty rose.

I run my hand over the cloud-like fabric. "Prom is weeks away. That's *plenty* of time for me to find a new prom date."

Cara wrinkles her nose. "I still think it's bad planning to set up your *prom date* with someone else. Even if you two are only friends now."

I shrug. Priya and I broke up four weeks ago, after being together for four months. I liked Priya a lot, but I was definitely putting more energy into the relationship than she was. I even staged the most epic, *romantic*, perfectly executed promposal our school had ever seen, complete with a dancing flash mob, a chocolate heart with her name in flowery script, and roses from my mom's shop. Priya was delighted with the spectacle and, of course, agreed to be my prom date.

After the promposal, I scoured every vintage and thrift store in the city to get coordinated dresses in the same dusty-rose shade that flattered both our brown skin tones. I did so much work, but I think I always knew that I deserved *more* out of the relationship. More heart-flutters, more can't-get-enough-of-each-others, and more this-could-be-forevers. And there was no way I would meet my *actual* perfect person while dating Priya. We still agreed to go to prom together with our matching dresses after I broke up with her though, because we're friends. Even in my wildest dreams I wouldn't have imagined that Priya would fall headfirst in love with Amber Reynolds only a week after I introduced them. I'm genuinely delighted for them both.

The fact that I don't have a prom date now isn't a problem. It's an *opportunity*.

I smile as I inspect a deep red dress with rhinestones on the straps. "Oh, this is pretty! Whoever wore it must have looked *stunning* at their prom." The dress smells a bit like mothballs, but it's nothing an airing out can't fix. I hang it on a rack. "Anyway, I can't be mad at Priya. Amber's a catch. It's funny, though. I've actually been ditched for Amber before. In grade ten Dawson Claymore dumped me for her because she had better boobs than me."

Cara snorts. "Did he actually say that to your face?"

Cara pulls out another dress, a long navy one with a slit up one side. She checks it for stains or tears.

I nod. "Yep. And honestly, they *are* better. So how do I find a new date? I asked some friends at school, but everyone's already paired up. Should I try apps?"

"Why do you even need a date? Go solo!"

"Because this is prom, Cara! I don't want my prom memory to be *alone*. You remember who you went with, right?"

I only ask that because I already know the answer. Cara will never forget her prom date, and the dreamy look she gets whenever she thinks about her on-again, off-again girlfriend is *adorable*. I turn to look at her and yep, there it is. "Of course. I went with *Hannah*."

Cara is also a hopeless romantic, but she'd never admit it. All her romantic energy is funneled to one person: Hannah Weatherspoon. They started dating in high school, but Hannah went to university in Massachusetts on a hockey scholarship while Cara stayed here in Toronto to study physical therapy at the University of Toronto. Cara and Hannah have broken up a few times, but they always get back together. I've never met Hannah, but I know Cara has it bad for her.

"You just wait," I say. "I'm going to find someone like Hannah to go with. Or . . ." Hockey players aren't really my type. "Or someone as unforgettable to *me* as Hannah is to you!"

Cara shakes her head. "Careful, Sana. I'm worried you'd settle for just about anyone right now to get your cutesy, *couple goals* relationship." Cara reaches into the garment bag that had the navy dress in it and takes out a navy floral fascinator. "Wow. Do you think someone really wore this to their prom?" She clips the fascinator to her black hair and bats her eyelashes at me. With her tidy pixie haircut and smoky eye makeup, she looks like a 1920s femme fatale.

I laugh. "You look hot. And I'm not going to settle. I can't end up with a prom story as bad as my mother's." Cara raises a questioning brow as she takes off the fascinator. "My mother's prom date was a twenty-two-year-old she met at a coffee shop," I explain. "She only went out with him because she liked his dog."

Cara laughs. "Your mom has the *best* stories. Seriously, she's epic. She should write a book."

Yeah, Mom is epic. Epically bad at modeling healthy, loving relationships for her only child. Which is why I want the *opposite* of what Mom wanted.

"How do I manifest a meet-cute? I saw on TikTok that burning bay leaves can help you meet a new love." I'm pretty sure Mom has dried bay in the apartment.

Cara rolls her eyes. "Sana, you're not in a romance novel. Real relationships don't start with cinematic meet-cutes." Cara wheels over another rack stuffed with more donated prom clothes, her chunky black boots reverberating on the old wood floor. Cara mostly wears vintage too—she's wearing a nineties rayon floral dress today.

"Relationships have to start somewhere. Why can't they start with a meet-cute?" I grab a garment bag from the rack. "I don't even remember how Priya and I first met."

Despite having a decent number of exes, I've never had a meet-cute worthy of the books and movies I inhale. I've had a few *almost* meet-cutes. I was once rescued by a very fit lifeguard when the cheap plastic oar on my inflatable boat snapped in half at Woodbine Beach. He had gleaming brown skin and white teeth. Plus, perfect abs. When we locked eyes after he dragged me and my sad little boat to shore, I was positive our story would end with a barefoot sunset walk with an alt-folk song playing in the background. But I never saw him again.

Then there was the time I was grabbing the last custard pineapple bun from the tray at my favorite bakery on Spadina, and my metal tongs hit the tongs of a cute girl wearing cat ear headphones and an anime T-shirt. We smiled at each other and even ended up sharing the bun. We talked about music and our favorite animes, and we exchanged Instagram handles, but other than the odd heart on one of the pics on my grid, I never heard from her again.

"I *live* on Love Street," I say. "How cool would it be if I met someone here?" I unzip the bag and am met with lush red fabric. "Ooooh, a jacket. Yay!" We tend to get a ton of donated gowns for the prom drive, but very little for those who want to dress in masculine clothes.

Cara's eyebrows go up. "Wow, that's a unique one. Is it velvet?"

I nod as I run my hand over the soft lapel. It's a slim-cut jacket that could be worn by any gender, in a shiny, deep red velvet. "It's *gorgeous*. It looks like a red rose. This person has *taste*."

"Yeah, exactly *your* taste," Cara says. "I'll make a time machine so you can ask them to your prom."

I laugh, but she's right. The deep red is the same shade as the corduroy skirt I'm wearing right now. I sniff the jacket and inspect it for damage. It's in great condition—it won't need dry cleaning or repairs before we donate it to the youth center. I check the pockets and dump the contents onto the counter.

A tube of generic lip balm, a little tin of hair wax, a wrapped condom, and a tiny slip of white paper.

Cara picks up the condom. "No action on prom night. Sad." She opens the hair wax. "Oooh, that smells nice." She holds the tin in front of my nose. It smells clean and a little spicy.

"Preparedness and safe sex are so romantic. As is good grooming." I pick up the slip of paper. It's a fortune from a fortune cookie. "Oh my god, it's a sign," I say after reading it. "Manifesting worked! I didn't even have to burn leaves!"

"What's it say?" Cara asks.

"Love is closer than you think. Its power is going to change you more than you expect." I beam at Cara.

Someone laughs behind me. "Of course *Love* is close. This is *Love Street*." It's Jenn, our boss, and the owner of Cosmic Vintage. She's been doing paperwork in the little office behind the counter all night and has clearly been listening to our conversation.

I've known Jenn my whole life since she and my mom are old friends from high school. Jenn's the one who told Mom about the flower shop for sale after my parents' divorce. She hired me at Cosmic two years ago, saying since I spend so much time in her shop, she may as well pay me.

I wave the tiny white slip of paper in the air, practically dancing in place. "This means that I *will* find love . . . and right here! Closer than I think!"

Cara takes an exaggerated step away from me. "Don't look at me."

I laugh. Cara is a lesbian, and I'm pansexual, but not once have I thought Cara could be my one true love. She has a definite type—*athletes*. I'm convinced that's why she wants to be a physical therapist. My idea of physical exertion is changing the record on Jenn's old player.

Speaking of, I go to the stereo and flip over the Cure album that's playing. "C'mon, Cara. This is fate, right? I *literally* found a fortune about *finding love* while I was talking about wanting to find love."

"Fortunes are supposed to come out of cookies, not velvet sport coats," Jenn says, finally coming out of her office. She's dressed how she always dresses—in tight black jeans and a band shirt from the nineties. She runs her hand over the soft velvet of the jacket on the counter. "This is a nice one, though."

Cara shakes her head. "Fortunes aren't supposed to come in jackets *or* cookies. You're as gullible as my grandmother. She gets ripped off by the same fortune-teller every year since she moved here from China. That woman couldn't predict what month will come next."

Cara may not believe in omens, but I do. I slip the fortune into the pocket of my skirt. It's a sign. I'm going to be as happy as Priya very soon.

Jenn's gaze sweeps across the empty store. "Did any customers come in since I started payroll?"

I shake my head.

"Ugh." Jenn cringes. "Sales are down again this week. We've taken a big hit since that boutique on Gerrard opened."

Love Street isn't very big, and only a short stretch of it has stores, all with apartments over them. After the shops, there's a small park, then houses until the street ends. Cosmic Vintage is the biggest shop on the street—and probably the most popular. People come from all over the city specifically for Jenn's curated vintage collection. Along with Cosmic, there are a couple of small restaurants, an adorable new café, a dog groomer, a European grocer, an empanada shop, a bakery, a used bookstore, and, of course, Mom's flower shop. Love Street is off Gerrard Street East, which has been gentrifying a lot in the last few years. It kind of sucks for the neighborhood. Toronto's original Little India is on Gerrard, and a lot of those old Indian businesses are being pushed out. Thankfully, Love Street isn't really changing. It's got its own personality—different from any other place in the city.

"It's felt kind of slow all week," Cara says.

"It's been slow on the whole street." Jenn pulls her dark blond hair into a ponytail. "I was going to start interviewing for a new part-timer this week, but now I don't think I even need someone. You two are coming to the BOA meeting on Saturday, right? We're going to brainstorm ideas to increase traffic to the street." The LSBOA—the Love Street Business Owner's Association—meets once a month, and Jenn is the president.

"Yeah, I'm coming," I say. The monthly meetings are in my favorite café, LoveBug, and I like seeing everyone from the street all together.

Cara nods, then wheels the now-empty rolling rack out of the way. "I can come too. What do you think the BOA can do?"

Jenn shrugs. "I dunno. Maybe organize some new flyers or advertise or something. Anyway, let's not worry about it now. Hey, maybe we can bring those seventies dresses to the front? Post them on Insta, and people will think we have new stuff."

"Yes!" I love merchandising. Cara changes the record to an ABBA one to get in the seventies mood, and we spend the rest of our shift redoing the mannequins and front stock with a disco glam vibe.

Like always, I let my mind wander while working, daydreaming about a meet-cute happening for me right here on Love Street. It *will* happen. I don't even care that much about finding a prom date—but I *am* going to find *love. I have proof*, I think, running my finger over the fortune in my pocket.

After work, I dig through my jewelry and find a big silver filigreed heart locket that I bought from Cosmic last year. I fold the fortune and press it inside the locket. Cara might be skeptical of signs and fortunes, but I'm determined. This fortune is going to come true.

CHAPTER TWO

THE MEET-NOT-CUTE

The next night Jenn joins Mom and me for dinner because after, Jenn's going to help Mom paint a whole bunch of pots for custom centerpieces for a wedding. We're at our small dining table, which is squeezed between our kitchen and living room. Zuri, my small black cat, is sleeping on the chair next to mine. While we're eating, Jenn and I tell Mom about the fortune I found in the velvet jacket.

"I'm going to wear this every day," I say, holding the locket around my neck. "I know this means I'll find someone new."

Mom nods with a faint smile, then takes a bite of food. She's not romantic like me, so she probably doesn't believe in fortunes. Mom made chickpea bowls for dinner—basically, whatever's in the fridge, plus a can of chickpeas, chaat masala, and yogurt. This time it's chickpeas, zucchini, kale, and shredded carrots. Mom's honestly not the best cook, probably because she doesn't actually enjoy cooking. We're both vegetarians though, so what Mom's food lacks in variety, she more than makes up for in veggies and canned beans.

Most of the time I love the fact that my mother is the furthest thing from a stereotypical South Asian mother. My other desi friends are super jealous that she lets me do my own thing, as long as I do okay in school and stay out of trouble. She's fine with me studying digital arts in an arts college next year and didn't do the whole *you must study science or math* thing. She didn't have an issue when I came out as pansexual and doesn't care who I date as long as I'm treated well. She didn't even flinch when she found out I'm not a virgin—just asked me if I was being safe, which, of course, I was.

We even look alike; we both have medium brown skin, curly black hair, and the perfect lip shape for red lipstick. People always think we're sisters, not mother and daughter, but that's probably because Mom, in her favorite denim overalls and T-shirts, doesn't look very motherly. Mom's a bit . . . different. She's the kind of person others like to call a "free spirit," and they don't mean it in a good way. She was a wild child when she was young—she's told me so many stories of her and Jenn sneaking out of their homes to go to all-night raves or hanging out in coffee shop parking lots when she was supposed to be at school. She even almost flunked out of high school and went to a community college for floral design instead of going to university, disappointing her traditional Indian parents.

She married my dad when she was only twenty-two, even though Jenn told me that their friends back in high school had a poll of which one of them was the least likely to ever get married, and Mom won by a landslide. My dad is, like, eleven years older than my mom, and they knew each other for only six months before their wedding. I really don't know why they got married because they're so different.

They weren't like . . . cold or anything to each other

when I was young, but Dad never snuck kisses or bought Mom presents, and Mom never made him special dinners or planned date nights. They never even vacationed together. I don't like to think about it too much because *ew*, they're my parents, but I was born seven months after their wedding, so they probably *had* to get married because Mom was pregnant, and they both have traditional Muslim parents. I'm not sure they ever actually loved each other.

Mom's been single since the divorce, but that's because she's always busy with some new hobby or project. She repaints our living room about every eight months. She built a huge deck behind our apartment. She's gotten into knitting, sewing, and even learned to play the guitar recently. She's always doing new things in her flower shop, too. She's very good at her job—her floral designs are *gorgeous*. She's busy, but I have no idea whether she's *happy*. She doesn't talk about herself to me much.

"Only Sana would find a fortune in a jacket," Jenn says, laughing. "Gorgeous piece. I wanted to keep it for the store instead of donating it." Jenn's phone buzzes, and she checks the text. "Mrs. Kotch again. She's reminded me three times to put the rising cost of butter on the agenda for the BOA meeting."

I chuckle. The Love Street BOA is great, but I'm pretty sure they have no control over dairy pricing.

Mom shakes her head. "This is why I don't want to be on the BOA board. Constantly getting complaints for things you don't have the power to fix." Mom pauses. "I think people need to accept that we can't control everything on this street."

I look at Mom. I can't read her expression—I don't know

if she's talking about her store or about something else. Either way, I don't like that negative talk. Like, why bother even trying if you don't think you can't control anything?

"Think positively, Mom," I say. "I know the BOA will be able to help. Cara and I are going to the meeting with Jenn to help brainstorm."

"I thought you were going to your father's for the weekend?"

I shake my head. Dad wanted me to, but I told him I *had* to be at this meeting because I don't want to spend the night at his house. "Just having Sunday brunch with them all. Noureen picked some trendy pan-Asian place." *Them all* is Dad, his wife, Noureen, and Noureen's daughter, Sarina. Noureen is really into brunching, and Dad does whatever Noureen wants. Sarina is a year older than me and in university, and I have no idea whether she enjoys brunching as much as her mother, but she does always show up.

Mom doesn't say anything but glances at Jenn, who's also silent. I wonder if they're taking their own advice. . . . If you don't have anything nice to say, don't say anything at all. I honestly don't have a lot of nice things to say about Noureen, either.

"Anyway, you should come to the meeting, Mom," I say while dousing my bowl with more hot sauce. "Maybe we can plan a cross-promotion or something to get sales up, like what you did with the bakery last year." That was super fun—Mom and Mrs. Kotch gave out coupons for each other's shops with any purchase. "I noticed less walk-ins at the flower shop last time I worked there."

Mom shrugs and refills her water glass from the vintage

pitcher on the table. Most of our dishes are from thrift stores. Noureen thinks we're cheap for always buying things used, but it's good for the planet and has a ton of personality. I love all our vintage glassware—in the evenings, when the setting sun comes through our front window, all the multicolored glasses and vases shine like gems. It's magical.

Mom tugs at the loose strands of black hair falling out of her messy bun. She's getting more gray strands in her curls. "*You* don't need to worry about the shop's sales, Sana. We're fine. My wedding business is doing great. I just met with a new bride. . . . I love doing Indian weddings. They want a fully floral mandap."

Mom starts telling us about the bride's ideas for the mandap—the wedding canopy that is used in Hindu weddings. Mom does so many weddings that she's an expert on all the different wedding cultural practices in the city.

After dinner, Jenn and Mom set up the clay pots and paint on the table. I offer to help them, but Mom tells me to work on my homework instead. I sit on the sofa with my history books to work on an essay due on Monday. It's a good thing I prefer working with background noise, because Mom and Jenn soon start arguing about what shade of pink to paint the pots.

"Sana," Mom suddenly calls out. "Can you pop down to the cooler in the shop and grab me a pink ranunculus stem? We're going to need to color match it."

"Sure," I say. I save my work and head downstairs.

The door to Morgan Ashton Flowers is right next to the door to our apartment. The space is painted bright white, with pale wood floors and a warm wood counter. I always find it funny that Mom keeps the store so serene even though our apartment is full of bright colors. I open the flower cooler in the back room and grab a pink ranunculus from a bucket, then head back to the apartment. But as soon as I open the apartment door, I hear Jenn say, "I think you should tell Sana about this."

"Not now. She doesn't need to know yet," Mom says.

What are they talking about? They must not have heard me open the door. I know I shouldn't eavesdrop, but Mom's clearly not going to tell me this. Which isn't a surprise—Mom never tells me anything serious.

"This affects her too."

"Sana's just a kid, Jenn. I don't need to worry her yet."

"She's a hell of a lot smarter and more grown-up than we were at her age," Jenn says.

They're both silent for a bit. I wonder if I should go upstairs . . . but then I'll never find out what Mom's keeping from me.

Finally, Jenn says something. "Are you going to accept the offer?"

"I don't know," Mom says.

"You may not have a choice. I heard that Rossi's wants to take over the vacant space next to it to open a floral and garden department."

Ugh. Rossi's is the chain gourmet store that opened nearby. If they start selling flowers, it would suck for Mom's business.

"That shouldn't affect me," Mom says. "My wedding and event business is keeping me afloat. No one goes to a chain grocery store for their wedding flowers."

"It would affect your walk-ins. They're already down," Jenn says.

Mom sighs loudly. "Yeah. If interest rates were lower, I wouldn't need to rely on walk-ins."

I frown. She's probably talking about her *mortgage* interest. Mom owns this building—with the shop downstairs and the apartment upstairs—and I know she had a meeting with the bank this week. I bite my lip. Here I am stressing about not having a prom date, and Mom's worrying about being able to pay her mortgage.

"Interest rates aren't going to change," Jenn says. "If your sales don't go up, you'll have no choice *but* to sell the building."

What? Mom had an offer to sell the whole *building* . . . including the apartment we live in? Why is Mom keeping this from me?

"Hopefully it won't come to that. They don't need an answer right away." Mom pauses. "Let's see what happens this summer. And don't worry. I'll talk to Sana before making any decisions."

I exhale a shaky breath. I can't keep listening like this. They only sent me to get a flower from the cooler. It shouldn't take this long. I call out, "Got a ranunculus!" as I loudly run up the stairs.

No one talks about interest rates or selling the business once I'm back. But it's all I can think about. I wish there were something I could do.

Mom starts cleaning up after Jenn leaves. "Can you cover the flower shop for a few hours on Sunday after your brunch?" she asks while she's washing the brushes. "I have to head up north. Nani and Nana need their gutters cleaned."

Mom's parents, my Nani and Nana, live about an hour

17

north of us. Mom gets called if there are any chores that need to be done in their house since she's the only one of her siblings somewhat close by."

"Yeah, of course," I say, still thinking about why Mom would keep this huge secret from me. "Mom, would it help if I left Cosmic to come work for you instead? You seem so . . . busy lately."

Mom shakes her head. "Absolutely not. Partially because Jenn would kill me, but also, I can't give you the hours she does. You're making money for school." Mom smiles, but it seems kind of forced. "You need to worry about *you*, Sana, not me. So, why do you need a prom date? I thought you were going with Priya? I hope you two work it out. She's such a nice girl."

Had she been listening at all at dinner? "I don't want to get back together with Priya," I say. "But seriously, I can at least cover more hours at the flower shop. I have time." I have no idea how else I can help, but I have to do *something* so she won't sell the building.

"You're such a good girl. I'm fine though." She yawns. "I'm meeting that bride again tomorrow. . . . I need to get some inspiration pictures together before bed."

"Okay." I reluctantly head back to the couch to study, even though I know there's no way I'll be able to focus on this essay now. I put my hand on the locket on my neck. Maybe this message isn't a good omen for me only, but for *everyone* here on Love Street, especially my mom. Because we all could use some good fortune right now.

I do a little bit of googling that night about interest rates and what would happen if Mom can't pay her mortgage.

I don't understand a lot of it, but it's clear that sales *need* to increase this summer—otherwise Mom might sell the flower shop and the apartment we live in. Hopefully the BOA can do something.

On Saturday I go home after my shift at Cosmic to get my history books so I can study at LoveBug before the BOA meeting. I see Mom at the workbench in the flower shop on my way out, so I pop in to say hi. Mom looks so pretty in her floral dress with Converse sneakers and a denim jacket. She has a beautiful little bouquet in front of her made with the pink ranunculus from the cooler earlier.

"That's so pretty," I say. "I love ranunculuses."

"Yeah, waste of time though. As soon as I finished it, the customer called saying they don't need it anymore." Mom sighs, shaking her head. "A theater company ordered it for a play, then decided to use silk flowers. At least they paid up front. Too bad I can't sell it—I'm about to close for the day."

"Oooh, if you don't need it, let me take it to LoveBug and take some pictures! I can put them up on the flower shop's Instagram."

Mom shrugs and hands me the bouquet.

"So, are you coming to the meeting?"

Mom nods. "Yeah, I'll be there. Jenn said it's my neighborhood duty."

I laugh. "Yay! I'll see you there."

The LoveBug café opened about a year ago, and I was utterly delighted when it did. In fact, the whole city was delighted. There was a ton of buzz from Toronto blogs and influencers, and the café is still pretty popular with people who want an adorable aesthetic for their social pics. With the pink floral wallpaper, pastel dishes, gold cutlery, and pale pink tables, LoveBug is the only *love*-themed business on the street. It's such an improvement over Donut Time, the café that always smelled like cigarettes and, despite its name, never actually had any donuts.

LoveBug is owned by husband and wife Ajit Patel and Julie Choi. The design of the café is all Julie, and the menu is all Ajit. The two seem so different until you talk to them and realize they are pretty much the same person. I seriously want to be them when I grow up.

Julie's wiping a table near the front when I come in, and she gives me a hug. "That bouquet is gorgeous!" she says.

"Stunning, right? Can I take some pictures of it here for my mom's Insta? I'll tag LoveBug too."

"Yeah, absolutely. You're staying for the BOA meeting, right?"

I nod. "I need to do some schoolwork first."

"I really hope we actually get something done this time," Julie says as she goes back to cleaning tables. "Something other than Mrs. Kotch complaining about prices and Grant going on about the bike thefts in the park. I get that bike thefts are a problem, but what can we do about what happens in the park?" Julie finishes wiping the table. "Want a pink chai?" She knows my favorite drink. I love the pink Kashmiri chai latte at LoveBug, not only because of the gorgeous light pink color but the sweet milky cardamom flavor, too.

"Yes, please. And a pistachio biscotti. Can you put it on my tab?"

"Sure thing. I'll get Charlene to bring it for you."

I drop my bag onto one of the pale pink café tables. "Who's Charlene?"

Julie beams. "My new part-timer! You have to see her latte art. She made a perfect Mickey Mouse on a matcha latte yesterday. She's studying biology at U of T."

I look over at the counter and see a dark-haired white girl with Ajit. She's pretty, with wavy hair, and is wearing plum-colored lip gloss and a pink sweatshirt with an illustration of a hamster on it.

"She's cute," I say.

"She's *lovely*. And she's working out *so* well. I didn't want to hire her at first because she's vegan—last time I had a vegan barista, they handed someone an egg and bacon sandwich calling it a 'chicken ovum and pig fat' sandwich. And they called a latte 'bovine breast milk and espresso.' Thankfully, Charlene isn't judgy."

I cringe. I'm a vegetarian, but I'm not militant like that. And if I were, I'd never take a job in a café that served animal products.

I grab a table near the window and pull out everything I need: my laptop, my history book, a new romance from the library (because I'll need a break, of course), and Mom's bouquet. Charlene brings my chai and cookie, and after about half an hour of taking notes, I decide that's enough history for now—time for that photo. I pick up the flowers. It's a self-standing bouquet, which means you can hold it or stand it upright on a surface, and it perfectly matches the aesthetic of this café. I arrange the flowers in front of my pink drink and half-eaten cookie, with the turquoise romance book in the background. When I stand to take a picture for my Instagram, I notice a guy I'd never seen before ordering at the counter.

It isn't the fact that he's unfamiliar that makes me take note of him, though.

Nope, it's because he's like . . . capital C *cute*.

His skin is brown like mine, and he has longish black hair pushed behind his ears. Plus glasses. Kind of nerdy, but in a cute way. He's wearing brown cords and a perfectly faded red T-shirt with black bands around the sleeves, and he's carrying a worn-out canvas messenger bag and a paperback tucked under his arm. When he turns, I see wide-set eyes, a perfect jawline, and full lips. *Nice.*

And also? I hear Charlene repeat his order back to him—a pink Kashmiri chai latte.

This could be the meet-cute I was waiting for. Maybe the reason I've never been in love is because I always go for people who are so different from me. Like Priya is a total overachiever, and I'm clearly not. Before Priya, I was with Noah, who was a complete jock, and before Noah was Dawson, who *hated* the color pink, flowers, or anything he deemed too girlie (except Amber Reynolds's extremely girlie breasts).

But this pink chai guy? He's hanging out in LoveBug and drinking Kashmiri chai, so he clearly isn't allergic to the color pink. He's got brown skin, so maybe he's Indian, like me. He's wearing cords, and I practically live in corduroy. And he loves to read! We have so much in common already.

I'm never afraid of talking to people I don't know, so I give the guy my most winning smile as he walks toward the tables with his clear mug of pink tea. I'm hoping he'll take the hint and sit at a table near mine.

Or even better—maybe he'll ask if he can join me. Maybe make a comment about our matching drinks. And I'll say something about how pretty the color is on such a gray day. Then he'll ask about the flowers, and I'll show him the bouquet that matches the café and the tea we're drinking, and he'll laugh and ask whether I planned that and if I like gardening, and I'll tell him that my mother is a florist and I grew up above a flower shop, and he'll ask where, and I'll tell him right across the street. . . .

My perfect meet-cute on Love Street.

My skin is buzzing with excitement, but the guy doesn't seem to take my psychic hints. He doesn't even look at me as he takes his chai to a table on the far side of the café. Nowhere near close enough to strike up a conversation.

No problem—maybe I need to work harder to make it happen. I touch the locket containing the fortune on my neck and take the flowers over to the cute guy's table. His head is down as he reads his book.

"How do you like the pink chai?" I ask.

Startled, he looks up at me. And yeah, he's even cuter up close. Deep brown eyes and curly, dark lashes. "What?" he asks.

I give him my best smile. "The pink Kashmiri chai, how do you like it? I don't work here or anything. . . . I'm curious. It's my favorite drink at LoveBug, and I don't see people drinking it much."

He looks at me with no expression for several seconds. Finally, he glances at his drink as if he just figured out what I'm talking about. "Oh . . . yeah, it's fine. A little sweet, but tasty." I like his voice. It's deeper than I expected it to be. And very smooth.

"Good thing I have such a sweet tooth!" I say, shooting him another winsome smile while he . . . continues to stare at me looking vaguely confused. "Hey, can you do me a favor? Can you take a picture of me holding these flowers in front of that wallpaper?"

The wall closest to us has pale blue wallpaper dotted with pink roses. And I happen to be wearing one of my favorite outfits from Cosmic, wide-legged dusty-rose trousers and a pale cream blouse with pink buttons. I know I look fabulous and match the flowers perfectly. I'll post the picture on Mom's Instagram, tagging both Cosmic and LoveBug, helping three Love Street businesses at once, and I'll have photographic evidence of my perfect meet-cute by having this cute guy take my picture.

"Just a couple of quick shots," I say. "It'll only take a second."

The guy still has that confused expression. Then he looks back down at his book. "Um, I'm busy," he says without looking at me.

Okaaay . . . I mean, if he doesn't want to take my picture or even stop reading his book, that's totally fine. But that was a little rude. I guess this wasn't the meet-cute I wanted.

The door to LoveBug opens then, and Cara comes in. Excellent. She can take the pictures. I don't say anything to the guy and go ask Cara for her help instead.

After Cara and I have a little photo shoot of me with the flowers, she sits at my table while I look over the pictures. "Who's that?" she asks, indicating the pink chai guy at the other end of the café. I had no idea he was still here. I shrug.

"He must work on the street," Cara says. No one would know it from her cool and aloof demeanor, but Cara is a total neighborhood gossip just like everyone else on Love Street. "Maybe at the bistro? Or Kozlaks'?"

I shrug again. I'm still irritated that he brushed me off so curtly, and I really don't want to waste any more mental energy on the guy.

"Maybe he's your future prom date?" Cara asks.

I roll my eyes. I wonder how long Cara is going to continue this one-sided conversation.

"He's exactly your type," she adds.

Now that, I *have* to respond to. I tilt my head. "Why, because we're both Brown? Priya's Brown, and she's nothing like that guy." Priya is the designer purse and shoes type. She hates messenger bags.

Cara gives me a smug look. "They are both *exactly* your type. You always notice high-maintenance girls and nerdy boys."

I laugh at that. I mean, my eyes were drawn to him the moment he walked in. "Okay fine. He's cute. But he doesn't seem interested in anything other than his book." I shouldn't judge. Maybe he's having a bad day and not looking to make friends today.

Jenn and my mom show up for the BOA meeting and Jenn sets up a folding whiteboard at the front of the café. Mom joins Cara and me at our table. I show Mom the pictures Cara took, and we pick one to post to the flower shop's Insta, tagging the other two businesses. Alain, the bistro owner, comes to our table to talk to Mom about flowers for his restaurant, while several people line up to get coffee from the carafe Ajit placed on the counter. I look over to the cute pink chai guy. He's still there, reading his textbook. Maybe he *does* work on the street. *Ugh*. It will be annoying to see him on Love Street all the time.

Jenn asks everyone to take a seat, and I notice that one

of the rude waiters from the bistro sits next to the guy, so maybe Cara's right and he works there. It would explain his attitude—everyone at the bistro, especially *that* waiter, has that French snobby attitude perfected.

The café is pretty crowded—since the meeting is open to everyone who works on the street, not only the actual business owners. A lot of people *love* working here, so the meetings become a social thing. After going over regular business, like dues owed and Mrs. Kotch's butter problem, Jenn starts talking about the sales decline on the street. She explains that Cosmic Vintage, as well as other shops like Second Story Books and the empanada shop, have all reported a noticeable drop in sales since the newer trendy stores opened on Gerrard. Other business owners pipe in to agree. Ina Kozlak from the Eastern European grocer says she had sausages go bad because they sat unsold for too long. Mrs. Kotch complains no one is buying her lovingly made authentic German cakes since they can now buy a grocery store one from a display case around the corner. I wonder if Mom is going to mention the decrease in walk-ins at the flower shop, but she doesn't say anything.

When Jenn opens the floor to ideas for what can be done to get customers buying again, people start talking over one another.

"Can we make a petition to force the Rossi's store to close?" Mrs. Kotch asks first.

Someone scoffs behind me, and I recognize the deep voice. Pink Chai Guy. I do agree that Mrs. Kotch's petition idea would never work because the grocery store is already open and has every right to exist, but Mrs. Kotch has run that bakery for over thirty years. Her livelihood is being threatened, so of course she's a little irrational.

I turn to glare at the guy. He's still at the same table with that waiter. "You can't force a store to close because you don't like it," he says.

I don't like that patronizing tone he used on poor Mrs. Kotch.

I lean into Cara. "Why does Alain hire such tools at the bistro?"

She shrugs, a sour look on her face. "Who knows, but I think you were right about him not being your type."

Mrs. Kotch and Alain both start talking at the same time. I'm pretty sure Alain's suggestion of how to take care of the grocery store is highly illegal, so Jenn shuts it down. "Serious ideas that we can actually implement only."

"We *can* actually implement that," Alain says. "I know a guy."

Everyone starts shouting out ideas again. The empanada shop's owner suggests putting tables on the sidewalks to make the street look busier. But Pink Chai Guy says they'd need a city permit for that. Someone else suggests closing to car traffic, like they do on Kensington Avenue once a month. But, of course, Pink Chai Guy tells everyone that the application process for that could take years.

This guy is getting on my nerves. I raise my hand to suggest cross-promotions on social media, like my post of Mom's flowers with Jenn's vintage clothes, taken here at the café. Julie pipes in agreeing that it's a great idea and that LoveBug's success is mostly driven by social media. Pink Chai Guy, of course, makes a comment that not everyone is tethered to their socials.

I turn to glare at him again. I don't know why I thought he was cute when I first saw him. It was probably the pink drink that made him look good. That chai has magical properties—it makes just about anyone look appealing. "Are you going to shoot down every suggestion anyone has?" I ask the guy.

He raises a brow at me. "Only the ones I know won't work. Honestly, I think you guys should do more research before jumping on an idea."

The guy from the bistro next to him snorts a laugh at that.

Ugh. That's it. I turn away from them. I should be focusing on how I can *save* Mom's store, not on this smug grump. New goal: banish Pink Chai Guy from my brain permanently.

I lean over to Cara. "*Well-Actually-Man* is getting on my nerves."

Cara giggles at my nickname for him.

"Why don't we highlight the history of the street," Reggie, the used bookstore owner, who's sitting in the front row, suggests. I'm not surprised. Judging by the number of historical books Reggie sells, he's a history nut. "Love Street was named after Lionel Osmond Love."

"Who's that?" someone asks.

That question makes Pink Chai Guy pipe in again. "You all work here. Shouldn't you know something about the street's history?"

Jenn, who finally seems annoyed by Pink Chai Guy, sighs. "Why don't you tell us?"

Pink Chai Guy stands and smiles like he was given a free puppy. Unfortunately, it's an adorable lopsided smile.

"Lionel Osmond Love was a prominent Toronto city councillor in the fifties. He was instrumental in challenging post-war urban renewal policies that were displacing lower-income workers from the city core. He was a major anti-poverty activist and championed diversity before it was common to do that. There *should* be a plaque about him in the park that's named after him. He's a hero to many in the city."

Huh. I actually *did* know that the street and park were named after a guy called Lionel Osmond Love, because the park's official name is L. O. Love Park, or LOL Park for short, which is hysterical to anyone under fifty. But I didn't know anything about what this Love guy did.

"There was a whole CBC Heritage Minute short film about him," Pink Chai Guy says when no one responds to him. He sounds positively incredulous that we're not up to speed on the life of this historical dude.

"Okay, but I'm not sure how we can get people to shop here by highlighting an anti-poverty activist?" Jenn asks, frowning.

Suddenly, an idea comes to me, and I stand and shout it out instead of raising my hand because honestly, it's pretty perfect. "No, he's right! We *should* highlight the name of the street. This is Love Street! *Love* is the common thread! Like love and romance!" It's so obvious that I'm kind of disappointed no one thought about it before.

April, who owns the pet grooming business, shakes her head. "This café is the only business here that remotely matches that theme. And I suppose the flower shop. No one else's store has anything to do with love."

I clap my hands together, excited. "So, let's make them

about love! Not, like, change everything in all the stores, but just like . . . a love promotion. Jenn can put some vintage wedding gowns in the window. The bookstore can put a romance section up front. Things like that."

Jenn's eyebrows furrow as she considers my idea. I beam at her, vibrating with excitement. When she and Mom were talking about interest rates and stuff, Jenn said I was smart. I *know* she'll consider my idea. "A *Love* promotion. That's interesting, Sana," Jenn finally says. "Anyone have thoughts on this?"

Everyone is silent for a bit, and then Alain, the bistro owner, suggests prix fixe date-night meals. Mrs. Kotch says she can do a promotion on wedding and anniversary cakes. Even Mom seems to warm to the idea and suggests selling small arrangements that people can give to their sweethearts.

"Can we broaden it to include platonic and family love? To be more inclusive," Cara asks.

"And pet love," April says. "I can sell T-shirts that say 'I love my cat,' or even cat T-shirts that say 'I love my person.'"

I nod. "Yes! The flower shop can make friendship bouquets, too!" I'm obsessed with this concept.

After everyone throws out more ideas for the promotion, Pink Chai Guy finally says, "It's kind of cheesy, isn't it? Do you really think people will come to the street specifically because of hearts and trite quotes on your social medias?"

I turn to glare at him. Figures he'd call it cheesy. He seems to dislike joy.

Surprisingly, my mother is the one to rebut him. "If we

make it visually cohesive, I do think people would come. We could even reach out to the media."

"I *know* people would come," I say. "LoveBug is always busy. If we make everything on the street pretty for pictures, people will flock here. Don't underestimate TikTokers and Instagrammers looking for the perfect backdrop for their grid." I look over at Reggie, the bookstore owner. "The bookstore can carry more romance—it's the highest-selling book genre in the world. Feature the books up front, and people will come."

Cara grabs my arm with excitement. "I wonder if we could get one of those big heart statues for LOL Park. The one at the Distillery District is always so busy."

Jenn had started writing these ideas down on her whiteboard and adds "statue for LOL Park" to her list.

"Pole banners on the streetlights!" someone says.

"Little flyers that each shop can keep on the counter that says what all the businesses are doing," April suggests.

This is such a great idea, and even Pink Chai Guy can't argue against it. Rebranding Love Street as the street of love *is* the way to get people to come here. And they'll keep coming back once they realize how amazing it is. Best of all, with the focus being on love, my mother's business has the most to gain, as it's the street's only florist. I smile at her, and she grins back.

Eventually we decide to form a subcommittee of the BOA for this Love Street rebranding project. Jenn asks for volunteers, and of course my hand can't shoot up fast enough. This was *my* idea, and I want to be involved. Plus, I'm going to be studying digital arts in college—any branding we do will be great for my portfolio. Cara, Julie, April, and Grant, one of the restaurant owners, also volunteer for the committee.

After the meeting ends, I turn to glance at Pink Chai Guy, but all I see is his backside leaving the café with that waiter from the bistro. It's a nice backside, but I'm glad to see it go.

Reggie comes up to me. "I think this idea of yours has merit, Sana, but I can't help wondering if this is all a ploy of yours to get me to carry kissing books?" He has a mischievous twinkle in his eye.

Despite his neglect of my favorite book genre, I like Reggie. He's a Black man with a salt-and-pepper beard and a faint Caribbean accent, and he always wears buttoned-up shirts and tweed or corduroy jackets. He reminds me of my favorite English teacher. I grin. "You're throwing away sales by ignoring the most voracious readers in existence."

He rubs his chin. "Well, now it seems we're entering the season of love. Fortuitously, I recently purchased a large lot of books in an estate auction, and there were quite a few romance novels among them. I'd planned to donate the romances, but maybe you could help me curate our first romance section instead? I'm afraid that I'm not well-versed in the genre. I would, of course, pay you for your time."

Ah! Curating a romance section in a bookstore! Dream come true! "Of course. I'd love to! I'll do it for free!"

"Oh no, my dear. I must insist. What would Lionel Osmond Love say about me using free labor to make more money for myself?"

I can't say no to that. This will be a ton of fun.

I have such a warm glow when I leave the café. This

whole rebrand is going to help Mom, Jenn, and the other business owners so much. Sales will increase, Mom won't have to sell the building, and we can all stay here happily on Love Street. I touch my locket as I walk out into the early spring night. Maybe Jenn was right—this fortune could be referring to Love Street, not my love life. This whole street is going to get flipped over by love.

And if I also find love while helping Love Street? Even better.

CHAPTER THREE

THE ONE DIRECTION BRUNCH

The restaurant my stepmother chose for Sunday brunch is playing an easy-listening cover of a One Direction song with an out-of-place country twang. It doesn't match the "Elevated Asian Fusion" the restaurant claims to aspire to, but I've come to expect that Noureen's restaurant picks are always more about style than substance. At least this place does have decent vegetarian choices, unlike last month's Tex-Mex brunch.

Noureen . . . isn't my favorite person. I didn't meet her until about a year after my parents' divorce, even though I know Dad was seeing her long before then. Maybe he didn't want to introduce me to Noureen because he knew she wouldn't like me. Or maybe he'd filed me in the "old life" category in his mind, and Noureen and Sarina were "current life," and he didn't see a need to combine them until necessary. It hurt—especially since Dad and I had a pretty close relationship before Noureen.

Noureen is different from my mother. She doesn't work; her life goals seem to be to have a husband and children. That's it. Like, I'm not sure if she has—or had—any career aspirations of her own. She does adore my father—or at least she adores being married to a successful man with his own company—and I think my father likes the way Noureen fawns over him because my mother's not the type to put anyone on a pedestal, not even her husband. I don't know if Noureen actively dislikes me, but she does seem frustrated that her attempts to fix me haven't worked yet. Noureen is a fixer. You can't mention anything to her, even things that aren't problems at all, without her giving her opinion on how to fix them. And I apparently have a lot that needs fixing.

Today she has already suggested I fix my wardrobe (*I assume that dress is used again? You would have a much better chance of finding clothes that fit if you bought them new.*), fix my hair (*You must try this new flat iron I bought Sarina! It would even smooth out* your *hair!*), and my grades. Well, she didn't specifically try to fix my grades because I know she sees me as a lost cause there. But she did say that I should look into transferring from the art school I'm going to in September to a proper university (her phrasing) after a few semesters. And she found a way to squeeze in the fact that Sarina got to choose between scholarships when she was deciding on her university options.

In my opinion, Noureen doesn't have the right to try to influence me or my life. She's done enough damage already.

"Sana, you should come home with us after brunch," my dad says after Noureen finally seems to accept that I'm not switching schools. "We can at least go over your course selections for next year."

"Can't," I say. "I have to help Mom at the flower shop." I sip my watery green tea. Thank goodness Mom gave me that excuse.

"I thought you stopped working at the flower shop when you started at the thrift store?" Dad asks.

"It's a *vintage* store, not a thrift store." Not that there's anything wrong with thrift stores, but Jenn spends a lot of time and energy curating and merchandising her stock, which thrift stores don't do. "And I help Mom out when she needs me."

"You can't have enough time for studying if you're working in two places," Noureen says.

"She's my mother," I snap. "I am always there for my family." I don't normally talk back, but ugh. . . . These brunches bring out the worst in me. And anyway, I'm planning to study while I'm at the flower shop, but of course I can't mention that because I don't want Dad and Noureen to know that the flower shop will probably have no customers. If they knew Mom's business was struggling, they'd use it against her. I also don't intend to tell them about the Love Street rebranding project because I know they would do nothing but poke holes in my idea. Now that I think about it, Dad and Noureen would totally get along great with that Pink Chai Guy.

Everyone is silent for a moment. "Well, maybe another time," Dad finally says.

I don't say anything. Brunch every two weeks is enough daddy-daughter time—I don't think we need more.

Dad and I used to be close . . . before the divorce. As a florist, Mom always worked weekends, and Dad used to take me out while Mom worked. He would keep track of all the festivals in Toronto: Taste of the Danforth, Taste of Lawrence, the Jazz Festival, the Festival of South Asia, even Comicon. Almost every weekend we'd be in a different part of the city, eating twirly tornado potatoes and cinnamon churros and riding cheap carnival rides. I'm pretty sure the tradition started because he had no idea what to do with a girl who didn't like sports, but we did have a lot of fun. I still kind of miss eating expensive food, people-watching, and getting to know all the different pockets of the city with my dad.

But then he married Noureen, who'd been divorced for years. And with Noureen came Sarina—a girl only a year older than me. Whenever I went to Dad and Noureen's, it was assumed I would hang out with Sarina, so no one planned anything special for me. No more fairs or festivals. Dad was probably relieved that he didn't have to find things to entertain me anymore.

Dad also became more judgmental after marrying Noureen. Probably because her kid is exactly the high-achieving, perfect and quiet child that Indian parents want, and it made Dad feel insecure about his own academically mediocre offspring.

"I like Cosmic Vintage," Sarina says suddenly. I look at her. I wasn't aware that my stepsister had ever been in the store before. I don't actually dislike Sarina, but we have pretty much nothing in common, and I admit, it's super annoying that Sarina is perfect in all the ways I'm not. "A really nice girl helped me there once," Sarina continues. "Short black hair . . . She was so great."

"That's Cara," I say. "She's one of my closest friends."

Sarina nods. "I've seen her around. I think she goes to my school. Fast fashion is so harmful to the environment. We should all be buying more secondhand."

I raise an eyebrow at my stepsister. I've never heard Sarina say something that conflicted with her mother's stance on anything, so this is pleasantly out of character.

Then again, I really don't know her that well. When we were kids, Sarina used to complain to her mother if I touched one of her toys, and she would make comments about me not being as smart as her, but it's been a long time since she said anything like that to my face. But even when we grew up and stopped the petty fights, we never managed to get close, despite all those weekends I awkwardly sat with her while she did her homework, practiced her cello, or did another Noureen-approved extracurricular.

"What are your plans for the summer, Sana?" Noureen asks, not acknowledging her daughter's comments. "You could work at your father's real estate office. Sarina works there part-time, you know. But there should be enough for you to do too. It would look much better on your résumé than the used store."

I shake my head. "I'm fine at Cosmic."

Noureen gives my father a glance like it's his turn to say something. He clears his throat. "Sana, this is a good opportunity for you to make some changes in your life," he says. "You'll be finished high school soon; you can't keep living this hippie-dippie artist life like your mother. It's time you looked and acted like an adult."

Hippie-dippie?

My jaw clenches as I glance down at my outfit. I'm wearing vintage, of course. A yellow blouse with pearl buttons and a rust-colored skirt, along with boots and a pale beige cardigan. My outfit is perfectly brunch-with-Dad appropriate. No hearts or rainbows to be seen, except for the heart locket, which still has that fortune in it. No tie-dye, either, so I don't know what about me looks childish or hippie-like.

"I have a job, Dad. And I was accepted to the best art school in the country."

"Why an art school, though?" Noureen asks, apparently not satisfied with how our discussion on this topic a few minutes ago ended. "It doesn't seem practical. Also, why not apply to schools outside the city? It could be a great learning experience to live on campus!"

Cost, mostly, but I don't say that. Also, OCAD, the Ontario College of Art and Design, is super hard to get into. They should be proud of me. "Dad's the one who pushed me to apply for digital arts!" I say. I wanted to major in drawing and painting, but Dad lectured me for so long about studying something with viable career options. I kind of saw his point, so the digital arts major was my compromise. But apparently Noureen still isn't happy. To her, I may as well be studying basket weaving. I cross my arms over my chest. "I'm not Sarina—I'm not going to study business."

I look at my stepsister, but Sarina says nothing. I can't read her expression.

Dad sighs. He takes a deep breath before talking again. Seems I'm going to get another Dad lecture today. "Sana, I wanted to speak to you at home about this, but you never come home anymore." He glances at Sarina for a moment, then back at me. Clearly Sarina knows what this is about. Which is weird. It's so odd to think my own father has a closer relationship with his stepdaughter than with me. "We would love to help you more with your education, so in September, when you start university, we would all be happy if you would come live with us instead of living with your mother."

What . . . ? He wants me to live with him? In Noureen's house? "In Vaughan?"

"Yes. We're not far from the subway. Sarina takes it to school every day. We could cover all your living expenses easily this way. Even give you a bit of an allowance."

I'm speechless. Why would I want to move in with the man who replaced his family with this better model? Why would I ever agree to live under Noureen's judgment and passive-aggressiveness? My jaw clenches.

"There's plenty of space in the house," Noureen says. "This is a good opportunity for change."

I can't stop myself from cringing. "I can't leave Mom."

"Your mother is an adult," Noureen says. "She doesn't need you babysitting her."

I squeeze my lips together. Of course, my mother is an adult. . . . She freaking owns her own business and the building it's in. Alone. And she's loyal, supportive, and honest. Noureen can only dream of being like my mother.

"Why don't you think about it," Dad says.

I'm not going to. Ever. Mostly because I don't want to live with Dad and Noureen, but also because I can't imagine leaving Love Street. Cosmic Vintage. The flower shop. Jenn, Cara, Julie, and the whole Love Street crew. But telling Dad and Noureen off now for suggesting I move in with them isn't going to help. They would be even more disappointed in me, which would only make these brunches harder.

"Okay, I'll think about it," I say, before downing the rest of my green tea.

On the subway back into the city, I do think about Dad and Noureen's proposal. There's no way I would live with them, but the fact is, Love Street is struggling. Mom's worried about sales and interest rates and is even thinking of selling the building. If she sells, where would I go? Maybe Mom would want to live closer to her parents up north, but that would be way too far of a commute for me. And I can't afford to live in my college's residence next year, not without taking out massive student loans, which I really don't want to do.

I'm a positive person, and I pride myself on finding the best in any situation, but an hour and a half with Noureen at brunch every two weeks is bad enough; there's no way I could live with Noureen and Sarina full-time without tearing all my hair out. And I like my hair. It's like Noureen is a vampire, sucking all the optimism out of me whenever I'm in the room with her.

I have to make this Love Street rebranding project work. If we can get more people to come to the street and Mom's sales go up, then she won't have any trouble paying her mortgage and she won't sell the building. And I could stay right where I am, living on Love Street, and working at Cosmic Vintage when I start university in the fall. Exactly where I'm supposed to be.

CHAPTER FOUR

A HATER OF TRUE LOVE

The next day after school, I head straight to the bookstore instead of going home or to Cosmic Vintage. Second Story Books is on the same side of the street as the flower shop and across the street from Cosmic Vintage. It's a small dark, overstuffed store, which, despite the name, is on the first floor of an old building. I think the store is incredibly romantic, with the smell of old books and all the hidden corners. Come to think of it, it would be a perfect place for a meet-cute among the bookstacks. But no. I'm not looking for a meet-cute anymore. My focus is *only* on the Love Street project.

Reggie bought the bookstore a few years ago, and he immediately increased the history and historical fiction sections. He also started carrying a small selection of used records. He, unfortunately, got rid of the meager romance selection, which was probably for the best since the only romances in the store back then were old paperbacks with questionable consent in them. I was disappointed that he didn't curate a better romance section, though.

But now *I'm* the one who gets to pick books for Second Story Books' new and improved romance section, and I couldn't be more excited. The bell on the door chimes as I walk in, and Reggie smiles warmly at me from the counter.

He once told me he used to be in finance before buying this store. I can't see it—this man was born to be a librarian or bookstore owner. He's like . . . an aging cinnamon roll romance hero. "Ah. Sana, lovely to see you on this gloomy day. You always brighten a room."

I beam at him. I'm wearing a pink and blue floral minidress, with blue tights and a white cardigan today. My hair's up in a curly ponytail. "Hi, Reggie! I love that jacket. No one wears tweed like you! I'm not working at Cosmic today. Can I look at those romance books now?"

"Ah, yes! Your timing is impeccable." He comes out from behind the counter. "I have Miles going through the auction lot right now in the back room. He's sorting the books by genre, so it should take you no time to scan through the romances and find the ones worthy of my shop. Look! I've already made a sign for the section!" He shows me a small wood frame with a white paper in it that simply says ROMANCE in neat printing. The wood on the frame is the same shade as the shelving and the wood floors.

"Perfect!" This is going to be fun. I adore going through old stuff looking for treasures. "Who's Miles?"

"My new part-time employee." Reggie guides me through the maze of overstuffed bookshelves with that intoxicating old-paper scent toward the back room. "He just finished his first year of university. Smart young man—he's a big history buff. Miles is helping me modernize this whole operation. We're expanding the online bookstore, too." Reggie pushes open the door at the back of the shop. "You may have met him at the BOA meeting? But there were so many people there! This little community is very loyal. It's wonderful to see that much engagement."

The first thing I notice in the storeroom is shelves filled with even more books. Practically enough to fill an entire store again.

Then I notice a person, Miles, I assume, sitting on a step stool with a box of books in front of him.

And dammit. Miles is the *Pink Chai Guy*. Because of course he is. My upper lip involuntarily curls into a shocked expression.

"Miles, Sana's here to go through the romance books," Reggie says. "She's been after me to carry more kissing books, and with this Love on Love Street promotion, there's no better time!"

Pink Chai Guy—*Miles*—blinks at me like he's never seen me before in his life even though we had a literal conversation about tea at LoveBug two days ago.

"Hopefully there are enough gems in this lot to fill a few shelves up front," Reggie continues. "Miles can show you the process. You two will be great together!" Reggie leaves the storeroom.

This is fine, just dandy. Whatever. Maybe it's an opportunity to redo that terrible first meeting with the guy. He could have been having a bad day and is not normally a total douche nozzle. And there's no reason I should be as rude as he was then anyway. Shaking off my shock, I walk toward him, smiling. "Hi! I'm Sana Merali! I think we got off on the wrong foot when we met at LoveBug. I work at Cosmic Vintage, and I'm volunteering on the Love Street rebrand project."

The guy stares at me blankly for several long moments. This is the closest I've been to him, and yep, unfortunately he's still as cute as he was the first time I saw him. Actually, he's one step above cute even; Miles is downright hot. He's wearing jeans and a yellow Second Story Books T-shirt, and up close his warm brown skin is clear and smooth. His hair is silky and rich black and looks like he just ran his hands through it. And he smells clean . . . and . . . yummy. Like cardamom and rose water. I wonder if he had another pink chai this afternoon.

His eyes sweep over me. Starting from my black Mary Jane shoes, up my legs and dress, before finally landing on my glossy pink nails with big red hearts painted on them. I can't tell if his expression is approval or derision, but it's unnerving either way. This guy has a very intense gaze.

"I'm Miles Desai," he finally says. He's not quite smiling, but he doesn't look annoyed with me. He almost looks . . . pleasant. Did I just feel a spark when our eyes met?

I give Miles my best smile, so glad that I'm wearing my new favorite pink lip gloss. "So nice to formally meet you! This is going to be fun. I'm a huge romance reader."

My mind starts racing with possibilities. Maybe that meeting on Saturday *was* a meet-cute after all. An enemies-to-lovers, opposites-attract kind of meet-cute. Or maybe this, sorting romance novels together in a dusty bookstore, is our perfect meet-cute. We have so much in common! We work on the same street and both for businesses that are great for sustainable consumption. We both like Reggie. I know I decided not to manifest a meet-cute right now, but maybe a meet-cute found me anyway. Right here in the back of Second Story Books.

I put my hand out to shake his, and he drops a big stack of books into it. My other hand scrambles to catch the books before they fall, but two paperbacks drop to the worn wood floor with a thud. He doesn't even flinch at the noise. "These are romances. The rest are in those boxes over there." He points to a stack of boxes in the corner. "I have no clue if any of them are popular or have a chance of selling, but you can connect to the store Wi-Fi if you want to look up any titles. I'll be here sorting the rest of the auction lot." He tells me the name of the website the store uses to determine resale value, so I can look up whether a book is worth keeping or not. Then he turns away from me and picks up a book from the box in front of him.

Okay, definitely *not* a meet-cute. That's fine. I pick up the fallen books. At least he's not being condescending, so this is still an improvement over Saturday. I touch the heart locket around my neck. I can't let myself get carried away and forget the reason I'm here: to work on rebranding Love Street. *Wait.* What did Reggie say earlier? "Love on Love Street"—a great name for our promotion. I make a mental note to mention Reggie's suggestion at our first committee meeting.

I pull over another step stool to sit on, plant myself in front of the boxes of romances, and start going through the books.

"Oh my goodness!" I say after a few seconds. These books are . . . good. Lots of new and popular books, all in excellent condition. Some older ones, too—but all romance classics. I don't need to look up the value. I *know* these books will sell. Romance readers will love them. "This is an awesome collection! There's a BBC miniseries tie-in copy of *Pride and Prejudice*! Colin Firth on the cover and everything! I'm buying this." I put the book aside.

"This is, like, my favorite book ever. So amazing."

Miles glances my way for a second, then turns back to whatever he's doing. Man of few words, it seems. "There are some fantastic books here," I say. "Where did Reggie get these?"

"He bought them from an estate auction. A rich lady died, and I guess her family didn't want her library full of books. Looks like she didn't even read many of them."

"Goodness! I hope she didn't suffer! Not getting to read her books would be painful enough." I'd assumed Reggie bought the stock of a store that closed—not someone's personal collection.

Miles looks at me with his eyebrows raised. "Did you say 'goodness'?"

"Yes. What's wrong with 'goodness'?"

"Nothing. Never heard someone under the age of fifty use that word, that's all. Guess it goes with your clothes, though."

Is he seriously *insulting* my outfit? I mean, it's likely that the original owner of this dress is now over fifty. But there's nothing wrong with that.

I will *not* let this guy get under my skin. I give him a tight smile, then go back to the box of books. It feels sad now, knowing that someone bought all these and died before she could read them. I hope my *To Be Read* list doesn't outlive me.

"How did she die?" I ask.

"I don't know. Natural causes probably."

"Maybe we should dedicate the romance section to her," I say, brushing my thumb over the cover of one of the books. I feel Miles watching me. "What?"

His brows are knit together. "Nothing. Just never saw someone get so sentimental about stuff from an estate sale."

"Well, sue me for caring about people." I really needed to stop trying to talk to this guy. I've given him too many chances—all to my disappointment.

We pass the next few minutes in silence, but when something from the pile catches my eye, I can't help but clap with delight.

"Oooh, there's a whole set of this shifter series!" I put them in the "keep" pile. I'm a huge fan of this author—I might want to buy these for myself in addition to the copy of *Pride and Prejudice*. Good thing I agreed to let Reggie pay me for this.

"Shifters?" Miles asks. "What are those, romances about people who do shift work?"

I shake my head. "Nope! But shift-work romances sound fun too. These are romances about people who change into animals."

"Seriously? I guess there's something for everyone. Probably don't sell a ton, though."

My jaw clenches. Is that a dig at romance readers? "Most people love this stuff," I say.

He gives me an incredulous smirk. "Most? Hardly. I really doubt *most* people are into animal love stories."

I roll my eyes. "I meant all romance books, not just shifter books. Romance is the most popular book genre." Going through these books was supposed to be fun, but fun might not be possible with this guy around.

"Is it actually, though?" he asks. I can't tell whether he's surprised or if he doesn't believe me. "Or are you all brainwashed by the romantic industrial complex? I doubt *most* people are reading the genre. It's just that romance readers read more books on average because they're easy to read and formulaic."

Brainwashed? Oh no. Now he's not only criticizing romance *books* but implying that romance *readers* aren't smart? "Have you ever read a romance?" I ask. He gives me a blank look, like how dare I even suggest such a thing.

I'm so exhausted by people crapping all over a genre I love without ever reading one book. People like this think that reading about joy is less important than reading about pain. "I know you're averse to love, but you don't have a right to criticize the genre if you've never even read one. I'm not here complaining about the comfort of"—I think for a second—"Second Story Bookstore T-shirts, because I've never worn one. If I try a few on and still don't like them, then I'd have the right to make the face you made." I'm pretty proud of myself that I kept my tone pleasant while I said that. "Besides, 'formulaic' is the weakest critique you could give. I don't know if you've noticed, but mysteries, thrillers, and fantasies are also formulaic. Interesting that we only ever hear that kind of criticism for romance, though. Wonder why. Maybe sexism?"

He stares at me and I stare back, daring him to say something. Miles is the first to break eye contact as he lets out a soft chuckle, his curls moving as he shakes his head.

Ha! I win!

"Fine, you've got me there, Merali," he says, and the nickname causes an involuntary charge up my spine. "And who says I'm averse to love?"

"You did. At the BOA meeting, you hated the idea of

rebranding the street with the love theme. You wanted to celebrate the LOL guy."

"Lionel Osmond Love," Miles says, annoyed. "He's an important figure in Toronto's history."

"I don't doubt that, but no one's going to come out to the street excited about— What did you say he was into? Urban renewal. People care more about their Instagram engagement." I cringe. Ugh. Now I'm crapping all over something *he* loves, like he did on romance books. Miles Desai is bringing out the worst in me.

Miles takes a breath, like I offended him to the core. "Love was a *critic* of urban renewal projects; he wasn't *into* them. He advocated for mixed-use neighborhoods with both commercial and residential zoning instead of suburban sprawl. He pushed for neighborhoods just like Love Street."

Huh. That's . . . pretty cool, actually. I still don't think focusing on the man is the way to revitalize Love Street, but I don't want to argue with Miles anymore, so I go back to the books and start separating the historical romances from the contemporaries.

After a few minutes Miles speaks again. "It feels like we're disrespecting his legacy to turn this street into a big Instagram prop. I can't imagine Lionel Osmond Love would be okay with all these twee hearts and flowers for social media cred."

I put the book in my hand down. "Do you always have to have the last word?" He looks blankly at me again but doesn't speak. I exhale. "I assume this Love guy is dead, so no need to worry about offending the man. And if he really did love neighborhoods like ours, wouldn't he be into an idea that helps keep Love Street alive? Why wouldn't people—even the LOL guy—*adore* that the street is celebrating joy and happiness?" I take another breath, and I feel my blood boiling. "And what's wrong with flowers? My mother is *literally* a florist. A very good one too."

He shoots a look at me, and I think I see a touch of regret for being rude. "Okay, I'm sorry, there's nothing wrong with flowers. I shouldn't have said that. It wasn't a slight against your mom's work."

I relax. *See? He can be understanding.*

"But I don't think your saccharine vision is right for the street," he adds.

Spoke too soon. I glare at him, mentally daring him to say more.

He, of course, takes the bait. "You're turning Love Street into a carnival attraction of cheesy sentiments and hearts everywhere! It will be the fad of the week—it won't be a *sustainable* improvement."

I grit my teeth. "Love isn't a *fad*. Everyone *always* needs more love in their life, so if we do this right, people will keep coming to Love Street because of the great time they had here." Miles has no idea why I'm so committed to this—to save my mother's store. He thinks all I care about is the *aesthetic*.

Setting down the books in my arms, I walk right up to him, staring him down. "The residents and business owners need this. . . . The BOA isn't doing it for vibes and social cred. They're doing it because their livelihood is being threatened. You've worked here for what, a week? I've *lived* and *worked* on this street since I was nine, so don't tell me that you know what's best for Love Street better than I do." I shake my head. "You're way too judgmental and stuck-up to see the potential of this neighborhood. I'll be back to finish sorting these books later . . . when *you* aren't here."

I turn and walk out of the storeroom. There aren't a lot of people in this world who I actively dislike, but I think I can safely add Miles Desai to the list.

CHAPTER FIVE

THE INAUGURAL LOVE ON LOVE STREET MEETING

The first meeting of the Love Street Branding Committee is a few days later. We meet in Miracle Egg, a restaurant a few doors down from Cosmic Vintage that specializes in egg sandwiches with Asian influences and is only open for breakfast and lunch, so it's a good place for our five o'clock meeting. The owner, Grant Yu, is on the committee and seems like an okay guy, but I don't really know him that well. If his personality is anything like the decor of his shop—painted entirely in a sunny yellow and full of old Hong Kong and Bollywood movie posters—then we'll get along great.

Me, Cara, Julie, April, and Grant sit at one of the bigger tables in the restaurant. I've already presented them with Reggie's name suggestion for our promotion, Love on Love Street, and most people agree it's perfect.

"Sounds kinky," Grant says. "But maybe we want that?" He wags his eyebrows suggestively at Julie. Yuck. Julie is *married*. I'm thinking Grant and I aren't going to get along after all.

Julie, who doesn't seem to notice Grant's gross attempt at flirting, shakes her head. "No, it's perfect." She writes Love on Love Street on the top of her notebook page since she offered to take minutes.

"This whole thing is supposed to celebrate *love*," Cara

says. "I mean"—she side-eyes Grant—"we don't want to be lewd, but physical love is part of love, isn't it?"

April huffs a laugh. April is Black, and she always wears scrubs with some cartoon animal print on it. Her makeup is always on point, and she keeps her hair cropped short. She once told me that she hates dealing with her own hair since she cuts and styles dog and cat hair all day. "Y'all need to be careful. We want to attract *families* to the street. If people think this is all a free sex kind of thing, they won't come."

"Most of the promotions we talked about are for *couples* more than families. Like date specials at the bistro and small bouquets at the flower shop," Grant says.

We argue a bit about who our target demographic should be, when the door to Miracle Egg opens. Grant immediately calls out, "Sorry! We're closed. Open at seven tomorrow!"

My back is to the door, so I don't see who's there, but I don't need to see him. I recognize his deep voice the moment he speaks. "Oh, I'm here for the rebranding meeting? I thought that was today."

Miles. Apparently telling him off on Monday wasn't enough to make him not want to be anywhere near me.

"Yes!" April says, standing and pulling another chair to our table. "Everyone is welcome! You work at the bookstore, right? You helped me find that Dog Whisperer book last week!"

Unfortunately, since I'm at the end of the table, April puts the extra chair next to me. Miles is in worn jeans again today. And another graphic T-shirt, but this time with an unzipped burgundy hoodie over it. His hair is still a mess, but the kind of mess that some guys spend good money at top stylists to achieve.

Ugh. Why does he have to be so good-looking? I don't remember his lips being so . . . full. He squeezes into the seat, barely even glancing at me, and I catch his scent. He still smells annoyingly good. Like soap and something else. Not spices like in the bookstore. Something I've smelled before but can't place. I turn my chair toward Cara so my senses aren't invaded by Miles.

He called my ideas "saccharine" in the bookstore the other day. I should not be finding him so attractive.

We keep talking about the kind of people we're hoping to attract to the promotion, but Miles doesn't add to the conversation. I sneak a glance at him. He looks . . . bored. Why is he even here? Did Reggie force him to come to the meeting? When I say there must be a way to be inclusive to all while still focusing on romantic love, I'm pretty sure Miles snorts under his breath.

I ignore him. When we start discussing the promotions that were suggested at the BOA meeting, he's silent.

"We can't forget the statue at LOL Park," Cara says. "Have you seen the lineups to get a picture at the heart statue in the Distillery District?"

"Yes!" I say. "We totally have to put something like that in the park. A heart, or even a rainbow!"

This time I *know* Miles snorts.

I turn to look at him. "Do you have a problem with a statue in the park?"

"No. But you guys don't seem to have any idea how much something like that would cost. Like, thousands and thousands of dollars. At least. And the park belongs to the city—you can't just plop a statue in it. There are permits and applications. It's completely impossible."

I exhale. I'm not going to let this guy bring me down. I know he's probably right, but he sounds so . . . *antagonistic.* How do we know for sure it's impossible before we even try?

"I think we should be *optimistic* and explore all options," I say. "But whatever we do, we need to consider that the *aesthetic* is what's going to get people here. Julie, what percentage of your customers come to LoveBug because they saw a post on Instagram?"

Julie thinks a moment. "New customers? I'd say about eighty percent. But they keep coming back because of Ajit's delicious food and drinks."

"Exactly. Get people in the door, or on the street, because of the look . . . and they'll keep coming once they realize we're awesome."

"You'll need more than just vibes," Miles says. I can't help but notice that every one of his snarky comments is after *I* say something. I throw an annoyed look at Cara, mostly because I don't want to look at his infuriatingly cute face, and she shrugs.

"He does have a point," Grant says. "I mean, I like Instagram bait as much as the next guy, but I know that it's not always enough. We're a little off the beaten path here. We need a *bigger* draw. Something that will get people in from all over the city. Something like . . ."

An amazing idea comes to me. "A festival!" I say excitedly, clapping my hands together. "We can have a street festival celebrating love!" Like all those festivals Dad used to take me to. They were always so busy.

April raises a brow, skeptical. "A festival. . . . Can we do that?"

I nod, vibrating with excitement. "Yes! Like close off Love Street to cars and have events in front of our stores. And maybe get some rides or something in the park. And a statue! Like—"

"Street festivals need permits," Miles interrupts. "Plus at least a year of planning and securing sponsors. This isn't like planning a party for your friends. There's no way you can pull this off in a few months."

I want to scream, *Would you like to see me try?*

I grit my teeth. "I *know* it would be hard. But what's the harm in trying? If we can't pull it off this year, then we're just in time to start planning a festival for next year. But if we *can* make it happen . . . I think this could be exactly what Love Street needs."

I put a positive spin on it, but what I don't say is that next year might be too late. Mom needs more sales *now* so she won't have to sell; her *business* is on the line here. And not only Mom's, but also Jenn's, Mrs. Kotch's, and even Miles's own boss, Reggie's.

"Okay, okay," Julie says. "Why don't we take a vote? Who's in favor of exploring the feasibility of a street festival?"

Every hand shoots up except Miles's. And I don't give him a smug look because I'm better than that. I think smug thoughts, though.

"Perfect," Julie says. "Sana, this was your idea. Do you want to be in charge of the preliminary research?"

I nod. "Absolutely. I can do that."

April looks at me. "Do you have time for this? Aren't you in charge of your school's prom?"

"There are lots of people on the prom committee. I have

time." This is way more important than prom anyway.

"I can help you research," Cara says. "I've only got one assignment, and then I'm done with school for the term."

"Okay," Julie says. "So, the girls will look into the possibility of a Love Street festival. We'll put a hold on other activities until we find out if we're able to do this festival or not. Sounds good?"

Everyone agrees, and Cara and I tell them we'll keep everyone posted on our research. Miles gets up from his seat and leaves the second the meeting is done.

"What's his problem?" Cara asks, watching him leave.

"What do you mean?" Julie asks as she closes her notebook.

"I mean, why was he here if he disagrees with everything anyone says?"

I'm glad Cara is saying what I'm thinking. I don't understand why Miles even came to the meeting.

"Ah, cut the guy some slack," Julie says. "Ajit got to know him a bit—he apparently grew up in a mansion in King City, but he's got a screwed-up family. He's having trouble adjusting to the city."

I cringe. King City is just north of where Dad and Noureen live. Poor Miles to have to grow up there.

"Did you see his watch?" April asks. "Those are about five hundred. Brave to walk around wearing that. You should see his fancy bike."

I didn't see his watch. I was purposely avoiding looking at his arms because I discovered how nice his forearms are when we were sorting books together. I'm not going to let Miles Desai's nice arms or contrary comments ruin our progress tonight. This festival idea is *perfect*. It's just

58

the thing to get people to come to Love Street.

"Wanna come over and we can start the research tonight?" I ask Cara when we finally leave Miracle Egg.

Cara frowns. "Maybe. Hannah just got back from Massachusetts."

If the love of her life is back in the country, why is Cara frowning? "Isn't that a good thing? You guys don't have plans?"

She shrugs. "I dunno. She didn't want to get together tonight." All of a sudden a massive grin transforms Cara's face as she sees something in the distance.

That must be Hannah—I don't think anyone else could give Cara that expression. As she gets closer, I finally see what Hannah Weatherspoon looks like, and wow. She's gorgeous. Hannah has the exact figure I would expect from a top hockey forward—tall and strong with broad shoulders and long legs. She's wearing black leggings with a purple stripe down the sides and a bulky sweatshirt that says AMHERST COLLEGE on it. Her wavy blond hair looks like a shampoo commercial, and she has perfect skin.

"There you are," Hannah says when she reaches us. She kisses Cara senseless, practically lifting her off the ground. When Hannah and Cara finally come up for air, Hannah seems to notice me for the first time.

"Oh. You're Saba, right?" she asks.

"It's *Sana*." I smile. "Nice to finally meet you, Hannah. Cara, we can talk about the festival later. Have fun tonight!" I wave and start heading down the street. I can do some preliminary research on my own—clearly Cara would rather be with the love of her life.

It looks like it might rain, so I inhale deeply. I *adore* the smell of rain. It's so . . . sultry. It makes me think of spring flowers, moody storms, and of romance. I wrap my pink houndstooth coat around me and, without really thinking about it, I walk past my apartment instead of going home. I *should* go home—but I know Mom will be there, and I don't really want to see her right now.

Things have been kind of weird since I overheard that conversation between Mom and Jenn. I haven't said anything to Mom about it, and of course she hasn't talked to me about her business struggles. But I wonder if there have been signs for a while that Mom's been stressed. She's always been such a busy bee. Painting the apartment, canning vegetables, restoring old furniture. She used to have friends over all the time to work on art projects or make pickles, or even just hang out. Now she only has Jenn over, and when they are doing a project together, it's always for either Mom's or Jenn's business.

I go to the park, figuring I'll go sit on my favorite thinking bench. LOL Park is pretty small, with a parking lot on one side, a playground on the other, and a patch of grass between them. The playground was put in last year when the city finally agreed that the old one was a bit of a death trap. The park is empty now. Give it another month or two, and there will be kids in the playgrounds and people walking their dogs on the winding paths at this hour. I can't wait—I love people-watching in the park in the summer.

As I walk on the path, I visualize what the festival could look like. We could have a stage on the grass, some vendors selling things like flower crowns, macarons piped into hearts, and milkshakes with two straws for sharing. And, of course, we'd get the big art installation sculpture for pictures. Maybe that could go near the bike racks?

And, honestly, I know I said I wasn't going to focus on my love life right now, but I can't help thinking about how a love festival is the perfect place to find love. That would be the most epic story ever. The ultimate meet-cute.

As I get closer to the bike rack, I see a person crouched near the bikes. Love Street, and LOL Park, are mostly safe, considering they're smack-dab in the country's biggest city. But still. I'm a teenage girl alone in a park when the sun is setting, and the only person here looks like they're getting ready to pounce on me. I should run away.

Or, more likely, this is the LOL Park bike thief, and they're in the process of stealing a bike. Well, not on my watch, they aren't. I'm not going to let anyone terrorize my community. I step forward and start recording the guy.

"Stop what you're doing right now," I say. "I'm recording you." I move closer and zoom in with my phone until the recording is clear enough for me to make out who it is. Blue jeans and a burgundy hoodie. And messy hair.

"Miles, what are you doing? I'm telling Reggie his new bookseller is stealing bikes."

I'm only a few feet away, so I can see his expression quite clearly as he rolls his eyes at me. "Go away, Sana. I don't need your snark now."

I don't know why I'm surprised he said my first name. Or surprised he's pronouncing it correctly . . . *Sun-a* instead of *Saa-na* the way most people say it. Still, can't get distracted here. He's stealing a bike! Is this how he got the expensive one April saw him with? "If you don't leave, I'm calling 911 to tell them I found the Love Street bike thief!" I wouldn't actually call 911, but he doesn't need to know that.

"I'm not stealing a bike," he says. "This is mine. I'm . . ." He sighs. "I'm . . . trying to inflate the tire with my mind." He looks pissed. Actually, he looks dejected. Like his already terrible night is only getting worse.

I step closer to Miles. The bike he's crouching in front of looks new and shiny. Also, the tire is very flat.

"Go ahead. Call the police on me," he says.

"Why would I do that now? You said it's your bike."

"Yeah, but you clearly don't like me."

I shake my head. "Dude, you're Brown. Do you really think I'd turn you over to the police unless I'm absolutely positive you're actually committing a crime? And even then I might not."

He huffs a laugh, then looks back down at the tire. After a few seconds, he drops to the ground, his butt falling onto the dirt surrounding the bike rack.

"Are y-you . . . ?" I stutter. "I mean, do you need help?"

"Not unless you have a tire pump in that bag of yours. Actuall . . ." He stands and briefly brushes the dust off his rear end. And I can't help it—I look. He's got a nice rear end. He then leans down to unlock the bike. "Do you know if the gas station on Gerrard has air?"

"That station is, like, miles away. You're going to walk the bike all the way there?"

He looks at me. "I don't have much of a choice. I can't afford a cab." His statement is punctuated by a loud rumble in the air. Thunder.

So . . . the rich kid from the suburbs has money troubles? "It's going to rain," I say. I'm not sure why I'm stating the obvious. . . . I sound like I'm rubbing it in that he's going to be stuck walking a bike with a flat tire on a busy road during a thunderstorm. "C'mon," I say, motioning him toward me. "My place is about a minute from here. I have a bike pump."

He looks like he's about to say no, when another loud thunder rumbles.

"Look, it's about to rain, so I'm going home. You can come, or not come. I do have a bike pump and a covered balcony."

He exhales right as the first drop of rain falls. "Okay. Lead the way."

It's raining hard by the time we're at the end of the park. My rayon dress is sticking to my legs, and I can feel my hair getting stringier with each step. I don't bother to check whether Miles is actually following me when I start running toward the flower shop.

When I get there, he's right behind me, holding on to his bike and looking like a drowned rat. His hair is in wavy clumps around his head, and his sweatshirt is so saturated that it looks nearly black. I motion for him to follow me down the narrow alley between Morgan Ashton Flowers and the empanada shop. Behind the flower shop is a small car pad where the flower shop delivery van is parked next to the wood stairs up to my balcony.

"Carry your bike up there," I say loudly. He nods, then effortlessly lifts his bike and climbs the stairs. I follow.

The balcony of our apartment is big—almost as big as the apartment itself. Well, not really, but it's at least as big as my bedroom and Mom's combined. Mom had a friend who's into metalworking help her build a corrugated aluminum roof covering about a third of it. He also built a metalwork grid bolted to the wall. That's where Mom and

I lock our own bikes to protect them from the elements. I yell at Miles to put his bike there, then use my key to unlock the back door and motion him into the apartment after me.

The back door opens into the kitchen, which is good, because at least we're dripping onto the linoleum instead of the wood floors in the rest of the place.

I don't see Mom. Maybe she went out with friends. I'm kind of glad she's not here to see me inviting Miles into our place. Not that she'd have an issue with me having a boy alone in the apartment, because that's totally not her style. But . . . I don't know. I don't want anyone, even my own mother, to have an opinion on what's happening here.

And what exactly *is* happening here? The balcony is a little noisy, but it's dry. I could just pass him the bike pump and leave him to it. But here he is, in my house. I don't know if my kindness has anything to do with how cute I find him.

But if I think about it more . . . maybe it's what he said out there in the park—that he couldn't afford a cab despite his expensive watch and bike. There's clearly more to Miles than what's on the surface. And he's now a part of the Love Street community. We help out our neighbors here. Even when they're supremely annoying.

"I hate rain," he finally says after we've been staring at each other awkwardly for several long seconds.

"I love it," I say.

He smiles kind of fondly. "Why does that not surprise me?"

I chuckle, drying my hands with a kitchen towel. I hand him a clean one from the drawer near the sink. "Seriously.

Especially spring rain. It smells so mysterious and makes everything look so shiny, but also spooky. It's like . . . everything is the same all the time, but then suddenly water falls from the sky, and it makes you see everything in a new way. It feels . . . romantic. I don't love what rain does to my hair, though." I laugh as I pull my hair back using the hair tie on my wrist. "Welcome to my apartment. Do you want something to drink? A bigger towel?"

He's taken off his wet hoodie. The blue T-shirt under it is mostly dry. "I'm fine." He looks in front of him into my living room, and I can't help wondering what he's thinking. This little place is about the furthest thing possible from a King City mansion. His house is probably a lot like Dad and Noureen's.

I love our place. It's just small. And cluttered because there isn't a lot of space since there are plants on every surface. It feels like there are more plants up here than downstairs in the flower shop. The kitchen, where we're standing, is narrow and long. Cabinets line one wall, and open shelves line the other for pantry stuff like spices and countless cans of chickpeas. The bathroom is next to the kitchen, and thankfully it's pretty big. Right after the kitchen is our tiny dining room with a table covered with a busy floral tablecloth pressed up against the wall. Then our small living room. It has a big window, and the walls are a raspberry-pink color right now. Mom's and my bedrooms are off the living room. Mine is a bit bigger than Mom's—she gave me the bigger one so it would fit a desk for my schoolwork—and it has a bay window overlooking Love Street.

Miles has slicked his wet hair behind his ears, and

somehow the rain has made his lashes even curlier. "I think the rain has already slowed down," he says.

I tear my gaze away from him. "I'll get the bike pump." I open the last kitchen cabinet, the one Mom and I call the garage because it's where we keep all the things we'd keep in a garage if we had one. After finding the bike pump, I hand it to him.

"Thanks," he says, taking it. "I appreciate it."

"No worries. I couldn't leave you stranded, could I?"

"Yeah, w-well . . . ," he stammers. He runs his free hand through his hair, which makes it messy again. He can't seem to keep his hands out of his hair. "I'll go pump up my tire."

I open the door and move aside so he can head out. "Do you need help?" I ask as he steps onto the balcony.

"No. I think I can figure it out."

"Okay. I'm going inside," I say, then close the door. I sit at the dining table and start unlacing my Converse hightops. I'm pretty soaked, so once my shoes are off, I go to my room and quickly change into a pair of purple leggings and a cropped black sweatshirt. I peel off my wet socks and throw them in the laundry hamper.

When I come back out into the living room, Miles Desai is standing alone in my kitchen, looking a little lost and a lot adorable. Damn that Cara for putting the idea in my head that he's my type. It's true—I *do* have a thing for nerdy Brown boys.

"I think your cat hissed at me," he says. My cat, Zuri, is at his feet, glaring suspiciously at Miles.

I laugh as I scoop Zuri into my arms. She immediately climbs onto my shoulder and wraps herself around the back of my neck, purring. "Storms make her nervous."

"It stopped raining," he says.

"How's the bike?" I ask.

He shakes his head. "I think it might have a leak. I tried to put air in, but it doesn't seem to be filling. Do you know a bike shop that can repair a tire around here—and cheap?"

Miles is clearly having money problems . . . just like the rest of the street. I wonder why his wealthy King City family isn't helping him. "It's probably a hole in your inner tube," I say. "I heard bike thieves are puncturing tires so people will leave their bikes in the park, and then they steal them in the middle of the night when no one's around. If you're short on cash, why don't you fix the tire yourself?"

He looks at me like I just suggested he perform open-heart surgery on himself.

I laugh. "You don't know how to fix an inner tube? I have a patch kit you can use." I kneel to open the garage cupboard, and Zuri jumps off my shoulder.

Miles is still looking blankly at me, then runs his hands through his hair again. "I've never done it before."

I shrug. "No biggie. I can show you." I take the patch kit—a small plastic box—and the toolbox out of the cupboard and slip my bare feet into some slides.

He shakes his head. "No, it's not necessary. I—"

I turn to him and put one hand on my hip. "C'mon, Miles. I know you think I'm vapid and superficial, but trust me. I *can* fix an inner tube. I've been doing my own bike maintenance since I was eight."

His brows knit together. Miles Desai also has nice

eyebrows. Too bad they're always furrowing. "I never said you were vapid and superficial."

"You thought it," I say lightly. I smile at him, hoping to make him trust me. "Seriously, you don't have to like me to let me help you."

He gives me one of his blank stares, and there's the Miles I know. That lost wet-puppy look was confusing me . . . making me think he's more attractive than he is. I'm on familiar ground with his sour mood. "What makes you think I don't like you?" he asks.

"Um, just about everything you've said to me, plus all your body language since we met? You called my ideas trite and saccharine, and you implied the only thing I cared about was the way a thing *looks*. You think I only want to rebrand the street for the *vibes*."

His eyebrows furrow. "Well, you called me judgmental and too stuck-up to understand you or this community!"

I exhale. I don't think anyone has been able to push my irritate buttons more than this guy. "That's because you act like you know what's best for Love Street better than the people who have been here forever. You pick apart every idea any of us has before we can even find out if they are feasible! We're being optimistic and hopeful, and you're only shooting us down!"

He shakes his head. "There's optimism, and then there's delusional thinking. What's the point of working so hard on something that won't make a difference!"

I shake my head. I should tell Zuri to hiss at him some more. This is exactly what my mother said about the BOA—that there was no point working with them since they had no control to fix anything. I have no idea how people can be so pessimistic. "C'mon, Mr. Glass Half Empty. Let's fix your stupid bike before the sun goes down."

He recoils. "You still want to help me with my bike?"

"Of course I'm still going to help you. You work here on Love Street, which means whether I like it or not, you're a member of my community. I'm not going to let a member of my community get ripped off by the bougie bike shop on Queen East."

He stares at me for a while. Why is this guy always staring at me instead of speaking? Finally, he sighs. "All right, fine. Show me how to fix it."

I toss him an oversize sweatshirt that was hanging on a kitchen chair as I walk past him to open the back door again. "Here, put this on. It's getting cold out."

If we're going to be doing this, then I need him to cover up a bit. With his hair drying into thick waves and his strong forearms on display, there's a distinct hazard that I'm only going to grow even more attracted to Miles Desai while helping him with his bike . . . which would really suck considering how much I dislike the guy.

CHAPTER SIX

A GREAT BIG PLAN FOR LOVE

Thankfully, it's not raining at all by the time we step outside. Not that it would be a problem if it were since the metal roof would keep us dry, but the roof only covers part of the balcony, and I don't love the idea of being squished next to Miles while repairing his tire.

After he unlocks his bike, I use my tools to start removing the back wheel. It's clearly a new bike . . . and April was right—it looks expensive. "You should get a better lock for a bike this nice," I say. "It's a wonder it hasn't been stolen yet."

"Yeah, it's on my list. Next paycheck. That's the first time I locked it up in the park, though. I used to lock it behind the bookstore, but the accountant upstairs got a car, so there isn't room anymore."

Expensive bike, short of money. I suspect he's living on his own for the first time. Lord knows rent in this city isn't fair to anyone's budget.

After showing Miles how to get the wheel free of the chain and gears, I lean the bike up against the railing. "My mom taught me basic bike maintenance when I was a kid," I say. "My grandfather actually used to work in his father's bike shop back home before he immigrated to Canada."

"Where's back home?" Miles asks. I'm surprised he wants to make small talk.

"Tanzania," I say. "My grandparents moved here in the seventies." I hold the tire in front of us. "Next we need to get the inner tube out." I squeeze around the tire to loosen some slack to make it a bit easier, then use two tire levers to pry the tire out from the rim. "It's easier if you have three levers. I don't know where the third lever is." When one side of the tire is free from the rim, I show Miles how to get the inner tube out.

He's not saying much, just watching and listening intently while I'm working. When I get the tube out, I hand it to him and then get a bucket from the other side of the balcony. Thanks to all the rain, it's full of water. After showing him how to use the water to find the hole in the inner tube, I dry the tube and mark the hole with a piece of chalk from the repair kit.

"So, how'd you end up here?" I ask. His silence is starting to get to me.

His eyebrows furrow. "Like, on your balcony?"

"No. I mean how did you end up on Love Street? Reggie told me you're a university student."

He nods. "At Toronto Metropolitan. Finished my first year."

"What are you studying?"

"Planning."

I raise one eyebrow. "How can you be planning to study something when you're already done with your first year? You changing your major or something?"

He shakes his head. "No. I mean that's what I'm studying. *Planning*. I'm doing a bachelor's in urban and regional planning."

"Oh. What's . . . *planning* about?"

"It's like, guiding land use and infrastructure to maximize quality of life and economic development while protecting natural resources."

I snort a laugh at his tone. "Okay, thank you, Mr. Textbook." I have heard of planning, now that I think about it. I remember reading a romance about urban planners.

After putting some glue on the tube, I tell him it needs to set up for a few minutes. "What are you planning to plan?" I ask. He looks confused, and it makes me laugh again. "I mean, what's your career goal? What do you want to do with your degree?"

"I want to be able to, you know, affect change in communities. Work in transit, housing, or government to make places livable and fair for all the people who want to live in them."

Huh. That's actually really cool. I respect people who know *exactly* what they want to do with their lives. Like me. I always knew I wanted to work in art. Even though my father convinced me to choose a practical major instead of fine art, it's still art. "Is that why you're so into the Love guy? What did you say, he pushed for mixed-use neighborhoods, right?"

Miles nods. "Yeah. Like Love Street. It's a good example of a vertical mixed-use neighborhood. Buildings have commercial on the street level and residential above. There should be more residential than only one level, though."

"That's only on this side of the street," I say. "There are four floors of condos above the stores across the street." The building that Cosmic and LoveBug are in is a condominium about fifteen years old. Jenn and her partner, Mark, have a unit on the top floor. I'm happy this Love guy would have approved of the neighborhood named after him. "Why are mixed-use neighborhoods better?"

"They encourage walking and biking, which leads to healthier lifestyles. And they help foster diverse, close-knit communities and more engaged residents."

"That's why I love Love Street so much," I say. "Everyone knows everyone. It's like . . . a Hallmark romance movie small town but in the middle of a big city."

He chuckles. Probably because I said the word "romance." "Yeah, I'm learning how close-knit this street is. I mean, you don't even like me, and you're helping me because you say I'm part of your community."

I flash a mischievous smile and put my hand to my chest. "Who said I don't like you? Anyway, aren't you from the land of suburban sprawl . . . ? Why do you care about these mixed-use communities?"

One of his eyebrows shoots up, and there's a small smirk on his lips. Turns out that Miles Desai *is* capable of amused expressions. They're hard-won, though. "You'll notice I'm not *there* anymore?"

I chuckle. No, I guess he isn't. I assume that if he's been biking to work, he's living somewhere nearby for the summer. "So, is that why you came to the BOA meeting and joined the rebranding meeting? You want to help Love Street thrive for this guy, Lionel Love?"

He turns away, looking at the alley behind the building, then looks back at me. "Yeah. Well, I mean, no. I didn't volunteer for the committee *just* for Lionel Osmond Love. I . . ." He runs his hand over his hair, which manages to look shiny in the dimming sun even after getting caught in the rain. I'm sure my hair is a frizzy rat's nest. "I moved to the city for school and because things were crappy at home. And I never really liked living in the suburbs. When I got the summer job on Love Street, I thought it was a sign. I wrote a paper about Love—the guy—in school, and I thought it was cool to be able to work on the street named after him. Also, I figured a bookstore in the city would look better on my résumé than the chain bookstore I worked at back home. I'm supposed to get an internship for next year, and I don't really have relevant experience. Or connections."

"Why are things crappy at home?" I ask. He doesn't say anything. "I mean, you don't have to tell me if you don't want to," I add.

"It's fine. My parents are separating. It's . . . messy."

I cringe. "Sorry. I know what it's like to be in the middle of a messy divorce. My parents split when I was nine."

He nods. "And it was . . . tumultuous?"

"Yeah, it wasn't pretty." I don't talk much about my parents' divorce or about how it felt to have the world torn out from under me with little warning. It was a long time ago, so I'm over it.

I show Miles how to attach the patch to the inner tube, pressing it down with the back of a screwdriver to make sure it's sealed. Then we put the inner tube back into the wheel, and I show him how to tuck the edge of the tire back into the rim.

"Thanks a lot," he says as I pump air into the tire. It's actually inflating now, so the patch worked.

"No problem. You're probably shocked that a naive child knows some life skills," I say.

He exhales. "I don't think you're a naive *child*." He runs his hand through his hair again. Guy's going to be bald before he's twenty-five if he keeps doing that. "I'm sorry I . . . implied I do. I haven't been very nice to you. I don't have great people skills. My mother says I have *foot-in-mouth-itis*. I'm sorry."

I laugh at that. I sometimes blurt out my thoughts without thinking too. "I've got a pretty thick skin. I know people think I'm shallow and twee because I wear pink and read romances and stuff. I'm well aware that I'm an acquired taste for many." I give him a sultry look, batting my eyelashes. "It's a taste people usually *do* acquire once they get to know me, though."

He laughs. And it's very cute. He looks . . . looser. I wonder if his crabbiness is just stress.

"I think I misjudged you too," I add. "I don't really like that guy you were sitting with at the BOA meeting, and I thought you were like him. You guys friends?"

He cringes, shaking his head. "No. That was the first time I met him, and I agree he's a jerk. Maybe you and I can start over?"

"Maybe. One question first. Do you really *hate* my idea of a festival? I thought you wanted Love Street to succeed."

He moves to the edge of my balcony, sitting with his back against the railing. "I *do* want Love Street to succeed. But grandiose plans will fail if you don't follow processes and procedures. People spend years planning a festival. To do it in only a few months is nearly impossible."

I grin as I sit across from him, my back against the brick wall. "You said *nearly*. Which means it *might* be possible."

He shakes his head. "You're impossible." He's smiling, so I know he doesn't mean impossible in a bad way. I like Miles so much better when he's smiling.

"No, I'm *determined*. And optimistic. I used to go to neighborhood festivals with my dad every weekend. They were always so busy, and everyone was so happy. Love Street needs that. So, tell me, how would you tackle it, Planner Boy?"

"Tackle what?"

I stretch my legs in front of me. "Planning a festival in only a few months."

He tilts his head, thinking a moment, and it really looks like he's giving the idea serious thought. "I think your biggest hurdle will be permits. The applications for summer permits are put in months in advance. You could try reaching out to the city councillor and have her fast-track the application. You'd need a proposal for why the community *needs* the festival and how it can help the whole ward, not just Love Street." He pauses, his eyes unfocused. "Su Lin Tran is the councillor for this ward. She's big into progress. She'd want to see how a festival like this could impact the area economically as well as culturally. She's also a huge diversity advocate—so I'd highlight the diversity of the businesses on the street and how the event would be inclusive to all."

This information is golden. Cara and I have no idea about any of this stuff. I feel like I should be taking notes.

An idea comes to me. I move my legs so my feet are next to his. "You should join our festival committee. You're all strategy, and Cara and I are all ideas. We're like yin and yang."

He raises a brow. "Seriously? You want to *work* with me?"

I grin, nodding vigorously. "Yes! C'mon. Planning a neighborhood festival would be perfect for your résumé! The city councillor will see our kick-ass proposal and *bam*. Now you have connections in city government."

He shakes his head. "I don't know." With the sun setting, his face is defined in light and shadow. The thought pops into my head that I would love to sketch his face one day, but I shove it back down.

"Is it because you don't like the love theme?" I ask. He doesn't answer the question. "Wait, are you aromantic or asexual? I'm pansexual . . . but I get that not everyone is interested in romance for themselves." I probably should have asked him before. I hope I haven't said anything offensive to him.

He shakes his head and looks down. "No. I'm straight. Not . . . asexual, either. I've just seen too many so-called perfect relationships go up in flames, causing destruction for everyone in their wake."

I recoil at that. *Flames* and *destruction*? What happened to this guy? "Are you talking about your parents' split?"

"Partially." He looks at me. "Why are you obsessed with romance if your parents had a messy divorce too?"

I shrug. "My parents never had . . . I don't know . . . a *loving* relationship. Maybe if they did, they would've been able to make it work. But they're not *romantic* people. I mean, my mom went to her prom with a guy only because she liked his dog."

Miles shrugs. "Prom's just a dance. I don't get why society tells us it should be as important as our wedding."

I shake my head. "Prom *is* important. It's like the . . . symbolic end to your high school years. I'm the chair of my prom committee, so I know. And anyway, a few relationships not working out doesn't mean love isn't the best thing in the entire universe. There's a reason ballads are written about love! All those songwriters can't be wrong."

Miles snorts, rolls his eyes, and shakes his head at me. A full trifecta of disdain. "My parents *did* have the hearts and flowers kind of romance, and the end is *ugly*. That's the thing. Love *changes* people—and not for the better. It's destructive more often than it's not. I don't see why our society puts so much importance on something that inevitably causes pain, not just to the couple but to everyone around them too."

I blink. Did he basically say that there's no point to falling in love because love always ends? I give him a sympathetic smile. "Your parents shouldn't be letting *their* ugly split affect *you*. I'm sorry you're going through that. But society says love is important because falling in love is the best feeling in the world! My parents didn't prioritize their relationship, and it ended, but that's their issue, not mine. And it makes me even *more* sure that true love—real, actual love with the right person—is *magical*." I don't want to end up like my parents—alone or with a wife who doesn't care about hurting people to get the "perfect" family she thinks she deserves.

Miles shakes his head. "You're too influenced by the commercialization of romance. Romance is a billion-dollar industry. Movies, books, music, weddings, and even Valentine's Day have convinced you that 'true love is real, and it beats all.' It's to get you to spend more money."

Wow. This guy was clearly messed up by his parents' split. My heart kind of breaks for him. Maybe he had a breakup of his own too? "Have you ever even been in love?" I ask.

Miles doesn't say anything, but the look on his face tells me the answer. Yes, he has. And it also ended in disaster. Which is probably further contributing to his cynicism now. But Miles is wrong. True love *is* real, and it's as wonderful and important as I've always believed it to be. I may not have experienced it, but I have *felt* it while reading books, listening to songs, and watching movies. Love isn't *commercialized*; it's *magic*.

I grin, an idea striking me.

"So you never said," I say, still smiling. "Are you going to help us with the festival?"

"Are you sure you want to work with me?"

I laugh. "Yes! We need your knowledge on this permit and bureaucracy stuff! We may have . . . *opposing* ideas, but our goal is the same—we both want Love Street to thrive!"

"Are you always so . . . *positive*?"

"Yes." I wave my hands at my bright smile. "It's like my whole thing, and I'm not ashamed of it." I kick the side of his sneaker with my shoe. "Come on, Miles. I want to prove you wrong. Love is real, and it's the best thing in the world. Once you see how much everyone loves the love festival, you'll see I'm right."

"Hardly. If the festival's a success, all it would prove is that everyone else in the city has been indoctrinated like you."

"Maybe so," I say, keeping my tone light because I'm

about to suggest the second-best idea I've had today, after the festival idea. "Or maybe you'll let me change your mind about love."

He raises a brow. "How?"

"Let me set you up with someone." I managed to find someone for Priya to fall in love with. I know I can do it for Miles, too.

His eyes go so wide that he looks like Zuri when she hears the can opener. "Seriously?"

"Yes, seriously! I'm an excellent matchmaker—I always set up my friends! You're only skeptical because you haven't met the right person yet! I *know* I can find you someone who will make you fall head over heels."

A little voice in my head tells me that this idea could backfire on me, I mean, I'm now dateless for my own prom because I set Priya up with Amber. But I shush the voice.

Miles shakes his head, eyes still enormous. "I don't know about this. I don't want to go out with randoms I've never met before."

"I'll come along if you want. They don't have to be *formal* dates, just a bunch of friends going out."

Miles is silent for a while, clearly thinking. I know this idea is perfect, and I really hope he sees it too. Miles isn't actually a bad guy, just a guy going through a rough time who needs to be knocked off his feet in love. And also? He's much, much too cute to be single.

I scoot forward onto my knees and put my hand out to shake on the deal. He stares at me for several long seconds before finally exhaling and shaking my hand.

"Fine. Go ahead and fix me up with someone," he says.

I beam, our hands still touching. "And we'll work on the festival together too?"

He nods, taking his hand back and rubbing it on his jeans. "Yes, I'll work on the festival proposal with you, too."

This is going to be so much fun. I love a summer project. Two in fact. Planning this festival to save Love Street, and make Miles Desai fall stupidly in love. I can't wait.

CHAPTER SEVEN

THE DATE WITH THE FLYING FISH

Miles and I talk a bit longer on my balcony before he leaves. I try to get him to tell me his type to help with my search for his true love, but he says if I'm such a good matchmaker, I should be able to figure it out. He has a point there. Eventually he leaves, after thanking me again for helping with his bike. I grin as I watch him carry it down the stairs. I have such a good feeling about this. Who knows, maybe Miles and I are actually going to be *friends*.

But all my warm and fuzzy feelings for Miles Desai evaporate about five minutes into our first official meeting of the Love on Love Street Festival planning committee. Me, Cara, and Miles are in LoveBug, and I can tell right away that Miles already regrets agreeing to work with us. He's punching holes through every idea we have. When I suggest we get a vendor to sell love locks for the chain-link fence at LOL Park, Miles asks us if we know how heavy those are and says they will cause the fence to buckle.

"They removed all the locks from the Pont des Arts bridge in Paris, you know," he says. "All the extra weight made the bridge unsafe. Plus, they are terrible for the environment. People always toss the keys on the ground or in waterways, which hurts the wildlife. Not to mention—"

I shake my head. "Okay, but they're so *romantic*. The locks signify an unbreakable bond."

"You think the city is going to let us keep them on the fence?" Miles asks. "We'll be the ones with the bolt cutters *severing* their so-called unbreakable bond after the event."

Cara laughs at that. I glare at her. I don't know why Cara doesn't find Miles Desai as irritating as I do. It's probably because Hannah being back is making Cara see through rose-colored glasses. Cara and Hannah have been spending almost every waking hour together when Cara's not working, and Cara is walking around with rainbows and hearts in her eyes all day. It's adorable.

"Well, I don't see how we can have a festival of love and not have love locks," I say, adding it to my list anyway. "I also think the statue is important. There must be a way to do a temporary version of it. It could be a big draw. Like . . . our signature attraction, you know?"

"I'm with Sana," Cara says. "I think we should explore options for a sculpture."

Miles shrugs. "We should really be finding sponsors first. Then we'll know how much money we have to work with."

"What's the point of getting sponsors if we don't even know what we want?" I ask, frustrated.

"And shouldn't we be getting permits first to know if we're having a festival at all?" Cara asks.

"I guarantee, the first thing the city will ask is how we will pay for it," Miles says.

"The BOA is paying for it. It's coming out of their budget." I tell them the amount Jenn said could be allocated for the festival.

"That's not nearly enough," Miles says. He has a condescending look on his face. Ugh. Why did I want to work with him again? He has good points, but he's just so negative. He doesn't want to work on finding solutions, just problems. I need to loosen him up somehow. I think it's time to start on Operation Find Miles a Match.

"Hey, I have an idea," I say. "We should all *go* to a neighborhood festival. For research. It's a bit early for festival season, but there's a small one in Little Portugal this weekend."

Miles shrugs. "Sure. We can see what works and what doesn't."

I grin, clapping my hands together. "And it can be your first blind date! I know exactly who I'm going to ask to come along." I don't actually know who I should invite yet, but I want to gauge his reaction before asking someone.

Miles rolls his eyes while Cara laughs. I'm irked to see that my friends have so little faith in me. "Come on, you said I could set you up, Miles! Let me prove to you that the theme of this festival is worth all this energy. And, Cara, you and Hannah have to come too!" Miles seeing Cara and Hannah's perfect love will also prove my point that true love is more than commercialism.

Miles does that staring blankly at me thing for a few seconds, but then his expression breaks and a small smile sneaks onto his face. "Yeah, let's all go to a festival. But first, take a look at these event proposals I found online. This will give us an idea of how to structure ours." He hands Cara and me some stapled stacks of paper.

I take the paperwork. I have a busy week—with a prom committee meeting plus working in both the flower shop and Cosmic, and of course, actual schoolwork, but I have every intention of working my butt off on this proposal too. This festival *needs* to be a success.

At school the next day, I'm in the cafeteria when I catch sight of a grade eleven girl I don't know very well, Abbey Santos, dropping a full can of soda onto the floor. She jumps out of the way, then freaks out a little and starts cleaning it up with napkins. I've seen Abbey around but never really thought twice about her. She's Filipino, a little quiet, and kind of bookish. Abbey seems the complete opposite of me, actually. I doubt anyone like me would be Miles's type, so Abbey might be his perfect match.

I go up to her. "Hi, Abbey! Do you need some help?"

She looks at me with a complete Disney-doe-eyes caught-in-the-headlights stare. She still doesn't say anything when I grab more napkins from the dispenser and help her clean her mess. And she only nods when I ask her if I can join her for lunch.

"I don't think we've ever spoken before," I say. "I'm Sana. I love that T-shirt. It's the perfect shade of pink for your skin." Abbey's brows knit together as she mumbles a thanks. She's really pretty with long dark hair and smooth tan skin. She has an innocent, angelic kind of vibe.

Eventually, through a series of one-word answers to my questions, I discover that Abbey likes reading, cooking, and is single. Also, she doesn't seem to have strong opinions on neighborhood festivals or the romantic industrial complex. She likes books; Miles works in a bookstore. Also, she's quiet and steady, and I get the impression that Miles thinks I talk too much and am too enthusiastic. Abbey will be a welcome change for him.

When I tell Abbey that I think she'd be perfect for a friend of mine who is a first-year university student, she seems open to it. She agrees to come with us to the festival in Little Portugal on the weekend.

Everything is perfect. The weekend can't come fast enough.

Six of us meet at a subway station to go to Little Portugal on Sunday: me, Cara, Hannah, Miles, Abbey, and Abbey's brother, Thomas, who I didn't know she would be bringing along. Thomas turns out to be two years older than me and is super cute. He has a wide smile and white teeth and is much chattier than Abbey. He sits next to me on the subway, which makes me wonder if this date is going to be two meet-cutes for the price of one: Miles and Abbey and me and Thomas.

But by the time we get to the festival, I'm pretty sure I'm not meet-cuteing with Thomas Santos. He will *not* stop talking about the stupidest things. Government conspiracies, cryptocurrency, and how he's trying to make millions as a streamer instead of going to college. Thomas is a complete blowhard.

And he won't stop talking at the festival, either. I can't even eavesdrop on Miles and Abbey's date because Thomas keeps going on and on. Nor can I roll my eyes and complain about this crypto-bro to Cara, because she and Hannah are several paces behind us. Probably to escape Thomas.

I sigh, throwing a longing look behind me. Cara and Hannah look so cute in their matching yoga pants and sweatshirts. Though, when I think about it, it's actually the most dressed down I've ever seen Cara. Usually she's like me and pulls together a statement-making outfit.

We finally all get food and sit at one of the tables set up in the middle of the street. Abbey and Thomas get grilled sardines and fries, Cara and Hannah split some skewers with salad, and Miles gets an enormous Portuguese chicken sandwich. And since there aren't a lot of vegetarian options, I get a couple of pastéis de natas—Portuguese egg tarts—and a coffee. I'm sitting next to Cara and Hannah on one side of the table, with Thomas sitting across from me, Miles next to him, and Abbey next to Miles.

"So, what do you think of the festival?" I ask the group after taking a big bite of my tart. It's delicious. Sweet and creamy, with a caramel flavor from the browned top. "Oh my goodness, we need these for our festival. Do you think they have a food truck?"

Cara shakes her head. "We have to make sure the food is on theme. Egg tarts don't work for Love on Love Street."

"So you're only going to allow cupcakes with hearts and flowers?" Miles asks, his nose wrinkled.

"No," I say. "We will have cupcakes with hearts and flowers, but also cookies with hearts and flowers. And . . . heart-shaped pizza?" Are there heart-shaped hamburgers? I have no idea.

Thomas shakes his head, laughing. "Dude, it all sounds so lame. *Love* festival . . ."

Great. Not another anti-love guy. I expect Miles to voice his agreement with Thomas, but when I glance at Miles, I see that he's glaring at Thomas. I think his eyebrow is even twitching. Weird. I need to work harder to spark the love connection between Abbey and Miles. First step, get Abbey talking.

"Abbey," I say turning to her. "I'm so glad we did this! You told me you're into reading. Miles works in a bookstore, you know. What kind of books do you like?"

She blinks, confused. "Um, I don't read books. I like . . . magazines."

Oh. Had she mentioned that when we had lunch? It's fine. So what if she's not into books like Miles? "What kind of magazines?"

"I like celebrity magazines from the drug store. Like gossip ones."

I exhale. Maybe Abbey actually isn't right for Miles.

"Hey, Sana, are you going to your prom with anyone?" Thomas asks. "Abbey said it's in a hotel, so I assume you have a room for the night. I can free up my schedule if you need a date." He flashes the grossest smile. Was I supposed to find his offer attractive?

"You're an ass, you know that?" Miles says. Which, true, Thomas is an ass. But telling him that to his face is certainly a choice. All Thomas did was ask me to my prom.

Abbey looks at me with a worried expression. "I like books with animals too. I read one about whales once."

"Oh, that sounds fun," I say, hoping to defuse the tension between the guys. "I read a book with a cat—"

"What's your damage, bro?" Thomas practically growls at Miles.

"I'm not your *bro*," Miles says. "And my damage is that you've been talking out of your ass since we got here with your crypto crap, and I don't know why you think I'd approve of that rude gesture you made about Sana when she was getting food. You're a pig—you should go see if they'll roast you on a spit."

Ew. What exactly was this gesture? But also . . . Thomas is considerably larger than Miles and looks incredibly pissed off. The last thing we need is physical violence at our festival committee's first research trip.

Abbey still seems to want to defuse the situation. "You have to try this fish! It's so good!" She spears her sardine with a fork and points it at Miles with such force that it flies off her plastic fork and hits Miles in the face before landing on his lap.

Everyone is silent for a moment. Did that really happen?

"Did you just throw a fish at me?" Miles asks Abbey. He doesn't sound angry, more shocked.

"Oh no!" Abbey says. "I'm sorry! My sardine got away from me. Here . . . let me . . ." She reaches to get her grilled fish from Miles's lap, and in the process knocks down her orange soda, which spills onto both hers and Miles's laps.

Miles scrambles out of his seat and wipes his lap with a napkin. Which causes the fish to fall to the ground in a puddle of orange soda.

"What the hell did you do to my sister?" Thomas yells at Miles.

Now Miles looks angry. His eyebrow is still twitching, and his nostrils flare. "She threw her fish at me!"

"It was an accident," Abbey says.

Thomas stands. "Yeah, but this isn't." He takes a handful of fries out of his box and throws them directly at poor Miles.

I stand. "What the frick!" I yell at Thomas. Miles was *defending* me from this creep. He doesn't deserve fish, fries, or orange soda thrown at him. I whip my second pastéis de nata at Thomas. The tart hits him in the chest with a thud, creating a large splotch of custard and pastry on his T-shirt. He looks like a combination of anger and shock. Maybe I shouldn't have done that.

Cara laughs at Thomas, then throws a handful of salad greens at him. A leaf of arugula sticks to the custard on his chest, which only makes him angrier.

"Hey," a voice says. I turn and see a guy wearing a festival volunteer shirt, standing with a uniformed security guard. "Knock it off. I'm going to have to ask you kids to leave."

Thomas, still furious, glares at Cara, then at me, then turns to his sister. "This isn't worth it. Let's get away from these weirdos, Abbey. Who plans festivals for fun, anyway?"

Abbey nods, then gets up and leaves with her brother without even looking at me or Miles. The rest of us apologize and start cleaning up our mess before we leave. I can't believe we got kicked out of a neighborhood festival. The Love on Love Street Festival planning committee is off to a terrible start.

Soon after we're done cleaning, Hannah says something about meeting her friends downtown, and Cara goes with her. Which leaves me alone with Miles to walk to the subway.

"You have fish skin on your cheek," I say, handing him a napkin. "Oh, and a french fry in your hair." I pick it out. I feel so bad—this was my fault. I'm the one who invited Abbey.

"That went well, don't you think?" he deadpans while wiping his face.

I squeeze my lips so I won't laugh, but it's unnecessary

because Miles starts laughing himself while using the napkin to wipe his jeans.

Even with fish on his face and french fries in his hair, Miles is still adorable. Especially laughing.

"I'm sorry," I say when his laughter eases a bit. "I had no idea Abbey would bring her brother. Or that her brother would be the definition of douchey crypto-bro."

Miles chuckles as he tosses the napkin in a trash bin. "At least the food is good. I'm glad I finished my sandwich before someone threw it at me."

"I shouldn't have thrown that tart. Thomas wasn't worth it." What a disaster. Although Abbey didn't seem too bad. Just a little clumsy. "So, when her brother wasn't being a blowhard, do you think you and Abbey hit it off? Like, did you talk on our way there at all?"

Miles shakes his head. "I tried to talk to her, but she only gave one-word answers." We get to the subway station, tap our cards, and rush to get the train that is rolling in.

Once we're seated, I smile at Miles. "Abbey is a bit quiet, but I thought you'd like that. She's so pretty. You didn't feel a spark?"

He raises a brow. Miles has really expressive brows. Like he could tell a whole story with his eyebrows. And his eyelashes.

I have to stop staring at the guy's eyes.

"Why do you think I'd want someone quiet?" he asks.

"Maybe because you think I talk too much?"

"I don't think you talk too much. I like talking to you. Even if most of the time we're arguing."

I look at him. I've been trying to tamp down this extremely inconvenient attraction I seem to have for Miles

Desai, and it would be much easier if he didn't say things like he enjoys talking to me. "Okay, so you want someone who never agrees with you and who is philosophically opposed to everything you believe in?"

He laughs, shaking his head. "I like people who speak their mind. Who have opinions on things. I think this setup idea is ridiculous, by the way. If the next date throws a fish at me, I'm done."

I laugh. "Fair enough. I need to find someone with a mind of their own, conversation skills, no dickwad family members that they bring on dates, and who will not throw, drop, or launch a fish at you. Piece of cake."

We spend the rest of the ride home talking about what we liked and didn't like at the festival. Coming to this thing was a great idea, even if Miles didn't have instalove with Abbey. I know I'll do better next time.

The following night at home I'm trying to get some work done on my final project for my painting class, when I hear Mom call out for me. I wash my paintbrush and find her at the dining table with her laptop in front of her. Zuri is curled up in a ball on the table.

"You look like one of those lo-fi YouTube videos with the cat and all those plants," I say. "You just need a scarf."

Mom looks up at me, frowning, then takes her glasses off her face. Her curly hair is in a messy bun on her head again. "Can you watch the store tomorrow evening? My flower wholesaler's in town."

"Sorry, I'm at Cosmic tomorrow."

She exhales. "Okay. I'll figure something out."

She puts her glasses back on and looks at her computer.

"Mom, are you okay? You look . . . stressed."

She doesn't take her eyes off her computer when she answers me. "Aren't we all?"

I sit at the table. Zuri notices me and stretches out, so I scratch under her chin. "Yeah, I guess we all are." I wonder if it's time for me to tell her that I know she's thinking of selling the building.

Mom takes off her glasses again and looks at me carefully. She's always been gorgeous, but there are dark circles under her eyes and some new lines around her mouth.

"Are *you* stressed, Sana? You're working hard at Cosmic, plus the prom committee and the Love Street project. It's your very last month of high school—you should be enjoying it."

I shake my head. "The fact that school is almost over is why I *should* be focusing on Love Street. In a month I won't be at that school anymore, but I'll still be here, won't I?" Unless Mom sells the building. But that won't happen because the festival *will* save the street.

Mom shakes her head. "Don't give up your youth for this, Sana. How was the festival in Little Portugal?"

I chuckle. "A disaster. I brought this girl from school, Abbey, as a date for Miles, but she brought her asshole brother. She accidentally threw a grilled fish at him, which started a food fight, and we got kicked out."

Mom laughs. "Sana Merali, you are a drama magnet. Why did her accidentally throwing a fish start a food fight?"

"Her brother started it. He was a complete creep to me. Like, he asked me to take him to my prom but *only* if I have a hotel room for the night." I shudder.

"Oh dear. Can I assume you put him in his place?"

Mom knows full well that I don't tolerate that kind of thing.

"Actually." I pause. "Miles told him off. Which is how the whole fish-launching happened." I don't think I really processed the fact that Miles came to my rescue.

Mom nods appreciatively, laughing. "Good for him."

I giggle too. The whole thing *is* funny, actually. "Back to square one in finding Miles a girlfriend, though."

"Why do you need to find him a girlfriend? Let Miles be."

I shake my head. "He needs to fall in love! The guy seriously doesn't have a romantic bone in his body. He actually called love locks pollution."

"They technically are, aren't they?"

"Mom, not you, too!" I know my mother isn't *romantic* . . . but I thought she'd be on my side.

"Okay, okay, Sana. But have you considered that the guy might actually be interested in *you*?"

First Cara, now my own mother thinks me and Miles should be together? "Seriously, Mom? I love grumpy heroes in romance novels, but not in real life. He's way too pessimistic—we'd be terrible together! Miles Desai has only two things going for him: he understands the bureaucracy to get the approvals we need for the festival, and he's committed to maintaining communities like Love Street. That's why I want to *work* with him on this. My focus is only on the festival right now, not on my love life. Miles's two positive traits aren't enough for me to forget what's important."

Mom shrugs. "He's got nice hair."

Fair point. "Okay, three positive traits. It's still not enough."

"It might be enough for you one day, Sana."

I doubt that very much.

CHAPTER EIGHT

A CREATURE WAS STIRRING

Miles texts the next night in our festival planning group chat that he has a draft of the event proposal ready and asks if we could get together to work out some details, but we can't seem to find a time this week when we're all free. Eventually we decide to meet on Friday at seven, after I'm done at the flower shop. Neither Cara nor Miles is working, so I tell them to meet me at LoveBug.

Cosmic is dead on Thursday, so Jenn asks Cara and me to change the windows again. She thinks the eighties stuff might be bringing bad memories and preventing people from coming in, so we're going nineties beach bunny.

"I can't believe how bad Miles's first setup went," I say as I slip a Hawaiian shirt on the male mannequin. "I'm kind of surprised that he's letting me set him up again, actually." The shirt is way too big, but I love the color. The purple and green are so inviting. "I can't believe we got kicked out of a festival on our first research trip! Or that Abbey accidentally threw a fish at him!"

"The date was dead even before the fish incident," Cara says. "Her brother was terrible."

I nod. Thankfully, Abbey hasn't said a word to me at school since our trip to Little Portugal. And I'm not planning to tell anyone about the festival food fight.

"Abbey's not the right girl for Miles, anyway," Cara adds. Cara is wearing jeans and a pink and gray flannel today—uncharacteristically light colors for Cara, but she still looks great.

I pin the back of the Hawaiian shirt, but that makes it drape weird. I shake my head. This shirt isn't going to work.

"Try that orange and blue one," Cara suggests. She's put a purple bodycon dress on the girl mannequin, and it fits like a glove. I'd picked the purple and green shirt to coordinate with the dress.

I grab the other shirt. "Why don't you think Abbey is right for Miles?" I agree with Cara that Abbey and Miles are a bad match, but hearing another person's opinion may help me pick better next time.

"She was sweet . . . but maybe too sweet? I think she was too quiet for Miles. Maybe because her brother is such an ass, she learned to be invisible." Cara suddenly takes her phone out of her pocket. She looks at it for only a moment before putting it back. I can tell that whatever she saw upset her, but she's trying not to let it show. I wonder if it's Hannah. I got a weird vibe from her at the festival. Hannah didn't really talk to anyone except Cara. I have no idea if there is trouble in paradise between Cara and Hannah, but if there is and Cara doesn't want to talk about it, I don't want to force it.

"What kind of girl do you think would be better?" I ask. I love matchmaking, but I'm kind of stumped with Miles. I can't picture who would work for him. "Abbey's so pretty and seemed harmless."

Cara shakes her head. "Beauty is in the eye of the beholder. Just because you find Abbey pretty doesn't mean Miles will. What did he say about her?"

"He said he didn't like that she talked so little. He likes . . . *invigorating* conversation." Actually, what he said was that he liked talking to *me*, but I'm not sure what he meant by that.

"Makes sense. Miles needs someone who can challenge his brain, not just agree with everyone."

"So . . . someone smarter? Someone who he'll match with on an intellectual level more than a physical level?" Cara nods. I smooth the new Hawaiian shirt I've put on the guy mannequin. "But also, someone that *looks* good with him," I add. "Because someone who looks like him deserves someone equally . . . hot."

Cara laughs. "You seem pretty preoccupied with how attractive Miles is." She looks at the shirt. "That actually looks pretty good with the purple dress."

I step back to look at the couple together. They do look good. Not matchy-matchy, but complementary. "Yeah, I like it too." An idea suddenly comes to me. "Charlene! She's studying biology at U of T! She's perfect for Miles!"

"The girl who works at LoveBug?"

I nod. Charlene has been very friendly and chatty every time I've been in LoveBug. And she seems so smart—I saw her textbook once, so I asked her what she was studying, and she started going on way over my head about complex genetics.

"Ever notice she always has rodents on her clothes?" Cara asks.

I hadn't noticed that. "What do you mean?"

"Every time I see Charlene, she's got mice, or hamsters, or something like that on her shirt."

"She's a bio major. She likes animals. Maybe she wants

to be a vet." I clap my hands together, delighted. "Where should we go? It needs to be *romantic*. But not, like, obviously romantic, because Miles doesn't buy into that stuff." What's romantic but also, like, a normal thing to do?

"A walk on the beach?" Cara suggests.

I shake my head. "It's still too cold."

"A fancy meal? Sunsets? Ballroom dancing?"

"That's it! It's *perfect!*"

"Really? No offense, but Miles totally doesn't seem like the ballroom dancing type."

"No, not that—*sunsets*. We can go to Riverdale Park to watch the sunset." Riverdale Park is a cute park not far from here that has a big west-facing hill. At sunset the view of the Toronto skyline from the hill is absolutely gorgeous. "I'll set it up. You'll see. Miles and Charlene won't be able to resist the beauty of a Toronto sunset. Or each other!"

I go to LoveBug during my break at Cosmic, and thankfully, Charlene is there. I tell her I want to set her up with Miles from the bookstore, but only if she's interested. I heavily imply that Miles is interested in her, which makes her face light up. Charlene is totally into the idea, which doesn't surprise me. Miles is good-looking and smart. He's a total catch. I text him as I'm leaving LoveBug.

   Sana: Change of plans. We're moving the festival meeting to Riverdale Park tomorrow.
   Miles: Why? How are we going to have a meeting in a park?
   Sana: Charlene wants to see the sunset. I'll bring snacks. Do you have a picnic blanket?
   Miles: Who's Charlene? Not another blind date.

Sana: It's not a blind date, because you know her. It's a visible date! Charlene from the café. She's into you.
Miles: The girl with the rat T-shirt?

I make a face. Why has everyone noticed Charlene's rodent attire except me?

Sana: She's studying bio at U of T. She's smart, and a great conversationalist.
Miles: I still don't know why I agreed to these setups.
Sana: Because you can't say no to me. I told you that you would acquire a taste for me.
Miles: You weren't kidding when you said you were determined.
Sana: Come on, Miles. It will be fun. The sunset view at the park is unmatched, and since Charlene works on Love Street, she'll have ideas for the festival. She's lovely. And she's vegan, so she won't throw fish at you.
Miles: Fine. I know where Riverdale Park is. I'll meet you there. What time?
Sana: Seven. Don't forget a picnic blanket.

On Friday after school, I prepare the most perfect date food for the picnic. I pack fancy cheese cut into cubes, a sliced baguette, hummus, gingerbread cookies, some grapes, and some dried dates. I know Charlene's vegan, so she won't eat the cheese, but there's plenty of other stuff. I even have a cute little pint of fresh strawberries, which are without a doubt the most romantic food in existence. I consider dipping the strawberries in dark chocolate, but I don't have time.

I dress in high-waisted, wide-legged pink jeans and a white T-shirt, topping it with a fantastic cardigan Mom made me out of variegated yarn in all the colors of the sunset—orange, red, yellow, white, and a touch of purple. I add a cute yellow bucket hat to finish my "early spring picnic in the park" style. I look in the mirror. "Perfect," I say to Zuri. She meows in return.

With my backpack stuffed with food, I rush to grab a streetcar to the park after I leave the flower shop. Everyone will be meeting there, since Hannah and Cara are having dinner with Hannah's friends first, and Charlene will be coming straight from her school, where she works in the lab. Miles isn't working—and I still have no idea where he lives. I check my watch once I board the streetcar. I'm going to be a bit late.

When I get to the park, the hill is crowded with people. This is a popular place to watch the sunset in the city, and now that the weather is milder, I guess a lot of people have the same idea as me. I scan the crowd and see Miles and Charlene sitting on a blue tarp on the grass. Perfect. I briefly consider waiting before joining them to give them more time alone, but this bag is heavy. And honestly? We *do* have work to do on the festival plan tonight. I head toward them.

"There you are! Hope I'm not interrupting anything!" I plop down on the tarp next to Miles. Charlene is on the other side of him. "Oh my goodness, Charlene, you look amazing! I *love* that sweatshirt! Isn't purple totally her color, Miles? It makes her skin glow!" Charlene's sweatshirt is a pale lavender with an illustration of . . . yep, rodents on it. Gerbils, I think. I admit, it's an odd quirk. But the fact that the girl likes small animals is hardly a red flag. And she looks so good next to Miles. He's in a blue checked cotton shirt with jeans, and I can see his messenger bag at his feet. He looks like he dressed up for this. Good. Charlene did too. She has a lace collar coming out the neck of her gerbil sweatshirt. There's a cream backpack in front of her, and I decide not to look too closely to see if there are rodents on it.

Charlene beams at the compliment. "This is my favorite sweater! I love yours, too. Did you get it at Cosmic?"

I tell her that my mom knit it, and we talk about clothes while I settle myself on the tarp. It's not quite the picnic blanket I was envisioning, but it works. And the fact that Miles brought it proves he's *invested* in this date working out.

"You're at U of T, right?" I ask her. "Miles goes to Toronto Metropolitan University. He's studying planning. It's such an interesting field. It's like, planning neighborhoods and cities and stuff. What are you studying?"

Charlene tells us that she's in her second year in a biology program and says she's hoping to go to veterinary school in Guelph after. Miles mentions that he has a cousin who goes there, and soon the conversation carries on about grad schools, career choices, and their impressions of their universities. They have such an easy rapport that I may as well not even be here, which is *fantastic*. I predict that Miles and Charlene will be in love in a month, and Miles will be so utterly enamored that he'll be even more into romance than I am.

I wish Cara could see how well this is going. I text her that it's okay that she's running late because the setup is going so *perfectly* that I'm thinking about escaping to let them be alone. Cara writes back some kissing emojis, then says she and Hannah are still at dinner with Hannah's friends but will be leaving soon. I start taking the food out of my bag and laying it out on the tarp.

Miles looks at the containers as I put them in front of us. "I thought you were just bringing a snack. I figured chips or popcorn."

I laugh. "I am *so* not a chips or popcorn kind of entertainer." I clap when all the food is out. "There. I have bread from Mrs. Kotch's, Havarti cheese, grapes, strawberries, vegan cookies, and dried dates. Oh, and lemonade!" I take a thermos and some clean metal cups out of my bag.

Charlene plucks a cube of cheese from the container. I thought she was vegan? "Havarti! That's Agnes's favorite!"

My eyes widen. Who's Agnes? I glance at Miles, and he shrugs.

Charlene opens a zipper on her backpack, and I notice for the first time that it has a mesh front. "Come out, Agnes! Sana brought you cheese! No, not you, Roland. You like cheddar. Havarti is *Agnes's* favorite."

Um . . . I raise a brow. Who is Charlene talking to?

Agnes, it turns out, is a small white mouse, who sticks her head out of the backpack to get her cheese. I quickly close the containers of food. I didn't do all that work to feed *vermin*.

"There's a mouse in your bag?" Miles asks.

Charlene beams. "Three of them, actually! This is Agnes." She picks up the small white mouse in her hand. It's got red eyes, and honestly, the way it's holding the cube of cheese is kind of cute. But *no*. I'm a cat person. Which makes me decidedly *not* on team mouse. "Inside are Roland and Albert."

Miles looks at me with both eyebrows raised. And yeah, I agree with him. This is no longer a cute quirk. "I rescued them from a lab at school," Charlene says. "I take them *everywhere*. See? They have a little house in my backpack. I even take them to class."

"You don't bring mice into LoveBug, do you?" I ask. That's a health code violation. Julie and Ajit's café could be shut down.

Charlene doesn't answer that. "Look how cute Agnes is." Charlene actually kisses the top of the head of the tiny mouse. The mouse doesn't seem to care; she's just focused on the cheese.

Miles suddenly points to the backpack. "Watch the other one!"

One of the other mice, Roland or Albert, climbs out of the zippered opening and stands on top of the bag. It stares at the three of us for a moment, then scurries down the backpack and onto the tarp. Charlene seems to want to reach out and try to stop it, but Agnes is still in her hands. I can see the moment in her eyes where she considers which mouse means more to her, Agnes or whoever the runaway mouse is. She decides on Agnes and clutches the little Havarti-eating vermin tightly to her chest. Miles reaches out to grab the runaway mouse, but it's too fast for him. It scurries off the tarp and onto the grass.

"Roland!" Charlene calls out. "Get him!"

I most definitely do not try to get the mouse. Honestly, it's taking everything in me not to stand and scream like a 1950s housewife. Why did this girl bring three mice with her on a *date*?

As Miles and I watch the small white mouse run down

the hill, Charlene finally gets Agnes secured in the bag with Albert, then hurries down the hill, weaving between picnickers and sunset watchers. "Roland!" she yells. "Rolly! Come back, Roland!" She asks people sitting on the hill if they've seen a white mouse.

Miles looks at me. "Should we help her?"

I mean, *probably*? If we were at a park with a friend who lost their pet dog, I would help them. The fact that the pet is a mouse shouldn't change anything, should it?

I sigh, then stand. Pointing to Charlene's backpack, I tell Miles, "Keep an eye on Agnes and Albert." I feel ridiculous but call out for Roland as I head down the hill.

"Did you see a small white mouse come this way?" I ask a couple on a pink blanket. The girl shakes her head while the guy looks at me, horrified that I would even ask. Dude, *I know*.

I keep asking people if they've seen Roland as I follow Charlene down the hill. Many people look at me like I've lost my mind. At least one person squeals and jumps when I say the word mouse. But most just shake their head.

Once I'm at the bottom of the hill, I turn and ask people on my way back up the hill. After I ask a cute couple sitting near our tarp if they've seen a white mouse, one of the men points to the other, who is taking a picture of something on the edge of their picnic blanket. It's Roland. He's eating a small piece of what looks like cheddar cheese.

"Charlene! The mouse is here!" I yell out. Everyone looks at me. Charlene, who is several meters away, yells, "Grab him!"

Oh God, I'm going to have to touch the thing. I wince . . . reaching out. *It's fine*, I tell myself. It's like a cat, but smaller. It's just a pet—it doesn't carry the plague. But . . . it was from a biology lab. Maybe it carries . . . I don't know. Experimental diseases.

Just as I'm crouching down to grab Roland, a green plastic berry basket lowers on top of him, trapping the mouse with his chunk of cheddar.

It's Miles who trapped the mouse. "I dumped the strawberries in with the cheese," he explains.

The two men whose blanket we're invading clap with glee. "The mouse is trapped!" one of them announces loudly. Which makes many others on the hill clap along with them. Presumably the people who had the heebie-jeebies about the fact that there was a mouse on the loose.

I look at Miles, wincing. This is ridiculous. This date might be an even bigger disaster than the last one.

But Miles's face isn't showing anger, like after the fish incident. Or annoyance. Or even his usual smugness. His whole face has transformed into the biggest smile. And then he bows with a huge flourish as everyone cheers that he caught the runaway mouse.

I laugh. Disaster date aside, I managed to make Miles Desai enjoy himself.

CHAPTER NINE

SUNSET IN THE PARK VIBES

Once Roland is safely zipped into his backpack house along with Agnes and Albert, Charlene, who looks like she was just reunited with her lost child, tells us she needs to get the mice home.

"No, stay," I urge her. Despite this rodent fixation, a part of me is still kind of hoping Charlene and Miles could have something. Miles likes animals—or at least I think he does. He didn't seem to have an issue with Zuri, even when she hissed at him.

Charlene shakes her head vigorously. "You don't understand the *trauma* these babies have *already* gone through." She leans in to speak closer to us, presumably so the mice won't hear. "They came from the *psychology* department." She shudders. "I don't know what studies they were in, but I know they have lasting damage. I need to get them back to their safe space." She puts her backpack on and starts climbing up the hill toward the streetcar stop. From the mesh screen on the front of the bag, I can see Agnes, Albert, and Roland looking at us. I wave goodbye to the mice.

"Your friend is a little strange," someone with a faint European accent says. It's one of the guys Roland stole the cheddar from. The people who were sitting between us and them seem to have left. Probably not mice fans either.

"Oh, she's not really a friend," I say. "We work near each other. I didn't know she'd be bringing mice."

The second guy, the smaller of the two, laughs. He's really cute with curly black hair. "Honestly, it's not that weird for Toronto." This guy's accent is pure Toronto local. "Remember, this is the city that birthed the Ikea Monkey."

I continue to chat with the two guys for a bit. The European one, David, is new to town—he's from Denmark and moved to Toronto for a job. The other one, Ali, has lived here his whole life and is an artist who owns a custom T-shirt business. They're on their second date and look so happy. We exchange Instagram handles.

When I tell the guys to enjoy the sunset and turn back to Miles, I fully expect him to say we may as well leave too. But he doesn't. He looks at me curiously. The sky is doing that thing where it brightens a bit before the sunset, and the slightest pinky-orange color is high in the air.

"How do you do that?" Miles asks.

"Do what?"

"Make everyone your best friend after minutes of conversation."

"I'm a people person. But"—I smile—"I didn't make *you* my best friend when we met."

He blinks. "Yeah, no one would ever call me a people person."

"I think you are. You just need to warm up to people a bit."

We're both silent for a while. Maybe I'm not always a people person because I have no idea what to say to Miles about Charlene.

"So . . . Charlene seems . . . nice," I finally say. "Really smart, right?"

He raises a brow. "Um, I don't think bringing mice to a park is a very *smart* thing to do. What if someone brought a snake?"

"Okay, so Charlene has a small quirk, but you have to admit, I did better with her than Abbey. You two seemed to be getting along great until she opened her backpack. I now know your type. Next time I'll do even better."

He chuckles, stretching his legs in front of him. "I think the rodent obsession is more than a small quirk. And I don't think there was much of a spark anyway. Before Roland's escape, all she talked about was school. And she spends all her free time in the animal labs."

"So, you'd prefer someone more well-rounded?"

He laughs at that. "You're zero for two, Sana. I thought you were an excellent matchmaker."

"I am an excellent matchmaker. . . . I just don't know *you* that well yet." I'm still positive I can find someone Miles will fall headfirst for and who will make him rethink his stance on love and romance. I need to find someone smart and who has various healthy interests. I reach into the container and take a cube of cheese.

"Well, I'm an open book," he says. "Hey, that's a really cool view." I wonder if he's been here before. He's focused on the cityscape in front of him.

I feel like I could look at Miles's face forever when he's this deep in thought. There's a lot of intensity in Miles's eyes, but his jaw softens. Like his tension fades when he's looking at something beautiful, like the sunset.

But lately he hasn't been nearly as tense as when we

first met. He laughs a lot now. He looks so . . . relaxed on this hill that I wonder why I ever thought he was an uptight grump.

"Where's Cara?" I ask, mostly so I'll stop staring at Miles's face. I pick up my phone and text her. She responds right away.

Cara: Not going to make it. We're at Hannah's friend's volleyball game. Hope Miles and Charlene are cozying up together! If it's going well, you should leave the lovebirds alone too.

I sigh. I don't even know if I should answer that. "Cara's not coming," I say.

Miles lifts an eyebrow at me. I understand his way of communicating now—that means, *Oh really?*

I text a quick, **Okay see you tomorrow** to Cara, then toss my phone onto the tarp. "Question," I ask Miles. "What do you do when you suspect your friend is walking into a train wreck but you know she won't hear it?"

He exhales long. Sounds like Miles has experience with this exact problem. "You don't like Hannah for Cara?"

"I *barely* know Hannah. But . . . I get the distinct impression that Cara is more invested in making Hannah happy than the other way around." I sigh, wrapping my arms around my knees. "I don't see Hannah . . . *cherishing* Cara the way she deserves. And Hannah doesn't seem to want to get to know Cara's friends, which, I guess is her prerogative." I think about the lighter colors Cara has been wearing when she's with Hannah. The outfits that look nothing like her usual style. "But what do I know about healthy relationships? None of my past relationships have worked out. Maybe completely losing yourself is what's *supposed* to happen."

"I got the impression last week that Hannah didn't want to be there with us. And no, you're *not* supposed to lose yourself completely in a relationship. Trust me."

I glance at him. It almost sounds like Miles is going to open up to me there, but he doesn't. He takes a long sip from his water bottle, then looks back at the view.

"Well, it looks like tonight's festival meeting is a bust just like your date," I say. "If you want to leave, I get it."

He shakes his head. "I'm staying for the sunset. It was on a list of the top ten cheap things to do in the city. I paid a dollar twenty-five for this tarp, and I want to get my money's worth."

"Okay, then." I smile and put the snacks between us. "Hope there are no more rescued lab mice with psychological trauma to steal our cheese."

He laughs again and pops a cube of cheese into his mouth. I can't believe how many times Miles has laughed tonight. He's got such a cute laugh. Who would have thought that the grumpy Pink Chai Guy I first met at the BOA meeting would be such an easy laugher?

"So . . . what's your origin story?" I ask.

He frowns. "What do you mean?"

"I mean what's your cultural and ethnic background? I know it's an awkward question because usually when people ask me that, they mean 'why aren't you white?' But we're both Brown, and I already told you that my mom's family is South Asian from East Africa. My dad's the same, except he was actually born in Uganda."

"My mom's Indo-East African too," he says. "Her family is also from Tanzania. Dad's family came from India—he was eleven when he left Mumbai. Oh wow . . . that's amazing." He gestures to the sky. It's turning darker shades of pink and orange with grayish-blue clouds near the horizon. The buildings of the downtown skyline are glowing as they reflect the light of the low sun.

"Seeing the city like this reminds me how lucky I am that I get to live here," I say, leaning back on my hands to tip my head up to the sky. "Did your parents meet in Canada?"

"No." He sighs. My dad's family lives in Florida, and they met there." He sounds a little dejected, so I look at him. He's looking at the sky, but his jaw is tense.

"Mine met in the prayer hall here in Toronto," I say. "We're Ismaili Muslim."

He turns to me, a small smile on his face. "I thought so—my mom's Ismaili. I've heard the name Merali before."

"Seriously?" I ask, smiling. I'm surprised. It's a small sect of Islam, and the name Miles isn't common in the community. Neither is Desai, actually. But I suppose he got his surname from his father.

He nods, still smiling. "My mom's whole family is Ismaili, and I was raised in the religion too. My dad's Hindu." He leans back on his hands like me and stares in front of him.

The Ismaili community is pretty close-knit in Toronto, so I ask him some questions to see if we know any of the same people or are even (god help me) related, but we can't find any connections. He grew up in the suburbs, while I've always lived in the city. We talk a bit about growing up in the religion and about how both our mothers seemed to grow less devout as they got older. He asks me if I consider myself religious.

I shrug. "That's a tough question. I loved growing up in a tight group, and it's nice to have . . . answers for questions about the universe. But I was nine when my parents divorced, and Mom was judged pretty harshly by the community and Dad's family, so the two of us kind of pulled back from the religion."

"Why was your mom judged?"

"Oh, you know. Gender double standards. Dad was the upstanding member of the community, and Mom's always been . . ." I sit up straight. I don't want to say "a free spirit," because whenever someone calls Mom that, they mean it as an insult.

"What?"

I exhale. "Mom's *unconventional*. She was a wild child when she was young, and people called her a bad seed." I shrug. "And I guess she passed on her *hippie-dippie* ways to me."

"Who calls her that?" he asks.

"My stepmother. She says we're both hippie-dippie and thinks Mom should stop wearing overalls and I should get *new* clothes instead of only buying used ones."

"The fashion industry is terrible for the environment," he says. "We should *all* be buying secondhand."

"Exactly. Noureen also thinks I should work in my dad's real estate office even though I hate real estate agents, that I should go to a regular university instead of an art college, that I should straighten my hair, and that I should spend more time with my stepsister, probably because she hopes her daughter's perfection is contagious and fixes me."

Miles cringes. "That's ridiculous. You're great the way you are. Does your father think these things?"

I look at Miles quickly. Did he mean to call me *great*? He's still leaning back looking in front of him. "Um, I don't know," I say. "My relationship with my dad isn't the best. He doesn't have my back." I sigh. "Family is complicated."

Miles doesn't say anything.

I take a strawberry from the container. It's red and juicy and bursting with flavor.

"What are you studying next year?" he asks, taking a strawberry himself.

"Digital arts. But my stepmother thinks I should study accounting or business."

He chuckles. "I can't imagine you as an accountant."

I throw my strawberry stem into a napkin. "Yeah, no one can. I don't actually mind numbers—I've always been good at math. But I like art more. Fine arts would be a *dream* career for me. I adore sketching and painting, but I know digital art and design is more practical. I want to be an illustrator or graphic designer, hopefully with my own firm supporting small businesses." I tell him about the work I've done for Jenn and my mom on their websites and promotional material.

"That's really cool," Miles says. "I've always admired people with artistic ability. Probably because I have none. Even musicians—there was this girl at my high school who got all these scholarships for violin. Watching her play was mesmerizing."

I smile knowingly at Miles. Maybe I should track down this violin player for him. "Did you have a *thing* for her?" I ask teasingly.

He shakes his head. "When she wasn't playing violin, she was the nastiest bully in the school. She made the mean girls in that movie seem like saints."

I file away that information. No mean girls, but musicians are good.

"I should get you to do some mock-up sketches of the festival for the proposal," Miles says. He takes a bite of a soft ginger cookie. "Oh, these are good!"

"Of course they're good. I'm an excellent picnic packer."

"They remind me of these chocolate-covered gingerbread cookies my mom used to buy."

"Yum. And yes, I can absolutely do some mock-up illustrations for the proposal," I say. We discuss the visuals for the festival, and if we'll need a logo yet. He knows his stuff, and it's clear that he's done a fair bit of research on neighborhood festivals on his own. I'm a little surprised at that since he was so against the festival idea in the first place. But I'm learning that Miles is a little like me. When we decide to do something, we never do it halfway.

"This is when it's the prettiest," I say, taking a picture of the sky. The sun is peeking out between the buildings, and the whole sky is a glorious shade of orange. The CN Tower stands high, watching over the other buildings like a sentinel. It's all breathtaking. I turn so I can get a selfie with the sunset behind me. "Get in the shot," I say, motioning him to get closer.

He looks at me like I've lost my mind for a moment. "It's just a picture," I say. "C'mon, Miles, we're friends, aren't we?"

He finally leans in close to my head, and I snap the shot. He's smiling in it.

"Can I post to my grid?" I ask.

He nods and tells me his Instagram handle so I can tag him. I post the shot with the caption *Glorious sunset picnic with @milesaway.*

It *is* glorious. And actually, so is this night, despite the disastrous start. It's weird—seeing Miles like this, all loose and chill, has pretty much squashed my dislike of him. He doesn't always say something when I expect him to, and he may have a slight case of resting grumpy face. But he's funny, and nice, and really is so much less awkward when he's comfortable with someone. I'm starting to think Miles and I will work really well together on this festival project. And I guess he's right. I *can* make friends with just about anyone.

Mom's doing a Zumba class on YouTube when I get home.

"Oh," she says, not even pausing her dancing/exercising. "I thought you were at your father's this weekend. Do you want some leftover chili?"

Hadn't Mom noticed that I never spend the night at Dad's anymore? "Nah, I ate a ton of cheese at the park." I plop onto the armchair to greet Zuri, who is draped over the back of it. There's a big pile of fake flowers on the table. Mom buys them from thrift stores to practice new designs. "What were you working on here?"

Mom pauses the TV. She's in leggings and a tank top, and there's a sheen of sweat on her shoulders. "Was playing with some hydrangeas. Don't you think these would be *gorgeous* as hanging wedding centerpieces?" She shows me some pictures on her phone of hydrangeas made into large orbs. She tells me about her vision, and it sounds amazing.

"How's the festival planning going?" she asks after she puts the exercise class back on and gets into position.

I pull Zuri onto my lap. "It's going. Miles put together a draft of our proposal, but we couldn't talk about it tonight because Cara was a no-show. I don't know what's going on with her. She only does what Hannah wants lately."

"Young love," Mom says as she does this sideways shimmy, mirroring the lady on the TV. "It's consuming her life."

"I wasn't like that with Priya, was I?" I scratch Zuri's chin while I think about it. It's funny—all I could think about a few weeks ago was manifesting a meet-cute and finding a prom date. But with the problems on the street, and Mom thinking of selling the building, and putting together this festival, plus, of course, finding Miles a match, I've barely thought about my own love life lately. Maybe that's for the best, though. Seeing Cara lose herself in a relationship makes me think I should stay single for a while.

"It's a good thing you have Miles," Mom says. She's still dancing. "He's a smart kid."

I don't "have" Miles—haven't we had this conversation already? I change the subject before giving it too much thought. "Hey, do you know Nasrin Kanji? That's Miles's mother. She's Ismaili, like us."

Mom shakes her head. "I don't recognize the name." I tell her where Miles grew up to see if she knows his family, but she's zoned out, concentrating on the dance instructor's movements.

This is frustrating. I was fine with pretending that everything's okay and not telling her that I know about her money problems, but she's not even *listening* to me. Maybe she's trying to stay extra busy to keep her mind off her problems? I just wish the fact that she's thinking about selling the building was out in the open so I could ask her. Should I tell her I know?

"I bumped into Ina Kozlak today," Mom says suddenly. "She's going through a rough time."

"Oh no! What's wrong?" I ask.

"Sales at Kozlaks' are down. She can't compete with the large chains anymore. She may have to close. Did you know Rossi's has their own brand of pierogies?"

"Ugh. But there's no way they are as good as Mrs. Kozlak's." This sucks. I love Kozlaks'. They have the best European chocolates and cookies. "Maybe the festival will be good for them too."

"Maybe." Mom shakes her hips while doing this sweeping motion with her hands, but I can tell that her mind is elsewhere again.

I sigh. This festival *has* to happen. If not, this Love Street, *my* Love Street, won't exist anymore.

CHAPTER TEN

THE DRESS APPROPRIATION

On Monday I stay in my advanced painting classroom during lunch so I can keep working on my final project piece. My teacher, Ms. Carothers, stands behind me and watches me work.

"That's gorgeous," she says. "Is it a self-portrait?"

I squint at the painting. It does look a little like me. It's a watercolor of a woman sitting on a tall stool wearing a simple black dress, but instead of hair she has an enormous riot of colorful flowers cascading from her head. I think when I started the painting, I was loosely modeling her on Priya, but now that I look at it, I've definitely made her hips bigger, which is more my figure. And the flowers make her look like she has curly hair. Actually, if I'm honest, this looks a lot like my mother. She even has the same wide, unfocused eyes.

Ms. Carothers and I chat a bit about the work, and she tells me about a mural she's been commissioned to paint over the summer, which sounds super cool. While she's showing me some sketches of her mural project, I get a text. It's Priya, asking if I forgot that there's a prom committee meeting today. I *had* forgotten. I clean up my art things quickly and head to the library to join the rest of the prom committee.

As prom committee chair, there isn't a lot of work left for me to do. My role has mostly been in the ideas stage, plus being the point of contact for the banquet hall and making sure everyone else does their jobs. The committee is great, so everything's going fine. I listen to everyone's updates on how their duties are going. The girl in charge of communications just put up some teasers on the school's Instagram account, and students are saying this is going to be the best prom in years.

I meant what I said to Miles earlier—I *do* think prom is one of the most important events in high school. And I've been looking forward to mine for four years. I'm even the chair of the committee because I wanted my dance to be perfect. But now my prom is almost here, and there's so much else going on that I feel like I got cheated out of my prom experience. Like how can I get excited about the rotating 360-degree photo booth and cream puffs for dessert when the livelihoods of the people on my street are at risk? I don't even have a prom date because everything happening on Love Street made me put finding one on the back burner.

I'm putting all my faith in this festival to help the street, but I know that even with super-smart Miles working on the proposal, getting approval is a big long shot. And even if we *can* have the festival, will it help? Will people come to a festival on such a small street? And will they keep coming to the street after the festival? I may have no choice but to live with my dad if Mom has to sell the building, unless Mom moves somewhere else in town. And I still don't know how to talk to Mom about what I overheard her saying to Jenn. Or even if I should.

And no matter what, my life is going to change significantly in the next few months . . . and I have no idea whether it will be a good change or a bad one. Prom seems like the end of an era for me. And I don't know what life will be like after that era, so it's hard to look forward to that ending.

But maybe Miles is right. Prom is just a dance, and it doesn't need to mean the end or the beginning of anything significant. And actually, maybe he's also right about my head being in the clouds for thinking that *love* is going to be the answer to all our problems. I know he's right about love changing people, and not always for the better. Look at what's happening to Cara. Look at my father, who used to be a fun and attentive dad, until Noureen.

All this uncertainty is getting harder to ignore, and it's making it kind of hard to get excited about a carefree, happy dance with my friends. And the fact that I'll be *dateless* for my prom isn't helping.

After the meeting, Priya stops me as I'm leaving the library. She's positively glowing. Before, Priya always used to seem a little stressed and harried. Falling in love with Amber *did* change Priya for the better, so Miles is wrong that it always changes people for the worse.

Not all hope is lost.

"Sana! You've been holding out on me! Tell me all about the new hottie you're seeing! Are you bringing *him* to prom?"

I raise one eyebrow. What is she talking about? Or rather, *who*? "What hottie? I'm not seeing anyone."

"The guy in your Instagram."

Oh. She's talking about Miles. "He's a friend—we're not dating. He works at the bookstore a few doors down from me."

Priya frowns, looking genuinely disappointed, which is sweet. She does want me to be happy.

"I wanted to ask you something," she says. "You know

the vintage dress you got for prom that matches mine?"

Of course I know the dress. I found it at Cosmic and fell in love with the rose-pink tulle skirt and satin corset bodice. And then I'd scoured vintage and thrift stores all over the city to find Priya a dress in the same shade, so we'd match like we'd always planned to.

"Yeah, what about it?"

"Could Amber borrow it for prom? Or . . . could we buy it off you? You two are about the same size."

Priya wants my prom dress?

"I—I mean . . ." She stutters, probably picking up on the WTF expression on my face. "I assume you aren't going to wear it . . . because you probably don't want to match me anymore . . . and you work in a vintage store, so maybe you already found something better to wear? I don't have time to shop again, because you know . . . I have those college prep classes and my Indian dance lessons. But if you're going to wear it, then it's totally fine. I just thought—"

I shake my head. "No, it's fine, you can have the dress. I got it with my employee discount, so pay me what I paid for it."

Priya beams and wraps her arms around me. "Thank you thank you thank you!" She lets me go. "See! Amber said there was no way you'd give her your prom dress, but I knew you'd understand. This is why I adore you, Sana! I have to run . . . but I'll come by this week to pick up the dress!"

She smiles and leaves. I sigh, clutching my bag to my chest. Okay, so maybe Priya doesn't care as much about my happiness as I thought. Why did I say yes? Ugh. Now I need to find a new prom dress on top of everything else I have going on.

. . .

At Cosmic that night I scour the formal-wear section, but I can't find anything in my size that I like for prom. I tell Jenn my situation, and she says she'll keep her eye out for a dress. I know it's probably too late to find something vintage that would work—I may have to go to the mall.

When I leave Cosmic after my shift, I see Miles at the counter on his laptop in Second Story Books. He's looking out the window as I pass, so I smile and wave. He waves back but doesn't smile.

My new friend is *stingy* with his smiles. I keep waving furiously and smiling until he finally laughs, and I bow proudly before walking away. As I'm climbing up the stairs to my apartment, he texts me.

Miles: If you're free now do you want to go over the proposal?

I'm smiling as I write back.

Sana: Is that a ploy to see me, Mr. Desai? What were you doing in the bookstore on your computer?
Miles: I just saw you. I was applying for internships, but we can work on the proposal over the phone instead.
Sana: Okay, but I'm terrible on the phone. Do you want to work at my place?

He doesn't respond.

Sana: I'll tell my cat not to hiss at you.
Miles: Okay. When?

Sana: Give me 15 to change and get dinner.

Mom's still in the flower shop, so I quickly make two quesadillas with leftovers in the fridge and plate them with some salad. After taking one plate down to Mom, I ask her if she minds if Miles and I work in the apartment on the festival proposal. She says it's fine and that she'll be working late on a large funeral order.

After I change into sweats, I start eating on the couch when there's a knock on my door. When I run down and open it, Miles is there in worn jeans, a faded red T-shirt, and his old brown messenger bag on his shoulder. And a smile on his face. So much for being stingy.

I grin and motion for him to follow me up the stairs. "I'm still eating. Want a quesadilla?" There's enough black beans and roasted red peppers to make another one.

"No, I'm good. I just had a burger."

We sit on the sofa, me with my plate balanced on my lap and him with his computer, and start going over the proposal draft. He did a lot of research. In the community impact section, he wrote about how other festivals have helped revitalize communities. I add more personalized information about Love Street and how increasing visibility could strengthen the close bond the community members already have. We work together on the financial section next, covering sponsors, vendor fees, and the BOA budget for the event.

"Don't forget to add something about the statue we want to put in LOL Park," I say. "Maybe we can find a sponsor to pay for it." I did a bit of research, and, while I hate to say it, Miles was right all those weeks ago—it's not something we can afford without help.

Miles shakes his head. "It's going to be an enormous amount of work to get it approved, and the piece will cost tens of thousands of dollars. People will come for the street vendors and the performances. This big heart sounds so . . ."

I exhale. "So what?"

"Trite."

I can't believe we're here again. Why do we keep having the same argument? "I have no idea how I'm supposed to plan a festival of love with someone who doesn't believe in love," I say.

That comment makes his brows knit together. "I believe in love."

"Okay, then with someone who thinks love should have no importance in society and who thinks everyone who loves romance is indoctrinated into the capitalism machine."

"You're putting words into my mouth," he says. I can see that tension sneaking back into his jaw.

I shake my head. "I am not putting words into your mouth. I'm making an analysis of your opinions based on your actions and comments on the matter. You agreed to me setting you up on dates so that you'd see how amazing love is. If you were already a . . . love aficionado, I wouldn't have to do that, would I?"

A small smile appears on his lips. "Love aficionado?"

"Okay, okay, tell me one thing. How's Reggie's new romance section selling?" Maybe I should have insisted Miles *read* romances on top of letting me set him up to get him to change his tune. Lord knows the setups haven't worked yet.

"They're not selling more than other categories, but I admit they are doing better than I thought they would."

"Reggie hasn't advertised the romance section at all,"

I say. "But even still, people are buying. They can't *all* be buying the books because they've been brainwashed by marketing—they read romance because of the joy and hope in the genre. People want that in their lives. Just because you're a frigid fish doesn't mean others feel the same way." I exhale, regretting my words immediately. Name calling isn't helping anyone here. "I'm sorry. Forget I called you a fish."

Miles blinks at me. "Do you really think I'm frigid?" he asks. He actually looks hurt, and that was not my intention at all.

I close my eyes for a moment. I have no idea why this person sitting next to me affects me like this. Sometimes he's the easiest person in the world to talk to, but he also irritates me more than most people do. He makes me say things I don't normally say. I'm Sunny Sana, the eternal optimist. I don't call people names. But Miles Desai has thrown me so completely off my groove, and I don't know what to do with that. I turn to look at him. "I apologize. I shouldn't have said that."

"But do you think it?" he asks.

I bite my lip. To be honest, Miles has never seemed like a warm, affectionate, or even passionate person, but I don't think that necessarily means he's cold, either. I decide to be honest.

"I don't know. Sometimes, maybe."

After a few moments, he speaks again. "Not everyone's interpretation of love is hearts and Hallmark Christmas movies. That doesn't mean we're not capable of it."

"Have *you* ever been in love?" I ask. I asked him that question before, and he didn't answer me then. But now we're friends.

He exhales, then looks away from me. "I don't know."

"You don't know if you've been in love?"

He stares in front of him at the macramé owl hanging on the wall. "I had a girlfriend for a year in high school," he says. "I thought I was in love. But now I wonder if it was just . . . *convenient*."

"Ugh. Poor girl."

Miles huffs a laugh, looking at me. "Considering we broke up when I found out she hooked up with my best friend, I don't have a ton of sympathy for her."

"Oh my goodness! That *sucks*. I take it back. Poor *you*. That, plus your parents' separation. . . . It's no wonder you're so jaded."

He shakes his head. "I'm not *jaded*. My relationship or family history has nothing to do with why I don't see the point of pouring energy and money into a frivolous idea like a heart-shaped park installation. It's a waste of our resources."

I take the now-empty plate off my lap and cross my legs. "*Disagree*," I say.

"I guess we're at an impasse, then," Miles says. "It doesn't need to be in the proposal anyway. The next section is diversity."

We finish the rest of the proposal together, but the vibe between us is different now. I'd thought we were getting closer, or at least on similar wavelengths since we watched the sunset, but now I wonder if I imagined that. Our entire worldviews are different at, like, the molecular level.

"Should we send this to Cara before emailing it to the city councillor?" Miles asks after we've gone over the entire document twice.

"Yeah, let me text her." I grab my phone from the coffee table and fire off a text to Cara, but she doesn't answer. Because of course she doesn't.

"She's with Hannah, isn't she?" Miles asks.

"Probably. But don't you dare say that this proves your point."

"Why would I say that?"

I sigh, dropping my phone to the couch. "Because you're going to say that Cara has the lovey-dovey hearts and couple goals kind of love, and it's making her flake out on her commitments."

"I wouldn't have said that." He looks like he wants to say more but changes his mind.

"What?" I ask.

"I . . ." He hesitates. "I just wonder if Cara thinks she has the couple goals kind of love."

Neither of us says anything for a few moments. I have no idea what the answer to that question is. Cara has never told me she's unhappy. But maybe Miles has seen something I haven't.

"Question for you," Miles finally says. "Because we clearly need to understand each other better if we're going to work together. Have *you* ever been in love?"

I exhale, looking down at my lap. The answer is a little embarrassing. "Does it matter if I've been in love? I know what I'm drawn to, and I'm not the only one into hearts and romance. Corporate greed can't be the only reason Valentine's Day is such a huge holiday. The heart installation will attract people like me to the festival. It doesn't really *matter* if me and people like me are a bunch of delusional idealists, as long as we spend money here."

"I don't think you're delusional, Sana," Miles says

softly. I look at him. His intense gaze is focused only on me, and it makes my breath catch in my throat. He's only a foot away from me on the sofa, and his hand is close enough that I could touch it if I wanted to.

And the thing is, I do want to.

I take a slow breath. The air around us seems charged. I may not have been in love before, but I *know* what chemistry feels like. I *know* this fluttering of my stomach, this goose bumpy feeling.

But it's probably only on my side. Miles called my ideas "frivolous." He thinks my head's not in the real world. He's not feeling anything for me except annoyance. And it's so monumentally inconvenient that I've got these fluttery feelings for someone so different from me.

I turn away quickly. "So . . . you ready for me to find you another date? I think I know you well enough not to mess it up this time."

He doesn't answer right away, and I resist the urge to turn back to him because I'm afraid he's going to see my stupid attraction all over my face.

"Yeah, let's do it," he finally says. "Maybe the third time will be the charm."

He's definitely not into me like I'm into him. Which is good. Miles Desai and I are oil and water. We would never work out. We would be more opposite than my mother and father . . . and look how their relationship turned out.

Maybe finding Miles's true match is the best way for me to get over these feelings I have for him—because they are making planning this festival very hard for me.

CHAPTER ELEVEN

THE FIRST CASUALTY ON LOVE STREET

I work on the mock-up sketches for the proposal in the art room at lunch with Ms. Carothers's help. When I send them to Miles, he texts back that they're great, and he'll put it all together and email the whole proposal to the city councillor's office that afternoon.

After school I go straight to Kozlaks' since I haven't been able to stop thinking about Ina Kozlak struggling with her little store since Mom told me about it. The store has been here forever, long before Mom and I moved to Love Street. The white sign with KOZLAKS' painted in black block letters is such a landmark in this area.

Inside, it's a small space with a few shelves of Polish grocery items on one side, a deli counter for cured meats on the other, and a few fridges and freezers with cheeses and frozen pierogies at the back. I go straight to their cookie section and grab a blue bag of heart-shaped chocolate-covered gingerbread. When Miles mentioned chocolate-covered gingerbread at Riverdale Park, I immediately knew exactly where to get some.

I smile at Mrs. Kozlak at the counter, but she doesn't smile back. She looks . . . worried. "Mrs. Kozlak," I say after paying for the cookies, "I don't know if you know about it, but a bunch of us are trying to put on a street festival here on Love Street. Can you think of something your store can feature for the festival? Like something love and romance themed. Mrs. Kotch is doing desserts. Mom's going to do little love bouquets. LoveBug is—"

"When is festival?"

"It hasn't been confirmed yet, but we're aiming for the third weekend of July."

"We closed," Mrs. Kozlak says.

"What?"

"The store closed by then. For good."

My shoulders slump. "Oh no! You can't close Kozlaks'!"

She shakes her head. "We can't stay open. No one comes in anymore. Rent goes up every year, and sales go down."

"But this store is so great." She doesn't say anything to that. "When are you closing?" I ask.

"End of the month. I sell all this to Zensky's in Scarborough. Nothing can survive here." She sighs. "I have to find a new job now. Maybe Rossi's will hire me. Maybe I'll go live with my daughter in Calgary. This city is too expensive . . . I could have a *palace* back home."

I exhale. I really don't know what to say. "We'll miss you on Love Street."

"Here." Mrs. Kozlak hands me a second bag of heart-shaped gingerbread. "You're a good girl, Sana, and so young. You should be having fun. This? This is kicking dead horse deader."

I slip the cookies into my bag and head straight to Love-Bug to get a tea before my shift at Cosmic. I feel terrible and need the pick-me-up. Before now, all this low-level worry and dread for the street was just that. Low level. But now . . . this feels so much more real. This is the first small business that I know is *closing* because of the nearby gentrification and the rising rents. And it sucks.

If Ina Kozlak can't keep her store open because Rossi's is selling cured sausages and pierogies, then what will happen to Morgan Ashton Flowers if Rossi's opens a flower department? How will Mrs. Kotch compete with cheaper grocery store cakes? What will happen to Cosmic if more trendy stores open in the mall on Gerrard?

While Ajit is making my masala chai latte, Julie asks me what's wrong, clearly noticing my terrible mood.

"Did you hear about Kozlaks'?" I ask.

Julie nods. "That it's closing? Yeah. Heartbreaking. The landlord apparently wanted to increase the rent by twenty-five percent. I don't even know how that's allowed."

"Commercial rent doesn't have rent control like residential," Ajit explains. "Hopefully the same thing doesn't happen to us next year."

"Residential rent control isn't really helping anymore, either," Julie says. "And if those developers sniffing around Love Street build their new condos, the area will get even more expensive. Vultures. I don't blame her for leaving." We all sigh because what can we say?

"Let's not focus on negatives," I finally say, forcing a smile. "Miles and I finished the festival proposal yesterday, and it's amazing. I *know* things will turn around. You'll see."

"I hope you're right," Ajit says. "I'm so impressed with Miles. That kid is going to go places. And he loves Bollywood action movies! Kindred spirit, that one."

I laugh but then remember something I'd wanted to ask

Ajit and Julie. "By the way, why is your part-time barista obsessed with rodents?"

Ajit snorts a laugh, while Julie shakes her head. "I have no idea. I had to ask her to stop wearing clothes with rats on them while working. I'd rather the customers not even think about rodents while in our café. She swears she's never brought her pets into the store, but we've implemented employee bag checks."

"Smart move," I say.

I'm working with Cara that night, and Cosmic is surprisingly pretty steadily busy. I'm helping a customer find jeans in her size, when an unfamiliar upbeat voice behind me says, "Hi, Sana!"

I turn . . . and am shocked to see that it's Sarina. She looks cheerful, and friendly, and I'm not sure why I didn't recognize her voice. Probably because it's weird to see her at work. Or without her mother. Cara is next to her—also smiling.

"Look who's here!" Cara says. "I totally didn't realize *this* is your stepsister! I've seen her around school loads of times."

I feel like the worlds I carefully keep separated are colliding. "Oh, hey, Sarina." My customer comes out of the fitting room and stands in front of the big mirror. "Did you need me for something? I'm with a customer right now, but I'll probably be done in ten minutes or so."

She grins and shakes her head. Sarina is so pretty. She's tall and slim with enormous brown eyes, delicate features, and long straight hair. She's in jeans and a cream T-shirt today, and her hair is in a ponytail. "Help your customer. Don't worry about me. I was just in the area and thought I'd say hi. But now that I'm here . . . I kind of need summer clothes. Maybe sundresses?" She glances around the store.

"I'll help Sarina," Cara says. "You finish with your customer."

I give Cara a thankful smile. It would be strange to help my stepsister find clothes. Her mother's voice would be in my head the whole time.

I end up with my customer for another twenty minutes, as she wants to try on every pair of pants in the store. It's worth it, though, because she buys a ton. I can see Cara helping Sarina—Sarina tries on a few dresses, and Cara helps pin them so Sarina can take them to a seamstress.

My customer leaves right before Sarina is ready to pay. "So, you found stuff?" I ask while Cara is ringing up Sarina's purchases.

"Yes! With Cara's help. I never would have thought to try on a halter dress."

Cara smiles. "You have the shoulders for it."

After Sarina pays for her purchases, she gives me a big hug and thanks Cara again profusely before leaving the store. I watch her go, still a bit confused.

"That was weird," I say.

"What? She looked great in that halter dress. Did you see it on her?"

"No, I mean it's weird that she came in. And she was so nice." I wonder if Noureen sent her to spy on me.

"She seems really sweet," Cara says. "She's very easy to talk to. Why don't you ever hang out with her?"

I start putting the pants that my customer didn't buy

back on hangers. "Honestly, we're not really friends. We never socialize without our parents."

"Maybe she came here because she wants to change that." Cara suddenly smiles huge. "You know what I just realized? Sarina would be perfect for Miles."

I take a step back. "Seriously? Are you kidding?"

Cara nods vigorously. "Yes *seriously*. She's so nice!"

I exhale. Why does everyone think Sarina is *perfect*? "I don't even know if she's single."

"She is. She mentioned it to me. She's smart, too. And you know enough about her to know that she's not obsessed with rodents, and she probably won't throw a fish at Miles. Come on, don't you think she's totally the type to inspire love ballads? She's stunning."

Cara is right that Sarina is pretty. Plus, Miles mentioned how much he admired that violin player at his school, and Sarina plays the cello. They'd both mentioned to me how damaging the clothing industry is and said we should be buying secondhand. Honestly, on paper, Sarina *is* perfect for Miles. They have a lot in common.

But I don't know. I logically know that Sarina isn't her mother, but still. Setting up Sarina with Miles would mean me spending time with her. Which I know would make her mother happy, and I don't really like doing things that could make Noureen happy. Also? My self-esteem is usually fine, but spending time with my perfect stepsister could seriously test that.

Of course, the other issue with setting Miles up with my stepsister—actually, with setting him up with anyone at all—is that I unintentionally developed a little crush on the guy despite him frustrating me more than almost anyone else I know. But that might be the best reason to try Sarina for Miles's next setup. Because I imagine the best way to turn me off someone is to connect them to my stepmother and stepsister.

I sigh. "Sure. Why not. I'll call her tomorrow."

CHAPTER TWELVE

THE CHERRY BLOSSOM CALAMITY

The next day, after thinking of another perfect date spot for a committee meeting, I open a text to my stepsister. I decide not to tell her that this outing is a setup, because she may be less inclined to come if she knew. Her mother doesn't have a lot of faith in any of my abilities, and I don't know if Sarina feels the same.

Sana: Hey Sarina, great to see you yesterday!
Sarina: Hi Sana! Yes! I love your store.
Sana: Question—A bunch of us are going to High Park on Sunday afternoon to see the cherry blossoms, and Cara said I should invite you. My friend Miles is coming too. He's great—you'll like him. It will be the last weekend for the cherry blossoms.
Sarina: That sounds amazing! Absolutely I'll come. What time?

I give her the time and a meeting place near the park and say I'm looking forward to seeing her again. *There*. Now I just have to convince Miles to come. On my way to work at Cosmic that evening, I take one of the bags of chocolate-covered gingerbread to Miles at the bookstore.

"What's this?" he asks after I hand him the blue bag

of cookies. He's at the counter with his laptop in front of him again.

"Chocolate-covered gingerbread. I saw them at Kozlaks' and thought of you."

He inspects the picture on the bag. "They're heart shaped."

I try not to laugh at that. He's really, like, *allergic* to any romantic imagery. "That's not why I'm giving them to you. They're great cookies. Try one."

He opens the bag and takes a bite of one of the little gingerbread hearts. I can see his mood change as he chews. His brows unfurrow, and I swear his eyes almost roll back in his head.

I grin. "Good, right?" I'd been planning to keep the extra bag of cookies that Mrs. Kozlak gave me for myself, but now I think I need to keep them for Miles for when I need to soften him.

He smiles wide. "They're just like the ones my mom used to buy. Thanks."

"No problem. Now, question—what are you doing on Saturday? After the stores close?"

"Nothing."

"Good. We're all going to see the cherry blossoms at High Park."

Miles's smile disappears. "Is this another date?"

I nod. "Yep. This one is *perfect* for you. She doesn't even like mice." I think Sarina doesn't like mice. To be honest, I don't know.

He frowns. "Yeah, maybe the setups aren't such a good idea. I mean, the last two didn't work, and I'm kind of feeling—"

I put my hand up to stop him. "My stepsister, Sarina, *isn't* like the last two," I say. "You'll *adore* her. She's a business student at U of T. She's very smart. And even though she's my stepsister, she's like . . . normal."

"What do you mean, *normal*?"

I exhale. "I mean, she's not, like, weird." I pause. I don't know how to say this. "She's not going to bring mice or toss a fish at you. And she's not *eccentric* like me. She's great." I think I might be selling Sarina too much here, but I really need Miles to agree.

Miles stares at me for several long seconds. "What makes you think I have an issue with *eccentric*?"

I let out a nervous laugh. "I mean you said *I* was too *idealistic*. Sarina's not like that. She's . . . realistic. Grounded. She takes everything seriously."

He stares at me with this intense look in his eyes. I have no idea what he's thinking, but my stupid heart pounds faster the longer he goes without talking. I can't stand it.

"I'm going to invite Ajit and Julie too," I say quickly. "You and Ajit are buddies, right? The High Park cherry blossoms are *so* beautiful. I'll bet they are on your list of cheap things to do in Toronto, right? And this is a festival committee meeting, so you have to come."

He keeps staring at me. "Fine," he finally says, sighing. "I'll come." He looks down at his laptop. "By the way, I got an email from Alex, Su Lin Tran's assistant in City Hall. Su Lin now has our proposal."

I clap my hands together. "Yay! We're totally getting the festival! And we're going to High Park to celebrate! It's going to be perfect."

. . .

We don't hear back from the city that week, so the High Park party isn't *technically* a *celebration* party, but it is a party. Cara promised she and Hannah wouldn't ditch us again, and Ajit made a whole bunch of snacks to bring along. Sarina is waiting in front of High Park subway station when we get there, and the moment I see my stepsister, I know I made the right choice for Miles. Sarina looks as perfect as always. She's in pale blue jeans, which are rolled up to her ankles, white sneakers, a pink T-shirt, and a long gray cardigan. Her hair is loose, and the only makeup I can see on her is a touch of pink lip gloss. She gives us a shy smile when she sees us, then flips her hair over her shoulder like a shampoo model. Next to her . . . I feel like a short clown.

I'm wearing a cherry blossom dress I found in a thrift store last year. It's bright turquoise with branches all over it, covered with pale pink flowers. The dress is about mid-calf length, with a full circle skirt and a shawl collar. I'd thought it was perfect for this outing—until I saw Sarina's delicate, *understated* outfit.

But it doesn't matter what I look like next to Sarina. All that matters is what *Miles* thinks of her. I wave. "Sarina, come meet my friends! This is Julie and Ajit; they own the café on Love Street. Of course, you know Cara, who works at Cosmic Vintage with me. And this is Hannah, and Miles! He goes to TMU and is studying planning! So cool, right?"

I can't read Sarina's expression, but I hope she likes what she sees when she meets Miles, because he looks fantastic today. He's in jeans and a pale beige short-sleeved shirt that has tiny blue flowers on it. I need to remember to ask him if it's vintage.

Miles, of course, is fully aware that this is a setup, even though Sarina doesn't know. This way, if disaster strikes like on the other two dates, then Sarina will never know the true reason I invited her here, and Noureen won't complain about me playing matchmaker.

As expected, High Park is busy. The cherry blossoms, or sakura trees, in this park were a gift to Toronto from Tokyo in the 1950s, and it's the largest concentration of cherry blossoms in the city. They are only in bloom about two weeks a year, and of course, *everyone* wants to see them. "I wonder if the shops in the area see more business when the flowers are in bloom," I say to Miles while we walk toward the trees. Sarina is on the other side of me. Cara, Hannah, Julie, and Ajit are a few paces in front of us.

"Probably," Miles says.

"The trees are *so* romantic," I say. Too bad we can't get them for the festival. It would be cool, but I get that it's not possible. I grin playfully, turning to Miles. "What do you think, Miles? Should we plant cherry blossom trees in LOL Park for the festival? All this pink would be *perfect* for the aesthetic. I'm calling the city councillor to add it to our proposal."

He, as expected, gives me an incredulous look. "Do you have any idea how long trees take to mature?" he asks. "I doubt they even flower in their first year. We can't consider every whim that passes your mind. Getting trees would be completely—"

"Impossible," I say, interrupting him. I giggle and squeeze his arm briefly. "I know we can't get *trees*. I literally grew up in a flower shop; cherry blossoms take years to root. But I had you scared, didn't I?"

He huffs a laugh, rubbing the back of his neck. He's flustered and embarrassed and ridiculously adorable and . . .

I'm supposed to be setting him up with my stepsister, not teasing him.

I should leave Sarina and Miles alone. "Oh, I just remembered I need to ask Cara something." I speed up to catch up with the others.

"Wait up," Sarina says, running after me. "I need to tell her that halter dress fit perfectly after I had it altered."

Great. Now we've left Miles all alone. Ajit and Julie slow down to walk with Miles, leaving me and Sarina walking with Cara and Hannah. So far this setup isn't working. I don't think Sarina has said two sentences to Miles. Sarina compliments Cara's cream sweater—which . . . again, what happened to Cara's retro goth style?

Once we get to a heavy concentration of trees, our group scatters to take pictures. There are hundreds of people around us also taking pictures with their phones. I see a few people with more professional-looking cameras too, and lots of girls in pretty dresses posing with the trees.

The sakura trees are almost . . . magical. They are absolutely enormous, and each huge tree is entirely covered with small pale pink flowers that contrast perfectly with the cloudless blue sky. There are so many of these towering pale pink trees in close concentration that the breathtaking beauty in every direction is almost overwhelming.

I come to see the blooms every year, and they have never not left me speechless. As this is nearing the end of their bloom period, the flowers are losing their petals, so the grass below our feet is carpeted with the same pale pink as the branches. And with every gust of wind, more pink petals fall, swirling in the air like confetti.

I look for the others. Cara, Hannah, and Sarina are a few paces away, taking pictures. Ajit and Julie are a little closer, taking a selfie together. Miles is suddenly next to me. "Your dress has cherry blossoms on it," he says.

I look down at my dress, fake horror on my face. "Oh my god . . . it does! How did that happen?!"

Miles chuckles. "You were wearing sunset colors when we went to see the sunset."

I grin. "How observant of you."

"Do you regularly pick clothes based on a theme?"

"Sometimes." I position my phone in front of me to take a selfie of me with a tree. And of about twelve other people behind me doing the same thing.

"Do you want me to take it?" Miles asks, putting his hand out for my phone.

I give it to him and strike a pose in front of the tree. After he takes a few shots, he hands my phone back. "There are so many people around, I couldn't get you alone," he says.

"Why would I want to be alone?"

His forehead furrows. "Don't you just want you and the trees with your matching dress?"

I shake my head. "No! The very last thing I want to do is erase all these people. It's the coolest thing about this place. . . . Everyone came to see the same thing I'm here to see. Thousands come every year to see some trees bloom. I *love* it." I scroll through the pictures Miles took. He has quite an eye—the pictures are great. I start to upload a few to my grid right away, then look at Miles. "Come here," I say, smiling.

"Why?"

"I want a selfie with you. You're wearing flowers, too. We both match the trees."

He laughs, but then comes and lets me take the selfie of us with our heads leaning into each other, surrounded by the pale pink trees behind us. I upload the picture along with the others he took, tagging Miles again.

"Question," I ask as I put my phone down. "Did you wear that shirt with flowers on it because we were coming to look at flowers? Because I think I'm a good influence on you."

Miles laughs again. I can't get over how much his face changes when he smiles. It's almost as if there are two Miles Desais—the nonsmiling surly one who is irritated at about every third thing I say and this easygoing one who laughs a lot. *This* Miles looks like it matches the rest of him. Like his bright eyes match his expression for the first time.

I turn away, exhaling. I'm way too fascinated with my frustrating new friend. Maybe it's because he's so completely different from me. But I need to stop this. *Miles is my friend*. We're literally here because I want him to fall in love with someone else—my *stepsister*.

"I see your real reason for dragging me here, by the way," he says as we walk to the next tree.

"I have no ulterior motive," I say. "I wanted you to meet my stepsister. What do you think of her?"

He looks over at Sarina, then shrugs. "She seems nice enough. Quiet, though. But I mean why you brought us *here*, specifically. You wanted me to see how many people will come to a place just so they can post it on their social media."

I tilt my head. I actually hadn't thought of that, but yeah, the number of people here at High Park proves my point that we should have some sort of installation in LOL Park that people can post to their socials.

"Yes, exactly," I say, smiling. "We *need* something this photogenic."

He nods. "I don't see how we can do anything to this scale, but yeah, I see your point. We need a signature attraction. Social media bait."

I grin, clapping my hands together. "Yay! We can brainstorm ideas after we get the festival permit. We'll think of something *iconic*."

"*If* we get the festival permit."

I shake my head, poking his shoulder with my pink-painted fingernail. "None of this *if* business, mister. We're getting it. You and me? We're an unstoppable team."

He laughs, and again my heart flutters. I really shouldn't be craving the rush of making him smile so much.

"Where's Sarina?" I ask, looking around. I need to get them together again and then escape without her following me so Miles and Sarina can be alone.

I see her several trees over. She's not really *with* Cara and Hannah, but she's watching them. Weird. Cara and Hannah are standing under a tree with their arms around each other, and Hannah has an arm out to take a selfie. She kisses Cara on the mouth as she takes the picture. From my angle, I can clearly see Sarina grimace and take a step backward the moment Hannah and Cara kiss.

What is that about? I wonder if Sarina overheard Hannah say something not great to Cara earlier, so she doesn't like Hannah for Cara.

I'm about to go ask her what's wrong when Sarina takes another step backward and trips over a tree root. She falls quite spectacularly to the ground, knocking over two other tree photographers with her.

"Oh no!" Miles says, rushing to Sarina. I follow him, saying "excuse me" to the dozen or so people between us and Sarina.

When he gets to her, Miles kneels at Sarina's feet and asks if she's okay. I slow down to give them a moment alone. I love that he ran to her rescue immediately. But also, I feel a twang of jealousy of the attention Miles is giving Sarina, which is ridiculous. I brought Miles and Sarina here because I wanted *him* to fall for her, and the fact that he's currently helping her out of the dirt is a good thing. As is the fact that he's gently picking off the cherry blossom petals stuck to her sweater.

Then Sarina says something I don't hear that makes Miles smile. The same smile he just gave me. I step closer to them.

"I'm fine. I'm fine," Sarina says. "Just embarrassed. I'm such a klutz." She apologizes to the people she knocked down, who've already gotten up from the dirt. They look annoyed—especially the girl in the cream dress that now has dusty brown splotches on it.

Cara and Hannah come to see what's going on, along with Ajit and Julie. Sarina again assures us all that she's fine. But when she starts to walk, it becomes clear that she's *not* fine. She nearly falls again after taking only one step. Miles is still next to her and catches her.

"I just need to walk it off," she says.

Cara looks skeptical. She's studying physical therapy,

so she knows. "Let me look at your foot," she says.

While Sarina stands on one foot holding on to Miles for stability, Cara inspects Sarina's ankle. Cara turns it a bit, then asks Sarina to put her weight on it, which makes Sarina cringe with pain.

"I think it's twisted," Cara says. "It doesn't look like a break. But it might swell up. I'd stay off it as much as possible to let it heal."

Sarina's already-wide eyes go even wider. "Do you think it's okay for me to take the subway home to Vaughan?"

Cara shakes her head. "Can you get a ride or an Uber home?"

Sarina sighs. "Yeah, I suppose."

"We can split an Uber," Miles says quickly. "I'm going to King City to see my mom. Vaughan's on the way."

Great. So now Miles and Sarina will have a long car ride alone. I exhale. This is *good.* Sarina is smart and stable and is a perfect match for Miles. This could make them *both* happy. "That's a great idea!" I say, laying on the enthusiasm. "It's *so* convenient that you live near each other. This is why I wanted you to meet. You have so much in common!"

Miles is still holding Sarina up, but glances at me with an unreadable expression. Maybe I was laying it on too thick? I smile at Miles, but I wonder if he can see right through it.

After Sarina calls for a car, Miles and Ajit support Sarina as we walk to the main street to meet the Uber. Sarina still looks embarrassed, and the peaceful, serene look on her face seems to have left her. Probably because of the pain.

Miles barely even looks back at us after helping Sarina in. But when I call out that I'll text him later, he gives me a nod and a small, almost knowing smile. And then the car drives away with my stepsister and Miles.

I stare at the car as it leaves.

"She'll be fine," Cara says, maybe noticing my expression.

"Oh, yeah, I'm sure she will be. Sarina's always been clumsy." I have no idea if that's true. For some reason I want to sound like I actually know my stepsister.

We start walking back toward the trees, taking pictures as we walk, but I'm not in the mood for this anymore.

"You finally did it," Cara says.

"Did what?" Hannah asks.

Cara looks at her girlfriend. "Sana's been trying to set Miles up with someone all month. I think this date was the best one. That was a very Jane Austen meet-cute, wasn't it? Unless Sarina *did* break her ankle. That wouldn't be good."

I shake my head. "I mean, her getting hurt makes the date a disaster, but I guess this was still better than the others."

"Sarina's sweet, too," Cara says. "I don't get why you always complain about her like she's an evil stepsister. She's a bit normcore, but I like her."

"She . . . used to be kind of mean to me when we were kids."

Cara shrugs. "So? People grow up. She's great now."

Yeah, Cara's right. Sarina *has* grown, and she's probably not that bad a person. She doesn't really talk to me when we have brunch, so I figured we were polar opposites. But Sarina *is* more cheerful and chatty away from our parents. Today she has been perfectly pleasant—just a little clumsy. I need to stop resenting her like this. Why wouldn't Miles be into her?

I don't realize I'm clenching my jaw until Hannah speaks up.

"I don't think she's into Miles," Hannah says.

"Why not?" Cara asked.

Hannah shrugs. "She didn't look interested in him." She kisses Cara on the cheek. "You're coming back to my place after, right?"

Cara nods, smiling widely. She really does look happy.

We all hang out in High Park for about an hour more, taking pictures of the flowers, then eating the little veggie sandwiches and warm chai Ajit brought. As the sun sets, the hazy dusk adds a really cool vibe to the park. It's actually gorgeous.

But I don't enjoy it. I still feel down. I should be happy that I finally succeeded at setting up Miles, but I feel far from happy right now.

CHAPTER THIRTEEN

SAY WHATEVER TO THE DRESS

I text Sarina in the morning to see how her ankle is. She writes back right away.

Sarina: It's a bit swollen but so much better than last night. I texted a picture to Cara, and she said to keep off it and ice it, so that's what I'm doing!
Sana: I hope it didn't completely ruin your trip to High Park.
Sarina: No! I had such a great time. Miles and I talked the whole way back to my house. . . . You're right. He's so smart! Such a great guy.

I exhale. I wanted Miles and Sarina to hit it off, but now it feels . . .

Sana: Glad you had fun. We should do it again!
Sarina: Yes! Text me anytime. Well, in a few weeks when my foot's healed.

What exactly happened between Miles and Sarina on that Uber ride to Vaughan? Should I ask Miles? Did they exchange numbers? Are they going to date? After two failed setup attempts, one finally worked, and I can't enjoy it because I have a stupid crush on the guy now. *Ugh*.

I realized when I was looking at that picture of Miles and me with all those cherry blossom petals behind us that there's literally *no one* I like looking at pictures of more than Miles Desai. I like looking at him in person even more. I like talking to him, even when we're clashing on the festival plans. And I really like making him happy. A lot. It's shocking how much I've grown to like him.

I mean, I always thought he was cute—going right back to when I first saw him in LoveBug. I also found him arrogant and annoying back then. But now that I know him better, I realize that he's not a know-it-all, he just actually knows a lot and he wants to share that knowledge. He's an introvert, and maybe a little awkward, but he's not antisocial. He cares about sustainability, equity, and community engagement—all the same things I care about.

But I *have* to get over this crush. Because he doesn't feel the same way. If he did, he wouldn't let me continue to set him up with girls. Also, this festival is way too important for me to risk it by falling for the person I'm planning it with.

I need some space from him. If I don't see or talk to Miles for a while, maybe this crush will fade. And as for Sarina, I should avoid her, too. If they're meant to be together, they can figure it out for themselves. I need to focus on what's important—saving my mother's flower shop, and all the other businesses on Love Street. I'm officially retiring from matchmaking for Miles Desai. My emotions just can't take it.

On Wednesday Cara and I go through the formal-wear section of Cosmic one last time to see if there's a suitable prom dress that I somehow missed. Prom is on Friday—only two days away—so I already put aside a vintage dress to wear if I can't find anything else. But I'm not completely sold on it—it's very similar to the one I sold to Amber, but the pale blue color does nothing for my skin tone. While we're looking, I tell Cara I'm worried about what Sarina may have said about me to Miles on their car ride home.

"What is she going to even say?" Cara asks. "I don't get why you still don't like her. What did she do when you were kids?"

I exhale. "She just . . . I don't know. We were kids and we were forced to be sisters, even though we were so different. She used to say I wasn't allowed to touch her stuff because I would ruin it, and she made cracks about me not being in a gifted program like her."

Cara's head tilts sympathetically. "That *sucks*. Your father should have put a stop to that."

I shrug. "Probably. Anyway, Sarina's been fine since . . ." I pause. "Since I was twelve or thirteen, but we're *not* close. She *is* close to her mother, though. And Noureen is still very passive-aggressive to me. Maybe Sarina agrees with everything her mother says and is just too polite to say it to my face now."

Cara still looks sympathetic. "I'm sure she doesn't. What exactly does your stepmother say about you?"

I sigh. "Noureen and Dad think I need to grow up and stop this . . . *bohemian* lifestyle. They think I should dress more conservatively and give up on being an artist." I hold up a minidress with sequins in a peacock pattern. I like colorful clothes, but this might be a bit much for my prom.

"Bohemian? Sana, this isn't the 1960s. They're being

ridiculous. How you dress doesn't mean you're not serious."

I turn to look at Cara. Maybe she isn't the right person to talk to about this. She's dressed . . . *conventionally* again. Jeans and a polo shirt. I don't think I've seen Cara in all black once since Hannah came back to town. I hope she's not dressing *conservatively* for Hannah.

Anyway, I just need to put the whole Miles and Sarina situation out of my mind. "Hey, do you want to go to Kensington Market tomorrow night?" I ask. Neither of us is working tomorrow. "I'm sure I can find something for prom there."

Cara shakes her head. "I'm not sure Hannah would be into that."

I don't recall inviting Hannah, but okay. "If she's not into shopping, we could meet up with her after? How about dumplings in Chinatown?"

Cara doesn't look at me as she flips through dresses. "No, I mean I don't think she's into us all hanging out."

I blink. Is Cara telling me that her girlfriend doesn't like me? Which . . . fine. I'm not a huge Hannah fan either. "You can come without her, you know," I point out. "You two don't have to do everything together."

Cara shrugs. And is still quiet. I don't even know what to say. Is Cara not *allowed* to do things without Hannah?

Cara is so, so happy to have Hannah back in the city. I'd ruin our friendship if I told Cara that I think her girlfriend is controlling. Although at this rate I'm probably going to lose Cara as a close friend either way, since Hannah doesn't seem keen on Cara hanging out with me outside of work. Cara is such a great friend, I need to say something. Maybe Cara can't see what's right in front of her face.

"Cara, does Hannah *let* . . . I mean, is she *okay* with you doing things without her?"

Cara looks at me, irritation all over her face. "Of course I can do things without her. We're a couple. We want to spend time together. You would understand if you . . ."

I exhale. I would understand if I were in a relationship.

For a moment the only sound is the rustling of clothes as we swipe through our respective racks, until Cara says calmly, "We're fine. Hannah just likes spending time with me alone, that's all." Cara takes a beige off-the-shoulder gown off the rack and holds it up to me. I cringe and shake my head. I am not a beige person.

She puts the dress back. "Back to Sarina and Miles," Cara says. "Sarina's been in Cosmic more than once. I don't think she looks down on your wardrobe. And Miles . . . why do you even care what she says to him? You guys are friends, now, right? He wouldn't be more influenced by someone he just met over his actual friend."

He might if he had feelings for Sarina.

I sigh. I'm not going to tell Cara that my own feelings for Miles go way beyond friendship. Because maybe if I never say it aloud, the feelings will go away. "I don't want him to think less of me." I pause. "I admit—Sarina brings out my insecurities. I thought it would be fine if I saw her without Dad or Noureen, but maybe I've internalized everything Noureen's said about Sarina being better than me in every way."

"Well, that's ridiculous," Cara says. "Your stepmother is wrong about you."

"Thanks." I smile sadly. "I'm probably overthinking. I hate being in a funk. This prom situation is getting to me. I mean, I've been looking forward to prom for *four* years, and I've been planning it since September, and now here I am days away and I don't have a date or a dress. Pathetic, right?"

"It's not pathetic, Sana," Jenn says, making me jump. I totally hadn't noticed that she'd joined me and Cara at the formal dresses. She was probably listening to our conversation. "Sometimes life throws us curveballs, that's all."

I don't have pity parties very often. In fact, I pride myself on being a positive person, on finding the upside of every situation. But these days I just haven't been feeling like my usual sunny self. I exhale. "A few weeks ago I thought the fact that Priya didn't want to go to the dance with me anymore was an *opportunity*. I was *so* excited to find someone new. Didn't quite work out, did it?"

Maybe Miles is right. . . . Maybe society does place too much importance on romantic love. Maybe if it didn't I wouldn't feel so crappy about my lack of a love life.

Neither Jenn nor Cara says anything. I guess they aren't used to dealing with a pessimistic Sana. Heck, *I* don't know how to deal with it.

"Enough of this," I say. "I need to think *positively*. The perfect dress is here. I can feel it." I scan the dresses on the next rack. There's a bubble-gum pink dress that could work. I pick it up. It's clearly not my size. Cara cringes and shakes her head at the dress.

Jenn finally holds up a dress for me. I'd seen it on the rack and hadn't looked twice at it because it's not my style. I'm into big, puffy, and vibrant. This dress is dark plum satin and . . . slinky. It's sleeveless with a halter neck and a slit up one leg. It is gorgeous . . . but it's so *not* my usual aesthetic.

Before I can even say no, Jenn says, "Try it on. It should fit—I think you'd look stunning in it."

I nod. She has a point—how can I know it won't work without trying it? I take the dress to the fitting room, put it on, and come back out to look in the mirror.

The dress fits *perfectly*, except for being a little long. My butt even looks fantastic. I turn in front of the mirror. I still look and feel like *me*—just a different me. An older me. I exhale. It feels weird. Like, I said that prom is like the *bookend* to my teen years, and this dress somehow feels like a peek at who I'll be in the future. I can still be *me*, even if things change and look a little different. I smile at myself in the mirror.

Jenn comes up behind me and pulls my hair back. "Get a blowout so your hair is sleek. And just wear earrings . . . no other jewelry."

"You'll look stunning," Cara says. "I think this is the one."

"It's long," I say. "And there isn't time to send it to a seamstress."

Jenn smiles. "Let me get the pins. I can hem the dress." Jenn returns with a pin cushion and kneels to pin the hem. "You probably don't remember, but I used to sew you dresses when you were a little girl. Let me do this for you, for old times' sake."

I do remember. In fact, I almost tear up thinking how lucky I am to have had Jenn in my life since forever. I look in the mirror again. It's definitely not my normal style, but the dress *does* look good. And for the first time today, I feel like maybe things will be okay.

• • •

When I leave Cosmic that night, I go straight to LOL Park. I need to think, and hopefully a visit to my favorite bench will help push all this negativity out. What Jenn said is true—life has thrown a bunch of curveballs at me, but it's nothing I can't handle. I've dealt with stuff way harder than this before . . . like my parents' divorce. But this time my mind is going a mile a minute overthinking everything, and I'm stuck in a feeling-sorry-for-myself loop. I even had a whole pity party in Cosmic.

I sit on the bench near the path in the park. The sun is setting much later now, so it's still bright considering it's so late. I look in front of me. The green field is absolutely covered with yellow dandelions, and it's so mesmerizing. With unfocused eyes, I take in the bright yellow dots on the green grass. I should come paint the park at this hour.

Thinking about it now, this whole Love Street struggling thing *feels* like when my parents split. Maybe because when my parents told me they were breaking up, it felt like the rug was pulled out from under me. I had no control, and I was scared. That's how I'm feeling now. Like I'm about to lose everything I care about again, and I can't stop it from happening. Add in everyone telling me how wonderful my stepsister is, and it's no wonder I feel nine years old again. It's probably why I'm finding it so hard to hang on to my normal optimistic self.

The worst part about everything is that even if I focus on the positives: I have a gorgeous prom dress, we put together a kick-ass proposal for a festival that could save the street, and my stepsister and I are finally getting closer, there's still one big negative that I cannot ignore. I still don't have a prom date. The most important night of my high school career and I'll be alone, trying to keep my smile on my face.

"What are you doing here, Sana?" a voice says. It's Miles. So much for avoiding the guy.

He looks . . . concerned. And so damn adorable. His T-shirt is the same medium blue as the sky, and he's in his cords that look so good on him. I smile. "Needed a place to think," I say. "Why are you here?"

"I just got off work. Grabbing my bike." He stands in front of me, like he doesn't know whether he should join me, or keep walking on the path toward the bike racks.

"You're still locking your bike there?" I ask.

He nods, then sits next to me. "It's a wonder it hasn't been stolen yet. I think you were right about thieves puncturing tires. My other tire was hit last week. Thanks to you, I knew how to fix it. Pain in the butt to walk it home flat though."

"You could've fixed it on my balcony," I say. "Where do you live, anyway?" I'm not sure why I don't know this, considering how much I've seen him in the last month.

He smiles. "In a crappy, tiny room in a basement apartment with six other students. It's loud and it smells bad, but it's all I can afford. At least I have my own room—the others are all sharing."

I cringe. And here I was worried he would think my apartment over the flower shop was too small and shabby looking. I wonder why his parents aren't helping him get something better. "That's rough. Is it close by?"

"Not too bad. Half hour walk from here. I usually don't ride my bike to work because I don't want it to get stolen. I'll need that bike when school starts."

"You can lock your bike on my back balcony," I offer. I know I'm supposed to keep my distance from him, but he needs help. "Mom won't mind. It's safe up there—we have cameras out back."

He tilts his head, then smiles. "Actually, yeah, that would be great. Thank you."

"Not a problem at all. Is that why you're always working on your computer in the bookstore? Because your place sucks?"

He nods. "Reggie lets me stay as long as I need to get quiet work done. He's actually helping me with my internship applications—he has a ton of corporate experience."

"Reggie's a great guy," I say.

"He's the best."

Neither of us says anything for a while. I can tell things are strained between us, which makes me wonder if Sarina *did* say something about me in the Uber ride. I don't want him to talk about Sarina, but I can't stand this awkward silence.

"LOL Park is going to look so amazing if we get the festival approval," I say.

He nods. "Yeah, we'll have to come weed this field, though."

I scoff at that suggestion. "Why would we do that? Dandelions are beautiful. Hopefully they are at the seed stage then. . . . Those white wisps in the air are so romantic."

"Unless you have seasonal allergies."

I smile at that. We've had this argument so many times. He's called me idealistic, and I've called him uptight, and we end up in the same place again and again. I don't know why, but this time the disagreement feels *comforting*. It's like even though we're disagreeing, I feel like we both *value* our different opinions now. I turn to him, still smiling. "Antihistamines exist. Only you could look at that carpet of yellow and green and think it needs to be changed."

He chuckles at that. We sit silently for a while. I'm hoping he's trying to appreciate the dandelions in front of us.

Finally, he turns to me. "You okay, Sana? You're . . . quiet."

I shrug. "Not used to that, are you? I'm just in a tiny funk. I know it's shocking, but even Sana Merali has bad moods."

"You're entitled to feel down." He pauses. "Do you want to talk about it?"

I shake my head. "If I tell you what's bothering me, you'll think I'm brainwashed by the . . . what did you call it . . . the *romantic industrial complex*. You're going to think it's so cringe." I sigh, looking at him. Miles just watches me quietly, patiently, and I feel my heart skip a beat before I break eye contact. "I'm upset that I don't have a prom date anymore. I found an amazing dress, but I'll be alone at the dance."

He tilts his head with genuine compassion. "That sucks. I'm sorry."

Miles looks so kind that I'm trying not to feel a little breathless. I can't let him notice what he's doing to me, so I dramatically raise my brows. "This coming from the guy who said that it's *ridiculous* that society tells us prom should be as important as our wedding?"

His gaze turns to the bike locks in the distance. "I definitely think everyone's obsession with prom is a result of the romantic industrial complex," he admits before he turns his head to look back at me. "I—I think . . . I—I mean . . . ," he stutters. "Even though prom isn't my thing, I know it's important to *you*."

Welp, so much for not feeling breathless. My heart is pounding so hard that I'm sure Miles will notice my T-shirt moving. "Did your date *just* back out?" he asks.

I shake my head and stare in front of me. "No, it was a few weeks back. She's actually my ex, but we were still planning to go together as friends. That was before she got a new girlfriend. I was going to find another date, but I've been so busy, and now prom is days away and I'm alone." He doesn't say anything, and I don't want to look at him because he's sitting so close. I let out a shaky breath. "I'm the chair of the prom committee. . . . It's embarrassing that I'll be walking in alone while Priya and Amber are there in their matching dresses. But you're right—it's just a dance. It doesn't really matter."

"I'll go with you," Miles says.

My head whips around to look at him, and all I see are his wide brown eyes with a soft expression. I must be hearing things. "Did *you* just offer to go to my prom with me? You *hate* prom."

He nods. "Look, I know I said some stupid things to you before, and I'm sorry. But *you* care about your prom, so I'd be happy to take you."

I have no idea what to say. Honestly, I have no idea if I remember how to speak. My heart is pounding even harder, and my skin is tingling, and there's no way that Miles, who is only inches away, doesn't know that he's completely wrecked me. Has anyone, *ever*, done something that generous for me?

When I say nothing for too long, he adds, "I'll go as your *friend*."

I exhale. Of course he's asking me as a *friend*. That's all I am to him. But to *me*, he's a friend who I very much want to kiss. Going to prom with him seems like a bad idea. This will be utter torture.

"Showing up with a date will stick it to your ex, won't it?" Miles asks when I still don't answer. "Could you still get another ticket?"

Showing up with Miles on my arm would definitely be better than showing up alone, but I have a *crush* on Miles. Like, a *huge* one, and as hard as I'm trying to get over it, it doesn't seem to be going anywhere. Taking the guy to my *prom* certainly isn't going to help. And the fact that he insisted he would come as a *friend* means that's all he sees me as.

"I'm committee chair," I say, despite the voice in my head telling me I will get hurt. "I can get you a ticket. Do you even have something to wear?"

He nods. "I donated my prom clothes, but I have a suit. I'd just have to go up to my parents' to get it. When's your prom?"

"Friday night."

His face falls a bit. "Oh." He opens his phone calendar. "I have something that night, but I can cancel. I'd rather hang out with you." He smiles at me. "So, what do you say, Sana? Will you do me the honor of letting me be your prom date?"

The look on his face is hopeful . . . and it makes me wonder. Does Miles actually *want* to go with me? Like as a real date, not just a *pity for my friend* date?

No, he doesn't. He invited me as a *friend*. But that's still pretty amazing, because he hates prom and everything it represents. He's asking me because he cares about me being upset. I don't think I could say no even if I wanted to. "Okay, Miles Desai. Yes. You can be my prom date."

He grins, and we shake on it. And I ignore the butterflies in my stomach and the goose bumps on my skin the moment our hands touch. I have no idea whether this is a good or a bad idea, but I do know that at least now my prom will be memorable.

CHAPTER FOURTEEN

CAKE MAKES ANYTHING BETTER

I don't go to school on the day of my prom—I spend the morning setting up the banquet hall, then rush to get my nails done in a dark shade to match my dress, then go to the hair salon to get my hair blow-dried straight. After grabbing my dress from Jenn's, I do my own makeup in shades of plum and silver. I look amazing. Yes, the sleek hair and deep plum satin skimming my body isn't my normal vibe, but I still feel like *me*. I'm so glad Priya asked for my other dress, because I love this one so much more.

Miles picks me up at my apartment before the dance. When I open the door, I just stare at him. He's wearing a black suit that fits him very well, with a gray shirt and a deep plum tie—did he know what color my dress would be? His normally unruly hair is slicked down with a precise side part. He looks . . . like, classically handsome. Like an old Bollywood star. I honestly didn't know he had this in him. His expression is unreadable. Maybe confused?

When we're both quiet for too long, I smile. "Hi, Miles," I say. "You don't like my prom dress?"

He shakes his head. "No. I mean, you look amazing. You're not really dressed like you usually dress, that's all."

I preen. "And yet I'm still *fabulous*, right? Even I didn't know I could pull off sleek and sophisticated until I bought this dress on Wednesday."

He frowns. "You only got your dress on Wednesday? Why?"

"Long story." I smile. "You're looking pretty dapper yourself."

He shakes his head, like he's coming out of a trance, then smiles. "I thought it would be weird to get you a corsage because you live with a florist, so I made this at my parents' house when I went to get my suit," He hands me something out of a tote bag I hadn't noticed.

It's a corsage made with Lego flowers glued to an elastic wristband. It's so pretty, even though it's made of hard plastic. "Is that a Lego wrist corsage?"

He nods. "I have a lot of Lego. I kind of . . . collect it."

The flowers are pink with brown stems. I think they're cherry blossoms, like the trees we went to see together. How incredibly kind and thoughtful of Miles to make this for me.

My skin tingles as I put out my hand for him. "Look at you, embracing prom rituals. Thank you so much." He slides the corsage over my hand. The pale pink flowers work well with the dark plum of my dress.

"Now, shall we?" I say. "Warning, Mom will probably want to take a dozen pictures of us before we call the Uber. She's downstairs in the flower shop, so there's really no way to avoid her."

Miles just laughs as he smoothly lends me his arm to take, and I try to ignore the jolt of electricity as I slip my bare arm through his.

. . .

The prom looks fantastic. Our committee did an excellent job in planning, so the decor, the photo booth, the food, and music are all exactly as we envisioned. The theme is Starry Night—I know it's a cliché, but I love the van Gogh painting, and the deep navy along with bursts of gold and yellow make the banquet hall look magical.

Miles is a great date. Honestly, I can't even believe he's the same surly dude I first met at the BOA meeting, because he's nothing but pleasant smiles and attentiveness today. We're sitting with some of my art class friends, and he's personable and even chats with them when I have to leave him to go put out some fires in my role as prom chair. It's weird, when he asked me to prom, I thought it would be hard because of my massive crush on the guy, but this isn't hard at all. Maybe because we're not alone and are surrounded by my school friends, but honestly, nothing has ever felt easier than being on a date, even a friends-only date, with Miles.

He's just so nice to be around. Comfortable. Whether we're arguing about the festival or talking about our families, it feels effortless. I can completely be myself—be my real, positive, idealistic, and sometimes messy self, and I know it's not going to change how he feels about me.

When one of my favorite slow songs comes on after dinner, I don't even have to ask Miles to dance, because he asks me. I grin.

"I didn't know you danced," I say as I stand and take his hand.

He nods. "I did three years of modern Bollywood dance as a kid. Don't worry, I'm capable of keeping to the beat of non-Hindi songs too."

I laugh at that. As we walk arm in arm, we pass Priya and Amber, who are leaving the dance floor. I smile at Priya. She looks fantastic in the dusty-rose dress and matching pink makeup. "Hi, Priya!" I say. I honestly don't have any hard feelings about her canceling on me and taking my dress, because my night is turning out fantastic anyway.

But Priya only gives me a tight smile, then glances at Amber. And if looks could kill, I'd be dead on the dance floor right now, thanks to the glare Amber gives me.

They keep walking, so I shrug and head to the middle of the dance floor with Miles. I put my hands on his shoulders, and he lays his on my waist. The press of his hands through the soft satin of my dress shoots a current of electricity up my spine.

I take a shaky breath. He's so close. He smells like cardamom and rose water again—I have to remember to ask him what that is . . . when I'm able to speak, that is. The skin on his neck looks so soft, I just want to bury my face in it as we sway lightly to the soft nineties love song. Okay, this is the sweet torture I was expecting, but thank goodness I said yes to bringing him to this dance because I would not want to trade this moment for anything in the world, no matter what comes next. I lightly rest my head on his shoulder and sink into the sensations.

"Can I assume that was the ex who ditched you?" he suddenly asks. My head jolts up to look at him. His brow is furrowed with concern. "That girl shooting daggers from her eyes at you, that's your ex's new girlfriend, right?"

"How'd you know?" I ask.

"They were wearing matching dresses."

I chuckle lightly and nod. "Yeah, that's Amber and

Priya. Priya is my ex. I have no idea what that look was about. Amber and I are . . . were friends. I even introduced them."

Miles smiles. "You and your matchmaking. At least now you can retire from that little hobby."

I have no idea what he means by that. Does he mean I can retire on a high because Priya and Amber are in love? Or because I matched Miles and Sarina and it's going so well that I won't need to matchmake for him again? I clench my teeth. I really don't want to think about Sarina right now. I don't want anything to ruin this night.

"Did you really take Bollywood dance for three years?" I ask, changing the subject. This slow song isn't really showing me whether he has any impressive dance moves.

He nods, laughing. "I did. From when I was three to six. There were only two boys in the class, so we took turns being Shah Rukh Khan. My father's a huge Bollywood nut."

I grin. Despite being Indian, I never really got into Indian movies and music, but I love that Miles was more connected to our culture. "You must have been *adorable*." I'm imagining tiny and serious Miles with a furrowed brow focusing on complex dance moves.

He nods. "Stick around, Merali, and I'll show you pictures. I was nauseatingly adorable."

I laugh, squeezing his shoulder. He still is. And I don't know what he meant by stick around, but that's exactly what I want to do.

When I smile and wave at a friend coming onto the dance floor, he tilts his head at me.

"You're such an extrovert."

I raise a brow. "You're just figuring that out now?"

He shakes his head quickly. "No . . . and I don't mean it as a bad thing. It's just weird seeing you at a high school event. You know I barely talk to anyone from high school? And I only graduated a year ago."

"Why not?" I fully intend to keep in touch with many people from my school. Maybe not Priya, but definitely my art class friends.

He shrugs. "I feel like if I saw them now, I could only be one person with them. I like the idea of maybe trying to be someone else."

"What do you mean? Like you've changed since then?"

He shrugs. There's a small smile on his face. "I guess I have. I was quiet and a big nerd in high school. And then I was with my ex, Giselle, for a long time, so everyone thought of us together. She was definitely more popular than me. I don't know. I kind of like the option of people seeing more of me than who I used to be."

I smile. I assume this is the girlfriend who cheated on him, so I get that he'd want to distance himself from his identity as her boyfriend, or ex-boyfriend. And now that I think about it, it's kind of why I'm so comfortable with Miles. He has shown me that he *sees* more of me than just one thing . . . the cheerful but idealistic one.

We dance a few songs together, even some faster ones so I can see that yes, Miles is a good dancer. And he's clearly having a great time at a prom, of all places. Miles Desai is full of surprises.

When they announce that dessert will be served soon, we head back to our table completely out of breath. I start talking to my friend from painting about our final projects, when Miles suddenly says, "Holy crap. We did it."

I turn to him and he's looking at his phone, a huge incandescent smile on his face. He's practically lighting up the whole ballroom. He's breathtaking.

"What is it?" I ask.

He grins at me. "I got an email from Su Lin Tran's assistant. We got the approvals. The Love on Love Street Festival is going to happen this summer. They approved the road closure, the—"

"Oh my goodness!" I interrupt whatever he's saying to clap my hands together, laughing. "We got *approval*?" I'm so happy that I launch myself at Miles, practically climbing onto his lap and wrapping my arms around him in a hug. This is seriously the *best* news.

He laughs, then hugs me back. He feels warm and solid in my arms, and he smells so good up close. When I finally let him go, it's not because I want to. "We did it," I say.

He nods, still smiling widely at his phone. "It was such a long shot, but apparently Su Lin Tran agrees that something like this can add visibility to the unique street. She's completely on board. She wants to meet with our committee soon to go over the plans, but we got the hardest parts approved—the road closure for the festival day and the signage and pole banners."

I shake my head, grinning. "We should celebrate."

He nods. "Yeah, we should. I'll check with Julie and Ajit tomorrow—"

I shake my head. "No, let's celebrate *now*. I want, like . . . cake or pie or something."

Miles looks around the banquet hall. "Aren't they serving dessert?"

I nod. I know what dessert is—defrosted cream puffs and a scoop of cheap ice cream. This banquet hall isn't exactly top tier—the school couldn't afford better.

And besides, if we stay, I'm going to have to explain why we're so happy to everyone at the table, and I kind of want Miles to myself right now.

"Let's leave," I say. "Mrs. Kotch gave me one of her Cakes for Two to sample yesterday. It's in the flower shop."

Miles's eyebrows furrow. "You want to *leave* your prom?"

I grin. "It's fine. It's just a dance, right? I wanted the night to be memorable, and it definitely has been, thanks to you. But now I want to celebrate this huge accomplishment, and it's weird to celebrate here with my classmates. What do you say . . . ? Want to eat a German-style cake in a flower shop with me, or do you want to stay here for freezer-burned ice cream?"

He's got that intense thinking look on his face, but eventually he nods. "Sure. It's your night, so your choice. And how can I say no to cake?"

I beam at him. Miles Desai alone and cake. My prom night just got so much better.

When our Uber gets to Love Street, Mom's light is off. I have a key to the shop, and after I open the door, I disable the alarm system.

"Your mother doesn't mind you hanging out here in the middle of the night?" he asks as I turn on some lights in the main part of the store.

"Nah. I even used to have sleepovers in here. A friend and I would pretend we were fairies, and the back room was an enchanted forest. Mom used to make me flower crowns with her cutoffs." I take off my jacket and hang it on the hook in the back room. It's weird being in here in a floor-length satin gown, but I don't want to go upstairs because it will wake Mom up.

"Your mom is really . . ." He doesn't finish the statement.

"Artsy?" I suggest. "Strange?"

He shakes his head. "No, not strange. I like her. She's . . . *creative*. I was going to say interesting, but I thought you might assume I meant it sarcastically. But she *really* is interesting. She told me she took you to Thailand for four months when you were two."

When did Miles talk to my mother without me? "I wasn't even two yet. She bought the ticket on impulse when she realized that I wouldn't be able to fly for free for very much longer. My dad didn't even come. We went to Thailand again when I was twelve so I could remember the trip." I grab the cake from the flower cooler and put the pink bakery box on the counter in front of us. The plastic window shows a small square of cake decorated with white butter cream and a riot of pink hearts and flowers. I assume Miles, the skeptic of all things lovey-dovey, hates the look of this cake. I find two forks in the junk drawer under the counter.

Miles isn't looking at the cake at all. He's looking at me. I raise a brow.

"I should have said it before, but your hair looks nice," he finally says. I laugh and touch the strands draped over my left shoulder.

I smile. "You've never seen it straightened."

"It's longer than I thought," he says. "You look so different tonight. Still you, but different."

I grin. "And then I open my mouth and I'm still me." I open the cake box and carefully lift the cake out. "What do you think?" I ask. There are even more hearts on the sides of the cake, along with piped shells and swoopy lines. I cringe. "This cake looks more like me than I do tonight."

His eyes narrow, inspecting it. "It is a bit . . ."

"Even I agree it's a bit much," I say. "I think the Cakes for Two is a great idea, but we're going to have to talk to Mrs. Kotch about . . . understated elegance."

"I feel like I might get diabetes just looking at it."

I shake my head. "Mrs. Kotch's cakes aren't as sweet as they look. Her buttercream is as light as air. Have you had her black forest?"

He shakes his head.

I hand him a fork. "You're in for a treat. She's an *artist*."

Miles takes the first bite of cake. I'm not surprised to see that under the fluffy white frosting, the cake itself is red. Of course she'd use red velvet for a love cake.

He puts the bite in his mouth, and I watch his face to see his reaction. I can't believe I once thought he was stingy with his smiles. Sometimes his expressions are small, but he does smile. A lot.

And since I've become a bit of an expert on Miles's expressions, I can see the moment his eyes widen and his forehead smooths. Eventually, his mouth turns up slightly in the corners when he realizes that the trite red and pink cake is actually one of the best things he's ever eaten. He's so cute when he's genuinely happy.

"I told you it would be delicious."

He nods. "I think I need to try her other cakes." He looks down at the rest of the square of cake on the counter. "This looks more like a cake for four than a cake for two, though."

"It's *enormous*. I think we can rise to the challenge." I take a bite, and the cake is amazing. The frosting is light with a hint of tang from cream cheese, and the cake itself is tender with a delicate crumb and mild chocolate and vanilla flavor. I moan with pleasure. "This was such a good idea. I guarantee this is better than the cream puffs at my prom. I am most decidedly hashtag team cake."

He looks confused, so I explain. "Everyone is either team cake or team pie. Don't get me wrong, I love a good pie, but between a good cake and a good pie, cake will always win." I take another bite. Mrs. Kotch's cakes are always sublime.

Miles takes another bite. "I think I'm team cake too. Even though I usually prefer savory over sweet. But this cake is delicious."

I realize that even though two out of three dates I've set him up on revolved around food, I don't know what Miles likes to eat. Other than chocolate-covered gingerbread. And now, cake. "What's your favorite food in the city?"

He pauses, thinking. It's a hard question—Toronto has such a huge food scene. "Going to have to go with the papri chaat at my uncle's restaurant. I know I'm biased, but it really is *that* good. Better than I've had anywhere else."

I slap his arm lightly. "Shut. Up. You have an uncle with an *Indian restaurant*?"

"Yeah. My dad's brother has a place in the West End. Indian street food."

"Oooh, how's their pani puri?"

He grins proudly. "The best in the city."

"I'm going to have to try it. Pani puri is easily my favorite Indian dish. I usually get them from the sidewalk vendors on Gerrard, but I have to be careful not to get them too often because I can eat, like, two dozen in one sitting." That makes Miles tilt his head back and laugh, and I can't help but feel my insides warm. "Hey, mind if we sit?" I ask. "These shoes are killing me."

A few minutes later we're sprawled on the floor of the flower shop on top of a blanket that my mother keeps in the back room. We're leaning against the counter, and I have removed the strappy silver sandals I was wearing, and Miles has taken off his tie. The cake is between us, and we're talking while taking bites of it.

"So you work here and at Cosmic Vintage?" Miles asks me.

I shake my head. "I don't *technically* work here. But I help out when Mom needs me. She doesn't pay me, or anything. I've practically grown up in flower shops—Mom worked at another one in Markham before we moved here. I'm not as good as Mom, but I'm not bad at floral design."

Miles's eyes widen. "You're originally from Markham?" He seems surprised at that.

I chuckle. "Nope. Born and raised in Toronto—but we used to live in the North End."

"So you're here for the same reason I am."

It takes me a second to realize that the reason is our parents' divorces. "Yeah, I guess so."

"What happened between your parents?"

I take a bite before answering. "Oh, you know. Tale

as old as time. Man meets free-spirited woman. Falls in love. Gets married. Man disappointed to discover that free-spirited wife doesn't become a respectable suburban soccer mom after marriage. Divorce. Child support. New apartment and custody arrangements." There's more to the story, but I don't want to get into it now.

Miles takes a forkful of cake in his mouth. "So you know exactly what it's like to get caught in the aftershocks of your family imploding," he says after chewing.

I turn to him and see the resentment on his face. My parents' divorce was a long time ago now, and seriously, I'm over it. But I remember how hard it was when it was fresh. Everything changed so much, and so quickly. It really messed me up for a while.

I give him a sympathetic smile. "Divorce *sucks*. I remember feeling like everything I thought I knew about my life was a lie. Did your mom move out, or your dad?"

He cringes. "Neither. They say it's because of housing costs, but I think they're playing chicken. They'd rather make each other miserable than pay rent somewhere else. I couldn't take it anymore, so I'm the one who moved out."

"Oh, that's terrible. Why would they do that to themselves? And to you?"

He shrugs. "Good question. When they started to only speak to each other through me, I realized I had to leave. Thank goodness I got a job quickly . . . and I had some savings from working all through high school."

"Aren't your parents helping you with school?"

"They pay my tuition. But since it was *my* decision to leave home, they won't help with rent. And they both blame the other for me leaving."

I shake my head. That's so ridiculous. Miles is great—his parents should be *proud* of his independence. "Do you have siblings?"

"Only child, thankfully. I'd hate for them to have more kids to use as weapons against each other." He takes another bite of cake. He looks so hurt, my heart breaks for him. Maybe I should stop eating and leave the cake for him. He needs it more than I do. "It's so stupid," he says. "They used to talk about their deep and profound love all the time. Hell, they named me after their relationship." When I raise a questioning brow, he clarifies. "There's this song from when they were young, 'I'm Gonna Be (500 Miles),' and it's all about how far the guy would go for the person he loves. They also picked the name Miles because it's not a Muslim or a Hindu name. My dad's Hindu, and my mom's Muslim, and neither of their parents approved of the marriage. Eventually their families accepted each other, but they said they named me *Miles* to represent the miles they went through to be together."

"That's so romantic," I say. "But now they're miles apart. Even in the same house."

He nods. We're quiet for a while. I wonder if his parents loving each other so much is why they're so toxic to each other now. Like they're only capable of enormous feelings for each other. To be honest, I get why Miles is turned off by that kind of . . . *demonstrative* love and why he hated the festival theme at first. His parents ruined the concepts of love and romance for him. I have a lot of bitterness from my parents' divorce, but at least they never used me against each other.

"We're both named after songs," I say, hoping to lighten

the mood. "Mom named me after the Cream song 'Sunshine of Your Love' and the Beatles song 'Here Comes the Sun.' They are her two favorite songs, and she listened to them nonstop when she was pregnant. She says that's why I came out of the womb smiling. I was almost Sunshine Merali."

He squeezes his lips together, holding in a laugh.

"I *know*," I say. "It's terrible. Dad insisted on *Sana* instead because it's pronounced a bit like sun, and it's Arabic for "brilliant." Which is what the sun is."

Miles looks at me with those intense eyes, again, and there's the smallest hint of a smile on his face. I smile back at him. It almost feels like he's going to say something. I wonder if he'll say the name suits me. I want him to.

When the moment gets too intense, I change the topic. "If your name brings bad memories, you could change it," I say. "You're over eighteen."

"Nah, it pisses them off more than me. I like my name. It's short. Easy to spell."

I smile at him. "It suits you." I can't imagine him as anyone but Miles.

He still has that tiny smile on his face as he takes another bite of cake. I take one too. This is nice. Not just the cake, but the conversation. Even the silence is nice. This is much better than staying at prom. I was so worried that my prom night memories were ruined, but Miles saved them.

"What's the story with your prom dress?" he asks after a few moments. "Why did you only get the dress two days ago?"

I sigh. "Did you see the dress Priya's girlfriend, Amber, was wearing? The one that matched Priya's? I was supposed to wear that. We bought the dresses when we were still together."

Miles chuckles. "Wow. That's a little—"

"Yeah, I know. Cheesy. Anyway, last week Priya asked if Amber could wear my dress, since she and Amber are in *love* so they should match at prom, not me and Priya. I had a week to find a new dress."

He cringes. "Ouch. That's harsh. Why did you give her the dress?"

I shrug. "She had a point; it would have been weird to wear it. I sold it to Amber and found a better dress. It's fine."

"Well, I don't think that dress looked very good on Amber. That is *not* her color."

I laugh out loud, shaking my head with amazement. "Look at you, Miles Desai, fashion critic. I still have no idea why Amber gave me that look when we were on the dance floor."

Miles grins. "Here's what I think happened: Amber told your ex to get her your dress because she wanted to sabotage your night. But then the dress didn't fit her well, and you show up looking like . . . *that*. I'd say you got the best revenge."

I raise a brow. "What do you mean . . . like *that*?"

He looks at me. "You said it yourself, Sana. You look fabulous tonight."

"*I* think I look fabulous tonight, but I didn't think *you* thought it too."

"Are you trying to get me to compliment you?"

"Maybe." I grin at him. "C'mon, Miles, say it. I look *hot* tonight, and you have no idea what to do with that."

He rolls his eyes, but he's smiling. "You're impossible, Sana."

"I know. Would it be easier if I complimented you first?"

He laughs softly.

I turn my body a bit so I'm facing him. "We're friends now, Miles. And I'm the kind of friend who *always* tells my friends their strong points. You're *exceedingly* good-looking, and you look fantastic in that suit, but I think I liked you in the flowered shirt you wore to High Park best."

I swear, Miles Desai turns as red as the cake. He's . . . adorable. Too adorable. I exhale. I shouldn't have said that. This crush isn't going anywhere anytime soon. It's only getting stronger. I turn back and rest my back against the counter. I take another bite of cake. "This cake is seriously so good," I say.

We're both silent for a while again. It's not as comfortable as it was before. Probably because I made things awkward by flirting.

"I still don't get how you do it," Miles says.

"Do what?"

"All of this." He motions to the cake, then to the flower shop. "Your obsession with love. The romance books. The hearts. Aren't you at all *cynical* after your parents split? Or after Priya?"

I look down at the cake. "No, the opposite. Those relationships didn't work out, so I want to *surround* myself with love that *does* work, you know? It feels . . . good when I read or watch movies about people falling in love. I want to celebrate *happiness*."

"It must annoy your mother that you're all into true

love and romance, though. You said she's not a romantic person."

I shrug. Does it annoy Mom? She doesn't read romance. She's more into thrillers or thinky literary fiction. We sometimes watch rom-com movies together. Honestly, Mom doesn't seem to have any issue with her romance-obsessed daughter even if it's not her style. "Mom's cool about whatever I'm into. But I don't think she ever wanted the hearts and flowers kind of love. Ironic for a florist who specializes in weddings. She personally agrees with you that prom is just a dance, but since I care about it, she does."

Miles takes a bite of cake, then offers the last bite to me. "I actually *did* look forward to my prom. We even got matching outfits. Do you remember I told you that my ex Giselle cheated on me with my best friend? I found out *at* our prom."

I look at him, shocked. "Holy crap! That's why you hate prom!" This makes it so amazing that he offered to come to mine. He's mentally done with high school, is a total introvert, and had a terrible experience at his own prom. But he knew I was upset about not having a date, so he asked me anyway. And he went all the way to his parents' house to get his suit and made me a corsage out of Lego while there. Miles is *incredibly* thoughtful and generous. I can't believe he did all that for me. I put the bite of cake in my mouth, because my eyes sting a bit like they are going to tear up.

"Yeah, my terrible night was probably why I was so harsh to you about prom. I left the dance really early. The only saving grace was the takeout we ordered beforehand, because I didn't even get dinner."

"So was this a better prom night than your own?"

He chuckles. "Yeah, your prom was way better than mine. Especially this cake part." We're both silent for a bit again, the low hum of the flower fridges the only sound in the room. "You know," he says suddenly. "You never did answer the question I asked you back when we were working on the proposal. Have *you* been in love?"

I swallow the cake in my mouth. Moment of truth. "No."

"No? Not even with your evil clone, Priya?"

I laugh at him calling Priya my clone. "Not even with her." I sigh. "I've been the last relationship before someone meets their true love more times than I'd like to admit. I'm a cliché. I'm obsessed with romance and can't make a relationship last long enough to fall in love."

For a beat, he doesn't say anything. He uses the side of his fork to scrape some icing off the cake board and eats it.

"You know," he finally says. "For an optimist, you're not very nice to yourself. What did you say earlier? You're the kind of friend who always points out her friends' strong points? Maybe you should treat yourself as well as you treat your friends."

I look at him, surprised. I know I've been negative lately, but I wouldn't have thought Miles would call me out on it. When I don't say anything, he continues. "I don't think the fact that you haven't been in a serious relationship means you're, I don't know, a less *serious* person. Relationships are hard work, and we're both young, so it's okay if we don't have it figured out yet. That's one of the things I don't like about movies and books making love seem so *easy*. We both know from our parents' example that staying happy in a relationship while staying true to yourself is hard, and many people aren't cut out for it. I think it's so cool that you haven't given up on love and that you still want to see everyone around you happy. You're not a cliché . . . you're kind of an inspiration, Sana. And maybe you haven't found a person who is worthy of you yet."

I blink at him. I have no idea what to say to that. Miles just called me an inspiration. And I know he really means it. And also, he's right. Relationships are hard, and we're young. It's okay if we're still figuring them and ourselves out.

I smile. "You . . . you're a great friend, Miles." I mean that. Yeah, I have a massive crush on this particular friend, but really, more than anything else, I'm so, so grateful to have him in my life now. "You know, I was supposed to fall in love this summer," I say. "I found a fortune cookie fortune that said I would."

He tilts his head. "Your future doesn't come from a baked good, Sana," he says, holding in a laugh.

"You don't believe in omens?"

He shakes his head. "No, of course not. I believe in coincidences. Sometimes coincidences make people believe that fate is controlling their lives, but they're really the only ones in control. There's no magic to this."

I exhale. And that's why, even if we're friends, Miles and I will *always* be miles apart. He doesn't believe in fortunes or magic and thinks beautiful fields of flowers should be weeded. And he implied that he's given up on love. Even if he miraculously feels the same way about me as I feel about him, he'd eventually get tired of me because we're too different. Just like Dad got tired of Mom. Like my parents—we'd be a disaster.

But that doesn't mean we can't be friends. And tonight Miles has shown me how *amazing* a friend he is. I don't want to lose this. I yawn, then rest my head on his shoulder. "Thanks for taking me to my prom. I'm glad you moved to the city. Even if your apartment is crappy."

"You know what, Sana? I'm glad I moved here too."

I don't have to look at him. I can hear the smile on Miles's face.

CHAPTER FIFTEEN

WE HAVE OURSELVES A FESTIVAL!

Once we have the approval for the festival, we need to hit the ground running since we only have a little over a month to plan it. On Saturday, I put up a post in the BOA member group that the Love on Love Street Festival is happening, and anyone interested in volunteering for the planning committee can sign up below, and anyone available today should come to a meeting at seven thirty tonight at LoveBug.

I text Cara immediately after posting. She doesn't always check the BOA forums, so I want her to know about the meeting.

Cara: I saw that the festival is on! Congratulations! I'm not sure I can come tonight, but you know I'll help plan. Tell me what to do and I'll do it.

Sana: No worries! I know the meeting was last minute. Plans with Hannah tonight?

Cara: We're going for hot pot with my parents. I'm nervous . . .

Wow. Cara's parents can be pretty strict, and I know they weren't happy about Cara and Hannah being so serious while in high school because they wanted Cara to focus on her education. Hopefully her parents support them more now. I'm also hoping Cara only misses this one meeting—I still feel a bit bitter that she skipped out on Miles and me so many times when we were working on the proposal.

Sana: Okay! I'll message you tomorrow to tell you what you missed. Good luck!

Me, Miles, Julie and Ajit, April, Grant, Alain from the bistro, and Ben from the empanada shop show up to the festival planning meeting. Cara, Jenn, and a few others also sign up to help out but weren't able to come tonight. The first thing the committee does is decide on a committee chair. Almost everyone agrees that Miles and I should be cochairs, since we were the ones who put together the proposal and because we already have a relationship with the city councillor.

After going over some basics, Miles and I start delegating tasks. Surprisingly, the adults in the room seem pretty okay with a couple of teenagers telling them what to do, but when we start talking about the proposal, things get heated.

"I really don't like this section about outside vendors," Alain says. "If we bring in others, they will compete with the Love Street businesses."

Miles shakes his head. "Love Street can't be so insular," he says. "It has to evolve with the outer community. We should *welcome* outside vendors to our festival—from Gerrard and beyond."

Did he really call Love Street *insular*? I look at Miles. I'd thought I understood him better after prom last night. That we understood *each other* better. And I don't think

I'm being delusional or it's wishful thinking because of the huge crush I have on the guy—but it felt like we really *connected*. But we haven't talked since last night, and he's barely looked at me during this meeting. Earlier today he posted a picture on his Instagram of himself eating a Jamaican beef patty, and I commented with the emoji of a chili pepper, then a fire emoji. Because . . . he looked hot in the picture, and that's what I do when a friend posts a hot picture, no matter who it is. But Miles didn't respond. Or even heart the comment.

Right now he's sounding more like the Miles I first met than my cute friend. Miles says Love Street has to *evolve*, but to me, Love Street evolving means losing everything we have here. It means people losing their businesses. Or jobs. Or homes.

"But the point of the festival is to help Love Street businesses," April says. "Why would we bring in vendors that will take our customers?"

"Bringing in other vendors for the festival will get more people to come, which in the long run will help Love Street," Miles says. "What do the rest of you think?"

The door to LoveBug opens then, breaking the tension. It's Cara. She looks . . . dejected.

"Sorry I'm late," she says as she slides into the chair next to me. I raise one eyebrow at her, questioning, and she gives me a look that says she'll talk to me about it later.

The conversation continues, and we eventually decide not to approve an outside vendor that would *directly* compete with a Love Street business. So, no florists, dog groomers, or empanada shops. We assign some duties like who will put together the list of the rental equipment we'll need and who will find performers willing to perform for free. Eventually, when everyone has a job to do, we wrap up the meeting. Everyone seems excited and committed to the project, but that argument about vendors has reminded me of what's at stake here. This festival is going to be a ton of fun, but that's not why we're doing it. Love Street is struggling and needs this boost.

I hang back a bit after everyone leaves the café to talk to Cara. "What happened to dinner with your parents?" I ask her. "Did Hannah cancel?"

Cara gives me an annoyed expression. "Why do you assume it's Hannah who canceled?"

I exhale. I made that assumption because Hannah doesn't seem to enjoy Cara's friends, so I assume it's the same with Cara's family.

"Well, was it?" I press. Cara doesn't say anything, just crosses her arms and looks at the floor. Last time I dropped the subject, not wanting to push Cara, but I'm seeing a pattern now. "Cara . . . do you think, I don't know. Do you think maybe Hannah is being a bit controlling with you?"

Cara looks at me then, annoyed. "Not this again. Seriously?"

"I mean, she likes you to dress a certain way, doesn't like hanging out with your friends, and cancels when you have plans with your parents. If you need to talk—"

Cara rolls her eyes. "God, Sana, why do you have to insert yourself into everyone's life? First matchmaking, and now you're butting in where you're not needed."

I blink. That *stung,* and I'm not sure what to say. I'm not *inserting* myself into her life. I'm being her friend. "I'm only asking because I care about you."

But Cara doesn't seem to notice, or care, that I'm hurt. "You haven't had a relationship longer than what . . . two months?" She scoffs. "You really are a naive child sometimes. Reading romance novels doesn't make you a romance expert. How about you stop armchair analyzing everyone else's relationships and maybe start focusing on yourself?"

I swallow. Cara is *trying* to hurt me. Does she actually believe I'm naive enough to think that books and movies have made me an expert on romance? "I'm not armchair analyzing. I'm just worried that you're not seeing what's clearly in front of you."

Cara rolls her eyes. "Well, you don't need to worry. I am quite capable of *seeing* my own relationship, considering it's *mine*." And with that, she leaves the café.

I stand there for a few seconds, too shaken up to move. Cara has *never* said anything like that to me before. Does she really think I unnecessarily *butt* into other people's lives? Maybe I should have stayed out of her relationship. I know she's head over heels for Hannah, but I don't think Hannah is treating her well. Cara deserves to be treasured, not cast aside.

But now I'm the hurt one. Cara has been such a great friend since we started working together, and I'm afraid I've lost that friend because I stuck my nose where it wasn't wanted. I take a breath and pick up my purse. I may as well go home.

When I walk out of LoveBug, Miles is right outside the door, waiting for me. He looks concerned.

"You okay, Sana? Cara just ran out of here and didn't even acknowledge me."

I shake my head. "Yeah, we . . . Never mind." I really

don't want to tell him that Cara called me a naive child. I feel terrible. "What's up?"

"My bike is locked on your balcony. I thought we could walk together."

I really want to be alone right now, but since we're going to the same place, I don't have much of a choice.

"Are you free to go to City Hall with me next week?" he asks as he walks next to me. "Su Lin wants to have a meeting with just the two of us."

"Why?"

"She says she wants to put faces to the names of the kids who made the proposal. I said I'd check with you and send her assistant some possible times, but I told her you're in high school so it will have to be outside of business hours."

"I don't have a lot of free time," I say. "I basically have two part-time jobs, remember?"

He frowns. "We could probably do it before your shift starts one day—it wouldn't be a long meeting. Tuesday at five would work for me."

"I think I'm at Cosmic that night, but I'll ask Jenn," I say. It's hard to concentrate after having a huge fight with my friend.

"Are you okay, Sana?" Miles asks, looking at me with concern in his eyes. "Something *did* happen between you and Cara, right?"

I sigh. "Yeah, I guess. I kind of asked her if Hannah was being controlling, and Cara told me to butt out of her life. She was . . . mean."

"Ugh. That *sucks*. Why do you think Hannah is controlling?"

"She's just . . ." I sigh. "Cara was different before

Hannah got here. She dressed differently, she never blew off our plans, and . . ." I sound so self-absorbed. Of course she's going to wear what her girlfriend likes and spend more time with her than me. "Cara said I don't know a thing about relationships because I've never been in a serious one."

"Ouch," Miles says. After our conversation last night, he knows it's a sore spot for me.

We're at the flower shop by then, and I follow him around to the back of my apartment and up the balcony stairs. It's pretty dark on the balcony—looks like Mom forgot to turn the back light on. She's on-site at a wedding tonight but left a light on inside that's casting a dim glow through the sliding door. When Miles gets to his bike, he suddenly turns to me instead of unlocking it. In the low light, I can't make out his expression. Why is he looking at me like that for so long? Is he going to say something?

Finally, I can't take it anymore. This is awkward. "Did you forget your lock combination?" I ask.

He shakes his head. "I just wanted to say, I don't know Cara or Hannah well enough to comment on their relationship, but Cara is your friend. I think . . . I hope she'll realize that you said it because you're concerned about her."

I nod. "I hope so. I . . . I just don't understand why she'd be so nasty to me. It's not like her. I hope she's okay."

"People can be a little irrational when they're stressed," he suggests. "You could have touched a nerve. But Cara knows you. She knows you care a lot about the people around you."

"Thanks." I exhale. "I should apologize for sticking my nose in her business. It's not worth losing a friend."

He smiles. "And she may need you when she *is* ready to talk," he says, leaning against the railing just a foot away from me.

My eyes have adjusted to the dim light by now, so I can see that he's looking at me intensely, like always. But there's something else in his gaze. Amusement. He looks happy. "I wanted to ask you something else. . . . D-did . . . ?" He stutters. "I mean did you have a good prom night?"

I nod, my bad mood melting away thanks to his smile. "It was great. Thanks to you. And that cake." I take a deep breath in, smelling the dirt from the house plants Mom was transplanting earlier and the faint floral scent that always surrounds the flower shop. And Miles.

We keep looking at each other, and it feels like we're back on the dance floor at my prom. He's always looking at me like this. I feel like I could stare into his brown eyes forever. I have no idea what's going on right now, but I don't think I'm imagining it. Something *is* crackling between us, and I'm almost positive he's feeling it too. My skin is tingling, and my heart is racing, and it takes actual effort not to swoon like a historical romance heroine. Miles takes a step closer, and everything that isn't Miles Desai in front of me blurs to nothing.

He lets out a shaky breath while looking into my eyes. "I had a slick line I was going to use now," he says quietly. "But I can't remember it."

I chuckle softly. How is this guy so adorable? "What were you going to do after saying the line?" I ask.

"This," he says. And then he puts his soft hand on my cheek, leans down, and kisses me on the lips. Right there on my dark balcony in front of his bike and Mom's extra plant pots, Miles kisses me. Is this really happening? It takes too many moments for me to process it. To process how strong yet soft his hand on my face feels. Or how soft his lips are. Or how, up close, he smells faintly of rain, on top of the cardamom scent.

Eventually my brain catches up and screams at me that this is Miles! His lips are on mine! The lips I have been obsessing over since the first time I saw him at LoveBug.

I don't think I've . . . Actually, scratch that. I *know* I've never felt like this before. *Ever*. My skin feels like it's on fire, and my heart is pounding, and when he starts to pull away, I can't help it. I move even closer. I put a hand behind his neck and pull him down to me. . . . And I kiss him back.

Both his arms wrap around me as the kiss deepens. The skin behind his neck is soft and smooth. His hands are pressing my soft sweater into my skin. I get my own hands into that silky hair, and it feels so good running my fingers through it. It's like we're the only ones in the world—like this is what was always supposed to happen. This might be the best kiss I've ever had.

It's over before I want it to be. Miles's arms drop to his side, and I already miss when they were around me. I exhale. His eyes are a little glazed over, and the smile on his face is downright sultry. I feel like I was just hit by a truck and like I had a taste of the best caramel crunch cake in the world.

"Wow," I say. I blow out a long breath. "Now I really wish I knew what you were going to say."

He laughs softly, then turns to unlock his bike. I want to ask him, what did that mean? Why did he kiss me? But I'm still a little shaken up.

I step out of his way when he pulls his bike off the bike rack. He starts climbing down the wood stairs off my balcony. When he gets to the bottom, he looks at me. He's so . . . gorgeous. His eyes are so striking.

"Sleep well, Sana," he says. His voice sounds a little raspy. Like he isn't really thinking straight either.

I nod. "You too. I'll let you know about Tuesday."

"Okay. Bye." He gets on his bike and rides away. And I stand there, leaning on the railing for a while before I'm able to walk into my apartment on my wobbly legs.

CHAPTER SIXTEEN

SERENITY WINS AGAIN

Of course, I don't do anything when I get into my apartment except analyze and replay that perfect, breath-stealing, toe-curling kiss on my balcony. I can't even believe it.

Miles kissed me.

And it was amazing. Seriously like a once-in-a-lifetime kiss. And the way his adorable awkwardness just melted away the moment his hands were on my face. . . . Wow. Miles Desai has surprised me before, but never as much as when his kiss deepened.

But as much as I want to luxuriate in those sensations all night, my mind starts overthinking. Is the reason he doesn't want me to set him up anymore because he wants to keep kissing me? And what's supposed to happen now? Are we going to talk about the kiss? Are we going to carry on like it never happened?

By the time I shower and put on my pajamas, I'm still turning all the questions I have in my head over. I've never been in a situation like this—I'm usually confident and know exactly what to do or say when I'm into someone. Or when I'm trying to figure out if they're into me. But everything with Miles feels different. I feel . . . a little bit lost, a lot confused, and completely out of my element when it comes to Miles Desai.

But still. I'm Sana Merali. The extrovert. Talking to people—even people I'm really into, isn't supposed to be hard for me. I pick up my phone and call him.

"Question for you," I ask as soon as he picks up. "Did you remember what you were going to say to me on my balcony?"

"Um, yeah. I was going to tell you to pretend it was still your prom night, because that's how I should have ended our date. To make it more memorable for you."

"Oh." I pause. "That would have been a great thing to say. Why did you kiss me?"

"You're not mad, are you?" He sounds unsure and awkward again.

"Not even a little bit. I'm definitely not going to forget my prom now."

"Is that a good thing?" he asks. I wish he were here with me so I could see if there was a tiny smile on his lips.

"It depends. Was that a pity kiss because I didn't have a prom date, or did you mean the kiss?"

"Have you ever known me to do or say something I don't mean?"

"No . . . but I think I still need you to answer the question."

His voice lowers. "I meant it, Sana."

And goose bumps erupt all over me again. "Okay. That's good. I meant it too."

"That's good," he repeats. Now I can hear the smile in his voice.

"So what happens now?" I ask. "Can I see you tomorrow night?"

"Yeah. Oh wait, shoot, I can't. I'm free earlier, though. Lunch?"

"I'm having brunch with my dad. Monday?"

"Yes. Monday. Great. Call me when you're back from school."

"Great. Will do. See you then."

"Great. I'm looking forward to it."

I try to say something other than great. "Good," I say, then giggle. "I should go to bed."

"Okay. Good night, Sana," he says.

"Good night, Miles." I disconnect the call before we start saying great again.

After getting ready for bed, I pick up my phone again and fire off a quick text.

Sana: Sleep well 🌶️ 🖤
Miles: You too 😂 🖤

I have brunch with Dad and Noureen the next day. I kind of want to bail on them, but after last night, I don't think even Noureen could bring my mood down.

Noureen seems to be off her "brunches from around the world" kick and, weirdly, picks a restaurant near my place—only about a twenty-minute walk away, instead of near theirs. The place is called Dive, and it's the newest location of a chain of so-called dive bars. But they're not really dive bars, just hipster places masquerading as dive bars. I went to one downtown with some school friends once, and I wasn't impressed. When I walk in, I see that this location looks identical to the downtown one. Which . . . I mean, isn't the point of dive bars to be that they're one of a kind?

I find Dad and Noureen sitting next to each other at a four-person table near the front. After Dad gives me a kiss on the cheek and Noureen hugs me, I sit. I'm surprised Sarina isn't here. I'm about to ask where she is, when Noureen starts talking.

"My friend Farida told me about this place." Noureen is smiling wide. "I'm so happy this area is getting better dining options. Sarina is excited to try it too! She's on her way. Your little neighborhood is really improving, Sana! Look, they have turkey bacon! And chicken sausages!"

It's sometimes hard to find non-pork breakfast options, which we need since we're Muslim. But I don't think the fact that this chain restaurant has turkey bacon means that the area is getting "better." I mean, there are *plenty* of vegetarian and vegan places around here. Hell, there's a halal Chinese hole-in-the-wall spot in Chinatown East that has the best vegetarian mapo tofu in the world.

But Noureen would never set foot in a place like that. I look at Dive's menu. The only vegetarian selections are sweet. Pancakes, waffles, and French toast. No wait, the French toast comes with meat on the side.

After I order blueberry pancakes and a green tea, Dad and Noureen start with the usual questions. How's school going? Am I still set on the digital arts program, or am I considering transferring to a "normal" university? How are my final grades? They don't ask how Mom is, how my prom went, or how my job at Cosmic is going. They do ask again if I want to work in Dad's office over the summer. I don't understand why we have to do this every two weeks. We could easily cut and paste this conversation into an automated email.

"Have you thought again about living with us in September?" Dad asks. I cringe, thankfully hidden behind the server as they set our plates down. Dad and Noureen *ooh* and *ahh* over the turkey sausage hash and salmon omelet they ordered, before Dad casts an expectant look back to me.

I shake my head, steeling myself. "I want to stay on Love Street. Mom may need me at the flower shop, and it's so much closer to school."

Noureen gives me her *I'm judging you* face. "Your mother takes advantage of you—making you work in her store for free. You cannot work there and at the thrift store when you start college. You need to keep your priorities straight."

I don't even bother correcting her that it's a *vintage* store, not a thrift store. "I *have* my priorities straight. I would think you'd agree that helping family is a good thing to prioritize." I take a bite of my pancakes. And . . . they're dry. They look way better than they taste. Typical for these brunches.

Dad sighs. "Sana, we're only trying to help. You're always so combative when we talk."

I don't say anything to that, mostly because I agree with him. Sometimes I feel like a completely different person when I'm with Dad and Noureen. Honestly, it's not a person I like much. I take a breath, mentally preparing myself to smile and attempt an apology.

"You have to understand that we have more experience in the world," Dad continues. "We're trying to use that experience to lighten your load—"

"Sarina! You made it!" Noureen says, interrupting my father.

I turn, and yes, it's Sarina. She looks effortlessly gorgeous, of course. She's in wide white jeans and a flowered button-up shirt. She's freaking *glowing*. And not limping at all.

"Hey, yeah, sorry I'm late," Sarina says as she sits next to me. "I spent the night at a friend's in the city since we had book club last night. Hey, Sana! You look amazing!"

I'm in jeans and a nineties Dad sweater. I definitely don't look my best. Sarina starts telling her mother all about her friend's get-together in the city the night before. She seems . . . much more animated than usual. Where is my serene stepsister?

She's being so nice that I feel kind of bad that we haven't talked since I texted her the morning after that day at High Park. I was so jealous of her and Miles then, even though I was the one who set them up. And up until yesterday, I'd wondered if maybe they were . . . maybe not dating, but at least *talking* since their shared car back to Vaughan. But Miles kissing me last night kind of squashed that theory. "How's your foot?" I ask.

"Oh, it's perfect," she says. "Hurt for a few days, then was fine. Thanks to Cara for telling me to ice it right away. I have to thank you again for inviting me to High Park. Even if I got hurt, it was so great to hang out with you all."

Maybe it's because she mentioned Cara, but I suddenly realize that I've seen that floral shirt she's wearing. It's from Cosmic. Or, we had one just like it there, at least. I'd almost bought it myself because the flowers looked like cherry blossoms, but since I already had a cherry blossom dress, I decided not to. She must have bought it that day Cara was helping her.

With Sarina here, the topic of why I won't move in with them is dropped. Instead, they talk about the economics summer class Sarina's taking, and I take that as my cue to tune them out. But eventually the conversation comes back to our trip to High Park last weekend.

"Sana's friends are so cool," Sarina tells her mom. "Ajit and Julie are the sweetest! They own this cute little café that's gone viral on Instagram. And, Sana, you were totally right—Miles is amazing! He's so smart!"

I smile. "Yeah, Miles is great."

Dad nods. "It's a shame he couldn't come to dinner on Friday. We must reschedule." Sarina nods in agreement, like she knows exactly what he's talking about

Wait, what? Miles was supposed to go to my dad's for dinner? He never mentioned that. . . . He did say that he originally had plans on prom night, but he didn't say those plans were to go to my *father's house*. Why wouldn't he tell me that?

There must be a good reason Miles didn't tell me. I'm about to ask Sarina why Miles was joining them for dinner when she gets a text. She looks at her phone with a small smile.

"Good news?" Noureen asks.

"Yeah, just some plans for tonight coming together." Still smiling, she types something, then puts her phone face down. After a few seconds, another text comes, her phone vibrating loudly. I know it's petty, but I want to ask why she's allowed to text at the brunch table when I'm not. Noureen doesn't even want me to have my phone placed on the table.

I'm about to let my pettiness win out and say something when I get a glimpse of Sarina's phone and clearly see the name of the person texting her. My stomach drops.

It's Miles.

Miles: I still have the address. Reservation is for seven, right?

Sarina has a date with *Miles* tonight. My Miles. The guy who said he couldn't see me tonight because he had plans. And what's worse, Sarina has already invited him to meet her family.

Because why would he want me, the naive romantic who disagrees with him at every turn, when he could have perfect Sarina?

My mouth feels dry and my hands are shaking, and it's taking everything in me to keep my voice calm. "Was that Miles? I saw his name on your phone."

Sarina positively beams. "Yes! He really is the best. I'm so, so thankful you introduced us." She moves her phone so I can't see it and texts something else.

"Sarina, no phones at the table," Noureen finally says. "Now, Sana, I really wish you would reconsider working in your father's office this summer."

Noureen keeps talking, listing all the reasons I should leave Love Street and my mother and live and work in Vaughan instead. I tune her out and think about Miles. He said he wanted to kiss me to make my prom night memorable because he's a good friend and he knew how much the night meant to me. We never agreed to be, like, dating, or anything more than friends. So do I even have the right to be mad?

I take a big bite of my pancake. It's still dry, so I wash

it down with some green tea and burn my lip. I hate this restaurant. I need to stop coming to these brunches.

I wallow in my emotions that night, which I feel fully entitled to do in this circumstance, even though Miles and I didn't have a relationship or anything. All we had was one kiss. And maybe I can't really be mad that he's going out tonight with a girl that I *literally* set him up with, can I? But he ruined my prom memories after being so sweet and attentive and adorable, and I'm sad about that.

If he's dating Sarina, then why did he kiss me? I honestly would never have pegged Miles Desai as a player, and that's not because he's too awkward to have any game whatsoever. He's just too . . . *nice*. Asking me to prom in the first place. The Lego corsage. He's been kind when I'm down, and he even called me out when I was feeling sorry for myself. He said I was an inspiration and that I just haven't found anyone worthy of me yet.

I can't help but wonder if I've been caught up in a fantasy again. Maybe my idealistic, *romantic* brain filled in the blanks and saw more in Miles than he intended. But I don't think that's true either, because if Miles wanted to be just friends, why would he kiss me like that? That was not a friend kiss . . . at least not in my experience.

Ugh. Cara is right. I am a naive child. I wish I could talk to her about this. But I'm not sure Cara wants to talk to me. I pull out my phone and draft a text.

Sana: Do you have a second? I want to apologize for what I said yesterday. I was out of line and judgmental about your relationship. If you ever want to talk, I'm here.

The text shows as read, but Cara doesn't answer. Figures. I toss my phone on my bed and pick up Zuri. She immediately purrs and wraps herself around my neck.

At least I still have my cat.

At school the next day, I spend lunch in the art room again. It's the only place in school where I can quiet my overthinking, and right now I really need that. I don't have any more projects due, but I want to finish one last piece before school ends in a week.

Painting, or actually doing anything artistic, has always been my best coping method when I'm stressed. That's why I have stacks of full sketchbooks, some that I started before my parents even split up, with doodles and abstract drawings I made when I wanted to escape. I'd started working on this piece in oils after I finished the watercolor of the woman with flower hair. It was around the time I was making the mock-up sketches for the festival proposal, so this painting is a more detailed depiction of one of the sketches I made of LOL Park. I put a huge sculpture on the path, and because this is a fantasy, added cherry blossom trees all around it. The sculpture is a big rainbow heart-shaped arch with *Love Street* written in cursive on it. There are people in the park—some taking pictures with the sculpture, some walking on the path. The whole thing is done in a modern impressionist style, so I keep stepping back to see it from the ideal viewing distance.

I notice a text from Miles while I'm adding some yellow dandelions to the painting. All it says is **hi hope your day is going well**. I ignore it and mute all texts. I'm not ready to talk to him yet.

"I love this piece," Ms. Carothers says. I hadn't noticed her behind me. "Is this a real place?"

"Yeah. It's for that festival I was telling you about. I wanted to get a sculpture like this . . . but we don't have the funds. So this is my fantasy."

She tilts her head at the painting. "This is supposed to be a sculpture?"

I nod and she smiles. "This is why I love your painting style, Sana." She points to the arch on my canvas. "I thought these were flowers. Like vines growing on a pergola. You're so skilled at allowing your observer to add their own interpretation of your art without compromising the theme."

Ms. Carothers had a lesson recently about who makes art—the artist, but also the observer; it's the artist's job to ensure the observer's interpretation still says what the artist wants to say. *Huh.* Now that I think about it, it *does* look like flowers.

I smile as an idea comes to me.

"Hey, Ms. Carothers, if there was a big floral installation in a park, like what's in my painting, do you think people would come out of their way to see it?"

She nods. "Absolutely. Floral sculptures are very popular." She tells me about this international floral sculpture competition at an annual floral show in New York that attracts thousands. She pulls a stool over to sit next to me. "Tell me more about your vision. Maybe I can help flesh out this concept."

After we talk for a bit and look at some pictures online, Ms. Carothers helps me sketch out an idea for a large heart-shaped floral arrangement that would be as big as the sculpture I want. She suggests that I ask my mom where we could get the frame for it. I can't believe I didn't think of this before.

"The thing is," I start, after telling her more about the festival and the dreams I had for it—dreams that Miles always shut down, "I also want people to be able to do something, you know, tangible at the festival, something to commemorate their love. Like love locks, but better for the environment."

Ms. Carothers thinks about it for a moment. "What about painting a mural or a mosaic that people can add to? Of . . ."

An idea comes to me while looking at my painting. "A tree! Maybe with tiles as leaves!" In my multimedia art class last year, my teacher showed us this project where a whole bunch of people painted small tiles, and then they got combined into a mosaic mural.

She smiles. "That could work."

We brainstorm ideas for how to make the mural, and even sketch it out. By the time I go to my afternoon classes, I have a lot of ideas for both a flower installation and a tile mural for LOL Park.

When I get home, I go find Mom in the floral shop to tell her about the floral installation idea, and she shows me some vendors where we can rent the aperture, or frame, we'd need. She gives me an estimate of how much the whole thing would cost—and it's within our budget.

"I can sell the flowers to you at cost to get the price down," she offers.

I shake my head, excitement buzzing in me. "Nope. This is *so* much cheaper than the permanent statue I wanted. Charge the festival full price. Remember, the point of this festival is to bring business to local shops like yours. I want you to earn all you can from it."

Mom smiles at me, proud. "Well, I can't say no to that. I think this is something we should make together so it will align with your vision. We can make it the day before the festival. Remember when you used to help me with wedding centerpieces and large arrangements?"

I grin. I love the idea of helping Mom create it. "Yes! It will be like old times. I can't wait!"

Thinking up two great ideas in one day has me as excited as when we first came up with the festival in the first place, which is great because all these issues with Miles and Cara almost made me forget why we're doing this. I, and Miles, for that matter, don't need to *understand* love and relationships to plan an amazing Love on Love Street Festival. The festival isn't really about love. It's about this community. It's about making sure Mom doesn't lose her store, and Jenn can hire more people, and Mrs. Kotch can afford butter. It's about all the other business owners and all the work they've done to build this little neighborhood into what it is now. And even if I don't know a thing about relationships, I *do* know how to put on a kick-ass event.

I'm *not* giving up on the Love on Love Street Festival. Even if I have to plan it with a total player.

I feel my phone vibrate with a call as soon as I enter the apartment. It's Miles. I was supposed to call or text him when I was done at school an hour ago, but I didn't. I want to ignore this like I ignored his text earlier, but I'm more mature than that. "Hey, we still good to meet Su Lin at six tomorrow?" he says when I answer. "I can meet you at Queen subway station and we can walk to City Hall together."

"Yeah, that works." My voice is flat.

"I thought we could talk a bit tonight before . . . make sure we're on the same page. Maybe after the bookstore closes?" He sounds . . . normal. Not like he's kissing one stepsister the night before dating the other.

"I'm busy," I say. "I need to work on my ideas for the park installation so I can show them to Su Lin tomorrow."

"Oh, you have ideas for the park? What are you thinking?"

"Don't sound so shocked. The park installation was *my* responsibility," I say. If I sound annoyed, it's because I am. "I told you I'd think of something, and I did."

"And you don't want to tell me about it?" He's annoyed now too. *Good*.

"No. You'll hear about it in the meeting tomorrow."

I hear him exhale. "What's the matter, Sana?"

"Nothing's the matter. I have a lot of work to do. I'll see you at Queen station tomorrow."

He says nothing for a while. In fact, I wonder if he hung up on me. Finally, he speaks. "I have no idea why you're suddenly mad at me, but if you don't want to talk about it, fine. I hope it won't get in the way of our meeting tomorrow."

"I know how to be professional. I'm not a child." This time I end the call.

CHAPTER SEVENTEEN

SANA AND MILES GO TO CITY HALL

I end up staying up late to perfect my ideas for the park installations. I find a vendor online who sells eight-foot heart-shaped frames for floral design for only a bit more than renting one, and this way we could use it next year, too. As long as I keep to inexpensive flowers, the whole thing would still be under budget. The cost of the tile mural is a little harder to estimate, as I want reclaimed tiles, and the online prices for tiles from demolition are wildly variable. I eventually use a generous estimate, knowing that we can probably get the materials cheaper. I'm positive both ideas would be big draws to get people to the festival.

I have no clue what Miles will think of them though. Will he call the giant tree mural trite? Will he have an issue with the heart-shaped floral arch? These are all the kinds of things he was against for the park named after his precious Lionel Osmond Love. They are so . . . romance-y. But then again, he kissed me one night, then took my sister out a day later. Miles Desai apparently doesn't have a problem with "romance" at all.

When I get to Queen station, Miles is waiting for me outside. After a brief hello, we walk to City Hall, barely speaking to each other on the way. Which is fine, even though seeing him for the first time since he kissed me on my balcony is weird. He looks . . . Well, unfortunately, he looks hot. I guess he dressed up a bit for this meeting, because he's in dark pants and a dark button-up shirt rolled up at the sleeves. His strong forearms are on full display with their corded muscles covered with soft brown skin. He looks so good that I really shouldn't have been surprised that he turned out to be a player like every other good-looking eighteen-year-old in this city.

When we get to City Hall, a twentysomething South Asian woman meets us. She introduces herself as Alex, Su Lin Tran's assistant, and takes us by elevator up to the councillor's office. Su Lin looks younger than the pictures I remember from when she was campaigning a year ago. She's small and looks to be in her early forties. Her straight black hair is cut in a no-nonsense bob, and she's wearing dark pants with a black T-shirt and a royal-blue blazer over it. She smiles.

"Sana, Miles! So glad to finally meet you in person! Please, sit. Can I offer you a drink? I was about to get myself a coffee—I have a five-cup-a-day habit!" She laughs.

We tell her we're fine, and then she excuses herself and leaves us alone in her small office. I've never been inside City Hall before. Through the window, I can see Nathan Phillips Square. It's full of tourists and locals sitting by the water feature or taking pictures of the big TORONTO sign.

"You look different, again," Miles says finally. "Not used to seeing you in . . . beige."

I raise a brow. I'd put on my most professional outfit for this meeting—the same one I wore to meet prom vendors. A pale cream blazer—vintage, of course—with a pink blouse and dark dressy jeans. My hair is in a bun on the top of my head, and I have pink lip gloss on.

"I told you I can be professional," I snap, then sigh. I need to do a better job of masking the annoyance in my voice, because this *isn't* professional.

"I know. I didn't doubt you could," he says. I can't read his expression. He looks away from me, gazing out the window. "I've never met someone who looks that beautiful in anything she puts on."

What? I turn quickly to him, blinking. Before I can say anything, Su Lin and Alex come back to the office, each with a mug in hand.

Su Lin smiles as she sits at her desk. Alex pulls out a chair to sit next to her. "Now, I want to hear all about how the festival planning has been going. I was so impressed with your proposal! I'm here to help in any way to make this event a success."

Miles and I go over our plans so far. She saw our budget in the proposal, but we mention some changes we made to it since we got the approval. We show her April's draft of the website, my sketches of the logo, and our plans for entertainment.

"Oh, that's lovely!" she says. "What a smart idea to reach out to local music and dance schools for entertainment. What about vendors? Maybe some international food offerings?"

I nod. "We're putting a vendor application form on the website when it goes up. One thing we've decided is we don't want to accept any that are in direct competition with the Love Street businesses."

Su Lin frowns. "I wouldn't worry about a bit of competition. A variety of offerings will bring in more people!

Maybe check with Rossi's on Gerrard—they can make some custom cupcakes."

There's no way I want Rossi's—the chain store that cut into Ina Kozlak's profits—at our festival. Just as I'm about to mention how we already have an amazing bakery on Love Street that makes the best cakes in the world, Miles cuts in.

"Of course," Miles says. "We're happy to consider every application."

"Excellent." Su Lin flips to the next page of the plan. "What about the park? It says you've allocated funds for a major art installation, but it doesn't say what it is."

I smile. "I have it here." I pass out copies of my proposal to Miles and Su Lin and explain both the floral heart piece and the tile mosaic tree.

"The mural mosaic will be an alternative to the popular love locks that you see on bridges and fences," I explain. "We wanted to do something more unique and sustainable. We can get reclaimed tiles and cut them into hearts or leaves. People will buy a tile to write a love message on it, and they will all be combined into a mural by volunteers on-site. My art teacher has volunteered to supervise."

Su Lin flips to the sketches that Ms. Carothers and I made yesterday. Miles is studying his copy too. He looks at me, a small smile on his face. "This is the *coolest* idea, Sana."

Su Lin nods. "I agree. I love both plans. How lucky that your mother's a florist! If you want your mural to be permanently added to the park, you'll have to complete a mural application form with the city. Let me know when you submit it, and I'll make sure it's fast-tracked. And don't worry about using *used* tiles. I'm positive I can get the tiles we need donated from Danver Hardware. In fact, they'll probably donate some labor, too. I'll have Alex reach out."

Danver is a big nationwide chain of box stores. I'm about to protest. A partnership with a store like Danver is exactly what we *don't* want for the festival. But suddenly Miles's hand taps my knee, clearly telling me to shut up.

"I can contact them," Miles says. He's been taking notes on his copy of my proposal the whole time I've been talking, but I can't see what he wrote.

We go over the rest of the festival plan together. Su Lin looks genuinely impressed. "I think we should reach out to the media soon. It's such a great story—an event like this conceptualized and planned by two teenagers. Be in touch if there are any other ways my office can help; this is exactly what my constituents need. We're going to make the Love on Love Street Festival the *best* neighborhood festival in the city!"

After saying goodbye, Miles and I leave City Hall. Despite the tension between us, I'm so excited about the meeting that I can't stop myself from talking about it.

"That went so well, didn't it?" I ask as we head toward the subway. I need to rush to Cosmic so Jenn can go home.

Miles nods. The look of awe on his face tells me that it went way better than he'd imagined it would too. "Yeah. It's *huge* that we have that kind of support from someone in City Hall. We're very lucky."

I shake my head. "Not *lucky*. We *worked* for this. The Love on Love Street Festival is going to be a real, amazing thing, and it's going to be exactly what Love Street needs. We did this together . . . you and me." Even if he's a player, I have every intention of continuing to work my butt off with him for the festival. The street needs us.

Miles looks at me, clearly not knowing what to say. I know he's aware that I'm mad at him, but he doesn't know *why*. If I want to be mature and professional while we're working together, maybe I should tell him that I know he went out with Sarina on Sunday night. I should tell him that I will keep working with him, but our friendship, or whatever else he had in mind, is off the table.

Miles gets a text right when I'm about to say something. And his face changes from mild annoyance and confusion to a big incandescent smile after reading it. The kind of smile he used to give me.

"Who was that?" I ask. It might not be Sarina. It could be about the festival.

He slips his phone into his pocket. "No one. Personal stuff."

Yeah, that was probably Sarina. I really don't care anymore about being *professional*. If he's going to keep things from me, then he can figure out on his own why I'm completely done with him.

We're at the subway stairs by now, but there's no way I want to ride the train with him. Without even saying anything, I keep walking toward the next station instead of following him down the stairs. I don't even know if he notices.

So I'll be a little late for work—Jenn will understand.

Cosmic is pretty quiet that evening, so I'm doing homework at the counter when someone comes in. It's Alex, Su Lin's assistant. I smile and say hello and that it's nice to see her again so soon.

She smiles. "I don't live very far, and when you told me about this store, I knew I had to see it. You left this in Su Lin's office." She hands me Miles's messenger bag.

"Oh," I say, taking the bag. "Thank you. Want me to show you around? We just got some new stock in." I get off my stool behind the counter.

I end up helping Alex pick out a pair of wide-legged green pants and a tie-front blouse. They look fantastic on her. She'll be the most fashionable person at City Hall. She leaves right in time for closing, and I lock the door behind her.

I see Miles's bag, still on the counter. Does he even realize he left it behind? I know there's nothing valuable in it like his laptop or phone, but still. He might be worrying about it. I send him a text explaining everything and that his bag is here at Cosmic, and he answers quickly that he'll pick it up tomorrow. I take the bag to the back room for safety, but as I put it on the desk, curiosity gets the better of me. I know I shouldn't snoop in his things, but I *really* want to know what he wrote on my proposal. Did he actually think my ideas were good, or was all that writing just him poking holes in my plans like he always does? I'm not going to go through all his things—just the folder he had the festival paperwork in.

I take out the folder and open it. My proposal is right on top, and it's covered with his handwritten notes. His comments are neither nitpicky nor complimentary; they're just so . . . *Miles*. Like suggesting reaching out to a specific charity that resells construction goods for the tiles and plywood and making sure none of the flowers in the installation are toxic to the wildlife in the area. Detailed oriented and conscientious. I exhale. Even after I snapped at him today, he still took my ideas at face value and thought of ways to make them work. To make them better, if I'm honest.

I don't understand how someone so thoughtful and . . . well, *logical*, could be a player. But then again, I don't know for sure that he saw Sarina on Sunday night. Maybe there's another explanation. I close the folder, but when I'm putting it back into his bag, an envelope falls out of it. A familiar envelope.

It's my father's letterhead from his commercial real estate office. Why would Miles have a letter from my father? I can't help myself—I pick it up and look at it. It's empty and doesn't have a stamp or an address on the front, just my father's office address in the left corner. On the back in unfamiliar handwriting, someone has written an address sideways. I don't recognize the handwriting—it's definitely not my father's. The address is on College Street, and when I quickly google it, I see that it's a fancy tapas restaurant.

I remember the text I saw at brunch—Miles told Sarina that he had the address. Sarina, who works at my father's office, with easy access to his letterhead, could have given it to him. I close my eyes as a wave of nausea moves through me.

I put the envelope back in his bag and lock up the store. This is all the proof I need; I am 100 percent done crushing on Miles Desai. I open a text to him.

Sana: I'd appreciate it if you would stop commenting on my appearance when we're working on the festival. I want to keep things professional between us.

It takes a while, but eventually I get a response.

Miles: Understood.

CHAPTER EIGHTEEN
MAGIC IN THE BOOK ROOM

We have a festival committee meeting the next night, and I seriously consider skipping it because I don't want to see Miles. But I go. I sit as far as I possibly can from him at the big table at LoveBug, though, and barely look at him when he tells everyone about our meeting with Su Lin.

"This . . . this is so cool," Cara says, looking up at me shyly. "I'd . . . I mean . . . I can help with the mural . . . if you want."

I'm surprised— Cara might love fashion, but she's not what I'd call *artsy*. This is the first thing she's said to me since the meeting started. Things have been awkward between us. We haven't really talked since I called her girlfriend controlling, and she ignored my apology text. I assumed I'd ruined our friendship. But maybe her offering to help with the mural is her way of asking if we're still cool.

I give her a genuine smile. "Absolutely. Even though you always say you have the artistic ability of a capybara. It would be *great* to do it together."

Cara smiles widely, and I know we'll be okay. I won't bring up her relationship with Hannah, but at least we can be friends again.

Miles leaves immediately after the meeting without

saying anything. It's reminding me of the grumpy Miles I first met in LoveBug. I should have listened to myself when I thought he was a douche back then.

"What's going on with you two?" Cara asks. Jenn, Cara, Julie, and I are still at the table, finishing our tea.

"Nothing's going on," I say.

"There's a ton of tension between you," Julie says.

"Yeah, I noticed it, too," Jenn adds. "You guys were great friends. Did something happen at prom?"

No, nothing happened at prom. We had a lovely time. Something did happen *after* prom, but I really don't want to tell anyone that Miles pity kissed me even though he's dating someone else. "Prom was fine. But I realized that we're way too different. I want to focus only on this festival, nothing else."

Cara looks at me skeptically. I know I never confessed that I had feelings for the guy, but she looks like she doesn't buy any of what I'm saying. I shake my head and stand to take my mug to the counter. "Nothing significant happened. We're just not as tight anymore. Anyway, I forgot to say, I know a guy who has a T-shirt company. I could reach out to get a quote on the volunteer T-shirts?"

When I get to Cosmic for my shift on Friday, Cara and Jenn are both behind the counter. Cara immediately gets her bag to leave, saying she has plans tonight. She's glowing with happiness. I don't have to guess who her plans are with.

"Oh, Sana, before I go," Cara says. She glances at Jenn, who smiles. "Reggie was here earlier looking for you. He bought a bunch more romances in an auction lot.

He asked if you can go through them after closing so he can put the good ones on the shelves for the weekend."

I cringe. I can't go to the bookstore. I'm supposed to be avoiding Miles. "I don't know—"

"If you're worried about Miles being there, he's not," Jenn says. "Reggie's niece Tamara is covering some shifts this summer. She's going to help you with the books."

"Oh. Okay, then. I'll pop by," I say. I've met Tamara before and liked her. She's a huge romance reader. It would be fun to go through the romance books with her.

When I go to the bookstore after closing Cosmic for the night, Reggie is behind the counter.

"Sana, my dear. Look at you! I always love your colorful wardrobe."

I smile and thank Reggie. It's warm now, so I'm wearing purple high-waisted shorts with a sleeveless pink blouse with a lace collar. My hair is pulled back with a pink knotted headband.

"Cara said you had more romances for me to go through?"

Reggie nods. "Yes. As you know, I'm not very versed in the genre . . . but I'm getting better! They're on the desk in the back room. . . . You won't miss them. Unfortunately, I must finish this paperwork or my staff won't get paid."

"Is Tamara there now?" I ask.

He smiles widely. "Yes. You'll have company."

"Okay . . . I'll just put the good books in a pile."

As I head toward the back room of the bookstore, Reggie calls out, "Thank you, my dear!"

I open the door to the storeroom, and . . . I freeze. The only person I see is Miles.

He's sitting at a little desk near the wall, engrossed in a history book. He doesn't seem to notice me, and Tamara is nowhere to be seen.

Stupid meddling neighbors and friends. Reggie and Jenn lied to my face about Tamara being here, and I can't believe I fell for it. I'm about to turn and leave Second Story Books when I realize what book Miles is reading. It's *Pride and Prejudice*—my favorite book of all time. It's an old, worn hardcover edition, which is why I assumed it was a history book.

"Miles," I say, walking into the storeroom and closing the door behind me. "Why are you reading that?"

He looks up at me, startled. He's wearing his Second Story Books T-shirt, the same yellow shirt he had on the last time I was in this storeroom with him. That feels like so long ago. That was our first argument . . . or maybe our second if I count the original BOA meeting where we met. We've argued so many times since then.

I can't believe I'm feeling nostalgic thinking about our arguments.

I take a step closer so I'm a few feet away from his desk. We've also bonded many times. Over our family issues, our love of good food, and our love of this community. We've laughed about those terrible dates I set him up on. We've watched a sunset together while eating cheese and strawberries. We've ate red velvet cake at midnight in the flower shop. We've brainstormed and collaborated and built an entire festival together.

And we've kissed.

He looks at me with those rich brown eyes and doesn't say anything for a beat before he puts down the book and runs his hand through his hair. "Sana, what are you doing here?"

"I have no idea." There are no books on the only desk here—only Miles's laptop. "I think Reggie and Jenn made something up as a ploy to get me to talk to you."

Miles frowns. "Oh. That's why he told me to stay back here."

I lean closer to see the book. "So . . . *are* you actually reading *Pride and Prejudice*?"

He nods. "Yeah."

"It's my favorite book, and you mocked me for that. And now *you're* reading it?"

"I didn't mock you." He sighs. "Sorry if I did. It's a good book."

"Why did you even start it?" I pick the book up from the desk. It's an old edition, probably from this bookstore.

"Because you said it was your favorite, and . . . you said I was a cold fish."

"I said you were a *frigid* fish," I say. Which is really the same thing. But since I said that, Miles Desai has kissed all coherent thoughts out of me, so now I know he's the furthest thing from *frigid*. "So, what, you're reading *Pride and Prejudice* so you'll learn how to be less cold?"

He shrugs. "You said I don't know a thing about love and romance—and you're right," he says. "Although, if Mr. Darcy is your idea of a romantic hero, I'd say that I come pretty close already."

"Yeah, no, I've seen you dance. Fitzwilliam Darcy has nothing on you."

That makes him chuckle, and it's adorable as always. I shouldn't have said that. I forgot that I'm mad at him. I still have no idea whether he's *dating* my stepsister. Maybe it's time I asked him.

"Do you want to be more *romantic* so you'll be a better cochair of the love festival or so you'll be a better boyfriend to my stepsister?" I can't help the hurt seeping into my voice. Because yeah . . . Miles and Sarina together would sting. A lot.

But he recoils at my question. "Why would I want to be your *sister's* boyfriend?"

"*Stepsister*. You went out with her Sunday night to a place on College Street, right? I saw your text to her at brunch. And Sarina was so grateful that I introduced the two of you."

Miles shakes his head, a look of confusion on his face. He gets up from his chair and walks around the desk so he's standing in front of me. He exhales. "So that's why you're mad. I *did* go out with Sarina on Sunday. But it wasn't a date. At least not with me."

That doesn't make sense.

"Sarina told me after High Park that she was really into someone," he says. "And it's someone I conveniently know. So I invited them both out, hoping sparks would fly."

My eyes widen. "Seriously? You were setting Sarina up with someone? Like I was doing for you?" That . . . was not the explanation I expected. Like, at all.

He nods, a tiny smile on his face. Now that I know the truth, I'm allowed to think he's cute again. Because his tiny smiles are too adorable.

Fighting my blush, I ask, "Who is Sarina into?"

He shakes his head. "She asked me not to tell you. She doesn't want her parents finding out."

I almost ask him to tell me anyway, because I wouldn't tell Dad and Noureen. But if Sarina *asked* him not to tell me, then I'm not going to force him. It's probably someone from Vaughan or King City anyway. Or maybe someone in his university program.

And it's definitely not Miles.

"So, you and Sarina *didn't* hit it off when I set you up?"

He smiles, shaking his head. "No, we *did* hit it off. She's cool. We're friends."

"But not dating." I need him to say it clearly.

He takes a step forward so now there's barely a foot separating us. He takes his book from my hand and drops it back on the desk. "Sana," he says. His voice is smooth and sure—all his shyness from a few moments ago long gone. He's right here, and I'm surrounded by the comforting smell of old books. "I kissed you on Saturday," he says.

I blink. "I remember."

"I admit that I'm utterly clueless when it comes to relationships," he says, "which explains the last few days. But do you really think I'd kiss *you* on Saturday and then go out with someone else the next night? With your *sister*?"

"Stepsister." I don't break eye contact with him. His eyes are so beautiful. I could stare at them forever. "I don't know if that kiss, like, really *meant* anything to you. . . . I mean, you said you meant it, but it was just a kiss. And you said it was to make my prom more memorable."

He smiles. "So you thought I was . . ."

"I thought you were a player. Kissing me and dating Sarina."

He chuckles and steps even closer. I can feel his warmth.

I can feel his breath. I want to close the gap between us, but I'm still not sure this is really happening.

"I don't have the foggiest idea how to be a player," he says softly. "I have no clue how to go after someone I'm into—which is why I can't seem to do the right thing with you. But I *definitely* meant that kiss." He's still very close, but he's not moving.

"Do you still mean it?" I ask, and he nods, his eyes watching my mouth. I decide to take matters into my own hands. "Show me," I say. I put my hands behind his neck, pull him down to my level, and kiss him myself.

His arms immediately go around my waist to hold me close, and it's just like Saturday night. I go on my tippy-toes, feeling every nerve in my body singing for him. Miles kisses me like he's starving and I'm a rich slice of black forest cake. It's like there's all this explosive passion beneath the surface of him that only erupts for the right person. Me.

We kiss like that for probably longer than we should. He's crowding me against the bookshelves, and I'm grateful to have something solid behind me holding me up because I doubt my wobbly knees could take my weight. I can hear his heartbeat and feel his smooth skin on my cheek, and his hair feels soft and thick through my fingers. It's like he's consuming me, and I never want him to stop.

But eventually he does let me go when his phone vibrates. He picks it up from the desk and smiles.

"Reggie's heading out. He wants me to lock up when we're done."

I laugh, letting my head rest on his shoulder. "I still

can't believe your boss and my boss *conspired* to get us alone."

Miles leans down to kiss my neck. "I'm not complaining," he says, his voice on my skin sending a shiver down my spine. "Do you think I mean this now?"

"Yeah, I think that would be hard to fake." I pause. "That was the stupidest misunderstanding. Next time let's just talk to each other."

He laughs, then pulls me down to the floor. We sit very close, leaning back against the desk. And we're holding hands. I have no idea what any of this means. Maybe we're going to talk. Maybe kiss again. I hope so.

He squeezes my hand, then lifts it like he's going to kiss it gently, but then gives the back of my hand three loud sloppy smooches. I laugh because it tickles and he's silly.

This is another surprising thing about getting to know Miles like this. He's . . . playful. He's not stuffy at all. I was so wrong about him.

"You are, like, *easily* the cutest person I've ever met," I say.

He huffs and looks away. He's clearly not used to compliments. I wish I could find that ex of his and tell her off for not showering Miles with praise.

"You're blushing," I add. "Now you're even cuter."

He looks at me. "Brown people don't blush."

"Sure we do. Our blood is red, isn't it? Now be honest. How are you enjoying *Pride and Prejudice*?"

"I'm loving it. I'm almost at the end, but I'm going to read it again when I'm done."

I laugh. "Miles Desai loves a romance novel."

He nods. "I do! It's so . . . *witty*. And I love the exploration of class differences and how they can impact our first impressions of people."

I smile. I don't think I'd realized it, but Miles and I kind of did what Darcy and Elizabeth did. I judged Miles before I really knew him. I assumed that because he was an outsider—because he was new to Love Street and because he came from a suburban mansion—he and I would never have the same perspective. And he clearly judged me, too. Based on my clothes and my personality, he thought I was naive and immature.

"Darcy and Elizabeth figured out that there's a lot more to each other than what they originally saw," I say.

Miles nods.

"When did you stop hating me, anyway?" I ask.

He shakes his head. "I *never* hated you, Sana. I mean, I thought you were so pretty when I first saw you at Love-Bug that I could barely speak to you."

Amazing. I thought he was being *so* rude that day. "But then I started irritating you as much as you were irritating me."

"I think *challenging* is a better word than irritating," he says as he puts his hand on my waist.

I chuckle. "And I know you like to be challenged. Does the fact that you're enjoying that book mean you want to read more romance?" I ask.

He nods. "Maybe. I definitely want to read more Austen. Maybe more classics like that. The Brontë sisters?"

My face scrunches as I shake my head. "There's no *joy* in the Brontës. It's just depressed people crying on the moors. You should read *joyful* romances. Because that's what romance is supposed to be. *Fun.*"

He laughs and squeezes my hand. "I have a feeling that I'm going to have a lot of fun with you."

I turn to look at his face. "Is that what we're doing? Romance . . . ing?"

His brows knit together. "Is that what you want?"

"What do you want, Miles?"

He turns his body so he can take my other hand in his. "Well, first I want to do this." He kisses my lips again. "Then I want to ask if you'd let me take you out."

"Like on a date?"

He nods. "I plan it this time." At my surprised look, he continues. "I want to show you *my* skills."

"Yes, please. I want to see all your skills." I take the back of his head and pull him in for another kiss.

We break apart after I find myself fully on his lap. Reggie probably knows what we're up to, but we shouldn't get too carried away in his store. I lean my head on Miles's shoulder.

"We have a festival meeting tomorrow night. How about Sunday?" he asks.

"I'm working at Cosmic . . . but after five?"

He smiles. "Perfect."

"Hey, will this"—I squeeze his hand—"get in the way of us planning the festival together?"

"Maybe this means we won't disagree on everything."

I giggle. "I doubt that. We might disagree *more*. Maybe you'll be comfortable enough to tell me all the things you dislike about me."

He wraps his arms around my waist. "I don't think I'll be able to find anything. I think I like pretty much *everything* about you. A lot."

I smile. "I like you a lot too, Miles." I give him a kiss on the cheek. "I should have known this would happen the first time I saw you. I mean, we were both drinking pink tea. That was fate."

"Or . . . a coincidence." He smiles widely, then kisses my lips again.

And we don't talk much after that for a while.

CHAPTER NINETEEN
NO DOUBTS ALLOWED

That night I don't sleep well at all. My mind is too busy replaying that spectacularly romantic moment when Miles told me he *still* meant that kiss. And when he said he likes everything about me. That was a romantic moment for the *ages*. Better than any book or movie I'd seen. Who would have thought that Miles Desai would be the one to make my knees weak and my skin tingle more than anyone else? Honestly, Miles might be the most *genuinely* romantic person I've been with. The most *earnest*. I'd been obsessing over him for weeks, but the reality of being with Miles far outweighs my expectations.

I exhale. Usually hooking up with someone new *clears* my head and makes my mood even sunnier than normal. But . . . something about this thing, whatever it is, between Miles and me, feels different. Deeper. Maybe it's because he frustrated me so much when we met, which was only a month ago. Like, I have whiplash from how much my feelings changed.

Back then I thought he was an arrogant know-it-all who didn't care about my community. But Miles *does* care about my community. He wouldn't be working so hard on the Love on Love Street Festival if he didn't care. And rather than being an arrogant know-it-all, he's smart and interested in learning and willing to admit to his mistakes. He's pragmatic, but that doesn't mean he's not passionate.

At the festival meeting on Saturday, I'm way too distracted by Miles next to me to contribute anything useful. The purpose of this meeting is pretty much only to approve the website before it goes live, and while April shows us the site, I look at Miles instead. He's so . . . cute. But also, hot. Sexy. I thought he was incredibly good-looking the very first time I saw him, but somehow he's even better now. Smooth skin in the perfect medium brown. Full lips that I now know are incredibly kissable. And those intelligent eyes. Intense and thoughtful. He's looking so intently at April's screen and listening to her explain her navigation choices. He always does that. Listens to everyone. Learns from them. He gives everyone his complete attention.

But then he notices me looking at him, and he blushes a bit. I want to take out my phone and snap a picture, so he can see what his blush looks like. I smile small at him, as if to say "busted," and he shakes his head, a soundless chuckle on his lips.

Later, after the meeting, I linger as usual, but this time Miles does too. And so does Cara. She looks at me, then at Miles.

"Can you explain to me why the two of you were making goo-goo eyes at each other while April was talking about HTML code?" she asks.

I raise a brow. "Because . . . HTML is boring?"

Miles looks like he's holding in a laugh.

Cara shakes her head. "Okay, what happened? We all wanted you to talk out whatever you were fighting about, but I wasn't thinking you were going to . . . What exactly *are* you two doing?"

I hesitate. Miles and I hadn't talked about what we're labeling this yet. We'd kissed twice. Actually, more than that, but on two different occasions. And he asked me on a date and I said yes. Does that mean we're dating? If I say we're dating, would he freak out? Would I freak out if *he* didn't say we were dating?

Literally for the very first time in my life I have no idea what to say.

"We're . . . getting to know each other," Miles finally says. Which is true, at least.

"And kissing," I add. Because I'm me, and sometimes I can't keep my mouth shut.

Miles laughs, and I grin at him. He laughs so much now, and it makes me feel all warm and gushy that it could be because of me.

Cara looks at me with an incredulous expression. "Getting to know each other by kissing."

I nod.

"So . . . you're giving up on matchmaking him with others and decided that only *you* can teach him the true meaning of romance?"

Miles laughs again.

This is awkward. "Enough about me," I say. "What's new with you, Cara?"

Now it's Cara's turn to look awkward. Like she doesn't know what to say. Which I gather is because she doesn't want to talk to me about Hannah.

Finally, Cara shakes her head. "Nothing interesting. Same old."

Yeah, she's definitely still drinking Hannah's BS. I sigh. If never talking about her girlfriend is the way for me and Cara to stay friends, I can do that.

Cara suddenly stands and picks up her bag. "I need to head out. Don't do anything I wouldn't do, kids!" Cara waves and leaves the café.

"That was weird," I say.

Miles also stands, taking my and his mugs to the counter. "What was weird?"

"Cara. I think she doesn't want to mention Hannah to me." I exhale, standing. "I hope she's okay."

Miles shrugs, coming back to me. "I think Cara is smart enough to know what's best for herself in a relationship."

"I hope so." I look at Miles, smiling. "Want to walk me home?"

"Um, my bike's there, so I was going to either way."

I run my finger softly down his bare arm. It's staying quite warm in the evening now, so he's just in a T-shirt. He gasps softly at the touch. Huh. Interesting. I do it again with the other arm and watch goose bumps erupt on him. "How sensitive is your skin, anyway?" I ask.

He chuckles again. "Why do I feel like this summer just got a lot more fun?"

I laugh. "Down, boy. Mom's home. C'mon, though, we can hang out on the balcony."

Ten minutes later we're sitting at the small table on my balcony, eating a bag of organic chips and drinking a pot of tea.

"Everything for the festival is coming together so well," I say.

Miles nods. "Yeah, I keep waiting for a shoe to drop. It's almost going *too* smoothly."

I shake my head. "Nonsense. No shoe will drop. The festival is going to be *perfect*. This whole summer is going to be epic." I beam at him. I completely agree with what he said earlier—thanks to Miles, I suspect this summer is going to be a *lot* of fun.

We talk a bit more about the festival while we drink our tea. He's so easy to talk to, but it's getting late. And I can see my mother looking at me through the window. "I should go," I say. "Mom's chill, but she's still a Brown mom."

He cringes, then stands to unlock his bike. "We're still on for tomorrow, right?"

I nod. "I get off at five."

"Can you meet me inside Broadview subway station as soon as you're done work?"

"Sure. Where are we going, anyway?" I ask. And why would we meet at *Broadview*—there are a few stations closer to Love Street, and his place.

"It's a surprise. Just meet me there." He pulls his bike off the bike rack and leans it against the railing at the top of the stairs.

"How should I dress? Will we be outside?"

He shakes his head. "Dress for public transportation and a fast-casual restaurant."

Casual restaurant? I'm really curious. . . . Is this date going to be something from his list of inexpensive things to do in Toronto?

He gives me one of his wide smiles. "Trust me, Sana."

"Of course I trust you." I take a step toward him.

Through the window on the door, I can see my mother in the kitchen. She waves at me. I roll my eyes, then turn back to Miles.

"Text me when you get home?" I ask.

He nods, then wraps his arms around me. I freaking adore how touchy-feely Miles already is. "I want to kiss you," he says softly.

"What's stopping you?" I wrap my hand around the back of his neck.

"Um . . . your mother is staring at us."

I chuckle. "We should go to your place sometime."

He shakes his head. "My place is *disgusting*. And we'd have even less privacy." I frown, but it disappears when he gives me a quick peck on the lips, then a hug. "I'll text you when I get home."

"Bye, Miles." I watch him carry his bike down the stairs and ride away before heading inside.

Mom is in the kitchen and has the food processor in front of her. She must have made hummus—she does that about every three days. "Did I see you kissing Miles?" she asks.

I nod, swiping a cherry tomato from a basket on the counter. "He's adorable, right?"

Mom doesn't answer that. "I asked around about his mother."

"You did? Why?"

She shrugs, then scoops the hummus into a plastic container. "I was curious," Mom says.

The hummus looks different—it's reddish in color. I

take another cherry tomato and dip into it. "This is good."

Mom smiles. "Experimenting with a new recipe—it has roasted red pepper and pomegranate molasses in it." She scrapes the last of the hummus into the container. "The Ismaili Muslim community is small. I wondered if I knew his parents. I don't think I do. You could ask your stepmother. . . . She's from that area."

I freeze. My hand is holding another tomato, hovering over the hummus. *Does* Noureen know Miles's family? I suppose it's possible. That thought makes me feel a little off-kilter. Like my worlds are colliding—and not in a good way. But Miles and Sarina have become friends. One of them would have told me if their mothers knew each other.

"He's not very close with his parents," I say. "They're separating right now and fighting a lot. He moved to the city because there was too much tension at home."

Mom tilts her head with sympathy. "Poor kid. I like him. I think he's good for you."

"I think so too." I dip another cherry tomato into the hummus. There's no reason to have any doubts about Miles—we're still getting to know each other. This relationship is going to be great—the fortune told me it would be, and there's no reason not to trust a fortune from a velvet jacket.

CHAPTER TWENTY

THE EYE-OPENING STREETCAR RIDE

It takes me forever to decide what to wear for work on Sunday, since I'm going straight to my first date with Miles after. I want to look good, but it needs to be casual, too. Jeans would be the obvious choice for a casual restaurant, but I'm not really a wear-jeans-on-a-date kind of girl. A short skirt would be more me, but I hate wearing skirts to work because I'm always climbing ladders. I finally decided on pink vintage sailor pants and a white shirt with a little scarf around my neck. I wear my hair big and curly, put on my brightest pink lipstick, and, finally, grab a pair of white sandals to change into after my shift. The outfit looks like I'd put thought into it, but it's as comfortable as jeans and a T-shirt. After I close the store, I change my shoes and touch up my lipstick before heading to the subway to meet Miles at Broadview station.

He's on the platform when I get off the train, and I can tell right away that he put thought into his outfit too. He's in perfectly fitted black pants that hit just above his ankles, a pair of trendy loafers, and a short-sleeved blue button-up with a leaf print on it. I smile, admiring how that blue brings out the warmth in his eyes. Miles's clothes aren't as loud as mine, but they are . . . *colorful*. I love how he manages to look preppy and smart, but also stylish. We hug like we haven't seen each other in weeks instead of a day. I'm getting so attached to the feeling of Miles's arms around me. Taking my hand, he says, "You ready?"

I nod. "Yes. You going to tell me where we're going?"

"I'm taking you to my uncle's restaurant," he says. "Unless . . ." He runs his free hand through his hair, looking unsure. "I mean, unless you think it's weird to meet my family. We can go somewhere else."

"If this is the place that has the best pani puri in town, I'm in," I say, even though I am a bit nervous. Miles wouldn't introduce me to family that wouldn't like me, would he? He starts climbing the stairs up from the subway platform, and I follow, even though I'm confused. "You said it's in the West End. . . . Wouldn't the subway be easier?" I ask.

He shakes his head as we walk to the streetcar platform on the upper level of the station. "Getting there is part of the date. We're taking a streetcar." He explains more when we get to the platform. "When I first moved here a few months ago, I used to go to my uncle's place a lot because he'd give me free food. But one day there was a subway closure so I couldn't take the train. The 505 streetcar runs between Broadview and Dundas West stations—right near my uncle's place."

I nod. "It's the same streetcar we took to Riverdale Park." Toronto streetcars run much slower than subways because they share the road with cars. It would easily take over an hour to get to Bloor and Dundas from here on a streetcar but would only be about twenty minutes by subway. I understand Miles's choice, though. We'll be above ground, seeing everything from one end of the city to the other, for nothing but the cost of one TTC fare. It's a perfect first date.

When the streetcar arrives, we take two front-facing seats in the middle, with me near the window. Toronto streetcars are *long*, more like modern electric trains than old-fashioned trolley cars. I'd always taken them for granted, but Miles tells me this is one of the last first-generation trolley systems still in operation in the whole world, which is super cool.

During the ride we talk about equity and about how even in a city like Toronto, wealthier neighborhoods are better served by public transportation than neighborhoods with less money, even though those are the people who rely on it more. We see some unhoused people sleeping on the street, which gets us talking about the housing crisis and what can be done about it.

"It's weird that Toronto has all these areas that are just houses, but then areas where there are apartments and businesses together," I say. "Why can't they turn empty office buildings into housing? Or tear down two houses and put up an apartment building?"

"Because of zoning laws that were put in years ago. A huge percentage of the city is zoned for single-family housing only, which is ridiculous. We should have more mixed zoning."

I nod. I can't believe I thought he was arrogant about all his knowledge of this stuff—because this—the work he wants to do—is *so* important to make the city fair for everyone here. We eventually pass the busy square at Yonge and Dundas, with its enormous multistory billboards and jumbotrons. There are people and cars *everywhere*.

Tourists shopping, people leaving work, even students taking summer classes at the nearby Toronto Metropolitan University—the school Miles goes to.

We pass the Ontario College for Art and Design next, where I'll be starting school in September. I show him the building most of my classes will be in. We pass Toronto's main Chinatown, and I point out the best cheap dumpling place. We get close to Kensington Market, and I tell him next time I get to plan a date, we're going there for tacos and vintage shopping.

"How often do you take this streetcar?" I ask.

"I've done it a few times. It's so much better than being in an underground tunnel."

"You go to your uncle's restaurant a lot?"

He nods. "Rajit is my favorite uncle. And he always feeds me for free. As a poor student, I appreciate that."

"Are you worried about what your uncle will think of me?"

"I don't really care what my family thinks of you. I like you. And what others think isn't going to change that."

I smile. That was a good answer. I lean over and kiss his cheek, and he blushes.

"Anyway," Miles says. "I know Rajit is going to *love* you. Seriously. He's not strict or . . . *parental*."

"Parental meaning *judgmental*, right?"

He nods. "He's my dad's youngest brother, and he always felt more like an older cousin than an uncle. He won't even let me call him uncle."

I nod. I'm still nervous though. Because I like Miles so much more than I've liked anyone else in a long time, and I don't want this to fizzle away like all my past relationships.

"This is a nice ride," I say. My head is on his shoulder so I can't see his expression, but he squeezes my hand. "You were right—you're an excellent date planner."

When we finally get to Dundas West station, it's a ten-minute walk to his uncle's restaurant. The restaurant is called Juna, and it's pretty new, with a modern design. It's a far cry from the old Indian street-food places on Gerrard. After we sit, a Brown man comes toward us with a huge smile. This must be Rajit. He's younger than I expected—he doesn't look much older than Miles.

"Hey, Miles, my bro! Who's your *friend*?" He says the word "friend" with a little teasing lilt. I already like the guy.

After Miles introduces me to his Rajit Uncle (who also insists I drop the uncle bit because it makes him feel old), Rajit hands us some menus and tells us to order whatever we want. He offers mango lassis to start, which I can't say no to. I smile at Miles when his uncle leaves to get our drinks.

"I like your uncle. He's like . . . an *extroverted* you."

Miles laughs at that. "What do you want to eat?" I look at the menu. It's standard Indian street food: samosas, pakoras, chaats, and, of course, the reason we're here, pani puri.

Miles's uncle sits with us after we order a bunch of different things to split. I ask him how long he's had the restaurant.

"Two years. It's been my dream *forever*. I'm in a partnership with my two closest friends in the industry, and we're working our asses off, but also having so much fun. I started working in Indian kitchens when I was fifteen. I'm still pinching myself that I have my own place."

"Kitchens here in Toronto?"

Rajit shakes his head. "No, in Florida. That's where Miles's dad's family is from." Rajit is chattier than Miles, so I learn more about Miles from hearing his uncle's history. Apparently, Miles's father's family originally came from India and settled in Florida. Miles's father worked at Disney World as a teen and met Miles's mother when her family was there on vacation, which . . . talk about an epic meet-cute. The two kept in touch, fell in love, and he ran away to Canada to marry her. Miles's father's parents pretty much disowned his father for marrying a Muslim. Rajit said he himself took the first opportunity to leave Florida, too. He followed his brother to Toronto, and got a job in a kitchen here as soon as he finished high school.

"You don't have a relationship with your grandparents at all?" I ask Miles. That's sad.

He shrugs. "They did eventually accept my mother, but we've never been close. They've called me a few times since my parents split, but that's only because they want to complain about my mother to me."

"Does your dad talk to them now?"

"I honestly have no idea," Miles says.

I reach over and hold his hand. Rajit looks at our connected hands and smiles. "My parents—and Miles's father, too—have a lot of *issues*. But what do I always say, Miles? Found family is *way* better than blood. People who support you unconditionally because they *want* to, not because of some family bond, those are your real family. Like my business partners . . . They're are good as gold to me, and I've known them for less than a decade."

Miles raises a brow at his uncle. "You're saying this as my *literal* blood uncle."

Rajit laughs. "True, but you know I *chose* you. Even if we're related."

I must look confused, so Miles explains. "Rajit says he chose Toronto when he left Florida because he wanted to be close to his only *cool* nephew."

I wonder how much of that was because he knew Miles's parents weren't the best, so he wanted Miles to have some decent family nearby. I smile. I really like this guy.

"I always knew he was a unique one," Rajit says. "Miles is my kindred spirit. A sign reader, like me. Are you a sign reader, Sana?" I have no idea what Rajit is talking about. He laughs. "There are two kinds of people—sign readers and people who can move through the world without the unignorable urge to read every sign they see."

I'm still confused. "What kind of signs?" I glance at Miles, and he looks a little embarrassed, but he doesn't say anything.

"Any sign," Rajit says. "Street signs, new restaurants, billboards. This guy." He puts his hand on Miles's shoulder briefly. "He's big on historical plaques. I remember when we all went to Montreal when Miles was a little kid, and his mother had to ban him from reading signs. Every two steps in Old Montreal, he had to read the whole plaque about what happened there. Museums take three times as long with him."

Miles is still a cute shade of pink. I can totally see little Miles reading every historical sign he sees. I remember his comment so long ago about how there should be a plaque at LOL Park commemorating that Lionel Love guy.

"And it's not just historical signs," Rajit continues. "You know those signs that they put up at construction sites talking about what's going to happen? He'll cross a busy intersection so he can study those."

"Notice of Proposed Development Application signs," Miles says. "They're to let the public know that someone has put in an application to change the zoning for a site."

I smile. I get why Rajit is telling me all this. Miles's curiosity . . . his drive to understand everything about a place and its history and how future changes can impact the people who live there is why Miles is amazing. It's what makes him . . . *him*. It's only making me like him more.

Our food arrives then, and Rajit leaves us alone to eat. As Miles promised, the food is all excellent. The balance of flavors is completely on point—the right amount of acidity, the perfect amount of spice, and a touch of sweetness in the fresh yogurt that brings it all together. I moan after popping another pani puri in my mouth.

"Good, right?"

"Better than good. I wish this place were closer. Actually, that might be dangerous."

"Yeah, it's probably a good thing that I can't eat here every day."

"Rajit seems great."

"He is. I told you, he's more of a friend than family."

"I'm glad you have that here. I mean . . ." I don't know how to say this. I exhale. "I understand how horrible it feels when you're an afterthought to your parents. Finding someone who has your back *is* as good as gold."

Miles smiles at that. "Did your parents treat you like an afterthought when they split?"

"My father did." I sigh. "It's complicated. My mom and I get along, but we're not, like, super tight or anything.

And my dad . . . That's a whole other issue. I like what your uncle said—that the people who are real, who support you because they *want* to, not because they feel they have to—those are the important people. It's like my Love Street people. Jenn, Julie, Ajit, April, Cara. Even Mrs. Kotch. We have our own little found family. And now you're one of us too. Whether you want to be or not. You're stuck with us."

He laughs. "Somehow I think I should be grateful for getting stuck with all of you."

"All of us?" I ask coyly.

And he grins. "One of you more than others."

"I'm happy to be stuck with you, too, Miles Desai."

That night I have an idea. Something that I want to surprise Miles with at the festival. I do some research online to see if it's possible, and unfortunately, I don't think there's enough time.

Unless . . . maybe Su Lin Tran can help fast-track it for me. I send her an email.

This will show him how grateful I am to him. Miles deserves this for opening my eyes to all the potential in this city.

CHAPTER TWENTY-ONE

COMPLETE RELATIONSHIP BLISS

The next three weeks go by in a blur because we're incredibly busy with the festival preparations. Vendors are approved, rentals finalized, and entertainment is lined up. After the logo is approved, April and Julie do an amazing job on all the marketing assets, signage, and pole banners. We did have to pay for rush printing in order to get the items on time, but Ajit has an uncle with a print shop, so we still got a deal. We partner with Ali, that guy I met at Riverdale Park, to get official T-shirts made, and I put up notices at my school asking for volunteers for the day of the festival, so we have plenty of teens looking to get the community service hours they need to graduate lined up.

The park installation preparations are going well, too. Mom bought the eight-foot, heart-shaped floral frame, and ordered flowers in pink, red, and white with a few accents of yellow and purple. We decided to focus on inexpensive "filler" flowers to keep the cost down, but I have no doubt that we can make them into something spectacular. I do a digital painting of the planned sculpture and upload it to the Love on Love Street social media channels, which are already buzzing with excitement from so many Toronto bloggers and influencers.

Somewhere in those chaotic three weeks, I had my high school graduation, which felt weird. Anytime Mom and Dad are in the same room ends up feeling like that. They sat together, maybe to make a show of putting their dislike of each other aside for my benefit, but honestly, their tight smiles and fake civility were so transparent. Noureen's fakeness was particularly nauseating. I honestly cannot be expected to live in the same house with her in September.

Miles and I have also officially been a couple for three weeks. He wanted to come to my graduation too, but it seemed too soon to have him at a family event, and I didn't want to subject him to the awkward tension in my family, especially when he's got his own to deal with.

We see each other at the festival meetings, of course. And we squeeze time alone whenever we can, usually after work. We spend a lot of time hanging out on my balcony drinking tea at night. I wish we could be alone somewhere *indoors*, since Mom is usually waiting inside when we're out there, but for now the balcony will have to do. Despite the hectic few weeks, I don't remember ever being happier.

"I can't believe the festival is in *four* days," I say. We're sitting on the wood floor of my balcony, with him against the brick wall next to the door and me between his legs, leaning on his chest. I'm so content that I'm practically purring like Zuri.

"I know," he says. "I think a part of me never thought we could pull it off."

"Of course we could pull it off," I say, grinning. "We've worked our asses off and have a great committee." I'm super proud of what we've done. "It's funny, my dad used to say I was an *idea* person, not an *execution* person. It feels good to be *executing* my vision."

"What was he talking about? Like what kind of ideas didn't you execute?"

"Oh, tons of stuff. Like in grade six I wanted to start my own business selling hand-painted press-on nails and bought a bunch of stuff for it, but then school got busy and I had to help my mom with a few big orders in the flower shop. Oh, and before that it was friendship bracelets, dog walking, and cat sitting. Big ideas, no follow-through."

"Sana, you were like, what, twelve or younger for any of those. You were a kid."

"I'm still a kid. I'm only seventeen." I know Miles is only a year older, but it feels like there's a world of difference in that year. He's living on his own and working to pay his rent. I just graduated from high school and live with my mom.

"Yeah, but you work two jobs. You were the chair of your school's prom committee and the festival committee. Don't believe your father—you're one of the most driven and responsible people I know."

I don't know what to say to that. I'm not sure anyone has ever said it to me.

"Seriously, Sana," he says. "People assume you're shallow or flighty because you dress girlie and talk about romance all the time, but you're not."

"*You* thought that about me," I say.

Miles exhales, then tightens his arms around me. I don't think I'll ever get over how much I like being in his arms. When we're connected like this, it feels like the whole world around us disappears. "I was wrong," he says. "There's nothing shallow about you, Sana."

I turn so he can kiss me then, and it's as good as it always is. Better. I'm in so deep with this guy. Deeper than I thought was possible.

I'm smiling when we break free. "You're the sweetest person I've ever met," I say.

He's smiling too. "I meant it," he says.

"I also made assumptions," I say. "I thought you were stuck-up and smug. I'm glad I was wrong."

He shrugs. "I was a little smug when we met. But . . . you shouldn't *believe* all these things people—especially your father—say about you."

"I'm working on it." I exhale. "You know my father's not even coming to the festival? I told him about it. I don't even know if he's proud of me for this."

Miles kisses my cheek. "I'm proud of you."

I smile. "I'm proud of us both. We did this."

He responds to that by kissing me. And then kissing me again. And I completely forget what we were talking about because there's nothing more important than getting lost in Miles Desai's kiss right now.

When I finally go into the apartment, Mom is on the couch surrounded by scissors, twine, glue, and other craft supplies. "Oh, you finally came inside."

What's that about? "Yeah, Miles and I were out back. What are you doing?"

"I'm trying, and failing, to make rustic-chic vases for a barn wedding." She's still fiddling with the twine and isn't looking at me. "You're seeing a lot of him, aren't you?"

I raise a brow. A few weeks ago she was convinced that Miles would be good for me, and now she has an issue with me spending time with him? "I mean, that's kind of the point of dating someone, isn't it? *Seeing* them?" I sit on the armchair. Zuri immediately climbs into my lap and starts purring.

"Do I need to talk to you about preventing pregnancy?"

I roll my eyes. What exactly is Mom's problem tonight? "Mother, first of all, you know I'm not a virgin, and you know I know how to prevent pregnancy, considering you explained it to me when I was, what, eleven? And second, where and when do you think Miles and I are potentially making babies? Considering we're both working long hours *and* planning a festival, the balcony is the only place we've been anywhere near alone in weeks. And neither of us is an exhibitionist." I'm hoping to rectify the fact that we're never alone as soon as the festival ends, but I'm not about to tell my mother that.

Mom sighs and starts wrapping the twine around a mason jar. "Just . . . be smart. I see a bit of my relationship with your father in you two."

I scowl at her. So that's what's on her mind. "Miles is *nothing* like Dad. He likes and *respects* me for who I am. Don't project your relationship mistakes on me."

Mom puts her jar down and turns to face me. "That's not fair, Sana. I don't want to see you get hurt."

"And Miles *won't* hurt me. He's honest."

"I'm not saying he *would* hurt you," Mom says.

"But you think because he's more introverted and academic, he won't appreciate me the way Dad didn't appreciate you." I did worry weeks ago that Miles was too stuffy for me, but those doubts are long gone. "Miles is attentive, generous, and he *likes* my . . . positivity. He supports me the way I am."

Mom sighs. "I don't think Miles doesn't support you because I don't really know him. But I *do* know you, Sana, and I know you see things through rose-colored glasses, *especially* about relationships. That's not a bad thing. The rest of us could learn to be more optimistic. But I've seen more of the world than you. I don't want you to miss red flags because of those rosy glasses you wear."

"I'm not a naive child," I say. I'm totally capable of seeing issues in my own relationship. After all, I'm the one who broke up with Priya when we weren't working anymore.

"I know you're not a child." Mom smiles. "Hell, sometimes I think you're wiser than me. You're an idealist, and look what that idealism has accomplished this summer! I'm so proud of all you've done to make this festival happen."

"All Miles *and* I have done. We complement each other."

Mom nods. "You're right. You're a great pair. But remember, there's nothing wrong with being cautious with your heart. To protect it a little bit."

I don't respond to that because I don't know what to say. Mom's wrong. I *know* I can be a little wide-eyed, and I know I wanted a relationship so much a few months ago that I would have settled for less, but that doesn't mean my eyes aren't open to any issues that might be here now. Miles and I are great together. But I also know that arguing with my mother won't get me anywhere. Not when we're both stubborn.

Mom picks up her jar and paints some glue onto it. "The flowers for the heart sculpture will be in on Friday. I've set aside the morning to build it. We're both going to have a busy weekend—I also have a wedding on Saturday night. Thankfully, it's pretty small."

I nod.

"Sana, after the festival, on Sunday, how about you and I go for brunch? Just us."

Brunch is really more a Noureen thing, but I don't have plans with Dad on Sunday. "Why?"

"Why not? We've both been so busy. I think we deserve a treat."

I shrug. "Okay. Let's do brunch."

Mom smiles as she wraps twine on the jar. "Good. Everything is falling into place. By the way, I have a meeting up north after the store closes tomorrow, and I'll be home late. I'll eat at my parents'."

Despite her judgmental comments about me and Miles, Mom actually seems to be in a good mood this week. Maybe she's not worried about sales anymore? Or her mortgage? Maybe she got a big new wedding. I feel kind of bad—I've been so wrapped up in festival planning and my new relationship that I haven't thought much about Mom's money issues. But Mom has been super busy lately—I can't remember the last time she didn't have at least two big events in a week. Maybe the early festival promotion is already helping the flower shop business? I rub Zuri's head, then shrug. Maybe Mom will talk to me about how the store is doing when we have brunch on Sunday.

I smile as I realize something. Miles and I had plans to go to Chinatown for cheap dumplings tomorrow night, but now . . . maybe we should change that? I grab my phone to text him.

Sana: Wanna skip dumpling night tomorrow?

Miles: I was looking forward to it. Why?

Sana: Okay wanna relocate dumpling night tomorrow? Mom's going up to my grandparents after the flower shop closes. We can get dumplings from the grocery store and have them at my place. Alone. Or we can completely skip the dumpling part.

Miles: Alone?

Sana: Just you, me and Zuri. All alone. For hours.

Miles: Yes let's skip Chinatown. I have a meeting in the afternoon but then I'm free.

Sana: Meeting for what? Did I forget a festival meeting?

Miles: No nothing like that. A school thing. But now I know I'll be distracted. I'll only be thinking about seeing you later.

I grin. Tomorrow night can't come fast enough.

The next day I'm working with Jenn at Cosmic all day. She's in the back going through the pieces that she sourced specifically for Cosmic's booth at the festival, pricing them and steaming out the wrinkles to make sure they look their best, while I watch the front of the store, which is pretty busy for a Wednesday.

Whenever I have a free moment, I work on my laptop, finalizing the festival volunteer schedule, the duty list for all the committee members, and my own to-do list starting at six a.m. on Saturday. I'm so engrossed in my document that it takes me a second to realize that a customer is standing in front of me at the counter.

Wait, not a customer. It's Su Lin Tran.

She's with three people, and all of them, including Su Lin, are in business suits, and they're not looking like they're here for vintage clothes. I smile widely at them anyway.

"Hi, Ms. Tran!" I say.

"Please, Sana, call me Su Lin." She smiles warmly. "These are some associates, Robert, Kirsten, and Ashwin. I brought them by so you could tell them a bit about the Love on Love Street Festival."

Talking about the festival always gets me excited, so I tell them all about our plans and pass out our festival brochure, which lists all the events. I don't know who these people are . . . maybe other city councillors? They're probably the kind of people Miles needs to impress to get the connections he wants, so I make sure to mention his involvement with the festival.

I wasn't sure about her when we first met her at her office that day, but without Su Lin Tran, the Love on Love Street Festival wouldn't be happening at all. She's been great any time we needed to get through red tape or get permits quickly for the festival, and she even helped me get the super-secret surprise for Miles. She really cares about the festival and Love Street.

I try to size up the other people while I'm talking to them. Robert looks old, like my grandparents' age, but the other two are younger, closer to Su Lin's and my parents' age. They ask me a few questions about how we advertised the event and how many people we're expecting.

"It's so remarkable that their planning committee is chaired by two teenagers," Su Lin says. "It's a great feel-good story. We've reached out to the press about it—several big outlets will be at the festival. Miles and Sana are the city's future!" Su Lin always sounds like she's trying to sell something, but I've learned that's just how she talks. Politicians.

"An event like this could bring a lot of attention to this area," Kirsten says.

"That's exactly why we're doing it," I say. "The businesses on the street noticed that people weren't coming out here as much. I've lived here since I was nine, and it used to be so much busier."

Robert seems curious about that. "You live on the street too?"

I nod. "Yes, above my mother's flower shop." I point to Morgan Ashton Flowers across the street.

"Oh!" Ashwin says, his eyes brightening. "Of course! You're Sana *Merali*, aren't you! You probably don't remember me, but we met years ago. I'm a friend of your father's. You've grown so much!"

The other men and Su Lin smile and say things like "small world," but my mind races. How does this man know my father? Ashwin is South Asian and looks about my dad's age, but he doesn't look familiar at all.

"You must be excited about your mother's new venture," Ashwin says. "How wonderful that you're involved with the festival that's making this street even better. It won't be recognizable in a few years!"

My breath hitches. What is he talking about? Mom doesn't have a new venture. And why will the street be unrecognizable? Because it will be busier?

"Do you think the festival will make it easier to find tenants for new storefronts?" Su Lin asks.

"Absolutely," the oldest man says. "I have no doubt this neighborhood will be an East End hot spot. Everyone will want to be on Love Street—selling units and leasing storefronts will be a piece of cake."

The four of them keep talking, but I honestly don't hear them. My heart is racing, and the room spins. *What new storefronts?*

It suddenly comes to me. *Did Mom sell her building?*

"Um." Jenn clears her throat behind me. I didn't notice that she'd come out of the back room. "I need to speak to Sana urgently. I hate to be rude, but I'm going to have to ask you to excuse us."

Su Lin waves her hand. "Oh no, don't be concerned. We were done anyway. So wonderful to see you, Sana! And don't worry. I haven't breathed a word to Miles about your little surprise." She looks at the others. "Sana arranged for a historical placard about Lionel Osmond Love for the park! She wants to surprise Miles with it since he admires Love for all he did for the city."

"How amazing," Ashwin says. "This all makes perfect sense. When your father referred Miles for an internship, he said he was a friend of his daughter's and she spoke highly of him. You're absolutely correct. Miles *is* a remarkable young man. I'm so happy we had an opportunity for him!"

Wait. . . . My heart starts pounding in my chest. Miles is *interning* with these people? And *my father* referred him for the position? I clutch the counter with white knuckles.

Why didn't Miles tell me? Does Miles know that my mother *sold* her building?

Has anyone been honest with me in the last few weeks at all? Or am I just as naive and dazzled by my shiny new relationship as Mom said I was to see what's going on in my own life?

CHAPTER TWENTY-TWO

THE BACKROOM BETRAYAL

Jenn puts an arm on my shoulder. "I'm sorry you heard that, Sana."

I turn sharply and look at Jenn. "Mom *sold* the building, didn't she?"

Jenn nods, but she doesn't say anything.

I can't believe it. Mom sold her building and didn't tell me. Which I suppose isn't a surprise—I did overhear Mom and Jenn talking about it months ago. But that day Mom *also* said she wouldn't do anything without talking to me first.

"She's closing the store? Where are we going to live?"

Jenn picks up her phone. "This is something your mother should talk to you about. I'll call her."

After a short phone call, Jenn tells me that Mom will meet me here at Cosmic in ten minutes. She must be closing the flower shop for this. And I guess it doesn't matter, since she sold it anyway. I cross my arms and sit on the stool behind the counter. My hands can't stop shaking.

I know those people with Su Lin were real estate developers. The kind that Julie was talking about, ones who want to tear up Love Street. They said all the work we did for the festival would make the street attractive for *new* storefronts, so clearly they're kicking out the stores that are already here. I did all this work to keep Love Street the way it is, and those people saw it as a reason to destroy it.

Miles, too.

That man, Ashwin, clearly said Miles had an *internship* with him. Was that who Miles was meeting today? Why did my *father*, of all people, refer Miles for the job?

I don't think I've ever, in my whole life, felt as betrayed by the people I care about most. Mom, Jenn, Miles. Hell, even Dad. Maybe even Sarina knew. After all, Sarina and Miles have recently become friends. Sarina even asked Miles to keep secrets from me, whatever they are.

But my family has *never* talked about serious things with me. To them, I'm too immature to handle the truth, too sensitive for the hard reality of life, and too frivolous for important conversations. I'm used to it—I don't expect them to see the real me.

That's why what Miles did hurts the most.

Miles *did* see me. He respected me for my optimism and for my romanticism about my street. He knew how much I wanted Love Street to thrive. And most of all, he *promised* we'd be honest with each other. He broke that promise.

Mom was right. Miles is just like my father.

Mom walks into the store then, her face as white as a ghost. She's in her regular floral-arranging outfit of overalls with a bandanna around her hair. Classic crunchy granola Mom. But it turns out Mom's a sellout to developers after all.

"Sana, I'm sorry you found out about the sale that way," Mom says as she walks toward me, shaking her head. "I wanted to tell you myself . . . after the festival."

"Why *after* the festival?" I spit out, bitter. "Is it because you didn't want me to stop working on the event? The event that's only making the street more attractive to developers who are going to bulldoze it all to the ground?"

Mom shakes her head. "Sana, that's not fair."

"Why don't you guys go to the back room?" Jenn says gently. It's probably a good idea. There are customers in here. Jenn gives my arm a little rub.

I exhale. I know I don't have much of a choice but to hear Mom out.

The back room at Cosmic is bigger than the ones across the street where the flower shop is. In fact, all the stores on this side are bigger, and newer. Not exactly new—I think this building is fifteen years old. But the buildings across the street where the flower shop is are over sixty years old. And, of course, on this side there are already condos above the stores. Four stories of them.

I guess that's what they want to do across the street. Stores with condos above them. Except probably even more than four stories. One of those mixed-use neighborhoods that Miles loves. I sit on one of the chairs that Jenn keeps back here and put my head in my hands. I don't want to look at Mom right now.

"Sana, they aren't going to bulldoze Love Street to the ground," Mom says. "Everyone's goal here is the same. To turn this street into a vibrant, sustainable . . . *affordable* community."

I huff at that. No one is going to be able to afford brand-new condos. I look up at her. "Why did you do it, Mom? Without even talking to me. You didn't even give the festival a chance to turn the street around." I don't tell her that I overheard her months ago telling Jenn that she wouldn't do this without telling me. I don't want her to know I was eavesdropping.

Mom sighs and sits on another chair. We're surrounded by racks of clothes. I can see one rack only has red and pink pieces. That must be for the festival booth. "I've been getting offers to sell for a while," Mom says. "We all have on our side of the street. I always refused. I know how much you love it here, and this community is so special. But . . ." She sighs. "Sana, it's time. You're finished high school. Your grandparents are getting older. They need me closer to them. And, honestly, walk-in sales aren't high enough to cover the costs of the building."

I shake my head. "But the whole reason for planning the festival was for *us*! The flower installation in the park is specifically to bring new customers to the flower shop. And it will." Does she think of me the same way my father does? That I'm all vision and no execution? I'm hurt. I thought my mother had more faith in my abilities.

"I know, honey. I appreciate all you've done. Really." Mom reaches out and squeezes my arm, but I pull it away and cross my arms in front of me. I try to ignore the hurt look on her face. "I'm not closing Morgan Ashton Flowers, just adapting to a changing market. People don't wander into the neighborhood florist to get a bouquet for their sweetheart anymore. Everything is done online. I can run an online florist out of a warehouse space up north for a fraction of what I'm paying here. And a bigger space would mean I can do more large floral installations like what we're doing for the festival. I'm going to look at a space tonight actually. It's ten minutes from your Nani and Nana's house."

I blink. So that's where Mom's going tonight. Here I was, excited that Miles and I will finally have some time alone, not knowing my mom is in the middle of uprooting our whole lives.

"What does Dad have to do with this?" I shake my head, trying to process this giant blow. "There was a developer guy here who said he knew Dad."

"Your father brokered the sale. He's been trying to convince me to sell for years, but he knew I wouldn't while you still wanted to live here."

I make a sour face. "Is that why he asked me to move in with him in September?"

"He asked you to move in with him?" Mom's brows knit together. "I'm sorry, Sana, I had no idea. That's so . . . manipulative. He was probably trying to take away my opposition to selling. You don't have to live with him if you don't want to."

"I have zero intention of moving in with Dad and Noureen." But where *will* I live? It's more than I want to deal with right now. I'm starting university in, like, six weeks. "You know Dad's manipulative. Why are you selling to him?"

Mom shrugs. "I'm not selling *to* your father. He's only the agent on the deal. And, at the end of the day, your father's financial well-being is important to me, because my favorite person in the world is his daughter."

I don't say anything to that. My parents have finally figured out how to work together, and they're working to take away my home.

"These developers aren't the bad guys," Mom says. "I liked their plans. Even Jenn likes them. They are one of the few housing developers committed to providing medium-density, affordable housing for the city. The storefronts will all be modern and larger, and there will be fifty housing units above. There will even be units set aside for the rental market. One of the founders of the company used to be a planner for the city. They want to build a whole community—with commercial and residential together."

"We already *have* a community."

"Sana, it's all falling apart. The land is worth more. And there's a housing crisis in the city."

"They are going to *gentrify* Love Street. They're going to bring in chain stores and kick everyone out like Mrs. Kozlak, and the street will look like every 'trendy' new area with no unique charm." I'm pouting and rambling, but I think I'm entitled.

Mom doesn't say anything to that because she knows I'm right. I wipe away a tear. "I don't get why you didn't tell me. I'm not a kid. This is my life too."

After a few moments of silence, Mom finally speaks. "I know. I'm sorry." She sighs. "I *just* accepted the offer. I haven't even signed the final paperwork yet. You've been so focused on the festival; I didn't want this news to get in your way. And I don't want the other businesses on the street to know yet. I'm the first to sell."

I don't think that's a good enough excuse. I know my mother still sees me as a little kid, and I hate proving her right, but in this moment all I want to do is throw a tantrum.

"I hate change," I say. I wonder what people thought fifteen years ago when the old stores on this side of the street—where Cosmic Vintage and LoveBug are—were torn down. Were they upset that Love Street was changing? Were they angry about new condos in the area?

Mom smiles sadly. "I know, sweetheart. But things are going to change whether we want them to or not. This way we can at least have some control of what the future will look like."

The fact I can't deny is that I *know* Mom's been stressed. I *know* the flower shop is struggling. Switching to an online shop is a smart idea. And being closer to Nani and Nana will make things easier for Mom. If she does nothing, then her flower shop could go under, and she'd lose everything she worked so hard for.

I exhale, uncrossing my arms. "So where will you live? With Nani and Nana? It would take me two hours to get to OCAD from their place."

She shakes her head. "It wouldn't be that bad. There's a train into the city. Or . . ." She hesitates.

"Or what?"

Mom shrugs. "We'll figure something out, Sana. Something that works for both of us. You won't have to live with your father, but we don't need to think about it now. The festival is only a few days away. I didn't want to burden you with all this yet. And tonight you have a date with Miles, don't you? You need to enjoy that."

I shake my head. "Miles has been keeping this from me too," I say. I tell Mom what the developer said about Miles interning with them.

Mom frowns. "He didn't tell you that he took a job with them?"

"No. I knew he was looking for an internship, but I didn't know he was applying at *developers*. The man said

Dad referred him. Miles definitely didn't tell me that."

"How does your father even know Miles?"

I shrug. "I assume through Sarina." I remember Dad mentioning that Miles was supposed to join them for dinner once. I knew I shouldn't have attempted to set him up with my stepsister. "This seems like the kind of thing a guy should tell his girlfriend, don't you think? He's conspiring with the enemy."

"I agree he should have told you, but Sana, these people *aren't* the enemy. Neither is your father. Miles wants what's best for the city and the people who live here."

That's what I *thought*. I think back to that streetcar ride. I can't believe the person who talked passionately about all the things he loves about Toronto worked with developers to tear down my street. I don't understand why he didn't tell me. Why be secretive? Because he knew I wouldn't be happy about him working there? Or . . . he didn't see the need to really let a naive, idealistic romantic into the serious parts of his life.

"You warned me," I say. "You said he was like Dad."

Mom exhales but doesn't say anything. I don't think she wanted to be right about that.

"He lied to me, Mom," I add. Withholding important information is lying. Mom knows firsthand what it's like to be lied to by someone you love.

"This relationship is serious for you, isn't it?" Mom asks.

I let out a shaky breath. "It *was*." I wipe my eyes. "You were right, though. I ignored all the red flags. I feel so stupid. . . . I *should* know what I'm doing. I mean, I read enough romance novels to have a PhD in romance, right?

And yet here's another relationship failure for me."

Mom smiles sadly. "Real life isn't like the books, Sana. Relationships are hard and messy and complicated. I don't know what's going to happen with you and Miles, but I do know that each of you should feel like you can share all the parts of yourself with the other. If you feel the need to hold something back . . . to hide part of who you are to keep your partner happy, then it's not sustainable. It's not worth it. . . . Being single is preferable." She chuckles. "Look at me, trying to give parental advice. What do I know about anything?"

I shake my head. "No, this is good advice, Mom. Thanks." I finally lock eyes with her and give her a tearful smile. "It *almost* makes me forgive you," I joke.

Mom huffs a small laugh.

I wonder how much of themselves my parents hid from each other. It also makes me think of what Miles told me weeks ago—that love changes people, and not for the better. Dad changed after he got with Noureen. He's no longer the type to spend an aimless day at a festival with his daughter. And Cara even changed the way she *dressed* for Hannah.

Relationships *are* messy and complicated. They are more than just meet-cutes and swoony moments. And Miles was right. It *does* hurt so much when things go wrong.

Are relationships worth it?

"We should talk like this more often," I say.

Mom nods. "Yeah, we should. Sometimes I forget that you're all grown-up. I'm sorry I didn't talk to you before accepting that offer."

I'm not sure I fully forgive her, but I understand. "We're still a team, right?"

She nods. I notice that Mom's eyes are a little glassy too. "Two peas in a pod."

"Do you want me to come look at that property with you tonight?" I ask. Maybe it would help me understand this decision better.

She shakes her head. "No, I'll manage." She gets up. "But I should be going. The meeting is in a few hours. I need to finish some centerpieces first."

"Okay. Good luck tonight. Love you, Mom."

She nods, then leans down to kiss me on the forehead. "Love you too, sunshine."

CHAPTER TWENTY-THREE

MORE MIND-BLOWING REVELATIONS

I sit alone in Jenn's back room for a while after Mom leaves. That was a lot to take in. I don't think my mother has *ever* been so open with me, and I'm not used to it. I wish she'd talked to me before agreeing to sell, but I do understand why she did it.

That doesn't mean the whole situation doesn't suck monkey balls.

I hate the thought of living somewhere other than on Love Street. I want to be able to look out my window and see Cosmic across the street, or LoveBug on the corner. I want to say hello to Reggie as I walk past the bookstore or grab a cookie from Mrs. Kotch's when I need the sugar hit. I hate that Love Street will turn into a construction zone, which will suck for the places that will still be here.

My whole life was turned upside down when my parents divorced too. And the hardest part about both huge changes is that I have zero control over any of it.

I can't stay here in the back room of Cosmic forever. I check the time—my shift is over anyway. When I go out to the selling floor, Jenn looks at me, her head tilted. "How are you doing, kiddo?"

I shrug. "I'm not happy about it, but I get it."

"I'll still be here," Jenn says. "You know you'll always

have a job here if you want it. And not just because you're practically family—you're my best employee."

I shake my head. "That will depend on where I'll be living, won't it?" If I'll be commuting two hours to school every day, I won't be able to work here at Cosmic.

The door to the store opens. It's Miles.

Because of course it is. Tonight's our *big date*. We were finally going to be alone.

But now . . . looking at him, in his preppy blue button-up shirt with dress pants, I wonder again if his meeting today was with those developers. Why didn't he tell me?

A better question is why did I ever think someone like him was right for me? He called me naive when we met. And I guess I proved him right. A naive, idealistic child who thought she could preserve her idyllic little street just by planning a festival.

His expression tells me he has no idea that I know about his secret new job. His eyes are bright, and a small smile tugs at the corners of his mouth.

"You ready to go? We can walk over to the Asian grocery to get frozen dumplings."

I shake my head. I don't want to speak because I know my voice will betray how hurt I am.

His brows knit together with concern. "What's wrong, Sana? Everything okay?"

I exhale. "No, it's not okay." I look at Jenn. I don't want to fight with my boyfriend in her store. "I'll see you later, Jenn. Thanks for . . . you know."

I walk out the door, and Miles follows me. He clearly has no idea what's bothering me. Which pisses me off more. How long did he think he could keep this from me?

I walk fast. I have no idea where I'm going, or if I'm running away from him, but I feel like I have to keep moving. When I get to my favorite bench at LOL Park, I sit heavily and put my head in my hands. He's next to me with his hand on my back in seconds.

"Sana, tell me what's wrong. Did something happen?" His voice is gentle. Caring.

I have no doubt that Miles really does care about me. Like my dad really cared for my mom once. But it's not enough. They both lied.

I shake his hand off my back and glare at him. "Why are you pretending you don't know what's wrong, when all along you *knew* that developers were going to destroy half this street?"

"What? What are you talking about? What developers?"

"The ones you took an *internship* with."

He doesn't say anything for a few seconds. I turn away. I can't look at him. Because I'm afraid that one look at those big, concerned eyes is all it will take for me to forget everything.

So I stare at the park. There are wispy white dandelions gone to seed all over the patch of grass where there will be a stage in three days, just like I wanted. I look at the path where the flower heart is going to be. I look at the brick wall where the mural full of tiles will be installed. Where people will permanently declare their love for someone. Only, will it even be permanent? Or will that be destroyed too?

What was the point of even doing any of this?

"I'm sorry," Miles says. "I was going to tell you that I got a job. It happened so fast."

"When were you going to tell me, Miles? Were you going to tell me when I found out that my mother sold her *building* to them and is moving the flower shop? Or . . ." My voice cracks. I can't help it. "Or were you going to tell me when I moved away from Love Street?"

"Your mother *sold* her building?" There's shock in his voice, which I don't get. If he works there, shouldn't he have known that?

"Yes, to the condo developers that *you* work for. They are going to make a killing—now that the community is getting noticed because of all our hard work for the festival. Isn't that why they hired you? Because you increased their profits?" There's venom in my voice. I look to see his reaction.

Miles looks like he doesn't know what to say. He told me before that things in this city needed to change to be fair for everyone, because right now the city is failing the most marginalized. He said he wants the city to *thrive*. But now I wonder if he's including the *corporations* who will thrive and *profit* off all the work people do to make communities special.

I shake my head. "You're the one who said it," I say, waving my hand toward the shops on Love Street. "All this should be higher-density housing. And now it's happening. Developers and chain stores are *salivating* to get here. The people who live here now are never going to be able to afford brand-new condos, and the developers are going to make a killing. You and my father were twirling your mustaches the whole time, weren't you?"

He recoils. "Your father? I . . ."

"Yes, I *know* that my father referred you for that job.

I cannot believe you would keep that from me. Just like you kept the fact that you were going to have dinner at his house from me." Why did I ever think I could trust him when he *still* hasn't told me about that dinner? I shake my head. "I'm going home. It's been a long day, and I have to feed my cat."

He shakes his head. "I don't—Sana, please give me a chance to explain! I only accepted the internship today! I was going to tell you tonight. And—"

"Jobs don't fall out of the sky unannounced, Miles! How long ago did my *father* refer you for a position at his buddy's company?"

He doesn't respond to that.

"Okay, let's make the question a bit easier for you to understand. How and *when* did my father refer you for a job?"

He sighs. "After High Park, Sarina and I were talking on the way home. I told her I was having trouble getting an internship and said I was hoping to work either in the public sector or with an ethical developer. She said her stepfather knew a lot of developers, so when the car dropped her off, I went in and met him. I talked to him for about ten minutes about what kind of place I want to work at. He said he would ask around and wrote the names of a few developers he thought would be a good fit and—"

"And he put the list into one of his envelopes?" I ask. Miles looks confused. "I saw one of my father's envelopes in your bag. I thought Sarina gave it to you." Miles wisely doesn't say anything about me snooping in his things. "My father also once said you were going to join them for dinner at his house." I should have asked Miles about that right away. I don't know why I didn't. Maybe a part of me was afraid of this from the beginning. I realize something else. That man—Ashwin—said when Dad referred Miles, he said Miles was a friend of his daughter's. But Dad was talking about *Sarina*, not me.

Miles nods. "He invited me that day to come to dinner the next Friday. I said yes because . . . I mean . . . he was helping me find a job, and I needed a job. But then I canceled because I went to your prom that night. We didn't reschedule. He emailed me a few days later saying a developer friend of his had an intern drop out, and I should call him." Miles looks at me. "That's all that happened. I didn't speak to your dad again. I didn't tell you because I knew you would be upset. I know he's not your favorite person . . . but I was desperate. Sana, I *needed* a paid internship, or I'd have to move back home with my family. I can't do that."

I close my eyes. Moving back home would be torture for him. Exactly like it would be hard for me to move in with my dad and Noureen. I exhale, staring in front of me. I don't even know what to say.

"Honestly, Sana," he says. "I didn't know they wanted to build *here* on Love Street."

I open my eyes, but I still don't look at him. Does it matter if he knew? He still kept this job from me. Just like Mom kept the fact that she was selling the building from me. Just like Dad kept all of this from me. Plus, Jenn, Sarina, and Noureen . . . all keeping poor naive Sana in the dark.

I stand. All my sadness has turned to anger. "I've heard enough. You and I are *done*."

I walk out of LOL Park without looking back. Here's hoping that the festival on Saturday will be the last time I see Miles Desai.

When I get to the apartment, there's a note from my mother on the table that says she made some lentil soup and it's in the slow cooker. She must have left it before Jenn called her to tell her I was crying in the store.

This is why it's so hard for me to be mad at Mom for what she did. She's sometimes distant and needs to stop treating me like a baby, but she's my *mom*. She hates cooking, and she still made me soup. She takes care of me. She makes sure that I'm safe and okay. And she's doing the best she can.

That's what all of us on this street are doing—our best. Our best to keep afloat in this expensive city. Our best to look out for one another. Our best to keep the little community that has always had our back.

I hug Zuri close. I don't know how I'm going to leave this street. And I don't know how I'm going to forget Miles.

There's a knock on the apartment door. Keeping Zuri on my shoulder, I open the door. It's Cara, and she's holding some brown paper bags. Why is she here? "I have cake and empanadas. I heard you might need them."

"Aren't you supposed to be working?"

She nods, then comes in and closes the door behind her. "I *am* working. Technically on the clock. Jenn told me my duties for tonight are to support my friend who needs me. She called Mrs. Kotch and Ben and told them you needed some cheer-up treats, and they donated these day-olds. Ajit is currently making a masala chai for you and a matcha latte for me, and Charlene will bring them over when they're ready."

I shake my head, amazed. I love this community. Cara starts unpacking the food onto the table. Looks like we have two of Mrs. Kotch's Cakes for Two and four big veggie empanadas.

"Wow. This is a lot," I say.

Cara nods. "Yep. Grab some plates and then talk, because I have no idea what happened."

I get plates and forks, and we each take an empanada. Charlene shows up with our drinks, wearing a dancing hamster T-shirt. She smiles as she hands them to me, until she notices Zuri at my feet. She glares at my cat, then leaves quickly. I snort a weak laugh at that.

I hand Cara her latte and sit on my armchair with my food and tea. The sweet milky and lightly spiced scent of the chai calms me instantly. I relax after taking a sip.

"Okay, now, what happened?" Cara asks. "Something to do with the festival?"

I shake my head. "No. Well, sort of." I tell her about Su Lin and the condo developers' visit to Cosmic Vintage.

"Oh my god. She brought actual *developers* into the store?" Cara shakes her head. "She's got some nerve to bring those vultures through. No wonder you're pissed."

"There's more. One of them mentioned that they finalized negotiations to buy the flower shop and the apartment over it."

Cara's already-wide eyes grow about three times bigger. "Holy crap. *This* apartment?"

I nod. "Mom is selling . . . *has sold* this building." My voice cracks again. I still can't believe it.

"Damn. Are you moving?"

I nod.

"When?"

"Don't know yet." I sigh. "I feel betrayed. My mom, my dad, Miles . . . they all kept this from me."

"What does Miles have to do with it? Or your dad?"

"Miles took a job as an intern with the same developers. My father referred him for it. And my dad's the real estate agent who brought this opportunity to Mom." I tell her about Mom's plan for an online flower shop.

"Holy hell." Cara seems as shocked as I was.

"I know." I shake my head. "I get why she sold. I just wish she'd told me beforehand. And I can't believe Miles would keep this from me. I thought I knew him."

But I always knew, from the very beginning, that Miles didn't really believe in love. Not in the same way I do.

I take a bite of my empanada. It's filled with kale and mushrooms—my favorite. The slightly spicy filling and the rich, flaky dough are exactly what I need tonight. Carbs. Precious, delicious carbs.

"You had no idea Miles was hiding anything from you?"

I exhale. "Actually, I *did* know that he was keeping *something* from me," I say. "Something about Sarina being into someone that she didn't want me to know about. Maybe that was a lie, and maybe it was really about this internship? I should have known he would keep secrets from me. I'm such an idiot." I take another big bite.

Cara squeezes her lips together and goes very still. I feel that familiar thud of my heartbeat picking up again. She looks like she's hiding something too.

"What?" I ask.

"What, what?"

"What are you trying not to tell me?" I ask Cara. "Don't tell me you knew about this internship too—"

"No," Cara interrupts. "I promise, I had no idea about it. And I don't know if Sarina knew. It's just . . . I *do* know Sarina's secret. It's not about your dad or real estate or anything like that."

So Cara has been keeping something from me too? Cara . . . *my friend*. I put down my empanada. "Not you, too. Everyone I care about—my mother, Miles, my father, hell, even Jenn has been keeping stuff from me. Clearly no one actually trusts—"

"Stop, Sana. I . . ." Cara exhales, then looks at me. "Miles *did* set Sarina up with someone. Me. Sarina and I are . . . *dating*."

I blink, looking at Cara. Did I hear that right? "I must be hearing things because I know you didn't say you are dating my *straight* stepsister," I say. She doesn't answer. "What about Hannah?" Cara hasn't mentioned her hockey player girlfriend in a while, but I assumed that was because Cara knew I didn't approve of Hannah.

She shakes her head. "I haven't seen Hannah since she stood me and my parents up for hot pot. And Sarina isn't . . . straight. We've been dating pretty much since I stopped seeing Hannah."

"Holy crap." I shake my head. "Really? And *Miles* set you up?"

"She was apparently into me when we went to High Park that day. That's why she came—she thought you were inviting her for *me*, not Miles. She told Miles everything in the Uber because she was upset. She didn't know I would be there with Hannah. When things went bad between me and Hannah, he arranged a get-together with me and Sarina."

I exhale. "To a place on College Street?"

"Yeah, we went for dinner, then to a board game café." She's smiling small.

I shake my head. Cara and Sarina? *Dating?* On that day at High Park, Cara went with Hannah, but then Sarina hurt her ankle, and Cara came to her rescue. They had a freaking meet-cute. "And no one thought to tell me?"

"Sarina didn't want Miles or me to tell you because she was afraid her mother would find out. She's not out to her family."

I look out the window, hurt. I *wouldn't* have told Noureen or Dad about this, and I would think that my friend Cara would know that. But apparently everyone would prefer to lie to me than give me a chance to support them.

I don't say anything for a while.

"You're not mad, are you, Sana? Sarina's amazing. She's not like your stepmother at all. Really, you two have so much in common—"

My gaze jolts to Cara. "You, Sarina, even my own boyfriend all lied to my face." I shake my head. "Yes, I'm mad! I brought her there that day for Miles—"

"Yeah, but you're with Miles now, so everyone is happy!"

"Are we all happy? Because the way I see it, everyone is fine keeping me out of the loop on what's going on in their lives. Because, what . . . ? I'm not mature enough to talk to about heavy stuff? I'm Sunny Sana—fun to hang out with, but not the person you talk about your life with."

"Sana, it's not like that!" Cara says. "Sarina didn't want to come out to her mom. What did you expect me to do?"

Honestly, I kind of get it. I get why Sarina wouldn't want me to know. We've never been close, so she wouldn't know that I'd have her back. And it's messed up to out someone who doesn't want to be outed, so I get where Cara and Miles were coming from too.

It just hurts to know that everyone was okay with keeping me in the dark.

Cara looks at me for a few moments. "I'm sorry, Sana. Do you want me to go?"

I nod. I really don't want to see anyone right now who doesn't respect me enough to be honest with me. Zuri has never lied—all I need right now is my cat.

Cara takes her matcha latte and leaves my apartment.

I pull out one of the Cakes for Two and eat the whole thing in one sitting. Which is depressing, but it helps. It does remind me a little bit of Miles, but this is a vanilla cake, not red velvet, so the memories aren't that strong. Mom's still not home by the time I go to bed, which is not unexpected.

When I'm in bed, I check my phone. I'd muted Miles earlier, but now I can't resist knowing whether he tried to reach me at all. There are three texts from him.

Miles: I'm sorry. I know I screwed up. I should have told you about the position with the developer. I'm sorry.

Miles: I have to keep the job, though. I need it. I wish you'd talk to me, but I understand if you don't want to.

Miles: I hope we can still work together on Saturday. If you never want to see me again after that, then okay.

I shake my head. I can't avoid seeing him because he's supposed to work in the bookstore all summer just like I'm supposed to work at Cosmic. And Miles *loves* working at Second Story Books. He loves helping customers find their next read and talking about politics with Reggie. He even loves the smell of old books like I do. With this new condo development, the bookstore isn't going to be around for long, and I know Miles would want to be there while it's open.

I'm so mad at Miles for not being honest with me, and I'm mad at myself for falling so hard for someone who doesn't want to preserve Love Street the way I do. But . . . I don't want Miles to leave the Love Street community. I want Reggie to be looking out for him, and I want him to be doted on by Mrs. Kotch. I want him to shop at Cosmic and drink chai while talking about Bollywood with Ajit. Because he *needs* this community. Who else is going to support him every day? His parents care more about hurting each other than about taking care of their son. His uncle said that found family—people who are there for you because they *want* to be, not because of some familial obligation—is as good as gold. Other than that uncle, Miles only has his Love Street family right now.

I write back.

Sana: No. I'm not going to avoid you. We'll have to work together for the festival, and we'll see each other on the street this summer.

Miles: But you don't want to talk, right?
Sana: I need space.
Miles: Okay. Maybe one day we can be friends again.

I don't respond to that. And it's not because I'm too angry. It's because I'm not sure I can bear being *just friends* with him again.

CHAPTER TWENTY-FOUR

SISTERS ARE BETTER THAN MISTERS

I'm woken up way too early Thursday morning by a text. Miles is still muted, so I know it's not him. I check my phone. It's Sarina.

> Sarina: I'm sorry. Cara told me what happened last night. Can we talk today? I want to apologize in person. And clear the air between us.

I don't want to see my stepsister. I don't want to see anyone who's been contributing to all these lies. I want to stay with Zuri and eat that other cake for breakfast.

But . . . I'm not really mad at *Sarina*. I'm angry at Cara and Miles, but Sarina and I have never had a sister relationship. There are a hell of a lot of things I've never told her about my life, so I can't be mad at her for not telling me about hers. To be honest, I feel bad for her. I've always had a mother who's supportive of who I choose to date. It would be so hard not to have that. And considering how *not* supportive Noureen has been about *my* preferences, I have no doubt Noureen wouldn't love the fact that her daughter is dating Cara.

> Sana: Okay. I'm free today. Where?

Sarina: I can come to you. How about that cute café near Cosmic?

I really don't want to talk to her on Love Street. If we met at LoveBug, Julie or Ajit will come say hello, and Cara might come in for a coffee. Or Miles, for that matter.

Sana: No not there.

I text her the name of a new café on Gerrard that has an impressive tea selection and tell her I'll be there at ten.

The café is pretty empty when I walk in right at ten, which kind of makes sense since it's a Thursday and most people are probably at work. I see Sarina at the back at a secluded table, and she waves. I nod, then get myself a London Fog, which is basically an Earl Grey latte with vanilla, before joining her at the table.

Sarina has a mug in front of her, along with a little teapot with an infuser. She smiles, and the expression looks a bit forced. I sit on the plush red seat at her table.

"Hi, Sana. Thank you so much for agreeing to talk to me."

"No problem." I'm not exactly glaring at her, but I'm not smiling.

She looks down at the table, running her hand over the rim of her mug. "I wanted to apologize. . . . Cara told me you were mad at her. I'm so sorry I asked her to lie to you. It's totally on me. Don't be mad at Cara. Or Miles. Cara said I could trust you, but I was . . ." She looks at me. "I just . . . I made a mess of everything."

Her voice cracks, then her shoulders slump, showing me just how dejected she feels. I don't think I've ever seen Sarina like this. She's usually so calm and steady. But then again, I don't really know my stepsister that well. She still looks pretty, in a pale pink loose V-neck T-shirt, light jeans, and minimal makeup.

"You were afraid I would tell your mother that you're dating my friend," I say. My voice sounds flat.

She nods.

I shake my head. "I'm . . . Honestly, Sarina, that hurts. I know we haven't exactly ever been close, but how could you think I would do that?" I mean, Sarina knows I'm pansexual. Why would she think I wouldn't support her? I would never, *ever* out someone like that.

She exhales. "I was . . . I was scared. And . . . my mother always said that you would be . . ."

"Your mother said what?"

She looks at me with wide eyes. "My mother says you're jealous of me, and I shouldn't trust you. She says you want my life."

I raise a brow. Yeah, at times I get a little bitter about how perfect Sarina seems, but I have *never* wanted her life.

"I don't think that about you anymore," she says quickly. "I know I was a brat when we were kids. I'm sorry for that, too."

I shrug. "I wasn't exactly an angel child, either."

"I realized my mother's wrong about a lot of things when I started uni. Seriously, she messed me up so much. But she's still my mom. I know she means well—she just doesn't understand things outside her bubble."

I want to say that Noureen most definitely does not

mean well. She's never been anything but judgmental to me and Mom. She took away the chance for me to have a relationship with my father. And my stepsister.

This is messy. Trying to build a relationship with someone whose mother caused my family so much pain is probably not a great idea. Sarina's right; Noureen is still her mom. Sarina may have realized how wrong Noureen is, but I doubt Noureen ever will. But Sarina's eyes look so sad. It feels like this has been weighing on her for a long time. I can't imagine how hard it has been for her to have to keep her true self from her own mother.

I still say nothing, so Sarina keeps talking. "But now . . . I don't know. I see things differently now. I know you're not . . . my enemy."

"Then why didn't you let Cara or Miles tell me the truth?"

She looks down at her teapot and shrugs. "I should have. We were going to tell you at the festival. I . . . I was scared."

I look at her. She's never looked so . . . normal to me. Not the perfect or serene Sarina, just a regular girl who grew up kind of sheltered and who doesn't want to disappoint her mother.

Sarina has never been anywhere close to my favorite person. Inviting her to High Park that day was so hard for me—I really didn't want to do it. I was so insecure and sure that everyone would be wowed by her perfection that they wouldn't notice me. Actually, now that I think about it, it was Cara who pushed me to ask Sarina to come.

But that was the first time I ever tried to build a relationship with Sarina. And she was so sweet and friendly that day.

She said nothing passive-aggressive like her mother would have, and she got along fine with my friends. And then, the moment I heard that she hit it off with Miles on their ride home, I grew bitter about her again and decided not to contact her. Partially because I really wanted Miles for myself, but also, I was uncomfortable with the idea of perfect Sarina in my circle of friends. I thought she'd look down on me like her mother does. I thought she'd talk to Miles about me the way her mother talks about me. Despite Sarina not doing anything like that since we were kids, I didn't trust her or really give her a chance, either.

"I get it. I . . . I haven't done a good job making you feel like you *could* trust me. I mean, I was also judgmental of you," I say. "I was so sure you spent that whole Uber ride with Miles complaining about me. I guess I was influenced by your mom too. I'm sorry."

She looks up at me, a small smile on her face. "So . . . we're okay?"

I nod. "I mean . . . I think we'll be okay. I was . . . *am* upset that no one told me what was going on, but I get why. And I'm *not* upset that you're with Cara. It's hard to wrap my head around it because I've known you both separately for so long, but you two could be cute together. Especially compared to her and Hannah."

Sarina scowls at that. "Yeah. Hannah's not . . . nice. So we have your blessing?"

"You don't really need it, but yeah, you have it. And I won't tell your mother. Or my dad." I'm still a little annoyed at Cara, but Sarina is clearly so terrified of her mother that I can't blame her for not wanting to tell me. "Anyway, I think this news would have been easier for me to accept if

I hadn't *also* just found out that my mother, my father, and Miles have been lying to me about something else."

She gives me a confused look. Can I tell Sarina what happened? I don't like airing all this dirty laundry—about my mother's business not doing well and about my own boyfriend not telling me about his new job, but I kind of trust Sarina now. I feel like I can tell her these things. And weirdly I want to. I tell her everything that happened yesterday.

Sarina is clearly shocked and upset on my behalf. "Can't your dad stop this?" she asks. "I mean, if he's the one brokering the sale, can't he, like, cancel the deal?"

"Even if he could, as if Dad would do that for me. Plus, my mom *wants* to sell."

"Yeah, but your street is so cool! There must be a way she could keep the building and . . . I don't know. Rent out the space? You could ask your dad for ideas. He's pretty understanding."

I exhale. It's so weird, and wrong, that Sarina has a better relationship with my father than I do. But that isn't *her* fault either.

And there's another layer to all this. Miles. "Did you know that Miles *never* told me Dad referred him for jobs?"

Sarina shakes her head. "I had no idea it was some big secret. Miles only met your dad that one time after the cherry blossoms, as far as I know."

"Do you think Miles knew that the job was with the same developers who bought Mom's building? It seems like too much of a coincidence."

She shakes her head. "I don't think Miles is capable of being two-faced like that. He's so great. I was a mess in that Uber ride. I was so upset and embarrassed, and he was so gentle and kind. He's been a great friend since then. Honestly, Sana, he's *nuts* about you. I think . . ." She hesitates. "It was actually Miles who really made me see you differently. In the car I said you were a bit of a flake, and he defended you so . . . *vehemently.* He said it was sexist to think someone is less intelligent because they care about clothes, or makeup, or aesthetics. He's the one who made me realize just how wrong I was about you. I wish I had before."

I wish I had before too. I let my bitterness about my parents' divorce and Noureen's judgments and even our childhood rivalry get in the way of actually *seeing* who my stepsister is right now. And who she is *now* is friendly, cheerful, and pleasant to me. Even during all those brunches, Sarina didn't treat me like her mother does. Neither of us gave the other a fair chance. Maybe it was her mother comparing us, or maybe it was because we're very different people who never looked beyond those differences.

But Miles . . . he *saw* me. Way back when we went to High Park, he was already defending me for the very same things he judged me for only a few weeks before.

But he also kept something from me. Something big. I can't ignore that.

I shake my head. "Even if he wasn't *scheming* with Dad, he should have told me. He knew how I felt about condo developers and my street. And he knew how I feel about Dad. I wouldn't have stopped him from working there, but we *promised* to be honest with each other."

Sarina nods. "You know your limits. It's still sad, though. Miles was . . . *is* so into you. You two could have had something special."

I exhale. I thought so too.

Sarina and I stay and chat a little longer. It's . . . weird. Honestly, it's a little awkward. After having a non-relationship for so long, it's going to take a while for things to be chill between us. But I can tell she's trying, and so am I. She's dating Cara now, and I really don't want to lose my friend. And also? It's kind of cool to see another side of Sarina. She's so different when she's not with her mother. She's still kind of quiet, but she's also really sweet, and kind of . . . optimistic. She only has nice things to say about anyone. We could have—*should* have—done this years ago. I could have had a sister, something I always wanted. I decide that now, no matter what happens between her and Cara, and me and Miles, I'm determined to get closer to my stepsister.

When I leave the café, one thing that Sarina said stands out in my mind. She said my father . . . her stepfather . . . is a pretty understanding guy. Honestly? That comment made me feel like crap. I understand that people can be different with different people, but why does Sarina get the understanding, supportive stepfather, while I get the judgy, distant father?

He's *my* father, and he's the one behind all of this. He encouraged Mom to sell her building and asked me to move in with him so Mom would agree. He's friends with the condo developer and referred Miles, *my* boyfriend, for that job. I get why Mom had to sell her building. I don't like it, but I understand it. And I knew Miles needed an internship badly. But why didn't my father tell me? Or at least talk to me?

On a whim, instead of going home, I head to the subway

station and take the subway and then a bus all the way to Vaughan to my father's office. It's time I had a talk . . . *alone* . . . with my father.

I have only actually been to my father's commercial real estate office once—not long after he and his staff moved into this space. The office was boring—stark, white, and without personality. As I walk into the second-floor office now, I'm not surprised that it looks the same. Well, maybe there's new artwork—all done in pale pastels—but for the most part, it's white walls and white furniture. NAHEED MERALI REAL ESTATE BROKERAGE is printed in black letters on the white wall behind the reception desk. The receptionist is young—maybe in her early twenties—and has long highlighted hair and wears a formfitting blouse. She frowns when she sees me, clearly thinking that I'm not supposed to be there.

Maybe I should have dressed up for this, but I didn't know I'd be coming here today. I'm wearing pink and black plaid pants and a pink cropped T-shirt that says CLASS OF '82 on it in pink glittery script.

"May I help you?" the receptionist asks suspiciously.

"I need to see Naheed Merali," I say.

"Mr. Merali is very busy. Do you have an appointment?"

"No. But . . . he's my father. Can you see if he has a few minutes?"

She looks shocked when I say he's my father. Which . . . why? I know Sarina sometimes works here. But Dad has mentioned his *other* daughter to his staff, right?

The receptionist still doesn't say anything. "Just ask him if he as a few minutes for Sana," I say.

She motions for me to sit on one of the white chairs in

the lobby. Then I see her pick up a phone. Hopefully to call Dad and not security to have me kicked out.

After a few minutes Dad comes rushing into the lobby from one of the offices. "Sana, what's wrong? Has something happened?"

I stand. He's wearing dress pants and a blue dress shirt. No tie. I'm not sure if I expected him to wear a suit and tie to work, because that would be ridiculous in this day and age. But still. It feels weird to see my father at work. To see him without Noureen is strange too. "I . . . I needed to talk to you. Do you have a second?"

He looks at the receptionist. "Farzana, James Andrews is coming in at one thirty. Can you ask him to wait until I'm done with my daughter? We won't be long."

She nods but looks surprised that Dad is willing to speak to me. I wonder if she thought I was lying when I said he was my father. I want to give this woman an *I told you so* look, but instead follow my father down the hallway to his office.

Dad's office is sleek and white and looks like the reception area. He indicates a leather chair across from his desk, and I sit. He sits at a tall office chair across from me.

Despite my issues with the man, I can't deny that Dad is quite handsome for a fifty-year-old. He's slim and fit because he still plays on a recreational soccer team and runs daily. And he clearly cares about his looks—his skin is smooth, and his hair is always shiny with no grays showing.

He's like the polar opposite of my mother, who doesn't care at all about the errant gray hairs popping up in her curls. Honestly, I have no idea why the two of them ever thought it was a good idea to marry each other.

"Okay, Sana? What do you need from me?"

"Why do you assume I need something from you? Maybe I just wanted to see my father." I mean, I did need something from him, but it's rubbing me the wrong way that he thinks that's the only reason I would come see him. Even if it's true.

"Well, I would love to see you more often. But you've never come here before. Do you need money?"

"Of course not. I have a job, remember?"

He sighs. "I have an important meeting soon. Maybe we can talk on the weekend. We can move up our brunch date. Why don't you call Noureen—"

"Dad, why do we only see each other with Noureen? Why don't you ever want to do something with just us?"

He stares at me.

This is a disaster. I'm feeling raw from today and yesterday's revelations, and now my father's questions are putting me on edge. I take a breath. "There *is* a reason I'm here. I heard that you're the one who convinced Mom to sell her building."

His eyes widen. Clearly he wasn't aware that I knew. "I'm only the broker who brought the opportunity to her. Selling was her decision."

"How much money are you making off the deal?" He doesn't answer that question. "Did you ask me to move in with you so Mom would sell? She said she told you before that she wouldn't sell while I still lived with her."

Dad's brows knit together. "No, Sana. Of course not. Noureen and I want to see more of you. To help you."

I shake my head. "I don't believe you. I think you were trying to manipulate Mom's decision. What I don't get is, why did you go after *Love Street*? Where I live. Condos can be built anywhere. . . . Was this all to get back at Mom or something?"

"Sana, this is business. Not personal. And your street should be—"

"I know. I know. It should be higher-density housing. But at the expense of the people who call it their home now? Your daughter *actually lives* there. Your *only* daughter, remember?"

"Your mother *wants* to sell. This isn't on me. And as for remembering you're my daughter, I'm not sure what you want from me. We try to see you as often as we can. I pay child support, and I said we'd help with your college expenses."

That's it? That's all he thinks he needs to do to be my father? Biweekly brunches and money? I feel tears start forming at the corners of my eyes, and it makes me even angrier. "What do I want from you? I want my father back! Remember when we used to actually do things together? We went to all those festivals and fairs, and even Comicon every year? It felt like you *wanted* to spend that time with me." I swallow the shakiness in my voice. "I want you to *want* to see me because I'm your daughter, not because it's your duty. And not see you and *Noureen* for an awkward brunch every two weeks so she can tell me all the things I need to fix about myself before she'll accept me."

Dad doesn't say anything for a while. I should have said this to him a long time ago. "Sana, Noureen is my wife," he finally says. "And she's never done anything—"

I interrupt him. "Don't even think about finishing that sentence. I know exactly what Noureen has done to my family." My voice is completely cracking here, but I don't stop. I say the thing I don't think I've ever said aloud. To anyone. Ever. "I *know* Noureen started a relationship with a married man."

Dad stares at me. I can't tell what he's thinking . . . but he definitely didn't expect me to say that. "Sana, you don't know what you're talking about."

"You can't deny it. I know you were together long before you and Mom split up."

"You can't know—"

"I've known since the beginning." My stupid eyes are tearing up now. I ignore it, letting the tears fall down my cheeks. "I overheard you talking to her on the phone—*before* you and Mom separated. You said you couldn't wait to see her. You said you would be together soon. When you told me you were divorcing, you and Mom *promised* that it wasn't because either of you were seeing someone new. You were lying, weren't you?"

"Sana, you were only nine years old. You couldn't—"

I raise my voice. "When you said you weren't splitting up because of another person, were you lying? It's a simple question, Dad."

He shakes his head, angry now. "You don't have the right to come here accusing me like this. Does your mother know you're here?"

"No. Mom doesn't know I'm here. Hell, she doesn't even know I know about your infidelity." I exhale. "You destroyed my family once, and now you're doing it again with this real estate deal."

He looks at me for a while. I wipe my eyes. I can't even see any sympathy in his face. He doesn't care that I'm hurt.

"What is it you expect me to do?" he asks. His voice is quiet.

"I don't know. Maybe be honest with me? You *knew* all this was happening. That Mom was getting offers to sell. You *pretended* you wanted me to move in with you . . . just because of a real estate deal." My voice cracks there. I squeeze my eyes shut. I don't want to look at him.

"Sana, you don't understand how these things work."

I glare at him. "So *help* me understand, then. You all treat me like I'm too young and frivolous to understand serious things, but you never even give me the chance. You guys are my family, and you're supposed to want the best for me, but no one bothers getting my input about what is actually working or not working for me. You just sit there while your wife tries to turn me into her perfect daughter instead of getting to know who I am. You do whatever is best for you and your bank accounts without thinking about how it will affect your family."

Something in my dad's face softens then. The anger leaves and is replaced by sadness and real compassion. I haven't seen that expression on my father's face since . . . well, since a long time ago. Since I fell off my bike when he was teaching me to ride it. Since my first cat died when I was six.

Why did it take so long for him to actually look like he loves me?

He shakes his head. "Sana. I'm sorry. None of this was my decision. Your mother *wants* to sell. If not through me, it will be through someone else. But you're right—we don't spend enough time together. Let me cancel my afternoon appointments. We can have lunch and . . . talk. Just us."

Why? To wipe my tears? There was a time when I would have jumped at that offer. I wanted more than anything to feel important to him. But I won't let him disappoint me again. I shake my head and stand. "It's too late for us, Dad. You've let me down too many times." I turn and walk out the door before he can stop me.

"Sana, wait," Dad says, calling for me down the hallway.

I walk right out of the office and down the stairs. And my father doesn't follow me.

CHAPTER TWENTY-FIVE

NO LOVE ON LOVE STREET

I'm pretty much shaking the whole way back to the city from Vaughan. It felt incredibly cathartic to finally tell Dad that I know the truth about him and Noureen—that their relationship overlapped with his and Mom's. I feel like a giant weight was lifted. But I don't know. He didn't *deny* anything. He didn't apologize for the divorce, either. I know I probably just ended any possibility of ever having a relationship with him. Not that we had much of one anymore. It's weird—the same day I kind of patch things up with Sarina, I throw away my relationship with my father.

But I need to put all that family crap out of my mind for now. Because tonight is our last official committee meeting before the festival on Saturday. I'm dreading it. It will be the first time I see Miles since I broke up with him. I wish I could skip the meeting, but I meant what I said: I'm not giving up on the festival. Even if we're trying to save a street that can't be saved, I still want this festival to be perfect. Call it a send-off to what Love Street used to be.

When I get home, I spend too long staring at my closet trying to decide what to wear. Choosing the perfect outfit for the first time you see an ex after a breakup is an art form. I can't decide if I want to look sad, so he sees how miserable I've been. Or if I should look smoking hot, so he feels even more regret about how he screwed this up.

But nothing feels right. I just . . . don't want to play games with Miles. I only want to be honest with him. But when every outfit I've ever worn is curated, how do I look like I haven't curated it this time? I finally decide to dress how I feel and wear jeans and a plain black T-shirt. If he thinks I look sad, it's because I am.

I'm the last one to get to LoveBug, probably because I was staring at my closet for so long. Everyone is at the big table with drinks in front of them. I don't join them; I stand at the door watching them all for a while. Honestly, watching Miles. He's like a beacon, drawing my attention whenever I come into a room. He always was, even before we became a couple. And tonight he looks . . . different. He was never an incredibly expressive guy, but I got to know him pretty well in the months since we met. He might not smile much, but his eyes were always . . . active. Taking in everything. Reading signs, watching others while they talked, and fully connecting to the world around him. But that's not how he looks now. His eyes are downcast, even though Ajit is talking. He looks sad, too. I'm not happy to see him hurting. I still care about him.

That's when I notice what he's looking at. His drink—he has one of LoveBug's clear mugs on a gold saucer in front of him.

And it's filled with steaming pink Kashmiri chai.

"Oh, Sana, there you are," Julie says. She pats the empty seat next to her. I smile and sit. Julie immediately pours me a glass of lemonade from the pitcher in the middle of the table.

Ajit is talking about the food trucks that he was able to confirm on Saturday. Julie leans close to me and whispers in my ear, "You totally broke Miles. He's barely talking. And he hasn't looked at you at all since you walked in."

I exhale. I didn't want to break him. I look at him, and yeah, his head is still downcast as he stares at his tea.

April asks me about the park installations, and I tell them that my art teacher will be bringing all the supplies with her for the *Love You* mural and that Mom and I plan to work on the flower heart all day tomorrow. We'll bring it to the park in the flower shop van on Saturday morning. Miles finally speaks when everyone is talking about their individual store's preparations. "Second Story Books is ready. Reggie's niece is coming to help for the day."

The meeting wraps up soon after that. I feel confident that we're ready, and I doubt anything will go wrong at this point. But it seems a bit of a hollow victory. I came up with this festival to *save* the Love Street businesses and to keep this perfect, idyllic little street the same as it is now. But Love Street was always going to change. We never really had the power to do anything . . . to control the future at all.

I leave the café quickly because I don't want to talk to Miles. But Miles is at my side when I'm only a few steps away from the door.

"I need to get my bike from your balcony. Can I walk with you?"

I shrug. I can't exactly tell him *not* to when we're going to the same place. We walk silently for a few moments. I have no intention of speaking, so I'm kind of glad when he does, because this is awkward.

"I can't believe the festival is finally here," he says. "We've come a long way."

I nod. "Yeah."

"If you need any help with the flowers, call me. I'm free tomorrow afternoon."

"It's fine. Mom and I can handle it."

"Okay." He seems like he wants to say more but doesn't know how.

I exhale. This is weird. Days ago, there was never an awkward moment when we were together. We could talk for hours. When we get to the alley next to the flower shop, I don't turn. I can't go up the back stairs. I don't want to be alone on my balcony with him. The place where we drank tea and talked so many times. Where we kissed for the first time . . . and actually the last time, too. The place where I showed him how to fix his bike tire. The place where I felt closer to him than anywhere else.

I walk toward my front door without saying goodbye—because I'm afraid the words won't come out without my voice cracking.

"Sana, wait," he says. I knew he would. Because back when we used to argue every time we saw each other, he always needed to get the last word.

I look at him. Really look. And it almost makes my knees give out. He's so, so gorgeous. I mean, I remember how cute I thought he was the day I first saw him, but that's nothing like the Miles I see now. Now that I know that the little wrinkle between his brows isn't because he's mad but because he's always thinking. That the little mole on his neck is a perfect target to kiss, and when I do, he always shivers. I know how well those arms fit around me.

"I'm sorry again," he says. "I should have told you about that job. I wish things could be different."

I sigh. "I *know* you're sorry. I get it. It's a good opportunity for you. You knew how I'd react to you teaming up with condo developers and my father. You didn't want to upset me."

"Yeah. That's—"

I take a step forward. "Here's the thing, Miles. I *want* people to upset me. My parents didn't tell me for *years* that my father cheated on my mother, because they didn't want to hurt me. Maybe they thought me knowing the truth about the kind of person my father is would affect the way I see him. They wanted me to *love* him without really *knowing* him. And . . ." I hesitate. "You didn't give me a chance to understand why you wanted that job. I don't need to be coddled, Miles. I know you thought I was too naive and too idealistic, but I thought . . . I thought you didn't think of me like that anymore."

He blinks at me. I'm not sure what he's thinking. If he sees why I'm being so stubborn about this.

He finally speaks. "I didn't keep it from you because I thought you were naive."

"You kept it from me because you knew I wouldn't be happy." I pause, trying to keep my voice from cracking. "You could have given me the chance to see your perspective. Like on that streetcar ride, you got me to see the city through your eyes."

He looks at me for a long time. Finally, he sighs. "I'm sorry. I don't know what else to say."

I shake my head. "You don't have to say anything. Goodbye, Miles."

He nods, then heads down the alley, and I hear him climb the wood stairs up to my back balcony. Blinking away a tear, I go up into my apartment from the front door.

CHAPTER TWENTY-SIX
AVOCADO TOAST TO THE RESCUE

The flowers are delivered early, so Mom and I get started on the flower heart on Friday morning right after breakfast. We're working in the back room of the flower shop—where Mom does most of her bigger arrangements—but it's cramped. The size of this room is why she always tries to do wedding work on-site if possible. To make the heart, we first squeezed moss and floral foam into the frame. Then, starting with the biggest blooms, which are sunflowers, we fill in the heart with flowers.

We work quietly. I haven't told Mom that I went to see Dad yesterday, because I don't think she'd approve. Working with her in this tight back room emphasizes her point—Mom *needs* a bigger space if her business is going to focus on special events more than walk-ins. But I still feel so betrayed. Why did they do this behind my back? Like I said to Miles last night, maybe if everyone had trusted me enough to *tell* me what was going on, I could have had time to warm up to the idea.

I also don't want to talk to Mom about the other thing I confronted Dad about yesterday—him cheating on her. I have no idea if Dad will ever tell Mom that I know. I don't blame her for not telling me—she was the one wronged. And she's been the one who's been an active parent to me.

She may be distant, but she's been *here*. Which is more than I can say for Dad.

"This is going to be stunning," I say, standing back to look at the enormous flower heart after we'd affixed about half the flowers.

Mom nods. "I am, of course, partial to flowers, but I think this is so much better than the metal sculpture you wanted. And I love that we decided on a full rainbow of colors instead of just red and pink. It's going to be fantastic." Mom suddenly checks her watch. "Oh, I didn't realize it was so late. We should change—I made us lunch reservations at Fiona's."

Fiona's Garden is one of my favorite restaurants in the city. Mom usually only takes me for my birthday because it's a bit pricy. "Why are we going for lunch?"

Mom wipes her hands on her overalls and pulls out the scrunchie holding her hair on the top of her head. "Since Asha is in the shop today, I wanted to treat you . . . to thank you for being so understanding."

I raise a brow. Asha is Mom's occasional employee—she doesn't work very often, but Mom has her in all weekend to help with the festival. But this still sounds suspicious. I'm wondering if she's going to try to convince me to live at my grandparents' with her by feeding me my favorite food. I'm not about to say no to lunch at Fiona's, though.

After I change into a floral dress and add a bit of makeup, Mom and I walk to the restaurant since it's only about fifteen minutes away. Mom talks constantly along the way about the festival tomorrow and the smaller arrangements she's made for her booth. She sounds nervous.

When we get to the restaurant, I almost turn around

and walk right out again. Because my father is here. Sitting alone at a four-seat table near the window.

"No," I say. "I'm not eating with him."

Mom puts her hand on my arm. "Sana, hear him out. He called me last night; he was very upset about your conversation. I think it's long past time for the three of us to have a talk."

I look at Mom. She seems . . . sad. But also determined. Determined to air out all the crap this family has been burying for so long.

I take a breath. This is what I always wanted. For my family to actually talk to me. But now that we're here . . . I'm scared. I'm not ready for another emotional conversation, and I'm afraid talking to my dad will only make me as angry as I was yesterday.

I frown, then silently sit at the table with my father. I know I'm pouting like a petulant child, but I don't care. Mom sits next to me.

"We should have done this before now," Mom says.

I glare at them both. "Like you two would have *wanted* to have a meal together."

My dad sighs. "We don't hate each other, Sana."

The waitress comes by then, and I order a mango pineapple dragon fruit smoothie. Dad orders a coffee and Mom, a water. Mom says we need a few minutes to decide what we want to eat.

When the waitress leaves the table, my dad says, "I called your mother when you left my office."

"It's clear that all three of us should have been talking about this real estate deal," Mom says, "because it's affecting us all. This family has a lot of communication to catch up on."

"We're *not* a family anymore."

Mom shakes her head. "The moment we had you, we became connected for life." She sighs. "We've been doing a terrible job of it, though. So we want to talk. Openly. About everything."

The waitress comes back to take our order. I already know what I want—smashed avocado and roasted veggies on sourdough with a fattoush salad. Mom orders a grain bowl. Dad stares at the vegan menu, like if he looks at it long enough, a steak will appear on it. "Um."

I roll my eyes. This place totally isn't Dad's vibe. "The kale pesto pasta is really good. You can't taste the kale at all. And there's a lot of basil." I know my dad loves basil.

He smiles at me with relief and orders the pasta.

Once the waitress is gone, I wait for them to start talking. This "meeting" is for them to be honest with me for the first time, so they need to start doing that.

My dad clears his throat. "Sana, I'm glad you came to see me yesterday. You brought up a few things that made me realize how far apart we've drifted. We need to have a proper conversation." He pauses and swallows thickly like he's uncomfortable. Good, he should be. "You accused me of only asking you to move in with me so your mother would sell her building. That isn't true—I would love to have you at home with us."

I shake my head. "Yeah, right. Like—"

Mom puts her hand on my arm, stopping me. "Let your father finish."

I cross my arms in front of me.

Dad exhales. "But I admit, the *timing* of my invitation *was* so your mother would reconsider the offer I'd presented to her. It was a good offer. I negotiated the best possible terms for her—not because I wanted a bigger commission, but because I truly do want what's best for her. For both of you. This developer is fair. I've known Ashwin, one of the owners, for a long time. I know enough about the industry to know that this was going to be the best deal for her."

Mom nods. "It really is an excellent offer."

"Yeah, but you should have told me the truth from the beginning," I say. "You both kept this huge thing from your own daughter."

"You're right," Mom says. "We should have. If we could do it again—"

I shake my head. "But you can't do it again. I'm not nine anymore. I'm *seventeen*. Do you think I'm not mature enough to understand these things? Or is it because you don't want me to have a say on decisions you know I won't agree with?"

"Sana, I explained why I had to sell," Mom says. "I thought you understood."

"I *do* understand," I say. If we're all going to be open with each other, I should tell the truth. "I overheard you and Jenn talking a couple of months ago—that day you were painting those flowerpots pink. You said you'd had an offer for the building, but you weren't going to sell until you talked to me about it. But then you didn't talk to me."

Mom cringes. "I'm sorry you heard that, Sana. I just . . . I didn't want this to affect your work with the festival."

"But I suggested the festival to the BOA so you *wouldn't*

have to sell. I've been helping you more in the store. I did it all so we could stay there." Didn't make a whole lot of difference, though. I hate how powerless I feel. Just like when I was little, everything is turning upside down, and I don't have control over any of it.

"We're sorry we weren't honest with you from the beginning," Dad says.

I glare at my father. "It's not like you've ever been honest with me in the past."

Everyone at the table is silent for several long moments.

Mom finally speaks. "Sana, how long have you known that your father was with Noureen before our divorce?"

I shrug. "Since the beginning," I say. "I overheard Dad talking to her in his office a few times. He said her name . . . Noureen. He said they'd be together soon. Then, when you told me that you two were divorcing, it all made sense. I was young, but I wasn't an idiot. You both promised that it wasn't because you were with someone else. Which I knew right away was a lie."

Dad looks sad, but I know he doesn't regret what he did back then. Because, I mean, he *married* Noureen.

"I'm sorry you heard that," Dad says.

No one speaks for a while. This "family" doesn't know how to communicate, so why even try? But I *do* know how to talk. Maybe I shouldn't have kept this in for so long, waiting for them to be honest with me. I'm not going to keep it in anymore.

I take a breath. "You two shouldn't have lied to me." I look at Mom. "You shouldn't have forced me to go see Dad . . . a *cheater* . . . and his *mistress* every weekend. And you"—I point to my father—"shouldn't have forced me to have a relationship with Noureen. She broke up my family. And she doesn't even like me, anyway."

Dad shakes his head. "Sana, that's not fair. Noureen has been nothing but welcoming to you. She's—"

"She's not the one who needs to be *welcoming* me to your family!" I spit out. "You're my father—I had you first!" That shut Dad up. Mom puts her hand on my arm, and I appreciate the support. I take a breath. "Noureen might like me if I were smarter, dressed better, had smoother hair, and wanted to work a corporate job. Basically, if I were Sarina. I don't know why she thinks she has the right to judge the daughter of the woman whose husband she stole."

Mom shakes her head. "Noureen didn't steal anyone, Sana. I promise. Everything isn't black-and-white here. I know it would be easier if there were a bad guy and a good guy . . . but your father and I both made mistakes. And quite truthfully, our relationship was effectively over long before Noureen came into the picture."

"What does that mean . . . *effectively over*?"

The server shows up with our food then. It all looks delicious—too bad none of us has an appetite right now. After she's gone, Dad sighs. "Your mother and I wanted different things from our lives. She wanted to open her dream flower shop in the city, and I wanted a stable house in the suburbs. And I'm not proud of it, but we bitterly villainized each other for our differences for much too long."

"You guys never fought!" We were a happy family. My memories weren't all fake. My parents weren't particularly romantic with each other, but I don't remember them arguing.

Mom shakes her head. "We did fight. All the time."

"We didn't let you see it. We thought we were protecting you." Dad says.

I exhale. All this lying. Just to protect me. I remember that comment I made to Miles a while ago, that divorce is shocking because you realize all your family memories might be wrong. I take a bite of my salad. It's, of course, great, but I can't really enjoy it. It would really suck if this whole conversation ruins Fiona's for me.

"So does that mean Dad didn't cheat?" I'm looking at Mom when I ask that. Because . . . I feel like she's more likely to tell me the truth. But Dad is the one who answers me.

"We decided to permanently separate before we actually did. Before we told you. It was a mutual decision—neither of us left the other."

"How long before?" I ask.

"Six months. Give or take," Mom says. "During that time, I looked for opportunities in the city and eventually bought Morgan Ashton Flowers and the building."

Six months. While I was reading my teen romances and telling everyone my dreams to be an artist, they were making plans to break up our little family.

I turn to Dad. "And you got with Noureen during those six months." He doesn't say anything. Just looks at me with the blank expression he had yesterday. It makes sense—Noureen wanted everything he wanted. The suburban house, the respectable businessman husband, and the stability for her own kid. "You guys should have told me," I say to them both.

"You were so young," Dad says. "And I'm not sure you would have understood. You've always been such an idealist."

"You're like your father that way," Mom says.

I look at her sharply. "I am *not* like Dad. I'm like you, remember?" Two peas in a pod. A couple of vegetarian, hippie-dippie, free-spirited artists.

Mom chuckles. "You *are* a lot like me. But . . . you're like him, too. You both have an image about what life is supposed to look like, and you reject anything that deviates from that image. Now, mind you, your images are quite different. You want your eclectic and colorful life to stay the same forever, and he wanted two and a half children, a two-car garage, and granite countertops. You're idealists with very different ideals."

Dad smiles at that. "She's right," he says. "Your mother wanted to do something different every few years. You're like me. Once you find your happy comfort zone, you want to stay in it."

I scowl. I know Mom and I aren't the same, but I'm *not* like my father, either. I'm honest. But . . . it's true that neither of us likes change as much as Mom, who repaints her bedroom twice a year while mine looks exactly like it did when I was nine. "If you wanted things to stay as they were, why did you leave Mom?"

Mom turns to look at me. "Because he wasn't happy. Neither of us was."

I glare at my father. "So you took away my comfort zone in the search for your own?"

"Sana, you wouldn't have been happy with unhappy parents," my mother says.

I blink. Was I happy before their divorce? I'd *thought* my childhood was fine in that North Toronto house. True, I like Love Street better, but I don't remember it being miserable at home. But even if I was comfortable, I doubt it would have stayed that way. Not if the two people I was living with were so unhappy. Mom's right. All this isn't black-and-white. Relationships have lots and lots of shades of gray.

"Were you ever?" I ask. Both my parents look confused at that question. "Were you ever happy together? Or do you regret getting married?"

Mom shakes her head. "I don't regret it for a second," she says. Then she looks at Dad like she has no idea what he will say to my question.

"I don't either," Dad says. "We were young and impulsive, and your mother and I have changed a lot since then, but—"

"We were in love," Mom says. "*Truly*. And of course, we got you out of it. I fell in love with you even more . . . more than anyone else in the world. So how could I regret it?"

I don't say anything for a while. I think that's the most they've ever told me about their relationship. I know Mom loves me that much . . . but . . . I look at my father.

"Sana, I really am so glad you came to see me yesterday," Dad says, eyes soft. "I needed that kick in the pants. I'm so sorry I haven't made you more of a priority. You're absolutely right—we *should* see each other without Noureen and Sarina." He chuckles sadly. "That's my idealism—I wanted us all to be a happy family. You, me, Noureen, and Sarina."

Even if Dad wanted that, Noureen never did.

"I wasn't pretending when I asked you to move in," he continues. "I would *love* to see you more. I know we're not as close as we used to be, and I thought it would be good for us."

I take a bite of my sandwich. How could he think that me living with Noureen could ever be good for me? Does he listen to her at all when we're at brunch?

"After you left yesterday," he continues, "I thought long and hard about how I can make you more of a priority going forward. I do think I got the best possible deal for your mother in the sale, but I think I can still negotiate a better deal for *you*."

"What? Like, Mom wouldn't sell?"

"I technically *can* cancel the contract," Dad says, "but I won't. This is what your mother wants."

Mom nods at that statement. And I know that she's right—selling the building is what she *has* to do right now. Even if I hate it.

"But because we haven't signed the final paperwork," Dad continues, "it's not too late to negotiate some extra clauses in the contract."

"Clauses like what?" I ask.

Dad looks at Mom, and Mom nods. So he explains. "The developers need to buy at least three more addresses near your mother's before they can build anything. They are currently in negotiations and are confident they *will* acquire them, but it will be a while before anything is demolished. A year, minimum. But empty storefronts aren't good for the street. I can include in the final contract that they can buy the land, but they must lease the building to me at a fair price until construction starts. For a year or longer. I can easily sublease the storefront for a year. And I'd keep the apartment for myself."

My eyes widen. "You want to move to Love Street?" I try to imagine Dad and Noureen in my tiny apartment.

Mom laughs. "Sana, he wants to rent it for *you* to live in."

I blink. I could stay on Love Street? With Cosmic and LoveBug and Second Story Books and Mrs. Kotch?

Dad nods. "I understand why you don't want to move in with me and Noureen. Your mother will probably be moving up north. Your mother and I discussed it, and we'd be willing to cover your share of the rent while you're in school, if you want to stay there."

This is . . . actually perfect. I can stay on Love Street. Maybe not forever, but at least for now. I look at Dad. I honestly can't believe this was *his* idea. Yesterday I was so sure that there was no way I could ever forgive him, but him doing this shows me that he *is* capable of making me a priority. Maybe it's fueled by guilt, or maybe me yelling at him really did show him that he hasn't been fair to me. But he put me first. Finally.

I'm so delighted with the idea, I clap my hands. "That's so perfect. Yes, I want to stay on Love Street. I can get a roommate . . . another OCAD student, or maybe Cara—"

"Wait, Sana," Dad says. "The other bedroom—your mother's room—how would you feel if Sarina rented that room?"

Did I hear him right? "Sarina?"

Dad nods. "Her commute to U of T has been hard on her. She's wanted to move out for a while now. Noureen won't like it, but I suspect she'd be happier if Sarina was living with family instead of with strangers. I know you and Sarina have been spending a lot of time together lately and have become so much closer, which is wonderful. But this is completely your choice. I won't even ask her if you don't want it."

I stifle a laugh. *No*, Sarina and I haven't been spending time together. We've seen each other literally *twice* without Dad and Noureen in the last couple of months—that day at High Park and then yesterday at that café. I wonder if Sarina has been telling her mother that she was with me when she went out with Cara. The thought makes me smile. First step to sisterhood is covering for each other.

"Yeah," I say. "But does Sarina *want* to live on Love Street?"

"As I said, I haven't asked her yet. I wanted to ask you first."

I like this new communicative family I have. On one hand, living with my stepsister would be weird. We barely know each other. But after yesterday I know Sarina is someone I *want* to know better. I think living with her would be the perfect way to do that. Not to mention, she's dating one of my closest friends. "If Sarina is cool with it, I'm fine with it. Actually, it would be great."

Both my parents smile widely. I can't even believe it. . . . This is such an amazing solution. I still don't love that Love Street will change, but at least for now I won't have to go.

After that is settled, Dad asks Mom how her search for a new space for the flower shop is going. Mom tells us about the warehouse space she looked at the other night. Dad then tells us more about the condo builder who's buying Mom's property. He says they seem different from every other developer he's worked with, and it's so evident that one of the founders was a planner with the city first.

I exhale. I can't deny it—this company does sound like a good fit for Miles. Not that I'm over his deception or anything, but . . . he wanted to help with the festival so he could make the connections to get a good internship. And he did that. And maybe my parents are right—the developers aren't the bad guys here. Life isn't black-and-white, but so much more complicated than that.

Mom, as usual, can tell what I'm thinking. "It's a wonderful opportunity for Miles, isn't it?"

I exhale. "Yeah. He's always talking about zoning and higher-density housing and whatever. I wish it didn't mean destroying what we have for *their* profit."

Dad shakes his head. "I know I'm an evil real estate agent, but not all developers are terrible. This firm really is focused on sustainability and building community. They plan to offer the new storefronts to the displaced Love Street businesses first. And they want community involvement in the planning."

I don't like it, but yeah, I know housing is what this city needs. And putting a few more people above the stores on Love Street doesn't mean that Love Street has to lose what makes it great.

"Your festival will be so good for the area. Not just now, but for years," Dad says. "I'm so proud of you—I thought the only good thing to come out of all those festivals we went to when you were young was my lifelong love of churros. Who knew it could benefit you, too!"

I laugh. Dad gives me an expression that I haven't seen on him in a long time—pure mischief. Like only he and I are in on a joke.

After Mom insists I order dessert—the vegan chocolate

torte that's to die for—I smile. "We should have talked like this a long time ago. I probably should have told you I knew about Noureen."

Dad shakes his head. "You were just a kid. You didn't do anything wrong."

"Seriously, Sana," Mom says. "We're the only ones who should be apologizing. And . . . I hope you'll grant Miles the same. Let him explain his point of view before you give up on him. Because you two had something special. You *complemented* each other. If he can't be your boyfriend, maybe he can be your friend."

I take a long breath. I know Mom's right. I have to give him the chance to talk. I owe him that much.

Dad frowns. "Wait, Miles is your *boyfriend*? Since when?"

CHAPTER TWENTY-SEVEN

THE COOKIE'S FULL CIRCLE

I get dressed very carefully the next morning for the festival. Not only because I'm going to see a lot of people and will be on the stage for my speech, but also because today I *want* to play that game. I want the perfect curated outfit that will give me strength when I see Miles. After that lunch with Mom and Dad (still can't believe that happened—so weird), I'm not as mad at Miles anymore. It's not that I want to get back together with him—he *did* keep something huge from me, and I can't forget that—but I'm not going to avoid talking to him. And also . . .

This whole thing showed me that Miles and I aren't compatible as a couple anyway. I totally understand why he took the job now, and I get why Love Street has to change, but a part of me can't help thinking that Miles will always make the practical choice. He values change and progress. He's pragmatic. But romance is *sentimental*. It's believing in fate. Miles will never be a hopeless romantic, not with his girlfriends and not in his life. And that's okay, but it's not what *I* want.

After that talk with my parents, all I can think about is if Miles and I stayed together, one day our differences would make us miserable, just like theirs made Mom and Dad so unhappy. And neither of us wants to end up like our parents. But that doesn't mean Miles and I can't be friends. Heck, even my mom and dad are kind of becoming friends now.

My outfit starts with the Love on Love Street volunteer shirt. We had them made in either pink or red, and of course I chose a pink one. It's a perfectly fitted T-shirt with the festival logo screen printed onto it—a heart with the words LOVE ON LOVE STREET in the middle, made to look like a neon sign. I pair the T-shirt with wide-legged dark jeans and my floral six-hole Doc Martens. And I add my silver filigree locket as a choker—the one that still has that fortune about love in it. I smile, remembering the day I found it right before we started working on this festival. It said my life was going to change because of love . . . and it was right. The Love on Love Street Festival changed my life more than I would have imagined.

Mom and I drive the flower heart in the van to LOL Park at about seven in the morning. It's weird. All that . . . communicating at lunch yesterday made things feel different between us. We're, lighter with each other. I'm seeing her differently—not like my flaky mother, or as a struggling, divorced woman, or even as a woman whose husband cheated on her. I'm seeing her as the person she's always been. A kick-ass, brilliant businesswoman who knows what she needs and goes after it. And who loves me fiercely.

By the time we have the flower heart in place, April shows up with the volunteers assigned to the floral heart. Their job will be to protect the floral installation and to manage the crowd if a lot of people want pictures of it— which I'm really hoping will happen. After giving them instructions, I go see Ms. Carothers, who is setting up the tile mural on the wall at the other side of the park.

"Sana!" she says when she sees me, and then she gives me a hug, which is weird because she's my teacher. Or I suppose she used to be my teacher. I keep forgetting I graduated from high school. She's wearing jeans, a red volunteer shirt, a red bandanna as a hair band, and red lipstick in the same shade as the T-shirt. "This is fantastic," she says. "Look at this wonderful festival you've put together. I always knew you were a special kid, but this is phenomenal."

I grin. The table has already been set up, and she has a few volunteers—all art students from school—helping her. Some are using tile nippers to cut reclaimed tiles into leaves and hearts, ready for people to purchase and write their message on before a volunteer helps them paste it on the mural. The mural will be built on a huge piece of plywood, not directly on the wall. This turns out to be a good thing, because now I know that this wall (which is actually the side of Mrs. Kotch's bakery) won't be here forever. I'm hoping we find a permanent place here on Love Street for the mural afterward.

While I'm looking at the mock-up painting of the mural that Ms. Carothers has set up on an easel, Mom comes over. After admiring my teacher's art, she turns to me.

"I took the van back to the store. All the street vendors have set up—go check them out. I think it will be chaotic after the gates open."

I bite my lip. I was glad that Mom and I drove from the flower shop to the park because it meant I didn't have to see Miles or Love Street yet. We're cochairs of this festival, but for the most part, the events and vendors in the park have been my responsibility, and the ones on the street have been Miles's. He's probably there right now making sure the tables are okay and helping everyone get set up. I do want to see him today, but also . . . I'm nervous.

Mom adds, "Miles and Jenn had to run up to the hardware store for duct tape or something. He's not there."

I exhale. "Okay. I'll go take a look, then."

I head over to the street.

The vendor booths are lining both sides of Love Street. Of course, all the businesses on the street have booths. I can see Mrs. Kotch, Grant from Miracle Egg, and April still setting up their tables. There are also a handful of outside vendors—like a local beekeeper selling honey and beeswax items, Ali's T-shirt shop, a handmade jewelry vendor, and a chocolate shop selling artisan chocolates. I stop at April's pet supply booth. She has a few stuffed animals wearing the I HEART MY HUMAN shirt, and pet scarves and leashes with hearts and the word "love" on it. Plus, more pet supplies and clothes.

"This all looks fantastic," I say.

April nods. "Thanks to you and Miles."

I shake my head. "Thanks to the whole committee. I love the consistency of all the tables having white tents and red tablecloths. And everything is so on theme."

"I thought Miles was being a little too hands-on micromanaging our tables," April says. "He spent over an hour with each of us last week to go over what we'd be selling and how it would be displayed. It paid off."

I knew Miles was in charge of the vendors for the festival, but I had no idea he'd worked so closely with each individual one. "Really?"

April nods. "He had a hand in each of these tables. He even found that jewelry designer who makes a ton of heart-shaped stuff."

I go to see the jewelry designer next, introducing myself as the cochair of the festival, and admire her pieces made of bent silver or gold wire. There are heart-shaped pendants, rings, and dangling earrings. My eyes lock onto a pair of hoop earrings made of wire bent into the word "love" at the bottom of the hoop.

"Oooh," I say. "I need these."

As I'm paying for the earrings, the artist compliments my heart necklace. My hands go to it immediately. "Oh, thanks. It's a vintage locket." I show her how it opens to reveal the tiny folded paper inside.

"Oh wow. I love lockets," the artist says. "Is that paper special?"

I nod. "It's a fortune cookie fortune I found once."

I move on to chat with the other vendors. As I'm chatting with Asha, Mom's occasional part-timer, I notice that the banners and signs at the entrance to the festival have been put up. I don't see Miles, so I go peek at the signs.

This is the first time I'm seeing them since they came back from the print shop, and I can't get over how *fantastic* they look. The big LOVE ON LOVE STREET sign with the logo is hanging high over the entrance, and there's a big standing sign that says LOVE FROM OUR COMMUNITY TO YOU, with a collage of pictures submitted by members of the Love Street BOA. This sign was Julie's idea, and she asked us to give her pictures of us that represent love. I find Julie and Ajit's wedding picture first, with Julie wearing a Korean hanbok and Ajit in an ornate South

Asian sherwani. There's a picture of April with huge nineties hair with her arms around a tall-haired boy from her prom. There's one of Alain in his restaurant with his arms around his eight-year-old sons, and an old picture, maybe from the seventies or early eighties, of Mr. and Mrs. Kotch outside an old car in downtown Toronto. There's one of Reggie barbecuing in a park with what I assume is his entire extended family around him, and one of Ben and his husband holding up an empanada. I laugh when I notice one of Cara and Sarina, with Sarina looking straight at the camera and Cara kissing her on the cheek. They look *so* happy. My father and Noureen aren't coming today, but I wonder if Sarina and Cara intended this picture as a way of going public with their relationship. And speaking of my father, my eye unexpectedly catches a picture of him smiling. He's sitting on an old sofa, with his arm around Mom. It looks to be about twenty years ago. Or almost eighteen, I suppose, because Mom is holding a white blanket-wrapped baby in her arms. Me.

I lean close because I've never seen this picture before. After my parents separated, neither of them had any old albums or frames accessible. Why did Mom submit this picture? A family that broke up years ago is *hardly* appropriate to represent love.

But I look closer, and there is so much love in this picture that I actually tear up. The way Dad has his arm around Mom and is smiling at her with complete and utter awe. The way Mom is looking at me like I'm the best thing that's ever happened to her. Yesterday they told me that they had been deeply in love when I was born, and I didn't really believe it. But their love is as clear as day in this picture. Even if they didn't have the big, swoony, epic love story, they loved each other. And they love me.

Then I see that Miles submitted a prom picture. I see why he submitted it, even if he and his prom date are no longer together either. In fact, I know they broke up that night. But the picture is such a perfect *cheesy* prom pic. His prom date, Giselle, I assume, is wearing a long red ball gown. (I snarl a bit at her picture for what she did to Miles.) And there's a big heart-shaped balloon arch behind them. Miles is even wearing red. I lean in to look closer at him. I know him well, so I can tell that he's not happy in this picture. He's stiff and uncomfortable.

But he's gorgeous, too. I was already teary from that picture of Mom and Dad, and now I'm even more teary. What my mom said was right—we did have something special. It's too bad Miles and I don't have a picture of us on this collage. Hell, I should have submitted *our* prom picture.

As my eyes take in everyone's pictures, I see it. A small picture of Miles and me at Riverdale Park, months ago, from my Instagram, with the Toronto skyline and sunset behind us, our heads touching. This was before we were together, of course. But we still look so happy—like we belong together.

Did Miles submit this too?

I had such a great time that day, once Charlene and her mice left. I know a lot has happened between us since we watched the sunset on that hill, but I really think that day felt like our beginning. And maybe he felt the same way if he submitted the picture.

I shake my head and walk away from the sign. I don't want to mess up my eye makeup before the festival even starts. I keep checking out the rest of the vendor tables. Cara is talking to someone at the Cosmic table. When I get close enough, I realize it's Sarina.

"Hi, roomie!" she says, grinning widely.

Last night she excitedly texted me, delighted with Dad's idea of her moving into my Love Street apartment in September, so yeah. She's going to be my roommate in a few weeks. After hugging me, Sarina puts an arm around Cara and grins. Cara looks at Sarina with an incandescent smile—bigger than I've ever seen on her.

Seeing them together for the first time is weird, but honestly, I kind of love it. Cara and Sarina look like the ultimate grumpy/sunshine pairing, with Cara back in her black ripped jeans and a red volunteer shirt with the sleeves rolled up and Sarina in a pink volunteer shirt with white jeans and sneakers. They are so clearly smitten with each other. They explain that Jenn asked Sarina to help out in the Cosmic booth for the day, since I won't be able to.

I grin at them. "Are you aware there's a picture of you two on the banner at the entrance?"

Sarina smiles, nodding. "Cute, right?"

I nod. "It's exceedingly cute. Does that mean you're not keeping all this a secret?"

"Whatever happens, happens," Sarina says. "I love that picture you sent in of you and Miles."

I shake my head. "I didn't send it."

"Miles probably did," Cara says. "You really did a number on him. He was such a grump, and you turned him into a hopeless romantic."

"No, I didn't. He's the furthest thing from a hopeless romantic."

Cara snorts. "Are you kidding? I mean, most of this"—she waves her hand at the vendor booths—"was his influence.... He's so *invested* in the festival."

"He's dedicated to the festival, but I'm pretty sure he still thinks the theme is cheesy."

A hopeless romantic wouldn't go behind his girlfriend's back and interview with a *condo* developer.... He wouldn't be so focused on changing everything she values. True, I see Miles's point of view a lot more now, but there's no question that he's single-mindedly focused on progress. Not romance.

Sarina laughs. "He's a *complete* romantic. Did you even see the bookstore?"

I shake my head. From afar I can see someone at the table outside the bookstore. It's *not* Miles—I could pick him out a mile away.

"Go see it, Sana," Cara says.

I shrug and head over. As I get closer, I recognize that it's Reggie's niece Tamara at the booth. And I'm shocked at the books I see on the table.

I expected that, somewhat reluctantly, Reggie and Miles would put out the rest of the meager used romance section that I helped curate, but also add a few history and literary fiction books. Hopefully books that at least have a romantic subplot.

But that's not what's on the table. First, these books are *new*. Second Story Books mostly sells used books, but Reggie does order a small selection of new award winners and popular book club titles. I've never seen a new romance book there, though. But the books on the table all are brand-new and firmly in the romance genre. After saying hi to Tamara,

I skim the bright covers. I've read a lot of these—there's a definite focus on diversity, and on Canadian authors, too. I pick up a green book that has an apartment building on the cover with a man and a woman each peeking out a different window. I've read the book—it's set in Toronto and has South Asian leads.

"I love that book," Tamara says.

"I've read it," I say. "It's great." I put it down and pick up a blue book next to it. The title is a donut pun. "Reggie did a fantastic job with this selection. Did you help him?" I then notice the framed sign above the display.

It's the Second Story Books logo, but it has the word "kissing" in red handwriting font before the word "books" and a red kiss mark next to it. "Holy crap . . . Second Story *Kissing* Books? This is brilliant."

Reggie comes out of the store then with a small stack of mass-market paperback romances. He smiles at me. "What do you think of our romance pop-up, Sana?"

"It's perfect." I see stickers and bookmarks that say FIND YOUR HAPPILY EVER AFTER ON LOVE STREET. "I need one of these."

Reggie hands me a bookmark, beaming. "And to think a few months ago I didn't even *carry* kissing books. Now look at us!" He shows me some more romance-themed bookmarks and stickers he ordered from small independent makers.

"You've totally outdone yourself," I say. "How did you even decide what books to get? Don't tell me you were lurking in the romance corner of TikTok?"

Reggie lets out a deep booming laugh. "Ah no, this is not *my* doing. Miles has been working on it for some time.

I believe he *read* most of the books before ordering them. I'm going to use this sign for the romance section after today. We'll have to increase the kissing books section! I mean, this is Love Street, isn't it?" He winks at me.

I can't believe Miles did this. And he *read* the books too? I know he read *Pride and Prejudice*, but he didn't mention reading any other romances. We could have been talking about romance books all summer. I look again at the books on the table, and I realize that Miles's touch is all over this selection. In addition to the book with the apartment building on it, I know several of these are set in Toronto. And there's so much diversity. I smile as I pick up a slim book with a light blue cover. I know the book—it's literally a romance between urban planners.

It's not a big romantic gesture like a dancing flash mob or filling my apartment with red roses. Miles's style is subtler. Quieter. More thoughtful. Just like Miles himself. I pick up another book, one I haven't read, and look at the badass Asian woman wearing a tiger jacket on the cover.

"Why didn't he tell me he was doing this?" I ask.

Reggie shrugs. "Perhaps he wanted to surprise you?"

It would have been an amazing surprise . . . if we were still together. If I walked down Love Street with Miles and unexpectedly saw this curated selection of kissing books out front and found out it was because of *him*, I would have kissed him senseless. It's actually the perfect gift for me. I would have been *delighted* with his new secret softy side.

But . . . I think this softy side isn't new. It was always there. I didn't see it because I was too busy noticing all our differences. He was *always* a romantic. Asking me to my prom when I was feeling sorry for myself was *romantic*. Making me that Lego corsage was *incredibly* romantic. He always cared about people, and that's what romance is about, caring about other people. He's just a different kind of romantic than I am.

True, he called romance novels formulaic a couple of months ago, but he was judging them before ever reading one. When I called him out on that, he started reading romances and found ones that worked for him. That's the biggest difference between us. When he realized he was wrong about something, he adapted his views. He was able to progress—something I wasn't able to do. When I was shown all the reasons a neighborhood like Love Street *has* to change to better serve the people who live and work here, I resisted the change. Even now, when I *know* all the reasons change is right for Love Street and know this developer isn't out to destroy the Love Street I love, I'm still resistant. I'm still unwilling to be in a relationship with someone who works for them. I'm still rigid in not really accepting it. Because it messes up my worldview.

But I was wrong in many ways. I thought my parents didn't really love each other because they didn't have a cutesy, swoony romance. But they *did* love each other. They didn't break up because their love was lacking. . . . They broke up because they wanted different things out of life.

I believed there was only one way to love someone—with big gestures. Hearts, rainbows, meet-cutes, and grand gestures. Not quiet moments drinking tea or long streetcar rides through the city together. I didn't believe that a quiet, thoughtful way of loving someone was as real.

I exhale. I *do* love Miles. And it's infinitely more real than I ever imagined it could be.

And he *is* romantic. I mean, hell, the fact that he submitted that picture from his prom proves it. It's the cheesiest, romancey-est thing I've ever seen. He even wore a suit that matched his date—a freaking red jacket and bow tie, at that. Clearly there's a bit of my brand of romance in him too.

I suddenly freeze. A red jacket . . . maybe a red *velvet* jacket?

I remember what he told me about his prom night. He said it was a disaster. He also said they got takeout before heading to the banquet hall. Could it have been Chinese takeout? With fortune cookies? I touch the locket around my neck. He said he *donated* his prom outfit. Would Miles pick a charity that provides prom clothes to kids that otherwise wouldn't have them?

I excuse myself from Reggie and Tamara and rush over to the sign at the entrance to look at the picture again.

The jacket is close. It's the same shade of red as the one from Cosmic. I see someone wearing a red volunteer shirt nearby. It's Jenn. Does that mean that Miles is back too?

"Hey, Jenn?" I call her over. "This picture . . . Do you think that's the same jacket you had in the store? The one that was donated to the prom drive?"

Jenn will know exactly what I'm talking about. I swear, she has a mental catalog of every piece of clothing that's been in her store. "The red velvet. I remember." She leans in, studying Miles's picture. "Could be. I got that jacket back, you know."

"What?"

"No one at the youth center wanted it. It wasn't really a red velvet sports coat kind of crowd. I put it out for the festival today. It goes with the theme, doesn't it?" She leans even closer to the picture. "So it was Miles's jacket the whole time? That's some coincidence."

I exhale. Or maybe it's fate. And that's when I realize it—the fortune *did* come true. But the fortune wasn't predicting *I* would find love. It was *Miles's* cookie. The fortune predicted *he* would fall in love, and maybe he did.

I take a deep breath.

"You should tell him," Jenn says.

I turn to her. "How do you know what I'm thinking?"

She smiles and pats my cheek. "I've known you your whole life, sunshine. Go get him. He fell as hard as you did."

I nod. She's right. It's time for me to go get Miles back.

CHAPTER TWENTY-EIGHT

THE LOVE ON LOVE STREET FESTIVAL IS HERE . . . AND IT'S AMAZING

I have no idea how, but I know that somehow I'm going to get Miles Desai back. Seeing all the work he did for the festival solidifies it for me—Miles has *always* been a huge romantic and was always willing to see my point of view. But I was too stupidly stubborn to accept it.

Change is inevitable. Neither I, nor any of us here on the street, can preserve this little oasis in the middle of a city that's evolving. But we're *not* powerless—we *do* have the ability to have an impact on what our home evolves into. That's why he's obsessed with all those signs—he wants to understand the past in those historical plaques, and he wants to have a say in guiding the city in a way that's fair for the people who love it. And if that's not romantic . . . if that's not sentimental, then I don't know what is.

There isn't only one way to love a person, or to love a place. Real love isn't meet-cutes and grand gestures—it's wanting the absolute best for the people and places you care about.

I get it now. And I need to make Miles see that. I rush back to the Cosmic Vintage table. Cara and Sarina are still setting up the accessories and clothes that Jenn picked out for the festival. I go straight to a rolling rack and find a familiar velvet jacket. I run my hands over the soft pile on the lapel.

"I love that piece," Cara says. "It's the same one we were drooling over when all those clothes were donated for the prom drive."

"I know. It was Miles's. He wore it to his prom."

Cara's and Sarina's eyes both open wide. "Seriously?" Cara asks.

I nod as I take the jacket off the hanger. It's definitely his—it even smells faintly like him. I slip the jacket on and push the sleeves up to my elbows.

"It looks good on you," Sarina says. "Red is your color."

I look in the mirror that Jenn set up in the booth. It does look good on me. Just like Miles was good for me. "I'm buying it," I say. "I need all your help. I need to show Miles I'm sorry. I thought he didn't really care about me or this street, but he did all this work for the festival because he wants to make sure the street changes in a way that is fair to the people here."

"Yeah, maybe he did this for the street," Sarina says, "but he also did all this for *you*."

Maybe—at least, I hope—he created the romance bookstore for me, but the rest of the festival? He did it for the city. And to make connections. "How do you know it was for me?"

"Um, because he told me?" Sarina says, laughing. "How did you *not* know? He was *smitten*. Like for a while. Since before High Park. He would have done anything for you."

I blink. Miles was into me that long? While I was setting him up, he was crushing on me? He told me that he thought I was pretty . . . but that I annoyed him. "I've screwed up everything, haven't I?"

Cara shakes her head. "No. Tell him what you just told us."

An idea comes to me. I smile. "Do you think anyone will mind if the love festival chair pours her heart out for her cochair during her thank-you speech?"

Sarina nods. "Yes! Do that! Shoot, I think the gates opened."

I look over, and there's a crowd near the entrance. It's ten o'clock, and the first annual Love on Love Street Festival is officially open to the public. I say a quick good luck and rush to my station in the park.

It's a bit of a slow start, but the festival soon finds its groove. Thanks to the committee's outreach, local influencers and a few news crews show up early to interview the organizers and report on the festival. Soon the park is absolutely bustling with people snapping pictures, checking out the vendors, and lining up at the food trucks. Ms. Carothers over at the tree mural has a steady line of people who want to declare their love on the Toronto Love Tree.

The flower heart is a hit too. I'm staying close to it, helping the young volunteers, because pretty much everyone wants to take pictures of themselves in front of the heart for their socials. We make sure there's an organized line, and I offer to take the pictures of the attendees with their phones. People keep praising the heart (I give away so many Morgan Ashton Flowers brochures), and everyone seems to be having so much fun.

I've always loved love, but this? Being the one to help all these people document their love for each other in front of a big floral heart that my mother and I made? It's *priceless*. I get why my mother loves to do weddings so much.

Eventually, Julie and Ajit come by. "This is beautiful," Julie says, looking at the heart. "I trusted you, but I was a little unsure what to expect from this installation. It's *spectacular*."

I smile proudly, then ask how business has been at LoveBug.

"Busy. We sold out of the pink chai already. Charlene had to brew more inside."

"Yay! Hey, can you help me out with something? I'm going to make a speech at noon on the entertainment stage before the first performance. Can you make sure *everyone* from the planning committee is there? Like you two, Cara, Jenn, April, Ben, and Miles?"

Ajit frowns. "Sure, why?"

"I want to thank everyone for putting this together. Make sure . . . especially . . ."

"That Miles is there?" Julie asks.

I laugh. "Am I that transparent?"

"Don't worry. I'll get him there," Ajit says. "Even if I have to drag him by the ear."

At almost twelve, Cara and I stand to the left of the stage, looking at the crowd gathering. It's mostly parents and family of the dance troupe that will be performing a tango soon, but a few Love Street residents and owners are here as well. My mom is there with Jenn, and I see the rest of the planning committee—except Miles.

I still haven't seen Miles all day. I've been in the park since the festival opened, and he was supposed to stay on the street to make sure everything there runs smoothly. Maybe he won't come for my speech. Maybe he doesn't want to see me.

"This is a bad idea," I say. I have my speech on my phone, and I just added a new ending, but if Miles isn't here, is there any point in groveling so publicly?

"Sana, you need to get on the stage. It's twelve," Cara says.

"He's not here," I say.

Cara shakes her head. "Just thank the committee and introduce the dancers. The crowd is getting anxious."

Forget the crowd. *I'm* getting anxious. I take a cleansing breath and nod. "Okay. Let's do it."

Some music starts playing. It's Cream's "Sunshine of Your Love," one of the songs I was named after. I laugh.... Jenn's partner, Mark, is in charge of audio today, and clearly playing this song was my mother's or Jenn's doing.

When I'm in the middle of the stage, I smile and take the microphone off the stand, and the music fades away.

I'm still wearing Miles's jacket. I inhale deeply and start. "Thank you, everyone! And thank you to all of you who came out on this beautiful day to the first-ever Toronto Love on Love Street Festival!"

I pause as the crowd claps. And that's when I notice Miles. He *is* here. Wearing a red festival T-shirt and jeans. His hair is messy, like he's run his hands through it many times. I suddenly remember the little tub of hair wax in the pocket of his prom jacket. Did he carry that on his prom night because of his habit of messing up his hair?

He looks amazing, but he isn't smiling. He's looking at me with his intense stare. And he's not alone. Su Lin Tran and the woman—*Kirsten*, from the condo developer company—are with him.

Damn it. I'm not sure I want those two to hear me pour my heart out today. Would they think I'm a lovesick teen? Would Su Lin take me less seriously? But I can't give up now. Miles is here. And this is a *love* festival—it's the best place to tell someone I love them.

"I'm Sana Merali," I say, surprised that my voice isn't shakier. "I'm one of the cochairs of the festival planning committee. We've put together a great day of food, entertainment, and some amazing vendors to celebrate our unique community here on Love Street. They say it takes a village to raise a child, and even though this street is in the middle of a huge, vibrant, diverse city, Love Street is *my* village. And it took all of us to raise this festival baby. I want to thank each and every member of the festival planning committee for putting all this together."

I call out the names of the committee members, and everyone cheers for them. I don't say Miles's name, though. I still can't read his expression. After thanking Su Lin Tran for her support and help in permit approvals, I take a breath for strength. "When we first came up with the idea of a festival celebrating love, the purpose was to bring attention to this corner of the city that we love so much. I'll be honest, part of the motivation—for me, at least—was *fear*. Fear that Love Street would get forgotten as the city grew and changed around it. Fear that people won't wander here on their own anymore, and the special little family businesses won't thrive like they used to. Fear that this little paradise where I both live and work will *change*. This place, this *street*, raised me. I wanted it to be here, exactly as it is now, forever.

"Even though this is literally Love Street, not everyone wanted to dedicate this festival to love. Some thought the theme was sentimental and cheesy. Some thought it diluted the legacy of Lionel Osmond Love, the prominent city councillor that this street, and this park, were named after. Lionel Love *always* advocated for those in our city who needed a little extra support. He imagined a city full of these little communities where people could live, work, and thrive . . . knowing your neighbor will always have your back. Love once said, 'Toronto is a community of communities, each one as important as the next.' And he fought to make sure each community had equal opportunity to thrive in this wonderful city."

I look right at Miles. "But I think . . . Actually, I *know* that the naysayers who were resistant to the theme of this festival kept an open mind and eventually learned that Love, whether it's the love of a city, of a community, or love for each other, is the perfect tribute for this street.

"The way things are now can't serve everyone in the future the way it has in the past. Change is sometimes necessary. If we sit back and let others dictate how our communities will change, what our communities will look like, then the people who need that little bit of extra support aren't going to get it. But if we stay engaged, we can guide the change to ensure these places can still be places where people can live, where people can work, and most of all, these places can still be full of love."

Everyone claps and cheers for me, and it gives me the energy I need to say the rest of my speech. "If you have a moment today, take a walk over to the other end of the park, where a new historical plaque has been unveiled today honoring Lionel Osmond Love. Learn more about him and his legacy, so while this community changes, we will all remember that it was created with a foundation of *Love*."

Everyone cheers for that. Even Su Lin. And Miles? He looks shocked. He had no idea about the plaque. I take a deep breath and open the locket on my neck. This is the new part of the speech that I just wrote. I take out the fortune with shaky hands. "True story. A couple of months ago I found this fortune—not in a cookie, but in the pocket of this jacket I'm wearing. It says, 'Love is closer than you think. Its power is going to change you more than you expect.' I don't think I could have imagined how much I would change after I fell madly in love this summer. So, a final thank-you to two people. One, Lionel Osmond Love, for inspiring this street and for showing me how important it is to engage with the change that we want to see for our city. And two, thank you to the person who opened my eyes to that and who I . . ." I pause, taking a breath. "And who I fell *stupidly* in love with this summer. Thank you to my cochair of the Love on Love Street Festival committee, *Miles Desai*."

Everyone claps. I stand there awkwardly, not sure what to do with my hands, when, strangely, the song Miles was named after, "I'm Gonna Be (500 Miles)" starts playing. Everyone claps. Ajit whistles, and I see Su Lin practically push Miles onto the stage. And then he's next to me, grinning ear to ear. He looks at me, then puts his hands on my cheeks and kisses me on the lips. Right here, on the stage, in front of my mother, my boss, his boss, and my whole community, he kisses me. And it's the sweetest, most loving kiss I've ever had.

When he pulls away, he whispers into my ear, "I love you too, Sana. And I want my jacket back."

Miles and I, of course, can't bask in the joy of reuniting for very long. Soon after, little kids dancing the tango replace us on the stage, and Miles gets a message that there's an issue with the vendor parking area. I need to get back to the floral heart anyway, where the poor volunteers are managing the crowd themselves.

On my way back to the flower heart, I see someone I was not expecting to see here—my father. He's eating from a paper bag of churros.

"Dad! What are you doing here?"

He smiles. "You reminded me how much I used to love festivals." He offers me a churro, and I take it.

I look around him. "Is Noureen here?" I wonder if I need to text Sarina to hold off on any PDA with Cara.

Dad shakes his head. "No. I wanted to come alone to see what you did here. I saw your speech. . . . It was phenomenal. I've never been prouder of my little girl. When did you get so . . . grown-up?"

Awkward. I have no idea what to say. "Um, thanks, Dad. I'm glad you came. I do need to—"

"You go." He waves me forward. "You're busy. I'm going to walk around a bit."

"Okay. Oh, and, Dad, if you see Sarina—"

"Don't worry, Sana. I saw her. And saw the pictures at the entrance. I have no intention of telling Noureen about *anything* on that sign." He shakes his head. "I know she wouldn't approve of that picture of me in a Canadian tuxedo. I really thought I was as cool as Justin Timberlake."

I laugh and head back to the flower heart.

Miles finally finds me again at about two o'clock and asks if we can take in the festival together as cochairs. I smile at him as I wave over an extra volunteer from the mural team to help crowd control at the floral heart.

Hand in hand, Miles and I walk around our festival. A few volunteers and committee members ask us questions, and we put out a few mini fires. We split an empanada and each get a strawberry matcha boba tea from LoveBug. But most importantly, we talk.

I start by apologizing. For not letting him explain why he took that job. For shutting him out as soon as things got complicated. I tell him that everything I said in my speech is true—I understand now that Love Street is going to change, but we can still have a say on *how* it changes.

"I loved your speech," he says. "Like, a lot. Thank you for . . . telling me that way."

I smile. "I wrote most of the speech last night. Up until I unveiled the historical plaque. I only added the last bit today." I pause. "A part of me thought that you didn't care about *us* as much as I did, because you didn't tell me about your job. And because . . . because I thought you didn't believe in all this romance stuff."

He squeezes my hand. "I'm sorry. I'm not great at talking about it, but really, I *do* care."

"Yeah, I know. Sarina told me . . . and I realized that you *are* romantic when I saw your perfectly curated selection of romance books. So I . . . I added the part where I said I love you."

He's turning pink again and smiling. "I read a bunch of those books, you know."

"Reggie told me. Are you now a romance lover?"

He lifts my hand and kisses the back of it. "I think I still prefer a good historical mystery, but I get the appeal now. I can't believe you've had the fortune I got on my prom night in that necklace all summer. How many times have I seen you wear it?"

I laugh. "Right? I had no idea it was yours until today. Now do you believe in fate? This *proves* we're soul mates." I beam at him, which makes him kiss my cheek.

He grins. "I almost believe . . . in coincidences."

I laugh at that and slap his arm.

We pass April's booth, and I point out the heart bow that I bought Zuri.

"I owe you an apology too," he says. "I *should* have told you that your father referred me for that internship. I didn't know that your mother was selling them her building, but I still thought . . . I thought you wouldn't approve. You hate developers, and you don't have the best relationship with your father."

"You were right. I wouldn't have approved. I was so . . . stubborn. My parents, strangely, are the ones who taught me that things aren't as black-and-white as I thought. I get the nuance, I mean."

He smiles. "Su Lin told me you were behind the historical plaque."

I nod. "I'm going to keep fighting for Love Street—and make sure it never loses the *essence* of why it's great, even if there are new people and new stores. It will still be my home."

"But aren't you moving?"

I shake my head, grinning, and tell him about my father's plan to have me and Sarina stay in my apartment in September.

"Oh!" He laughs. "That's great!"

"My dad's here, you know. He actually came. He said he loved my speech. I think he's trying to make up for lost years. He said he needed the kick in the pants. He's . . . stubborn and idealistic like me."

Miles freezes. "Um, are you saying I kissed you like that while your *father* was watching us?"

I nod. "Yep. Don't worry—he likes you, but I wouldn't really care if he didn't. Will you be staying in the apartment you're in now in September?"

He squeezes my hand again. "I wasn't sure. But now that I know you're staying on Love Street, I think I'll stay close by."

I squeeze his hand. "Maybe you can find a better place, though. Less stinky."

"Maybe," he agrees. "Hey, are we officially back together? Because I'd love to lock my bike on your balcony again. I've been rushing out to check on it every hour since I started leaving it here in the park."

I roll my eyes. "Is that all I am to you? A convenient place to lock your bike? I thought we had this great and profound love full of hope and joy and all you—"

He stops me with a kiss on my neck that almost makes my knees give out. How did I walk away from him? No one has ever made me feel like this.

"You know what you are to me?" he asks in my ear.

"What?"

"The love of my life."

Pure cheese. And there's nothing trite about it. I kiss him on his lips. Because he's the love of my life too. And just like the fortune said we would, we found each other right here on Love Street.

ACKNOWLEDGMENTS

Meet Me on Love Street is my ninth novel and my ultimate love letter to all things love and romance. It was such a joy to write a hopeless romantic character, and I am eternally grateful to the universe that I was able to bring Sana and Miles to life. In addition to the universe, there are many people I would like to thank for their help and support with this book.

A huge thanks to my literary agent, Rachel Brooks, for having enough faith in this project to find it a perfect home. Thanks to Dainese Santos, my editor at Simon & Schuster, for being one of the kindest and most enthusiastic editors I've had the pleasure of working with. Her editorial insight and earnest excitement brought this story to its best potential. Thanks to everyone at Simon & Schuster who worked on this book, including managing editor Kimberly Capriola, copy editor Penina Lopez, proofreader Jasmine Ye, the art team, the sales team, and the publicity and marketing teams. Thanks to my friend, writer Lily Chu, for reading an early draft and giving me excellent feedback.

A massive thanks to my son, Khalil, for reading a draft of this story to make sure I got the planning stuff right, and for inspiring me to write about an urban-planning student in the first place. Miles wouldn't exist if I didn't have an obsessive planning nerd in my life, making me really look at the places we call home. And thank you to the rest of my family: my husband, Tony, and daughter, Anissa (and cats, Darcy and Matcha), for putting up with my endless brainstorming, late nights, and messy house while on deadline. This book, and this career, wouldn't exist without you.

ABOUT THE AUTHOR

Farah Heron was raised on Bollywood, Monty Python, and Jane Austen, and has been weaving happily ever afters in her head ever since childhood. With a background in human resources and psychology, she now writes adult and teen stories full of huge South Asian families, delectable food, and most importantly, Brown people falling stupidly in love. She lives in Toronto with her family, plus two cats who rule the house. Please visit FarahHeron.com for more information.